PARAGON OF FIRE

Cover art by Michelle Ong

Edited by Amanda Dimer Silva

First Edition: April 2022

ISBN-13: 978-1-952145-19-3

PARAGON OF FIRE

SPECTRUM LEGACY BOOK TWO

BETH ALVAREZ

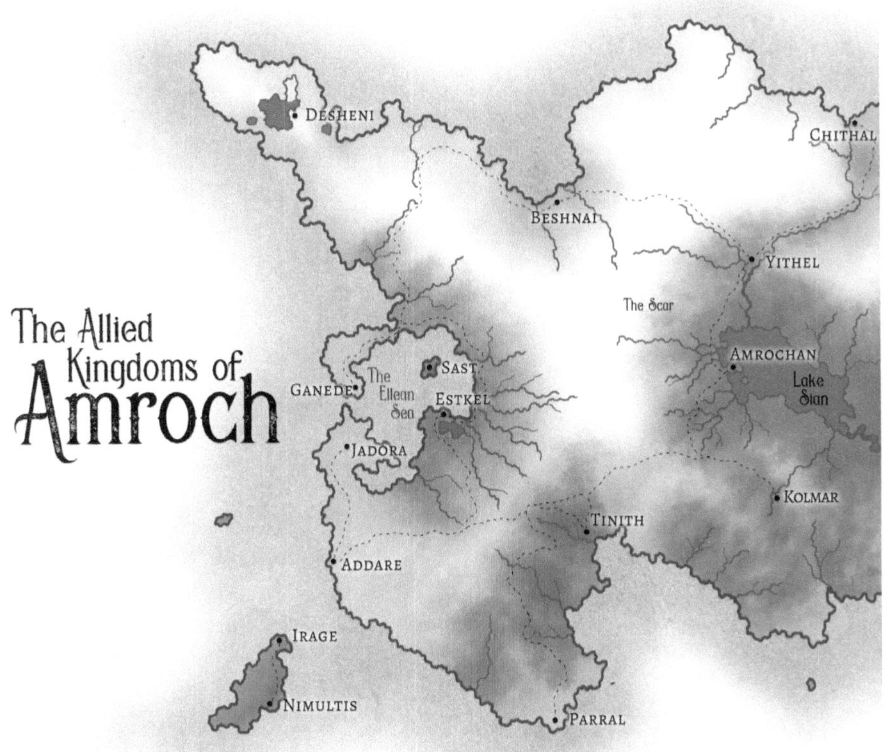

The Allied Kingdoms of Amroch
DESHENI
CHITHAL
BESHNAI
YITHEL
The Scar
AMROCHAN
Lake Sian
GANEDE
The Ellean Sea
SAST
ESTKEL
JADORA
KOLMAR
TINITH
ADDARE
IRAGE
NIMULTIS
PARRAL

CHAPTER ONE

THE TORCH FLAME rippled as Zaide swung it toward the shelves. It felt wrong to hold an open flame so close to the Elder's books, considering how much of Kolmar still smoked, but the only lantern they'd brought had refused to light.

"Here?" he asked as he pushed a few charred books aside. He'd never enjoyed his time as the Elder's apprentice, yet seeing the library destroyed still made his chest ache. In the wake of the attacks on the sleepy forest village, untold amounts of knowledge had been lost.

Resia squinted at the shelf. "No, not that one. I think it's one more to the right." She shuffled to the next bookshelf and scraped it bare.

Behind them, the rest of their meager party tried to find shelter under what remained of the library's roof. Blackened, skeletal beams arched over most of the building's ruins and a cold, heavy rain poured in. All of them were soaked, but Lark seemed to have found a reasonably dry corner. She paged through a book that had escaped the fire, uninterested in what they were doing.

"What exactly are you looking for?" Aren asked. He and Murk had posted themselves beside Lark, which meant neither managed to escape the rain. Both wore sour expressions and for a moment, Zaide wondered how uncomfortable their plate armor had become, now that they were wet. His borrowed leather armor chafed enough.

"A conversation I really don't want to have," Resia muttered.

Zaide blinked at her and moved the torch closer. "What's that supposed to mean?"

She gave him the sort of flat, unamused look only a sister could, then pressed something at the back of the shelf. A low thunk sounded somewhere behind it and the whole shelf swung forward.

His mouth fell open.

Aren's did, too. "The Elder had a secret passage? I always thought he was a boring old man."

"A boring old man who happened to lead your village and bear the most important burden of your people," Lark interjected. She snapped her book shut and put it aside. Soot left marks on her fingers and she crinkled her nose as she rubbed her fingertips together, then dusted her hand against her trousers.

Zaide caught the shelf and pulled it open wider. The space behind was framed by polished wood and lined with rough stone, and wooden steps descended into the earth. Despite the heavy rain, it smelled dry, the distinct scent of books strong in the air. A sense of betrayal surged within him. "How long have you known about this?"

"Uh, a while, I guess." Resia ducked her head and started down the stairs, a furrow between her brows. "Since before your Choosing."

"And you never told me?" They'd been best friends, foster siblings, and co-apprentices. How had she kept that sort of secret from him? Zaide thrust the torch forward into the dark and stormed after her.

"I was under very specific directions not to. I would say you should take that up with the Elder, but..." She trailed off and bit her lip.

He snorted. Their mentor's death absolved her of nothing. "Well, you're the Elder now, so that means I get to take it up with you. I was his apprentice too! Shouldn't I have known there was an entire secret tunnel in here?" With a latch hidden behind the books in the section devoted to curative magic, no less. A memory of Resia rearranging the library the day after he was made apprentice sprang to mind. New anger spawned at the realization she'd already known then, and had made sure to shelve books there that he could never use and would have no reason to read.

Resia shook her head, troubled, but unruffled. "It wasn't time. The Elder said he would tell me when the time came. He can't do that if he's dead, and there are things here that need to be taken to Amrochan before they're damaged."

"If you're dragging us down here to gather piles of records, I'll tell you right now that we won't be able to take them." Lark trudged down the stairs at Zaide's back, her arms folded tight across her chest. Aren followed close at her heels, but Murk lingered in the open doorway, establishing himself as lookout. They'd cleared the village proper of goborrins and Murk's scouting indicated the rest of the beasts were on their way out of the forest, but until Resia finished replenishing the magic that sheltered the valley, there were no guarantees.

"No records. But there are books about *that*, and I get the feeling we're going to need them." Resia turned her head just enough to nod toward the sword at Zaide's hip. It shimmered softly in the torchlight. Colors sparked and flowed endlessly across the blade. Its light came and went, but had proven enough of a distraction that Zaide already looked forward to getting it a scabbard. Wedged under his belt beside his usual weapon, it was more of a hindrance than a help.

"Oh, and it never occurred to anyone that I might need to know about this?" Zaide narrowed his eyes as they reached the floor and the ruddy torchlight spilled over hundreds of books that had been hidden away. After the exhausting expedition to recover the blade that had upended his life, the realization that information about the Spectrum Blade—and likely the artifacts he'd risked life and limb to recover—had always been within easy reach chafed worse than his wet leather armor.

His foster sister shook her head. "I'm not going to argue with you about this, Zaide. I was an apprentice, just following orders. Besides, it's not like I was allowed down here all the time." She cast his torch a doubtful look, then motioned for him to stay put.

He sighed and remained by the stairs while she vanished between shelves. She'd managed to relight the magic-fueled lantern in his bag when they were in the forest's temple, but after she'd begun to weave the powerful energy that would restore the Vale magic that protected Kolmar, it had extinguished and refused to light again. It wouldn't, she'd said, until the stronger force around it stabilized. Lacking magic as he was, he had no way of knowing when that would be.

Lark slipped past him to join Resia among the books. "What is it you hope to find here?"

Zaide shifted on his feet as Aren followed the princess, leaving him alone with the torch and unable to explore. He resisted the urge to sigh again.

"I'm not sure I can easily explain," Resia said. "When I touched the spring of power in the temple and it accepted me as Kolmar's Elder, it gave me visions. That's the only way I know how to describe it. It showed me what I must do to fulfill my duties. Restoring the power that protects the forest is only part of it. The other part is helping awaken the blade."

"Awaken it?" Lark asked, a note of surprise in her voice.

"Well, yes. Again, I'm not sure how to explain." She knelt at the edge of the light's reach and pulled a book from a shelf. Aren moved between Zaide and the girls, blocking all view.

The torch began to feel like a punishment. Zaide glanced up the stairs, but Murk no longer hovered in the doorway. With nowhere to pass it off, he was stuck, wet and cold and excluded from a revelation that affected him more than anyone. He transferred the torch to his left hand so he could brush his fingers over the hilt of the Spectrum Blade at his right hip. "It glows like the artifacts when it's doing something, and it's always got these swirls going. It doesn't look very sleepy to me."

Resia made a sound of displeasure. "Maybe that's not the right way to say it. When the blade was used to kill the last incarnation of Gadranus, its power was spent. Or, it dispersed."

"Returned to where it came from?" Lark suggested. Aside from Resia, she was likely the most knowledgeable person there.

"Yes, that's it. The Paragons are the ones who can restore it, draw its power back into it, and help it reach its full potential. Each of the Paragons represents an element, and the blade represents the harmony between them and the force that unites them. It's strong as it is, but I think if we can awaken it, our chances of ending this war would be better."

Zaide studied the sword at his side. After how easy it had made it to dispatch the goborrins, he wasn't sure he could imagine it being made stronger. "Is that something the magic water told you, or is that something you read in the Elder's forbidden books?"

Lark, Resia, and Aren all turned to give him dirty looks.

"Could you curb your bitterness for a moment and let the rest of us speak? You might be the new Bladebearer, but the rest of us have to put up with you." The princess glanced to the shimmering sword, more than a hint of resentment in her eyes.

Sullen, he grew quiet.

"If you're the new Paragon of the forest, Resia, does that mean you know how to do your part already?" Aren asked, the question a much more diplomatic way of phrasing what Zaide really wanted to know.

An uncertain smile pulled at the corners of Resia's mouth. "The spring of power showed me a little, but I remember reading something about the duties of the Paragons in one of these books."

"Considering the rain, we're going to need somewhere dry to

sit and read, and I don't think this is the best place to try to read by candlelight," Lark said.

At least that was something Zaide could help with. "Some of the houses on the north end of the village were left unburned. We'll set up there and read what we need. We might be able to scavenge enough supplies to cook something decent to eat, too."

"Now that sounds helpful." The look Lark gave him fell shy of approving, but he hardly cared.

"Just gather up what you need and let's go," Zaide grumbled.

Resia handed Aren a small stack of books. "We're going to need a way to move these without them getting wet. Any ideas?"

"Everyone empty our bags down here, move the books, and come back for the rest of our stuff?" Aren blinked as Lark added a few more books to the pile. "You aren't taking all of these to Amrochan, are you? You won't be able to carry it all."

Lark sniffed. "Of course not. We'll narrow it down to the most important volumes, and copy information out of the rest so we can travel light."

Even a few books would increase their load by a considerable amount. As far as Zaide knew, he and Lark were the only ones returning to Amrochan. They'd had no time to discuss matters in depth, but Aren and Murk had already agreed it would be best if they remained in Kolmar with Resia until her work was done. By her estimate, it would take close to two weeks to restore and fortify the magic over the forest. By then, Zaide and Lark would be in Amrochan and the Kolmari refugees in the capital could decide for themselves if they would return to the village or remain beneath King Sendassian's protective wing.

"By most important volumes, I hope you mean two books," Zaide said. "I hardly have room in my bag as it is."

"Then you'll have to carry another bag." Resia gathered her own armful of books, then murmured instructions for Lark to take another from the shelves. "Though I have to say, I'm not sure I want to trust you with any books after what you did to the Hymnflute's songbook."

Zaide raised a finger. "That was not my fault. Everything was fine until I fell into the river, and that only happened because those bugrak things were trying to kill me."

"But it was the second time you fell into a river after leaving Kolmar," Aren said. "Which is kind of weird. I've been out of Kolmar for more than a year, and I've never fallen into any rivers."

This time, he was the one to receive Lark's glare. "While I understand the desire to joke with your friends, we have work to do. Carry those upstairs and call for Murk to bring some bags to cover them."

"I could go get some," Zaide offered.

The princess frowned. "Then who will hold our light? Stay where you are. I want to look for one more thing."

He let his shoulders sag, but stayed put while Aren climbed the stairs. A moment later, Resia headed up, too. Zaide shifted and watched Lark pace up and down the rows of shelves.

"What are you looking for?" he asked softly.

"Before we left Jadora, Tula assisted me with a book that was the first to mention the blade. It had some useful information about the last Rise, when Gadranus reached Amrochan's walls. That Gadranus was the one who was sealed in the temple here. If your Elder's predecessor was the one to preside over the sealing, there should be a journal, or a log book, or..." She paused, tapping a finger against her lower lip. As prickly as she was, there were times her face softened and she seemed more approachable. Most of them revolved around books or knowledge.

Zaide tilted his head. "The Elder who took me as apprentice kept a journal, but it was in his desk. Do you think we should look for it? If it was in a drawer, maybe it escaped the fire."

She cast him a thoughtful glance. "Yes, that might be wise. Would you fetch it? I'll bring these up."

"All right." He started up the stairs, eager to escape the secret library and all the unpleasant feelings it gave him, but he paused halfway up to wait for her. He was still holding the torch, after all, and he suspected leaving the princess alone in the dark could be some sort of criminal offense. It had already happened once before, when he'd left her behind in the temple. That he hadn't known her identity at the time, he presumed, was all that had saved him from her wrath.

When she stopped near the top of the stairway, he slipped out into the space between charred shelves and checked the ceiling. After the rain started, most of the flames had extinguished, but they'd damaged the building enough that he wasn't sure it would remain standing for long. The moment one of the blackened beams shifted, they would all need to escape.

Resia stood in the somewhat-dry corner with Murk and Aren, cramming books into sacks that must have been salvaged from elsewhere in the village. Zaide only watched for a moment before he rounded the corner into what remained of the Elder's study.

Most of the furniture was scorched, some reduced to charcoal, but the heavy, lacquered desk appeared to be intact beneath a heavy layer of ash. Remnants of notes, no doubt. Zaide ignored them as he pulled the drawers open, one by one. True to his suspicion, the inside of each drawer had been insulated against the fire, their contents safe. He found the journal he sought and hunched forward to use his body as a shield to protect it from the rain. Then he shoved the drawers shut and returned to the front of the library. Lark had just finished foisting her burden off on the men, it seemed, for her hands were empty and she pushed against the bare shelf until the doorway to the hidden staircase clicked shut.

"I got it," he said. "Let's go dry off."

"About time," Aren sighed.

"Aye, that's about what I feel." Murk squinted at the sky, still dark and overcast despite it being the height of midday. "The rain was refreshing at first, but I've had my fill."

Resia hugged her sack full of books to her chest and nodded toward the door. "Lead the way. You and Aren have a better idea of what's left standing than I do."

Zaide nodded back at her and turned to step outside, the Elder's journal held tight to his body.

He slogged through puddles and mud to the north end of the village, where a familiar but sad-looking shack stood with the door slightly ajar. He hadn't had a chance to peek in, but he doubted what waited inside would be pleasant. After Kolmar had been overrun, the goborrins had taken residence in the houses. He braced himself as he lifted the door by its latch and hefted it back, used to the way the crooked hinges made it drag.

Inside, the thick coating of dry straw on the floor came as a welcome surprise.

"Huh." Aren all but shoved past Zaide to get into the dark building and out of the rain. "They look like animals. Didn't expect they'd sleep like them, too."

Resia followed close behind him. "I wouldn't mind curling up in some straw to sleep, myself. It looks clean enough. Maybe I will, once we're done."

"Don't get your hopes up, miss Elder," Murk remarked. "We might drip on it enough to leave the whole place soaked."

Zaide glanced back when Lark didn't enter.

She stood on the path outside the tiny house, staring at the building with an odd twist to her mouth. "What is this place?"

He gestured for her to move inside. "Home sweet home?"

Her nose crinkled. "Yours?"

He nodded.

"This is a hovel."

The distaste in her tone was so thick, Zaide couldn't help but snort. "Well, excuse me, Princess. We can't all grow up in castles."

Lark's expression did not change, but she squeezed past

Zaide to get inside. He pulled the door shut behind her. The shutters were ajar and let in a sliver of dismal light, but at least the house was dry, and the straw still smelled sweet.

"Aren, let me borrow the dagger." Zaide kicked heaps of the straw away from the hearth, where ashes sat so clumped and thick that he was convinced they were what he'd left behind when he'd departed Kolmar. The firewood he kept indoors remained untouched, piled beside the hearth and buried in straw, too. Perhaps goborrins didn't know how to use a fireplace.

A thud and grunt made him glance over his shoulder. Aren straightened, leaving his heavy sack of books on the low table that remained in the center of the room. "Sorry."

Resia left her own sack beside his and joined Zaide by the hearth. "We should push all the straw to the other end of the cottage, so no embers can land in it." She knelt to gather armfuls of it and move it to the far wall, opposite the hearth, where Zaide's pallet had been. Maybe it was still there, buried under the straw.

Aren passed the Molten Dagger to Zaide, then joined Resia in cleaning.

The wood was dry and well seasoned and it didn't take long to get a tiny flame going in a fistful of straw that served as tinder. The warmth of the obsidian dagger in Zaide's hand soon paled to the heat of the kindling, and flames licked up the sides of the log. He laid the dagger on the hearth and spread his fingers in front of the growing fire. "There's a comfort I didn't know how much I missed."

"Probably nice to be back in your own house, too." Aren flashed him a grin. "It's a little crowded, though."

"Well, it was never meant for visitors." Satisfied with the fire, Zaide stood and reached for the buckles of his armor. "We should try to dry out. You and Murk are going to rust if you keep all that plate on over wet padding."

The grunt Murk answered with was halfway between displeasure and resignation. With as seasoned a soldier as the man was, Zaide supposed it was possible Murk had experienced just that. He trudged closer to the hearth and began to remove his armor.

As Zaide peeled off his own and arranged the pieces to dry, he watched Lark settle beside the table and reach for the first book. She was soaked to skin and dripped onto the pile of straw that served as her seat, but her determination to push forward never faltered. In other times, he might have appreciated her duty-driven nature, but he was tired, hungry, and already knew that the long walk back to Amrochan waited on the other end of her reading those books.

Returning to the capital wasn't a problem. It was what came after they reached it that left Zaide worried.

When they'd departed from Amrochan, a heavy storm had followed close at their heels. It had been a relief, as the torrential rains offered respite from the fires the goborrin armies had started just outside Amrochan's walls. But they'd left the city by boat, and he and Lark would be returning on foot. Those armies would be there waiting. Even with the Spectrum Blade in his hand, carving through them would be a challenge.

As if aware of his thoughts, the colors on the sword swirled faster for a moment, flickers of light flashing wherever the iridescent shades met.

Lark glanced up to watch it. Her gaze grew uncomfortably heavy.

"You need a light," Zaide said, as if the statement freed him of her scrutiny. In a way, it did, because it gave him an excuse to turn and dig in a box that sat atop the mantel shelf. Most of his candles had been used down to nubs, but a nub would suffice. He jammed one into a small earthenware holder his foster mother had given him when he'd moved into the cottage, then knelt to light the wick from the fire.

When he sat the candle in the center of the table, he dared say the look on Lark's face was almost approval. "Thank you," she murmured.

That was almost amicable.

Progress.

Aren dropped the last of his armor beside the hearth and joined them at the table. "So, what's our plan? I mean, reading, yeah, but then what?"

Whatever cheer Zaide's candle offering had instilled in the princess, that question sapped it right back out. Her face darkened and she squared her shoulders, back to the cold, regal princess Zaide knew.

"That part should be obvious," Lark said. "First, we read."

Aren nodded. "And then?"

Her gaze hardened and in the firelight, her blue eyes looked black. "War."

CHAPTER TWO

WHEN THE RAIN finally ceased in the late afternoon, Zaide gathered his armor and strapped it back on. Hours spent reading beside the fire had done wonders for both his mood and the wetness of his clothes, and when he replaced the sword in the sheath at his side with the Spectrum Blade, he found that the odd size of the weapon bothered him less. It would still take time for him to grow used to it; it was lightweight and an awkward length, too long to be a short sword and not long enough to compare to the guard-issue weapon he had grown used to wielding.

"Think we have any chance of finding an empty scabbard somewhere in the village?" he asked as Murk and Aren donned their armor. Resia and Lark wore none, so both stood ready by the door.

"How many of the Kolmari do you think had swords?" Aren asked. "Chances would be better if we could stop by the garrison, but I guess I don't need to explain why that's a bad idea."

And it would remain a bad idea, at least until things settled outside Amrochan and Sendassian's army could push south to reclaim the outpost. The magic Resia had laid over the village and the temple nearby would keep them safe, but it wouldn't drive out the goborrins that had taken the garrison. That led to a new thought.

Zaide frowned. "The road runs right past the garrison. We'll have to find a way through the woods, loop around it and avoid being seen." Even with the advantage the Spectrum Blade seemed to bear over the monsters, he couldn't hope to face an occupying force alone.

"We'll figure that out tomorrow. Right now, we need to head back to the temple." Lark toyed with a curl of her golden hair while she waited for the men to prepare. It wasn't like her to show nerves, but he doubted she would appreciate any kind of attempt at comfort or reassurance.

The books Resia found had been helpful; several had been dedicated to the duties she now bore as Kolmar's Elder. One had detailed the ritual she was to perform in depth. The knowledge was useful, yet inconvenient. Had they the means to perform the ritual in his cozy little shack, he would have preferred to do it there and depart for Amrochan sooner. Instead, he found himself leading the way out of Kolmar to seek a trail he'd already grown tired of traversing.

"Are you sure we all have to go?" Aren asked as they began the uphill trek along the main path to the temple. "If it's just Zaide and Resia who need to take the sword to the spring, I could just stay behind and try to figure out some food."

"A valiant effort to escape responsibility, but we've run into trouble in the temple twice already. I want everyone ready, just in case." Lark tossed her head, her ponytail flicking out behind her like a whip. Murk ducked aside to keep from being hit.

Zaide would have preferred to return to a warm meal. The spring of power beneath the temple had become the new anchor for the Vale magic. As long as the new barrier was present, there was little risk. But Lark's insistence was the reason they'd come to Kolmar to begin with, and after a long night of travel and battle, he wasn't eager to pick a fight. They'd make do with cold rations if they had to.

Following the trail at a brisk pace, it took less time than ever to reach the temple grounds. Late afternoon sun peeked in through the clouds, bathing the mossy ruin with warm light. Unlike their previous visits, the forest had come alive. Birdsong and the chatter of squirrels filled the air, and between the opening in the ceiling and the front entryway they'd dismantled in the middle of the night, the sanctuary in the front of the temple was bright. The rope they'd used to descend from the hole in the ceiling still hung in the center of the room.

"Never getting that back," Aren remarked blandly.

"Not unless one of you feels like climbing to the roof and bringing it back down," Zaide said. "I'm beat." In some ways, he supposed he ought to be glad Lark wanted to delay their travel. A night in Kolmar meant a night under his own roof, and that meant the first decent rest he'd had in far too long. Maybe since he'd left the village to begin with.

Resia made a soothing motion with one hand. "This will be brief, don't worry. We won't have to linger. We'll finish, head back to the village, and then we'll all get a well deserved rest."

"In shifts," Murk put in. "And I'm not taking first watch."

Aren opened his mouth to argue, but Lark spoke before he could.

"If necessary, I will assign watch shifts after we've all eaten and made plans for what comes next. In the meantime, I would appreciate if all of you would focus on the task at hand." The princess glared at each of the men.

Zaide couldn't help but wonder what he'd done to be included in her ire this time.

Resia reached the altar room first and made a soft sound of surprise. It was enough to send a surge of alarm through Zaide's veins. He pushed forward with one hand on the hilt of his sword, ready to draw and defend.

But the surprise ahead was far from unpleasant. The strange

staircase that descended into the earth already stood open, a soft light marking the way they were meant to go.

The night before, it had taken the artifacts to open the way.

"What's this, then?" Murk managed to grumble, even when asking a question.

"The spring senses me coming," Resia said. "I can feel it. It opened the way as I entered."

Slowly, Zaide peeled his fingers from the hilt of his sword. "Is that a good thing?"

Lark shrugged and made for the stairs. "A necessary thing, I'd think. The Elder is supposed to maintain the temple, but only the Hymnflute is entrusted to the Elder's care. If it always took all three artifacts to open the path, none of the Elders would have been able to do their jobs."

That sparked a new thought, but Zaide worked to temper his small flutter of hope. "Does that mean the Hymnflute won't have to be left here? We can take it with us?"

"I'd already planned to send it with you," Resia said as she followed Lark down the stairs. "Now that its power has awakened, I figure it'll be more useful to the two of you. Even if you ruined the songbook that goes with it."

Which she would never let him live down, Zaide concluded. "The pages are still legible. Some are just stuck together."

She huffed. "Then it can be your job to unstick them and create a new copy by hand."

"Fair," he said. If he gave her that much, perhaps she'd cut him a little slack.

The tunnel they descended into was clear, but the path they took was not the same as what they'd traveled before. Instead of the ramp Zaide had inadvertently taken to the chamber where the Spectrum Blade had been sealed, Resia led them around a curve and down a flight of stairs that let out into the cavern where the pool waited.

When their feet touched the floor, Zaide looked over his shoulder twice. "That's the same stairway I came down, but—"

"But there was less falling involved," Lark said dryly. "I believe I'll let your sister lead the way more often."

Aren leaned close to share a whisper. "She's prickly, isn't she?"

"You have no idea," Zaide whispered back.

"I am also three feet away from you and can hear what you're saying." The look she sent over her shoulder was nothing short of frigid, but they didn't hold her attention long. Instead, she joined Resia at the edge of the pool and rooted in her bag to produce a book.

Resia lifted her skirt and slipped off her shoes. The water didn't respond when she waded into it, or at least not in a way Zaide could see, but it wasn't normal, either. No silt stirred from the gravel when she stepped into the pool. He glanced to Lark, then Aren. Both of them bore magic, if weak. Lark had claimed her power never manifested, but she was aware of nearby magic and its effects. Zaide had never thought to ask what Aren's power was, but all the Kolmari bore some sort of magical gift. He had no reason to think his friend was the exception.

Neither showed any sign that anything was out of place.

"I think I remember what the books said, but if it's all right with you, I'd like to make a record of what happens here. Perhaps assembling our own information about the rituals all in one place could be useful for future generations." Lark opened her book, its pages blank. Something she'd found in the remains of the Elder's library, he suspected. She certainly hadn't had that when they departed Amrochan. She drew a stick of graphite wrapped in string from her bag to go with it.

"That would probably be wise. I'm not sure where you'd find information about the other rituals." Resia worked her way across the pool to the fountain that spilled from the smooth wall. "Zaide, bring the sword here."

He preferred not to think of the other rituals at all. The books they'd carried to his cottage had answered Resia's questions, but said little of the other Paragons beyond their identities—the only piece of information they already had. He rolled up his pants and removed his boots and socks, then followed her into the water.

Murk and Aren posted themselves at Lark's side. She didn't seem to notice, already taking notes in her book.

Resia trailed her fingers through the water. "Draw your sword and kneel."

"In the water?" he asked.

She gave him a flat look.

Zaide sighed and unsheathed the Spectrum Blade. The water was cool when he knelt, but not unpleasantly so. He presented the sword to his foster sister, flat on his palms.

Resia grasped one of his hands and guided it to the hilt, where she wrapped her fingers around his. Slowly, she tilted the sword so the tip just skimmed the water. "Ready?"

"No, but let's get it done."

The smile she offered was a small comfort. She drew his hands back and tilted the sword beneath the fountain, so the water cascaded over the hilt and raced down the blade. "As we fill a vessel, so shall we refill this power. The strength of the forest, the force of the wind, the life-giving warmth of the earth. May you carry these gifts within your blade, so they might answer in your time of need."

As she finished, the water changed. A soft white glow filled the stream and illuminated the blade, radiating out through the pool in waves.

Something changed in the sword. A strange sensation flowed up Zaide's arms and coursed through him, much like the ripples of light that reached the edges of the pool and disappeared. It was warm, heady, but he couldn't have explained it if he tried.

His breath caught.

The light faded.

Shimmering colors raced over the Spectrum Blade, vibrant greens and yellows that soon settled back into their normal sleepy, rippling pattern.

"As the Kolmari Elder, I entrust you with this power," Resia said as she released his hands.

Zaide offered a nervous grin in return. "I didn't see that incantation in the books."

"Did you like it?" Her dark eyes sparkled with delight. "I made it up myself. It's not necessary, I don't think, but it made it sound really official, right?"

"Yeah, it did." He removed the blade from the water and tilted it. To the eye, nothing had changed, yet it felt different in his hand. He studied it for a time before Aren cleared his throat at the edge of the pool.

"Is that it?"

Lark elbowed him. "Be grateful it's something so simple. Zaide, how does it feel?"

He stood and gave the sword a gentle swing. Its tip sliced through the water, sending ripples toward the shore. "I don't know. It did something, I felt that much. But I don't know what it was, or what the difference is."

Resia perked up beside him. "You felt it? Like, felt the magic?"

Thus far, Murk had been quiet, but he glanced between them with a frown. "Was he not supposed to? I thought magic was the whole point of this little trip."

"Zaide's not a mage," Aren said. "He shouldn't be able to feel magic *anything* unless it's doing something to him."

Lark bowed her head and wrote in her book faster than before.

Murk grunted. "Isn't he the Elder's apprentice?"

Heat rose in Zaide's ears. "It doesn't matter, the Elder is dead." And his shortcomings as a mage's apprentice were the last thing he wanted to discuss with the old soldier.

"Can you describe the sensation you experienced?" Lark asked without looking up from her notes.

"Like sticking your arm in a giant bowl full of warm wheat porridge."

The blank faces that answered his description were about what he expected.

"Yeah, exactly." Zaide waded back to the shore and wiped the sword dry on the leg of his pants. His thighs, at least, were still dry.

Lark closed her book and cleared her throat. "Well, I suppose that's something to investigate through further study. Resia, did any of the books you read say anything about other places of power? Other springs? Perhaps if that's all there is to it, convincing the other Paragons to help us replenish the blade will be a simple matter."

"No, I'm afraid not." Resia followed Zaide to the water's edge and looked down at her soaked skirt, a hint of a frown marring her expression. "I'm not sure where else we would find that kind of information."

Zaide sheathed the sword. "Jadora."

"The Great Library," the princess agreed.

"Which means we're going to need our librarian."

The faintest hint of a smile curved Lark's lips. "Tula is still in Amrochan. If we can get through the front lines, we can take her back to Jadora and gain access to their records. Perhaps we can convince my father to come with us, now that we have something to show for our efforts. Even the busiest librarians wouldn't make an angry king wait."

"To Amrochan, then," Murk said.

Zaide nodded. "But first, dinner."

CHAPTER THREE

ZAIDE'S tiny cottage was cramped with five people sleeping inside, but the thick layer of straw made for a comfortable bed, and despite the snores and wayward elbows that jabbed his ribs, he slept soundly.

He woke not long after sunrise with Lark curled close to his side and Aren's knee precariously close to something he would rather not have kneed and for a long time, all he could do was blink groggily at the thin streak of sunlight that peeked in between the shutters. He hadn't taken the time to latch them properly. After they'd finished eating, it had been so late that no one wanted to do anything but fall into the straw to sleep.

Somehow, Murk had managed to hunt a rabbit in the woods without a snare or bow. Resia had found some potatoes and early greens in her family's garden, which was relatively untouched by the goborrins that had consumed everything else left in the village, and Aren had found a cook pot and some earthenware dishes who knew where. Zaide had provided savory herbs from a stash in the rafters of his cottage and between the four of them, they'd managed to make a proper meal. The pot sat among the ashes, where it would be kept warm, and the stew's aroma made his stomach growl.

With some cautious wiggling, Zaide extricated himself from his awkward sleeping arrangements and rubbed the back of his neck.

He'd been assigned a place in the middle, a buffer between the girls and the two stronger men. That they considered him an appropriate cushion made him wonder if they thought he wasn't strong enough to hurt them in his sleep or if they were convinced he was strong enough to protect them, and he wasn't sure which notion was worse.

On the other side of Aren, Murk's place in the straw was empty. He hadn't thought the dour man capable of sneaking about effectively enough to escape unnoticed. Then again, he'd been so tired that little had threatened his sleep.

Zaide dropped a log into the embers and stirred the fire back to life, then dipped a helping of stew out of the pot with a cracked bowl and licked the edge clean. It wasn't as warm as he expected —tepid at best—but it made it easier to eat right away. They hadn't found any cutlery, leaving him to try and sip his meal from the edge of the bowl. It had thickened, so when that didn't work, he scooped bites of stew into his mouth with two fingers.

"Your manners would make a goborrin proud," Lark commented quietly from the straw pile behind him.

He twisted to scowl at her over his shoulder, but she seemed unbothered. She slid from the straw without disturbing Aren or Resia and if her voice had woken either of them, it didn't show. Despite the sleeping arrangements, she managed to look unruffled, though she picked a few stray pieces of straw from her golden hair.

"Hungry?" he asked, barely above a whisper. He held out his bowl in offering.

Lark crinkled her nose. "I just watched you lick your fingers and stick them back in that bowl."

The urge to roll his eyes was strong. Instead, he picked up a mug with a chipped rim from the pile of dishes they'd created beside the hearth and offered that. She took it without a word and scooped up her own breakfast.

"Murk left just before dawn to scout," she said as she settled beside the table. "He's headed toward the garrison. He doesn't think any of the goborrins you ran out of Kolmar went that direction, but he wanted to see how many sentries they have posted and where before you and I depart. He was still sour about Resia's insistence we didn't need anyone to keep watch, so I figured it was best to allow him a chance to help through scouting."

Zaide nodded. "We'll need to find a good place to cross the river, too, now that the bridge is gone. Resia should be able to help with that, since she had to help the Kolmari escape when the goborrins took the village."

"We should leave as soon as he gets back. Start gathering your things after you're done eating." Her stew was just as thick as his and she squinted into her cup when it proved hard to drink.

Vindicated, he fished out a particularly large lump of potato with his fingers and ate it.

"Maker's mercy, would you two shut up?" Aren muttered. "Some of us are trying to sleep."

"And you'll get plenty of sleep after we're gone, so I'm having trouble feeling sorry for you," Zaide said. "Do you know how long it's been since I got some good rest?"

Aren lifted his head just enough to glower at both of them. "Yeah, because I was in Kolmar when everything happened, remember? It's not like I've been resting on my laurels since the Elder sent you to get the Hymnflute."

"Hush." Resia reached across the straw to swat him. "Just because you get cranky when you don't sleep well doesn't mean you can be short with anyone else."

He tucked in his chin and looked sullen. "Sorry."

She sat up and ruffled her dark hair with one hand. It stood up like a halo around her head, full of golden straw. "What was that about a bridge, Zaide?"

Out of respect for the way Aren turned over and tried to go back to sleep, Zaide kept his voice low. "How did you get across the river before, since the bridge is out? When you went to Amrochan and I found you in the marsh, and when you and the rest of the Kolmari escaped?"

Resia blinked at him twice, then offered a slight smile. "Don't worry about that. You won't have any problem crossing."

Zaide's brow furrowed, but before he could ask what she meant, the door creaked open and Murk stepped inside.

"Good to see you awake, Your Highness," the soldier said as he tugged the door shut behind him. It stuck in the dirt and he grumbled under his breath as he jerked it free.

"And good to see you've returned," Lark replied coolly. "What is there to report?"

"No sign of any goborrins anywhere near the village. No camps in the woods, and no sign of any trying to make their way here from the garrison, but..."

She raised a brow when he trailed off.

"But?" Zaide urged.

Murk frowned at him and turned to the princess. "Well, Your Highness, you're going to have to see this."

Zaide wasn't sure what he'd expected, but what greeted them at the edge of the river certainly wasn't it. He shifted his bag on his shoulder and rubbed the back of his neck. "You know, this kind of makes sense."

Where the bridge had been, a twisted mass of trunks arched over the water, a new bridge made of living trees spun together by magic. He recognized the Elder's work and studied it with a sense of awe, but it inspired less pleasant feelings, too. His foster father told him the escape to Amrochan had been taxing. For the

Elder, the price of that effort had been his life. But seeing the bridge and knowing how difficult such a work of magic must have been, Zaide felt a sudden wash of guilt, realizing his destruction of the old bridge had played a part in his mentor's death. Complicated emotions swirled inside him and for a moment, he wasn't sure he could move forward.

What he needed was rest. Time to sit by himself and think over everything he'd been through. He still hadn't done it, and every time he pushed the thought aside and carried on with his mission, the burden he carried in the back of his mind grew that much more precarious. Before long, he had to sort through his misadventures—and his failings.

"It's sturdier than it looks," Aren said beside him, mistaking his grim face for uncertainty.

Resia nodded. "Everyone in Kolmar crossed it. It has roots anchoring it on both sides. It'll grow this way forever, providing a permanent living bridge."

"One the boy can't knock down," Murk added, giving Zaide a flat stare.

"What would you know?" Zaide muttered as he shifted his bag again and took his first step onto the bridge. "You weren't even there."

The trees were springy underfoot and moved oddly as he walked, but the interwoven trunks and branches didn't so much as creak as he crossed. The others followed, though the group stopped on the other side.

"This is where we part ways for now," Lark said. "I'm trusting both of you will take good care of the new Elder until some of the Kolmari can return."

Aren nodded and inched closer to Resia's side.

Murk only frowned. "Are you certain about this, Your Highness? Kolmar is safe, and—"

"And the fewer of us there are, the faster we can travel." The princess would not be deterred.

Zaide didn't disagree with her choice. "We've got all the

artifacts, and she's got the instructions on how to use them. We'll be fine."

"I'm sure she will be. It's your fool head I have to worry about. And mine, which Sendassian will have if you let anything go wrong."

Nothing he said would make a good argument against that, so Zaide shut his mouth and gave a stiff nod instead.

Resia stepped forward to wrap him in a hug. "Be careful."

He patted her back. Every time he had to say goodbye to his sister, it grew more awkward. "I will be." No matter how many times he promised, she would always request the same thing. After his expeditions to retrieve the artifacts Lark carried, his assurances he'd be all right had begun to feel hollow.

"We'll go south when we're a mile from the garrison, cut through the thick of the woods and make our way back to the road on the other side." Lark had no goodbyes of her own to say, aside from giving orders, and she faced the parting with such neutrality that she came across cold. Nothing unusual, Zaide thought. She'd never done anything to make herself endearing.

"Kolmar's magical protection ends before that point, from what I'm able to sense," Resia said. "That means they have regular patrols that reach beyond that mile mark, so be cautious."

"Of course. Thank you, Elder." Lark turned away and started down the road as if nothing remained to be said.

Zaide glanced after her, then back to the others. "Be safe." He wasn't sure what else to tell them. "Take care of her."

Resia snorted and slapped his arm. "I'll take care of myself, thank you very much. Donil's right, you're the one we have to watch out for."

He blinked. "Donil."

The sour look on Murk's face grew stormier than ever.

Zaide's brows climbed upward. "Is that so?"

"All right," Murk snarled as he spun back to cross the bridge.

"Get on with you, then. The Elder will be fine. You just worry about keeping yourself alive."

Zaide strangled a laugh so it escaped as a small cough instead. "Fine. Be safe, Aren. By the Maker's mercy, I'll be back."

"And if the Maker's got mercy on us, you won't be," Aren replied with a grin. "Better run. Your princess is leaving you behind."

That made Zaide straighten, and when he spun to look for Lark, she was already a good distance down the road. He fought back a sigh and ran to catch up with her.

She didn't so much as look at him as he fell in stride beside her. "You're a very sentimental person," she remarked flatly. "They'll be fine, no need to fuss. Resia's an exceptional mage. I got to see her work firsthand, you know. While you and Aren were raiding the village."

"And while you were sitting with Donil?" The name felt odd leaving his tongue and Zaide shook his head. It was mild and average. No wonder the man preferred his nickname.

"Yes. Your sister's quite good at ferreting information out of people, you know. I think she had his whole life story out of him within an hour. She'll make a fine leader for your people."

He, on the other hand, knew next to nothing about the soldiers he'd traveled with, despite spending days with them on the road. His brows drew together, but he caught himself and smoothed his expression. "Did she ferret out any information that might be useful while we travel?"

"No, I'm afraid Murk's report is all we have to go on." Lark sighed. Clearly, he hadn't been the only one who hoped for more. "If Resia believes the goborrins are sending patrols more than a mile into the woods, though, we should consider an alternate route."

"I can help with that." He'd only been to this side of the river once, but he trusted his skill with woodcraft. Verlin had been a good teacher. There would be game trails through the entirety of the forest, but the trees were thickest in the middle of the valley.

"I'll watch for a good place to dip off the road. When I see it, I'll let you know."

"How about there?" She pointed, then veered off the hard-packed earth to make for the treeline.

"Hey!" Zaide protested. He had to jog to keep up with her. "I thought I was supposed to be leading this leg of the journey?"

Lark snorted. "I don't know what gave you that idea."

"Our conversation this morning after breakfast? When we agreed on how this trip would progress?" It had only been a few hours ago.

"Well, as your princess, I'm in charge no matter where we go." She tossed her head and walked with a little more purpose, as if she knew exactly where she was headed.

"I don't mean to sound skeptical, Your Highness, but even I have only been over on this side of the bridge once." He ducked under a wayward branch and tried not to growl. She walked too noisily, her booted steps crunching loud enough the whole forest would hear. "Maybe we should slow down and try to find an easier path, before we—"

Just before him, she dropped out of sight with a shriek.

"Lark!" Zaide scrambled forward, but she was already out of reach. She cradled her head with both arms as she tumbled down the side of a ravine. Thick mud and slick, rotten leaves gave way to accelerate her fall.

He spat an oath and scanned the hill for a way down. The incline was steep, the earth spongy after the previous day's heavy rain. There was nowhere to make an easy climb. He grimaced and grabbed the most flexible sapling he could find, then started his descent. Careful steps let him control each slide so he landed at the foot of a sturdy tree. The roots offered good footholds, but the going was slow. At the bottom of the hill, Lark came to a stop and groaned.

She lay still for so long, he feared he'd have to go right back up the hill to fetch Resia. When he was no more than a quarter of the way from the bottom, she pushed herself to her hands and knees and Zaide released his held breath.

By the time his feet hit the ground, he'd gone from being worried to being angry. "Now do you think I should be in the lead?" He bounded the last few steps and stumbled on the muddy ground, but managed to stay on his feet.

Lark lifted her head and gave him the most baleful glare he'd ever seen. Mud spattered her clothing and streaked her face, and more than a few scrapes marred her tanned skin.

Zaide sighed and crouched before her. "Are you hurt?"

She shook her head and sank to sit. "Only my pride," she muttered.

"Yeah, that was pretty idiotic." He plucked a strand of gooey hair from her forehead, her locks more brown than gold from mud. "You're lucky you didn't land in the creek."

"Maybe not. I need to wash this off, now."

Somewhere farther up the ravine, the low, thumping call of a drumbird filled the air. Zaide raised a finger to his lips and craned his neck, listening with his better ear.

Lark grew tense beside him. "Zaide, the sword."

He glanced down. The Spectrum Blade fit loosely in the scabbard at his side, providing more than enough space for the light that swirled across its surface to shine out.

"Goborrins?" she asked in a whisper.

"Stay here." He stood and unsheathed the sword.

Something in it definitely felt different. His fingers tingled as they tightened around the hilt.

Another drumbird call answered.

They were closer than he'd expected. Not close enough that they were in immediate danger, but it meant the enemy was still closer to Kolmar than he'd realized.

Lark did not stay put. She dragged herself to her feet. "How far does that sound carry?"

"Not as far as I'd like." He considered telling her again to stay put and let him scout ahead, but it was pointless. She was going to follow whether he wanted or not. Her determination was admirable, he supposed, but it could have come at a better time. For now, all he could do was appreciate that she kept her voice quiet.

The sword in his hand glittered as he moved through the sun-dappled ravine. The colored swirls moved faster, writhing as if the sword expected a fight—as if it liked the idea. He'd already grown used to the artifacts reacting to their environment and to one another, but the movement on the blade made him uncomfortable. Unlike the other artifacts, which merely glowed or sometimes emitted pulsing light, the way the colors slid made him feel as if the weapon were alive.

Maybe it is, you don't know, he told himself. *Maybe that's how it knows when the right person touches it.* That thought gave him goosebumps and he fought back a shiver.

"You all right?" Lark whispered.

It wasn't like her to express concern. He glanced at her, then shrugged. "Bad feeling." She could make of that what she pleased.

Evidently, she took it to mean problems, for she drew her silver knives.

Zaide swallowed another useless protest and pressed onward. The drumbeats weren't frequent, nor did they bear any rhythm or pattern he could identify beyond knowing it was meant to be a drumbird. The number of repetitions had to mean something, or maybe the tone, but he hadn't been able to decipher any messages yet. Maybe it was better if he didn't.

Something moved ahead. Zaide hid behind a stout oak and peered out around it. The flabby pink flesh of a goborrin's exposed back caught the sunlight at the edge of the ravine. Lark saw it, too, and pressed herself against a tree trunk nearby. Instead of looking at the monster, she looked to Zaide, her expression asking what she was meant to do.

Stay behind, like I asked you to, he thought at her as he frowned. But thinking it did nothing, as evidenced by the way she sheathed a knife and opened her bag instead. A moment later, she drew her tiny crossbow.

He gave his head a vehement shake. *Don't you dare!* Not when they didn't know how many goborrins waited above, or where.

Lark pursed her lips, but lowered it.

When he looked again, the goborrin was gone.

Perfect. He swallowed hard, but didn't let himself breathe any harder. Slowly, he pushed himself away from his tree and tried not to let his footsteps squish.

The ravine snaked off to the south, a shallow creek at its bottom. Hoof prints showed where deer had come to drink and the occasional mark of a broad paw warned of wildcats, but nothing bigger had been down there. He'd seen enough goborrin tracks now to know the difference. Even the biggest wild boar he'd ever seen didn't have feet that big.

As they walked, the drumbird calls grew fainter.

After a time, Lark inched closer to speak in a murmur. "Aren't we going to fight them?"

"This soon? We've hardly left Kolmar. We have a long way to go, and we're not off to a great start." And if the situation outside Amrochan had not improved, they'd have enough fighting to do just to get through the gates. Zaide tried to keep a steady pace as he followed the creek around the bend. It meandered west after a while. He suspected it would take them back toward the road eventually, based on what he recalled from the Elder's old maps, but those maps were gone now and he had little to guide him until night fell and he could see the stars.

The princess said nothing, though he sensed her disappointment. It struck him as odd; Lark was competent with her blades but wasn't much of a fighter by nature. Seeking a fight didn't strike him as normal for her.

Then he recalled the sword he still carried in his left hand, ready for combat should any goborrin patrols find them.

Aren had been excited to tell the others how the artifacts

performed in battle. Lark hadn't seen the Spectrum Blade in action. Of course she'd want to see it, after Aren's vivid descriptions of the way it carved through goborrins like a good knife through a slow-roasted wood hen. He still wasn't sure what to make of the way it seared them, filling wounds with iridescent light and spilling no blood.

"We'll have plenty of opportunities to strike them down," Zaide said after a time, when it became clear Lark planned to say nothing else. "Right now, we need to figure out a good place to get out of this ditch."

"Fine," Lark sighed, none too enthusiastic, though she scanned the slope to her right in search of decent footholds.

He looked, too. Not far ahead, a portion of the hillside sported a terraced sort of look where tree roots clung to the earth. "There. Those are good roots, we can head up there."

Still quiet, Lark began her ascent without any assistance. Zaide let her progress for as long as she could without sliding. The first time her foot skidded in mud, he caught her arm and guided her steps.

They were both a little short of breath when they reached the top of the hill, but if his sense of direction was worth anything at all, he estimated they were relatively near the road.

Zaide lifted his head to check and met the eyes of a half dozen goborrins around a campfire, staring right at them.

CHAPTER FOUR

"Oh, excuse me," Zaide said. "We'll just go back down..." He motioned vaguely back the way they'd come.

Unplacated, the goborrins bellowed and surged to their feet.

Zaide gritted his teeth and flowed forward to meet the nearest monster as it spun on him with its weapon raised. The Spectrum Blade flashed in his hand as he plunged the sword into the beast's stomach. It gurgled and fell back, only to be replaced by another goborrin swinging its club for his head.

Lark bounded to his side, daggers drawn, but the goborrins ignored her. Instead, the remaining five swarmed around Zaide, fixated on the shining artifact he held. She took advantage of the oversight and went in low, cutting deep into a monster's side. Coppery brown blood joined the mud that spattered her when she jerked her blade loose.

The monsters were big, their size a hindrance to them in close quarters. Zaide ducked between two goborrins and stabbed another. It cut so easily that his blade sank to the hilt and protruded from the monster's back before he pulled it free. Light glowed in the bloodless wound as the sword came loose and the goborrin collapsed.

"Stay down!" Lark snarled.

Zaide spun toward her. The goborrin she'd felled wasn't dead yet, its thick hand wrapped around her ankle and its teeth bared. She tried to stab it again, but it pulled her off her feet and she went down with a squeak.

He bolted in and raked his sword across the monster's throat, leaving a searing streak of white. Then he caught her by the arm and dragged her back to her feet.

The remaining three goborrins converged on them. Zaide went right and Lark went left, both tearing into their beasts with all the strength they could muster. Zaide's went down first and he rounded on the last of the monsters. It swung a rough sword at his chest. He pulled back and then launched himself forward, and his sideways slice cleaved the goborrin almost in two.

"Maker's mercy," Lark panted as she dispatched hers and stared at the fading shimmers of light Zaide's sword left behind on his adversaries. "It cuts through them like butter!"

He swallowed hard and struggled to catch his breath.

Six goborrins on the ground. The two of them untouched.

Several weeks ago, when he'd faced his first goborrin and taken it down, he would have thought such a feat impossible.

Lark cleaned her daggers on a goborrin's trousers and sheathed them. She brushed her muddy hair away from her equally muddy face and reached for Zaide's arm.

He almost asked what she was doing, then recalled she couldn't touch the sword. "It's clean," he said, unsure what she hoped to see. He let her take his wrist, twisting and turning his hand without touching the Spectrum Blade's hilt so she could inspect it.

"Incredible. How does it do that? Does it feel like anything when you fight?"

"Like a sword that's smaller than what I'm used to. That's about it." Despite how ordinary it felt, the iridescent swirls on its surface struck him as agitated with the way they churned.

Lark made a soft, thoughtful sound. "I just don't see how this can be. It's not like the rest of the artifacts. I can feel them, I can sense their magic. But this... It doesn't feel like anything to me, yet it's obviously more powerful than all three of the others."

"Maybe it's a different kind of magic. Something you can't feel." Zaide couldn't deny that he had felt something when Resia had blessed it, or whatever the term for what she'd done might be. But aside from magic, he didn't know what that sensation could have been.

"I don't believe anything like that exists, unfortunately. Remarkable. It doesn't draw blood at all? Can you cut yourself with it?"

"I don't know. I haven't tried, and I don't think I'm going to. Right now, I think we need to get out of here before other patrols come through." Their campfire looked relatively fresh, so it might be some time before the group they'd killed was due back somewhere. Even so, Zaide wanted to be long gone when that time came.

A small, wistful sigh escaped Lark as she let go of his hand and allowed him to sheath the blade. "Can I look at it more when we stop for the night?"

"Sure, but we have to be going before we can stop." He turned her by her shoulders and pointed west.

She started off without needing further direction and together, they ducked back into the trees.

"We should stay close to the creek for now. It's more muddy, but we're also more likely to evade detection." Zaide offered a hand to help her back down the slope, but she walked straight past him and began her own cautious descent. This time, they reached the bottom of the ravine without any scrapes.

"I hardly see why we should worry about being spotted. After seeing the way that thing cuts through those monsters, it almost feels like..." She trailed off and offered him a smile that bordered on shy. "Well, like we have a chance."

"That's the whole point, isn't it?" It had certainly seemed like it. Retrieve the artifacts, retrieve the sword, destroy Gadranus and his entire army. The need to visit the Magister in Jadora and the Desheni Shaman curbed his enthusiasm somewhat, but for the first time since Amrochan, it seemed as if he might finally get a chance to do something of value.

That he could be chosen as Bladebearer had never crossed his mind, never a possibility he'd realized existed, yet that served to temper his expectations, too. The sword might have chosen him, but he hardly knew what that meant.

"I suppose." Lark scraped mud from her hair as she followed the creek's bank farther through the ravine. It was too steep to trail along its edge in some places, and once they reached a point where wide, gravel-rich spaces of the creek bed were exposed, she stepped down to walk along the creek's bottom instead.

Zaide didn't like the deep footprints their boots left in the soft creek bed, but it wasn't as if they hadn't left any signs of their passing behind elsewhere. There was only one place they could go, besides. If the goborrins were half as intelligent as he expected they were, they'd know to find them on the road, no matter how they got there. "You sound like you're not sure. Is there something you want to tell me?"

Her hesitance said enough on its own. Eventually, she scuffed her heel against a pit of gravel and gave a shrug. "I guess it doesn't hurt to admit I was never sure of what we were doing. There was enough evidence in the books I read and the legends I'd heard to support the existence of the artifacts and the blade, but I was never certain we'd be able to retrieve them, or that they really held the power we needed."

"You risked our lives on an uncertainty?" It sounded harsher than he meant when it came out like that, but the princess seemed unbothered.

"A chance seems like enough, doesn't it? A chance to end a war, to save the people you care about, to protect the kingdom? I knew it was dangerous, but the biggest risk seemed to be the waste of time, if I was proven wrong." Again, she shrugged. "Yet time hardly matters. If we hadn't set out to gather these things, what difference would we have made?

We're just two people, too young to make a difference any other way."

Zaide tilted his head and squinted at the sky. It was hard to envision things turning out differently, harder to imagine what might have been if he hadn't encountered Lark in the woods on the day of the Spring Choosing. The goborrins would have razed Kolmar either way. As the Elder's apprentice, he would have been sent to the temple for the Hymnflute no matter what. "Maybe we don't make a difference. Maybe everything we're doing is inevitable."

The princess spun on her heel and paced along backwards, frowning at him. "That's grim, don't you think? You don't believe that, do you?"

"If I'm being honest, Your Highness, I'm kind of shaky on what I do and don't believe right now."

Her expression softened. "I suppose that's understandable." She turned back the way she was headed and raked her fingers through her hair again. Her ponytail clung to her back, resembling a snake. She shook it loose with a small sound of annoyance.

"You don't deal with that?" He couldn't imagine anyone experiencing what they had and not questioning things, but she shook her head and didn't look back at him again.

"I don't think the situation has been as challenging for me as it has been for you. I grew up in Amrochan and spent my whole life studying things like this. My father largely dismissed the Rise as a legend surrounding the war he inherited, but I had plenty of educators who made it clear the reincarnation of Gadranus was a genuine thing to expect. No one could tell me what exactly would happen or what things might be like, but being taught your whole life to prepare for the unexpected has a way of making one habitually open-minded."

The implication that he was not prickled, but he tempered the initial rise of annoyance and reminded himself her criticism wasn't often delivered in such a breezy tone. She had been sharp plenty of times before. "I don't think I'm not," he said slowly. "I'm just..."

"Sheltered?" she suggested. This time, when she spared him a glance, her rich blue eyes twinkled. The expression was so warm and unlike her that he stumbled in the gravel.

"Yeah." Caught off guard as he was, he didn't know how else to reply.

Lark didn't seem to hear him. Instead, she scanned the trees and pointed at a slope ahead that seemed a little less threatening than the rest. "Think we can go up there? We should be far enough away from that camp to find the road, right?"

"I think so. I'll check it out. " Zaide trotted ahead to climb before her. The slope was shallow enough that he was able to climb with one hand on his sword. Above, only the normal sounds of the forest carried on in the endless chatter of birds and other woodland creatures. He peeked above the rim of the ravine and searched the horizon. The woods were thick, but wide game trails marked the way down to the creek. Satisfied, he waved for the princess to join him.

Her climb was a little more graceful this time, though she relied on branches and the trunks of saplings to keep her upright as she made her way up.

Out of pure instinct, he offered a hand as she grew near. To his surprise, she took it, and he pulled her up so they could climb out together. Her fingertips were cold. He gave them a small squeeze with his warmer hand before he let go. "The road should be that direction. Once we get there, things should be much easier."

"Good. I've already had my fill of misadventure for the duration of this particular trip." She sniffed and made for one of the game trails, already back to her haughty self.

A puzzle, Zaide decided. One the Maker set before him either as a challenge, or simply to confound him. He could think of no other reasons for their fates to have become entangled so easily. "You'd be spared some misadventure if you'd let me lead," he reminded her as he jogged ahead to put himself in front.

Lark sniffed again, but did nothing to stop him. For now, it seemed he'd won that fight.

They remained quiet as they trekked through the dense part of the woods. There were no drumbird calls here, but after the surprise of finding the goborrin camp in the clearing before, it seemed unwise to carry on with conversation where they were easily seen.

Eventually, the trees fell away and the road was revealed, as wide and hard-packed and welcome as Zaide remembered.

"We should set a hard pace," he suggested.

Lark walked a little faster, supporting his choice.

Now and then, the soft echoes of drumbirds reached his ears. Most were real birds, but a few were the not-quite-right cadences and timbres he'd come to recognize as goborrin communication. Now and then, when a call went on a long while, the princess looked at him as if in question. He didn't know how to respond. The beats had to mean something, but they were another puzzle, one he was no closer to figuring out than he was to figuring out Lark. In the end, he merely shook his head and let them carry on in silence until the forest fell away behind them and night's shadow stole over the sky.

"There's something I meant to say earlier," Lark confided when they finally settled and Zaide showed her how to start a fire with the Molten Dagger. "When we spoke of the artifacts and being unsure."

"I hope you're not going to say something sappy right now, because we still have to walk for a few days and I'd prefer the trip not be any more awkward than it is." He pushed the small tin cup from his bag closer to the fire and sat back while he waited for the water inside to warm.

Lark's snort told him how likely that was.

"Sorry," he muttered when a stony silence followed. "Go ahead."

"The sword."

Zaide glanced at the blade sheathed at his side, but it shone no more brightly than usual.

"I mean, it's what made me sure. Earlier, fighting the goborrins. Seeing what it was capable of, what a single strike could do, was what made me sure we're on the right path."

"We're also on the only path."

"I didn't mean the woods."

"Neither did I." He tucked in his chin and stared at the fire. The evenings were not as cool as they had been when he'd first left Kolmar, but a distinct chill still sat under the trees after dark. "I don't think we have other options. After seeing everything in the temple, I..." *You what?* He asked himself. He hardly knew how to articulate how things had changed.

To his good fortune, elaboration seemed unnecessary. Lark nodded and scooted closer to the fire. "Nothing compares to seeing the truth with your own eyes. I can't pretend to understand why the Elder sought to keep knowledge from you, but there has to be a reason."

"Maybe the reason was he hated me and wanted me to stumble around making a fool of myself when I made it out into the world." He poked a finger into the water. Its mild warmth was a comfort on his skin, so he retrieved the cup from the fire's side and produced a scrap of cloth from his bag. He'd packed it with the intention of using it to polish the Spectrum Blade, but nothing ever seemed to mar its surface. He wasn't sure cleaning the blade would be necessary. A good thing, considering his record. He folded the fabric into quarters, dipped it into the water, then extended it toward Lark.

She raised a brow.

"For your face," Zaide said.

"Do I look that awful?" She sounded more resigned than insulted, and she took the cloth from his fingers to scrub her face clean. At first, all it did was smear the dirt around, but eventually the crusted mud began to wash away.

He passed her the cup so she could keep going. "You look like you fell down a muddy ravine. But we're headed to Amrochan, and I'd rather not show up with the princess looking undignified. I don't get the feeling Sendassian liked me, and I'd prefer not to give him any reasons to have my head."

"My father doesn't like anyone," Lark murmured. "Frankly, I don't think he likes me, either."

"He liked your mother. Didn't he? Or else you wouldn't exist."

The look she gave him made him regret opening his mouth. "You know very little of how things work among royalty."

Zaide shrugged. "Apparently I know very little about everything, from the Shattered Lands where I was born to what kind of currency is used anywhere in this entire kingdom." And perhaps the Elder was to thank for that. Or revile. He hadn't decided which was more appropriate, but he'd taken to leaning toward the latter. Whether or not the Elder had reasons for keeping him in the dark, it certainly seemed malicious to let Zaide fumble around the holes in his own knowledge.

"We'll work on that." Lark rinsed the cloth with what remained of the water in the cup, wrung it out, then sat both cloth and cup near the fire to dry. "We'll have to, since the Spectrum Blade only chooses one wielder."

"Was that in the Elder's books?" It seemed a safe bet, given how little Lark seemed to have known about the blade before they found it.

She nodded. "Once it has chosen the hand it wishes to have wield it against Gadranus, it cannot change hands until the Bladebearer is rendered incapable of wielding it anymore."

"So if I die—" Zaide started.

"It would select someone new to carry it. Yes. We wouldn't be rendered hopeless just because its chosen carrier was slain. Based on some of the history detailed in the Elder's volumes, it has happened before."

"Reassuring."

"It's war, Zaide. Nobody should expect to make it through alive."

He sobered. "I don't." He'd considered his own mortality plenty of times, even before he'd set out from Kolmar at the Elder's behest. "I've thought about that a lot since leaving home."

Lark raised a brow, invitation to go on.

There was plenty to say. The trip itself had brought a number of reminders, all of which stirred to mind as he watched the flickering fire, but one had hung in his thoughts since he'd made his way back to Amrochan with the last of the three artifacts in his possession.

"When I left Beshnai, after getting the Captured Spring, I met a merchant. She caught a farmer and asked him to help me. I rode with him to Yithel."

"Kind of them," she said, tone gentle but encouraging.

Zaide agreed, but the shadow of the woman's reasons still weighed on him. "While we traveled, the farmer said she'd asked him to help a lot of young people go join the war. Her husband had been a soldier. Her son wanted to follow him, like I wanted to follow my father. He left Kolmar when I was an infant, never came back. The woman—Orla—her son's friends were all a bit older than him, and she felt bad for him having to watch all of them leave before he could join them. So she'd send supplies with all of them when they left, and the farmer helped them halfway to Amrochan."

In the pause that followed, Lark said nothing, but the way she stared made it clear she was listening. Waiting. He rubbed his hands together and then held them toward the fire, a sudden chill stealing his warmth. "In the fall, when he made his last trip, the farmer finally took her son. Orla was proud of him, and he was excited to finally have his way, now that he was old enough to join the guard. He sent her a letter every week. They came in with merchants, the farmer said she always met them at the edge of town, excited to see news of the difference he was making in the war. And then one week, no letter came."

"Delayed?" the princess suggested.

Zaide shook his head.

For a time, things were still, but the burden of his thoughts grew heavier in the silence.

Eventually, he closed his eyes. "I've spent my whole life wanting this. What we're doing now. A chance to go to Amrochan, to follow my father's footsteps, to join the war and hope I could help finish it. The whole world has been consumed by this fight. Amroch is all that's left. We're the only hope anyone has to stop this. Why wouldn't I want to be part of that?"

"Are you saying you don't want to be?" she asked softly.

"No," Zaide replied, the response so fast and heated that he embarrassed himself. Heat stole up his neck and into his ears. The docked one always felt so much hotter when he flushed. "I do. I just... I never had any questions about it before. About what I would do or why. I never asked myself if it was the best thing to do. And now that we're going, and I've got the Spectrum Blade, I feel like I'm finally doing what I wanted to do all along. But after I heard that, heard how Orla spent all winter looking for someone to send in hopes she'd hear word from someone that her son was still alive, I just..."

"Have doubts," Lark finished for him.

He swallowed, but nodded. "For the first time."

The princess scooted closer. When she raised her hand, he almost expected admonishment, but instead she touched his shoulder in a gentle show of reassurance. "There's nothing wrong with doubting yourself or your goals. It's normal to have questions or be unsure about the choices you're making. It doesn't mean you're on the wrong path, or that you need to change course."

"Easy for you to say," he grumbled. "You're the princess. Future queen of Amroch. You're the one who decides if the course you're on is right, you get the privilege of making it right. The rest of us have to bend to what the world gives us."

Her brows climbed. "You think I don't? I'm a mage whose power never came to fruition the way it should have. Power I need in order to do what's expected of me. If my father can't end this war, it falls on my shoulders, and I'm not exactly a warrior princess."

"You're plenty capable with those knives."

"But I don't have battlefield experience. I'm... I am easily overwhelmed in combat, and before our expedition, I had only trained against people who would have been executed if they'd done me even accidental harm. At least your trainers were allowed to bludgeon you."

"And they did," Zaide said with a sheepish grin. He'd taken his fair share of knocks, always grateful that the practice blades they used were dull-edged wood.

"I overestimated some of my competence. That's difficult for me to say, but since we're being vulnerable with each other tonight, I suppose I can admit that much." She twiddled her fingers and looked away, as if too embarrassed to look him in the eye. "But even aside from that, it should be obvious I am not meant to lead. The Spectrum Blade chose you, after all."

For reasons he couldn't imagine. "It should have been you. The Bladebearer's supposed to be like a folk hero, right? It would be better for that to be royalty, not some..." He grasped at the air, unable to find a word that wasn't too self-deprecating. He understood why the broken-born were distrusted—sort of— but that was hardly what made him unfit to wield it. He'd overestimated his capabilities, too, and others had paid the price. "Some backwoods orphan who doesn't even know how much an Amrochan rui is worth."

Lark snorted. "It should have been me," she agreed. "The Bladebearer is supposed to be... well, I suppose that hardly matters. What does matter, though, is that I am not, and you are, and there's little sense in whining over it now. All we can do is move forward and hope for the best. I just hope you remain as pliant as you have been."

"Pliant?" Zaide repeated, startled.

"Malleable? I'm not sure that's the right description. Simply put, I hope you remain as cooperative as you have been. I realize this is not exactly what you dreamed your life would be, but if I cannot wield the blade myself, I hope you'll remain amenable to being wielded in its place."

Which struck him as a very complicated way of saying he was being used. Zaide mulled that over for a moment before he decided it would be better addressed in the future, when the sword at his side had been fully awakened and he saw what it could really do.

"Who says this isn't what I dreamed my life would be?" he said instead, unsheathing several inches of the iridescent sword belted to his side. "A few more days and we'll get to Amrochan, and with this thing, I'll finally get what I've always wanted."

Lark blinked. "Which is?"

A chance to pursue what he'd always felt he was meant to do. To honor his father's sacrifice and his refugee mother's memory. He touched a finger to the Spectrum Blade's edge and a hum of *something* ran through him. A sense of approval, he thought, which should have been disconcerting. Instead, it struck him as a comfort. He sheathed the blade again. "A chance to turn the tide."

CHAPTER FIVE

THIS WAS NOT what Tula thought life as one of Amrochan's librarians would be like. She leaned back in her chair and gazed wistfully at the tall shelves lined with thousands of books dressed in bright colors. Jadora's librarians preferred to keep things orderly and utilitarian. Seeing so many books with gilded spines and richly colored canvas covers made her heart skip, but since Dasienna's departure, she had yet to pull a single book from the shelves.

Instead, she sat at a table with more than a dozen other scholars, all of them older than her. Every last one of them sported a perpetual frown, the creases between their brows so deep that she wasn't sure they could come unfurrowed. Their downturned mouths had become contagious, too, and she found herself pursing her lips and then rubbing her face with both palms in hopes it would scrub away the sullenness. The expression left her face, but it did not leave her mood.

Amrochan's library was supposed to be an adventure, not another endless stream of work nobody wanted to touch. Although she supposed there was one difference there; in Jadora, the senior librarians pursued whatever they pleased, while the apprentices were left to tend less scintillating tasks. Here, every last librarian in the city sat perched around the same table, working figures and copying reports from the soldiers just outside the city walls. Important work, no doubt, but her fingers still itched to pull books from the shelves. Or at the very least, pull her notebook from her pocket.

How was it the books had never enchanted her when she'd had all of the Great Library at her disposal?

"Because everything you're not allowed is everything that's fun," she muttered to herself.

All around the table, Amrochan's librarians shushed her.

Tula resisted the urge to stick out her tongue. They were all so focused on their work. The air was thick with the constant scratch of pens against low-quality paper and smoother vellum, the tap of nibs against the mouths of inkwells, the rustle of clothing and the occasional cough to remind her all her companions were old. Where *were* all of Amrochan's apprentice librarians? She'd seen hide nor hair of anyone lacking gray at their temples.

Frustrated, she allowed herself to stretch in her chair before she slumped against the table. She pulled her notebook from her pocket and regarded it wistfully for a moment, then put it aside and took up her pen once more.

The city had enough barrels of barley to last eleven months. The supply of wheat would last almost as long. The figures were important, she knew, but there were enough scholars to work them without her. Yet they'd decided her assignment from Princess Dasienna meant nothing in the face of the siege, and she supposed she couldn't fault them for that. Amrochan had not been surrounded by goborrins when she escorted the princess back from Jadora, with a handful of precious books on loan from the Great Library to serve the princess's studies.

Had Dasienna remained in Amrochan, they could have studied together, but she also couldn't fault the princess for pursuing the blade they believed to be locked away in Kolmar's temple. Both of them were slaves to an unfortunate fate, and Tula could only hope Dasienna's expedition proved fruitful.

Perhaps they could resume study together once the princess returned—if she ever did.

News out of Kolmar had been grim even before the refugees arrived. Sendassian's forces had been thwarted, and now every blade was needed to hold a sea of goborrins at bay.

By the counts spread across papers that lay on the table, more than sixty thousand of the monsters had already been slain. Despite that feat, the army outside Amrochan's walls never seemed any smaller. How Dasienna was supposed to return through the storm of violence that raged in the fields, Tula didn't know. The ship rumored to have carried the princess and her party from Amrochan's harbor had been spotted traveling north. Everyone had expected Sendassian to have the ship seized and its crew questioned, but the war consumed every moment of his attention. The question of the princess's safety, it seemed, would have to wait.

The library's ornate lacquered door creaked open and a bespectacled figure stepped inside. Tula expected another armful of papers to be added to the heap of things they were meant to sort through, but the woman cleared her throat instead.

"The southern edge of the goborrin army has been breached," she announced.

Heads popped up around the table. A moment later, a chorus of complaints and questions filled the air.

Tula sat straighter and strained to listen over the voices. A change in the battle meant a lot of predictions and calculations would have to be rewritten, but the numbers mattered little to her.

The battle outside Amrochan had persisted without change for more than a week. The goborrin losses were always higher than those of Sendassian's army, yet neither side had made progress. For a shift to happen in the battle on the southern side of the attacking force, someone must have changed tactics.

No one had worked numbers for that.

The spectacled woman rattled off a list of numbers and places. A handful of scholars jotted them down as if it were the most precious information they'd ever been handed, while others launched directly into new figures. How many bushels of grain it would take to sustain the army under new possible outcomes. How many trainees would need to graduate and join the army to keep Sendassian's forces at full strength. How much steel would have to be imported for the blacksmiths to continue to forge swords, armor, and arrowheads.

Finally, someone closer to the door asked the questions burning on the tip of Tula's tongue. "Who's leading this attack? How many soldiers were required to cut into the southern edge, and from which direction did they strike the attacking force?"

There was a possibility, however slim, that the new attack hadn't come from Sendassian's army at all. Word of the attack had been sent to Jadora the very day the goborrin army arrived. Enough time had passed that a small band of fast-moving soldiers could have come from the desert. Tula meant no ill of the king's armies, but there was a ferocity in the desert's soldiers that was difficult to match. If they had already answered, perhaps the siege would end sooner than any of the scholars had predicted.

The woman at the door hesitated.

"Who is it?" someone else asked, sharper.

"Come with me," the woman replied, an answer that left every scholar at the table taken aback. "You're going to need to see this."

Tula leaped from her chair and darted for the door, earning herself more than a few dirty looks. A handful of others followed, though at a more sedate pace. Together, they wound through the hallways of the palace and emerged into the barracks grounds. Armored soldiers stood in rows while officers called orders. She twisted her head to watch them as the woman led the scholars to the far end of the grounds and up a tower, to where they could see the battlefield from the bulwark.

Smoke choked the sky and the roar of combat flooded the air, but to the distant south, a distinct hole had appeared in the southern edge of the goborrin horde.

"Like someone took a bite out of a biscuit," Tula murmured to herself as she leaned against the parapets and squinted into the distance.

The other scholars fanned out behind her, whispering between themselves as they took in the sight.

In the middle of the gap, something flashed, sometimes white, sometimes colors she couldn't quite define, but it carved a steadily growing gap into their enemy's ranks.

Tula squinted a moment longer, then clapped a hand to her mouth. "I know what it is."

"I beg your pardon?" a stuffy-looking woman beside her asked.

Tula spun to beam at her, a new surge of hope flaring in her chest. "I know what it is!" She shoved past the scholars and bolted for the stairs.

She'd left her notebook behind, and this had to be recorded.

The marsh had been quiet, even the marsh-wisps frightened away by what raged outside the city. Zaide supposed he should be grateful it had made travel easy. They'd rested well at night and arrived sooner than expected. He'd tried to bolster himself for what he knew lay ahead, but when they'd come close enough to see smoke on the horizon, uncertainty had begun to gnaw at his stomach.

"What's the best way to do this?" Zaide squinted at the battle at the bottom of the slope. The landscape was blackened, nothing left to char, but fires still churned smoke into the air. A battle tactic, he decided; the fires were all behind goborrin lines.

Perhaps the smoke didn't offend their lungs the way it did Sendassian's men.

"Charge in and start cutting them down?" Lark suggested.

"I said best, not most dangerous." After how far they'd come, it would only figure that he might get himself killed on Amrochan's doorstep.

She frowned. "I don't think there is a best way. There's no way to get to Amrochan's harbor from the south, so there's no way to get in from that side of the city. Either we fight our way to the front gate, or we don't get in at all."

Turning away was tempting, but that meant heading for Jadora without their librarian. He tilted his head as he thought. Tula wasn't necessary, but she would make things easier. On the other hand, they had no supplies to get them to Jadora, or even to Tinith—if the market still stood. They hadn't ventured near enough to tell if the market city had fallen victim to goborrin attacks.

"The fighting is thickest right against the walls," he noted. "It looks like they're trying to take ladders to the ramparts."

"And it's thinnest directly in front of the gates. See?" Lark pointed. "That's where my father's men emerge, so it's where their line is the strongest. If we can work our way up to that point, we can break through with the help of our soldiers, then make it to the gates to gain entry to the city."

"That also means going through an awful lot of goborrins. There are thousands of them down there."

"Maybe tens of thousands," Lark said.

Not reassuring in the least. He sighed and scrubbed a hand through his snowy hair. "But that might still be safer than trying to skirt the wall. If they bring hot oil out at some point, we'd fry as easily as goborrins."

"So we go straight through."

"Guess so." Zaide stood and shifted the bag on his shoulder. Fighting with his belongings strapped to his back would be cumbersome, but they couldn't leave any of the books Lark had crammed into his bag, nor could they abandon the artifacts that filled hers. She'd need both hands for her knives if they were to get through the goborrins, so making her carry his bag so he could fight unhindered was out of the question.

He squinted as a new thought sprang to mind. "Have you had any time to study working with the artifacts?"

Lark blinked at him. "What do you mean?"

"Using them. Resia used the Hymnflute to make a barrier when we were fighting that shadow thing in the temple. Can you do that?"

"I can try," she said, though she looked doubtful.

"You should. You keep the barrier up and we should be able to make it. I'll cut a path for us." He touched the hilt of the Spectrum Blade with his right hand and twitched when it sent a jolt up his arm.

The princess noticed. "What was that?"

He touched it again, tentatively. The sensation was still there. Not a shock, but a feeling that had caught him off guard. Something he should definitely discuss with her and their librarian, but something he doubted they had time for now. "Um... nothing. Just antsy. I mean, I've used it a couple times, but against that many enemies..."

"Oh." She seemed to have taken some sort of understanding, for she nodded as she reached for her bag. "Yes, I suppose there will be no hiding once you draw it. It seems to be like the other artifacts, reacting with light when its power is needed. With this many goborrins to fight, its glow will likely be blinding."

"Which should hopefully keep your father's men from filling me with arrows while we do this."

"Hopefully," she agreed.

Zaide made himself suck in a deep breath through his nose and released it slowly through his mouth. When he settled his left hand on the hilt of his sword, a wash of reassurance he wasn't entirely sure came from his own confidence flowed over him.

Any other time, walking into a field full of those monsters would have meant certain death. Now, with the Spectrum Blade's hilt in his hand and the Vale Hymnflute in Lark's, he was sure they could carve a hole into the enemy's defenses.

Whether or not they could push forward far enough to make it through was yet to be seen.

"Let's go." He gripped the sword and drew it from its too-long sheath. The metal sang as it came free. Colors danced down the blade's surface, snapping and sparking as a white-hot glow swelled from the middle of the blade to its razor-keen edges.

The goborrins ahead didn't see them advancing down the hill, occupied with the battle set before them.

Lark blew two uncertain notes before she found the best way to hold the Hymnflute. She followed close behind Zaide, adjusted her grip, and played.

He felt no magic, but a surge of wind spilled from the pipes, ruffled his hair and swept across the battlefield.

The gust caught the attention of the monsters ahead. By the time they turned, Zaide was already on them.

These goborrins were smaller than those he'd faced in the temple. These were closer to the first he'd felled, the size of a large man and clad only sparsely in scraps of armor. When the Spectrum Blade raked across the beasts, it tore through them like a scythe through a stand of wheat.

Wind poured around his legs and rushed outward as Lark finished the melody. A shimmer lit the air and a shield like a bubble welled up around them. Squalling pig-faced monsters stumbled back from the barrier, confused and angered, but they couldn't pierce it.

Zaide, on the other hand, was unimpeded. His sword flashed out through the shield of air, slicing through goborrin after goborrin. Light blazed in their wounds as they toppled, their bodies forced aside by the shield as they advanced.

A cluster of the beasts rushed at them from ahead and the music faltered. An uneasy ripple coursed through the shield.

"Keep it up," Zaide called over the roar of angry monsters. The smoke was thick down here, between the slopes. The Hymnflute's barrier kept the smog at bay, but it made it hard to see where he was headed, and Lark still followed his lead.

The notes steadied again and he continued forward. As long as Lark had breath to play, the monsters couldn't touch them. But she was unpracticed and the song faltered every time a new bunch of goborrins rushed them, and he wasn't sure how long he could count on its protection.

He swept forward to mow through another cluster. Around them, howls of pain and dismay filled the air. One goborrin staggered back when cut, clutching an illuminated gash in its shoulder. Tendrils of light crawled from the wound and crept over its flesh, like the cracks that had spiderwebbed out from the ice whenever Zaide fell in the ice cave.

Focus, he hissed silently at himself. He couldn't be distracted now. Whatever the sword was capable of, he'd see it all sooner or later. The blade was light in his hand, lighter than he was used to, and it made it easier to swing and lunge.

Behind him, Lark paused long enough to suck in a few gasping breaths before she resumed her song. The barrier shuddered around them.

"You're doing good!" He shifted east. They had to cut toward the gates or they'd never make it through.

The repeating song grew sharper, notes shorter. His own breath grew ragged as he plunged his sword through another monster. The ugly faces were all the same. He didn't know how many he'd already killed. "Keep going!" he urged, though he knew it wouldn't be long.

Where were they? Where was the palace? The Spectrum Blade's light flashed against the clouds of smoke as they reached one of the fires. The flames extinguished as the Hymnflute's shield passed over it. That was interesting.

"We're halfway there!" Zaide didn't know if they were or not, but he prayed the goborrins wouldn't make a liar of him. There weren't as many here. Some spun away and fled, their beast-faces stricken and confused. There was no order to the way they tried to escape, but it was only goborrins that surrounded them. No soldiers, no reinforcements. The realization made his heart leap into his throat. If the shield fell here...

As if to reinforce his fears, the song grew shorter, more strident. The barrier began to quiver.

"Hang on!" Zaide cried, but the plea made little difference.

Lark cut off with a gasp, pressed a hand to her head and swayed on her feet.

He spat a curse and doubled back.

The moment he caught her, the shield fell.

CHAPTER SIX

LARK ALL BUT collapsed into Zaide's arms, gasping for breath and digging her fingers into her temples. "I'm sorry," she panted. "I'm dizzy."

He didn't have time to reply. Goborrins surged toward them from every side, howling and swinging crude weapons. Zaide lowered the princess to the ground and spun to meet the first. Their swords clashed and the vibrations that coursed up his arms left him numb. His blade flashed, the colors on its surface churning faster than ever.

A second strike came faster, but the goborrin's speed worked against it and its sword skidded up the side of the Spectrum Blade, leaving it wide open. Zaide drove the blade forward to impale the beast, then lurched hard to the side. The sword tore free of his enemy in a blaze of light, leaving him free to parry the next blow, but goborrins advanced to his back and he knew he and Lark wouldn't last.

A few shrieking notes from the Hymnflute shot a wave of wind toward the monsters behind him, not enough to deter them, but enough to make them stagger. Lark fell back to the earth, fighting for breath.

Zaide braced his feet to either side of her and stabbed hard.

He missed his opponent's vitals and sliced off its arm instead. "Get up!" he roared.

The staggered monsters found their feet again and two rushed him at once. He struck one and ducked a swing from the other, but couldn't do more than that. His breath grew ragged, but he didn't have to hold for long. An instant later, Lark surged to her feet and drove one of her long knives into the attacker's side. It lurched and grasped for her head, but Zaide brought the Spectrum Blade down hard and drove its hand to the earth. The same tendrils of light sprawled out from the wound in its pierced hand, lancing up its arm. The goborrin howled and clawed helplessly at the magic. The light could be nothing else.

As Zaide jerked his sword free, Lark jammed the Hymnflute into his right hand. "Play," she pleaded.

He didn't know the notes. More goborrins were on them. He swung hard with the sword in one hand and the Hymnflute in the other. The sword ripped through one's leather armor while the artifact crashed into another's jaw with a hollow wooden thunk.

A cry of dismay tore from Lark's throat.

Not a weapon, idiot, he snarled at himself as he swept the pipes to his lips and blew. Two notes sounded, bright and clear. Not knowing what else to do, he slid the Hymnflute so his breath raked over the other pipes, notes climbing until they ended with a harsh, high shriek, and a shockwave of wind lanced outward from where he stood. Lark clung to his side to keep from being blown over.

"The shield's song, what is it?" he shouted.

She twirled to deflect a goborrin's strike. "Sei—"

"No notes! I don't—big or small! Big to small, what is it?"

With an exasperated huff, she swept the Hymnflute back out of his hand and played on her own. The barrier that spawned around them was shaky, but it drove the monsters back. Zaide turned to watch her play, committing the order to memory. He knew the sounds, not the names. All he had to do was connect the notes to the pipes from which they came.

He had the order down by the second repetition, but let her play while she could. "We have to keep going. Press forward or we'll never reach the gate." It would be easier if they could take turns, pass the Hymnflute and Spectrum Blade back and forth to fight and play. Both would be breathless that way, but neither so breathless they might collapse. A sensation of disgust shuddered up his arm.

I didn't say I was going to hand you off, he thought angrily at the sword before he realized what he was doing. It was just a weapon. It wasn't alive. Whatever feelings plagued him, they were his own, and he couldn't blame them on anything else.

They worked toward the east, carving a path through goborrins for as long as Lark could play. When she grew too winded, Zaide took over while she caught her breath. The sea of goborrins was too thick for them to press forward with the shield alone; it kept them at bay, but it couldn't push back so many. Perhaps it could, with the right song. For a fleeting instant, Zaide envisioned something like the shovel his foster father used to scrape snow from roofs, but made of magic and swooping goborrins out of his way.

Stupid, he snarled at himself. *Just play.*

Lark pressed a hand to her chest as she took a few more deep breaths and nodded to confirm she was ready. They had to make the switch fast; more than a second or two, and the already-weak barrier would fall again. She always took over more gracefully, and he threw his frustration behind every new strike he made against the monsters that surrounded them.

Bit by bit, they worked their way toward the city walls, but each press covered less ground. The muscles in his arms, shoulders and back burned from fighting, and a hint of vertigo had begun to lurk in the front of his head. Disconcerting as it was, he couldn't spare it more than an acknowledgment. Steady his footing, breathe deeper, will it to go away. Maker's mercy, but he'd never realized how much breath it took just to play a song. How Lark got back up after squeezing every last bit of air from her lungs each time it was her turn, he didn't understand.

"We're almost there," he lied as he hacked down another beast. How many had it been? He didn't know, numb to the bodies that littered the ground. He shut out the thought, unable to let his mind reel. The dizziness that spun in his head above and behind his eyes was bad enough without adding the thought of battle and death.

Voices unlike those of the squealing goborrins rose ahead and a flicker of hope lit in Zaide's chest. They *were* almost there. The line of goborrins was thicker here, dense enough to hold back a wave of Sendassian's men as they pushed toward their protective bubble.

Zaide willed more energy into his arms and his aching shoulders. "Hold on, we've got one last push!"

Lark couldn't stop playing long enough to do more than suck in a long, ragged breath.

Renewed by the reassurance of the voices ahead, Zaide surged to the edge of the barrier and threw everything he had left into the attack. Colors rushed over the Spectrum Blade like tongues of multicolored fire. He tore into the monsters, their attention now split between him and the soldiers on the other side of their line. Steel flashed reflections of his sword's light back at him as he plunged the blade through monster flesh and ripped it free.

Suddenly, human faces came into view, a cheer of triumph erupting from dozens of throats. The king's guardsmen spilled through the gap in the goborrin line, surrounding their bubble and driving the enemy back. Zaide caught Lark's arm and urged her onward as the wave of soldiers swallowed them.

A few steps more, and she almost collapsed. He eased her to the ground and knelt beside her as she gasped for breath. Behind them, the fighting continued as if nothing had changed.

"We have to keep going." Zaide tried to pull her up, but her eyelids fluttered and she resisted.

"I can't," she protested between breaths. Her voice was hoarse, uneven, her cheeks flush with exertion and forehead damp with sweat.

"You have to." This time, he didn't let her pull back. He hauled her to her feet and hoisted her arm over his shoulders. A moment later, some nameless shoulder joined them, taking her arm on the other side. Zaide nodded and the man nodded back. Together, swords still drawn and ready, they carried the princess across the smoky battlefield.

Amrochan's gates loomed ahead. He expected them to be closed, but the city was open, a seemingly endless stream of soldiers flowing in and out. After everything settled, he'd have to ask after their strategy. For now, it was all he could do to guide the soldier to the side of the main road so they could collapse against the cool stone of a building's foundation.

They made it.

Zaide leaned his head back against the rock and closed his eyes as relief and exhaustion overtook him in the same wave.

A moment later, he became aware of a nearby voice asking questions. The soldier. He forced his eyes open and tried to sort out what he'd heard. Were they okay? Did they need help? He thought he'd heard those. "We're fine," he croaked. "Just rest." What he wouldn't have done to have Resia present, with her healing magic and the ability to wipe fatigue from their bodies.

He raised a hand before the soldier could leave them. "Wait. The Kolmari?" Reporting to King Sendassian was important, but he had to let his foster parents know what they'd done.

The man seemed surprised by the question, but he pointed down a narrow side road. "The northwest district. They're all there."

Zaide nodded. "Verlin. Their acting leader. He's there?"

"He should be," the soldier said, and the fact Zaide already knew that name seemed to put the man at ease. There was no doubt he recognized Lark; his eyes kept darting toward the princess in some sort of panic, as if unsure whether he should offer help or flee before he was seen speaking to her. But Zaide was still a stranger here. Rumors of the former Elder's broken-born apprentice wouldn't have gone far.

"We need to go straight to the palace," Lark put in. She looked worse for wear than he did, but despite her weariness and how she'd played the Hymnflute until she'd collapsed, her voice was remarkably stable. And sharp.

"We need to speak to Resia's father," Zaide replied, his words flat in deliberate contrast. "He needs to know what happened in Kolmar."

"The Kolmari can wait. No one's getting through that to go anywhere." She jabbed a finger toward the gate, as if she could point to the battle outside.

Zaide looked at her hand, then at her face. The blankness of his expression must have struck a nerve, because she grew sober in an instant, a new question hovering unspoken between them.

After they retrieved Tula, how were they to leave the city to reach Jadora?

"I don't think we can get through that mess out there again," he admitted before she could say anything.

She nodded, confirmation she'd been thinking the same thing.

They'd get to that later. Zaide pushed himself up with a groan. "We can split up. You go see your father. I'll report to Verlin, then meet you in the palace so we can figure out what happens next."

The way her mouth twisted, it looked as if she'd tasted something bitter. "We go together. They won't let you into the palace without me."

"They'd let me into the audience chamber."

"I sincerely doubt my father is holding audiences right now." She waved a hand toward the battlefield beyond the city wall, then stuffed the Hymnflute into her bag and climbed to her feet. "Fine. Let's find your father, for now."

"Foster father," he murmured.

Lark's brow furrowed. "You draw strange and arbitrary lines, you know."

"Well, they're mine to draw, and yours to ask about later, when we're not right in the middle of a war." He started to turn, then stopped.

The soldier who had helped them was still there, shifting uncomfortably on his feet, and a small crowd had gathered around him. "Do, ah... Do you need help, Your Highness?"

She hesitated, then drew herself up to the best regal figure she could make with her hair and clothes still tarnished with dried mud and the brown blood of goborrins. "Take us to the acting Elder of the Kolmari, then report to your commanding officer."

"Of course, Highness." The man started to offer his arm, then looked flustered and headed for the narrow side street, instead.

Lark went after him and Zaide took up the rear, belatedly realizing he still held the Spectrum Blade unsheathed. That was what had drawn the spectators; the people clustered nearby on the street watched and murmured as he returned the sword to the sheath at his hip and hurried to close the distance between himself and the princess.

"How common of knowledge is the story of this sword?" he asked in low tones.

She glanced back, but appeared disinterested when she saw the blade was already sheathed. "Not very. Remember, Tula and I had to dig deep in the royal library to figure out what was missing. A fair number of people will have heard of the artifacts, I think, but the sword is less common knowledge."

"Sure is good at drawing attention, though."

Lark gave her head a toss, her dirty ponytail swishing clumsily at her back. "Can you blame anyone for staring? It's odd. And even without the colors, it's glowing."

Although not as brightly as it had been out on the field. Zaide drew it an inch or two, just so he could check and confirm it hadn't been a trick of his eyes as he grew fatigued. The blade bore a dim light in the shadows of the tall buildings. Nothing like the blaze it had been outside the city walls.

"I hope your library's got more information on this thing." He jammed it back into its sheath. "I've got some questions."

"We all do." Lark pointed ahead, to where people in the familiar clothing style of the Kolmari clustered outside a building.

Zaide had been there before; he hadn't recognized the route they took, but he knew the house he'd slept in after he'd returned to Amrochan the first time. Among the people, a splash of colorful clothing stood out. His brow furrowed. "Tula?"

She spun at the sound of her name, her fiery hair swirling around her shoulders. "I knew it!" The apprentice librarian rushed forward to join them. "I knew it the moment I saw that light from the bulwark. You got it, didn't you?"

"Yes." Lark did not elaborate at all. Instead, she slipped past the librarian to approach the Kolmari. "Is Verlin in?"

"Inside, speaking with soldiers," a woman answered. Her eyes widened with recognition when Zaide positioned himself at the princess's side.

He did his best to smile. He'd have to answer to a lot of neighbors before this was over. Instead of facing this one, he grasped Lark's elbow and gently steered her indoors.

"Zaide!" Sarma gasped as he appeared. "Maker's mercy, you're more ragged every time you set foot inside my house!" Her dark eyes widened when she got a good look at the princess, but she froze in place, unsure how to react.

In the corner, Verlin rose from a table where he sat with a handful of men in armor, a question on his face when he looked behind them and saw only Tula in the doorway.

Zaide let go of the princess. "Kolmar has been reclaimed. The temple is secure and the goborrins have been run out of the village. We couldn't do anything about the garrison, though."

"Where is Resia?" His foster mother wrung her hands and stood on tip-toe, as if that would help her see past the tall Jadoran girl at their backs.

"She must remain in Kolmar for now," Lark said before Zaide could answer. "The temple's spring of power has accepted her as Elder and infused her with new gifts. Until she finishes restoring the magic that protects your home, she cannot leave."

Relief flooded their faces.

"The Vale magic was not beyond hope, then," Verlin concluded. "You couldn't have brought us better news. But to reclaim Kolmar—just the five of you?" He'd been there when they departed, had helped them gather gear and set out.

"Actually, that was just me and Aren," Zaide said.

Sarma's mouth fell open.

Heat made his collar feel tight. He turned to display the Spectrum Blade and drew it partway. "We got this, and it—"

"It can cut through goborrins like they're nothing!" Tula clenched her hands to fists and hopped in place, a light of excitement in her eyes. "You should have seen it! They were visible from the city walls, the librarians went up to see. The sword was like a streak of lighting, striking down wave after wave of those monsters, cutting a hole through the army outside!"

The heat rose and Zaide ducked his head as color bloomed in his face. Claiming the feat shouldn't have been embarrassing, but in front of his foster parents, Tula's embellishment of events was awkward enough to steal the words from his mouth.

"That's nice," Verlin said with the patience of a man who'd raised more than his share of children. "But what is it, Zaide? What does this mean?"

The gentle redirection was appreciated, but Zaide still cleared his throat awkwardly and avoided eye contact as he put the sword away. "It's called the Spectrum Blade, and Princess Dasienna says it's the answer to ending the war."

"Which reminds me." Tula circled around to squint at the sword, her attention so scrutinizing Zaide felt compelled to grip the hilt in his right hand. "Wasn't the princess supposed to be the one who—"

"What's important right now is that we have it," Lark put in, cutting her short. "And she's right. We just cut through the army with me wielding the Hymnflute's power and Zaide wielding the sword. We're close to having answers, but I think what just happened outside is a good testament to the blade's power."

"And Kolmar is ready for people to return," Zaide added. "Aren and Murk, our other guard, stayed with Resia to ensure she'd be safe. The space around the temple has been cleared and is secure, so if the Kolmari wish to go back to the forest, I'm sure we can hire a ship to get you there." He glanced between his foster parents, hoping for some sort of reaction, though he wasn't sure what he expected.

Verlin and Sarma exchanged glances, both sober.

"We'll go back," Verlin said slowly, "when the time is right. I'm glad to hear Resia's safe. Aren, too. And the village. But moving that many people by ship, when we don't have any way to protect ourselves once we're there..."

"It may be better to wait." Sarma offered a smile.

Somehow, Zaide thought their refusal to leave Amrochan should have been more upsetting. But he'd just walked through an army of goborrins. Resia might have restored the Vale magic and replenished the unseen barrier that held the monsters at bay, but what if it was like the Hymnflute's magic? The shield they'd used to protect themselves had faltered more than once, and he had no doubt it could have been overwhelmed. If that many goborrins had reached the capital, who knew how many waited beyond Kolmar's forests, just waiting to storm through.

Perhaps the ancient magic couldn't repel them all.

"Where are our manners, though? Come in, sit down, eat!

The lot of you have to be starving." Sarma glanced them over, though her gaze lingered on Tula. The soldier who guided them had gone, and the librarian had squeezed inside to join them.

Come to think of it, why had Tula joined them? And why was she there? Zaide turned to frown at her. "What are you doing down here? Lark said you'd be in the library."

Tula pressed a hand to her chest, as if taken aback by the question. "I was! And then we went to see what was happening on the battlefield, and then I went to get my notebook so I could write down what I'd seen, because it's going to have to go in the history books for this Age when I get back to the Great Library."

A crease of confusion deepened between Verlin's brows.

"And of course I got a little lost, since the stairs here are all a bit confusing, and the first way down I found let out on the north side, which is extremely inconvenient, if you ask me," Tula continued, though her voice shifted toward uncertainty. "I was headed toward the library, but then I thought if I cut to the main street, maybe I'd see the princess as she came in with the sword, and..."

Zaide rubbed his palm over the blade's pommel.

The librarian cleared her throat. "And, well, now we're here. I didn't expect I'd see them somewhere like this, but I just had to see."

"This is normal for Tula, I assure you." Lark didn't smile, but a faint twinkle of amusement lit her eyes.

"Yeah. She's... excitable." Zaide ran his fingers through his hair and sighed. "But we can't stay. We need to see King Sendassian."

"Don't let us stop you then, lad." Verlin raised a hand as if to bid them goodbye, then sank back into his seat. It wasn't until then that Zaide noticed the soldiers he sat with. All of them regarded him with dark expressions, their eyes heavy, judging. That he stood with the princess should have alleviated him of some scrutiny, but they stared at him as if she weren't present at all. For a moment, he questioned the candor with which they'd spoken.

He ducked his head and took a step backwards. "Thank you. I'll be back."

"We'll be here," Sarma said. "There's always something in the stewpot for you when you're hungry."

Zaide flashed her a nervous smile, then retreated into the street. Lark and Tula followed close behind.

"Did you see the way those men looked at us?" Tula asked in a whisper.

"Hard to miss it." He looked toward the sky, hoping to catch sight of the palace and use it as a guide, but Lark set off before he saw anything. He jogged a few steps to catch up.

Tula trotted along at his side. "I didn't like it. It reminds me of the way some of the Magister's other guards look at the guardswomen."

"The guardswomen are almost naked, they should be embarrassed to be looking at all."

The librarian snorted. "By your standards, maybe. In Jadora, their state of dress is perfectly acceptable. Intimidating, even. Wouldn't you be frightened by a warrior who doesn't need armor?"

Zaide shot her a skeptical look. "Arrows don't care if you think you don't need armor."

"Well, bows are illegal in Jadora," Tula said.

"Lark had a crossbow on her when we entered the city."

The princess shot a glare over her shoulder. "Don't bring me into this."

At the same time, Tula huffed. "That's different!"

"How is that different? Crossbows are bows, and she had one in her bag. If she'd wanted to shoot one of the guardswomen, that skimpy armor wouldn't have stopped anything."

"It's different because she's the princess, and eventually she'll be the queen. She *makes* the laws, she can take a crossbow wherever she wants."

"Which means she could shoot a guardswoman, proving it doesn't matter how capable they are if they don't wear proper protective gear," Zaide argued.

Lark sighed, exasperated. "Would the two of you shut up?"

They quieted, though not without first exchanging sullen looks. Some small, rational part of Zaide's mind whispered that he was supposed to be kinder to the librarian when they crossed paths again, and he entertained it reluctantly for a moment before he decided Tula had instigated his newly soured mood. He could be amicable some other time, when she wasn't embarrassing them all.

The road which Lark chose widened as they approached the palace. Zaide's eyes traveled up the spires and peaks to the rippling flags and banners that splashed bold color against the sky.

"We'll go straight in," Lark said as she guided them to the front doors Zaide had passed through once before, or maybe twice; events blurred together in his head, and he could no longer remember. "Through the reception hall and straight to my father."

The guards at the door and in the entryway on the other side bowed as the princess passed them. The great hall in which Zaide had once waited for an audience with the king sat empty, its benches bare. Their boots clicked in the silence, the echo loud in the vast room.

Lark shook her head once, which set her ponytail to swaying. "Hurry. I'm sure my father has heard what happened outside the city by now."

There were no guards posted at the next set of doors. Zaide hastened ahead to open one for her.

He pushed open the door and a hand closed around his throat.

CHAPTER SEVEN

FURY FLASHED in King Sendassian's eyes. His grip tightened around Zaide's throat until the world threatened to go black. "How dare you?" the king snarled.

No matter how Zaide gasped or clawed at Sendassian's hand, his grip did not loosen. He felt the upward motion before he realized his feet were leaving the floor.

"Unhand him!" Lark cried. Her voice already sounded weak, distant, detached from reality.

Sendassian's iron grip came loose and Zaide fell to the floor. He sucked in as deep a breath as his lungs could hold, but the air made him choke and he coughed hard, clutching at his throat.

Lark's boot thumped down right in front of his face. Zaide remained on one knee with his hand against his neck. He already felt the flush of discomfort where bruises would form, marking each finger that had nearly squeezed the life out of him. A gentle hand grasped his arm as if to help him up. He lifted his head enough to see Tula beside him, then shook his head and swallowed hard.

"You greet us like this?" the princess demanded. "After everything we've done?"

"You defied me!" her father spat back. "You shame me with

your behavior, running away at every whim, then daring to interfere with—"

"With your battle outside?" She scoffed. "I left Amrochan to find a solution for this violence! Do you have any idea what we've risked to be here? What we've achieved because of it?"

The king's face crumpled into a scowl. "I ordered you to remain in the palace. I requested one thing, and you couldn't deliver. Your legends, your stories—"

"Are true!" Lark stomped her foot.

Zaide recoiled from her boot.

A mistake, as the movement drew Sendassian's eye. "How dare you aid my daughter in this folly? Who are you?"

"Blade, the Zaidebear—no," he coughed.

Tula buried her face in her hands.

Miraculously, Lark retained her composure. "You've met him before, Father. Zaide was the Kolmari Elder's apprentice. Now the Spectrum Blade answers his call, and he is my Bladebearer." Her voice grew fierce as she claimed him.

Startled by either her words or the intensity of them, the king drew back a step and straightened, his equanimity returned.

Unsure whether it was appropriate, Zaide dragged himself to his feet and positioned himself just behind the princess's arm. It hurt when he breathed, but he'd survive. In the back of his mind, he made a note to never accidentally cross the king, which meant the rapid formation of a list of incidents he could never speak of within the palace, lest they be overheard.

Sendassian watched him, his face melting from rage to an unreadable mask. Somehow, that was more frightening than the furious man who'd seized him by the neck the moment he opened the door.

"Please, just give us a chance to speak," Lark said as her father calmed. "Zaide just carved his way through the army outside so we could stand here. The least you can do is let us tell you what we've done."

The king said nothing.

She took it as an invitation to speak. "Centuries ago, our ancestors entrusted the artifacts to the three Paragons, knowing they'd be the key to someday ending this battle. They were the key to retrieving this, the weapon he now carries. Zaide?"

The sound of his name made him flinch. Surely she didn't mean for him to speak. He'd already opened his mouth and managed to place his foot firmly inside, his thoughts too muddled for his tongue to make sense of what he meant.

"Show him the sword," Lark said, and the order was a relief.

Slowly, Zaide curled his fingers around the hilt of the sword. Some part of him hoped for a zing of reassurance, some spark or tingle or sense this was the right thing, like he'd experienced the other times he touched the blade.

He felt nothing.

Unsettled, he drew the sword an inch at a time. All the while, he questioned the wisdom of drawing a blade in front of the king.

Instead of protesting, Sendassian stared as the Spectrum Blade slid free. His eyes grew wide.

Lark spread a hand toward it. "This was sealed away inside Kolmar's temple, buried with the remains of Gadranus's last incarnation. We fought a remnant of his power. Zaide defeated it and it was sealed within this crystal." She produced the deep purple gem from her bag and held it out for her father to inspect. Zaide couldn't help but stare at it, too. He hadn't seen the prism since that fight, when she'd pulled it from the bottom of the spring of power and stowed it in her bag. Something shifted inside it, like a plume of smoke or an impossibly dark flame.

Sendassian took the crystal from her hand and raised it to the light. Whatever surprise he'd shown at the sight of the blade, it was gone now, his cool, neutral mask returned to his face.

At Zaide's back, Tula released a quiet breath of wonder. As intrigued as Zaide was, he reminded himself all this was news to the librarian. Considering her excitement in front of the Kolmari, it was a miracle she managed to keep her mouth shut.

Lark went on. "By now you must have heard what happened outside, that Zaide and I fought our way through the goborrins. That the soldiers saw his sword alight and saw how he struck down dozens of goborrins on his own, while I shielded him with the magic of Kolmar's Hymnflute. That is the power of the artifacts, of this sword. The power we needed to strike Gadranus down and end this war, once and for all."

A shadow touched the king's eyes and he thrust the prism back into his daughter's hands. Before Lark could speak, he turned and reached for the Spectrum Blade.

"Don't," she choked out.

Sendassian grasped the hilt before Zaide could draw back. Light surged down the sword and a sharp crackle filled the air. The king jerked back with a shout and the blade fell from his grasp to clatter against the floor. He withdrew, cradling his hand to his chest as Zaide recovered the blade from the polished stone.

"Father—" Lark began.

"Leave us," Sendassian said.

She stared at him as if unsure what she'd heard, one hand poised as if to reach out to him.

"Go," the king snapped.

A tiny flicker of hurt pinched the corners of her eyes, but Lark nodded and inched backwards.

Sendassian turned his glare on Tula and she retreated alongside the princess. Together, the girls closed the door.

The king stared at the Spectrum Blade for a time before his deep voice split the silence. "So, I am to be scorned by my own fate."

Zaide stood with the shimmering sword in his hands and a prickle of cold crawling down his spine.

Sendassian's eyes slid up to capture Zaide's gaze. "Do you fear me, boy?"

"You have a powerful grip." Flippant as they were, the words were all he could think to say.

"You should." The king retreated a single step, then looked at his hand. The flesh was blistered. He flexed his fingers, but his face remained as smooth and cold as the stone tiles beneath their feet. "What has she asked of you, boy?"

Too many things to name now. Zaide stifled the thought before it reached his lips. "Her Highness wishes to travel to Jadora, to seek the blessings of the city's Magister. The sword has yet to awaken. She believes the blessings of the Paragons will restore it to full strength."

"Yet to awaken," Sendassian repeated in a murmur. "Yet it speaks so fiercely."

"Swords don't speak, Your Majesty."

The king sneered. "All blades do, in their own way. Were you an accomplished swordsman, you would know that."

Zaide could think of no way to reply. *Always short of wits when you need them.* Though wit was probably the last thing he needed to wield against the king, unless he wanted his head removed from his shoulders.

When he said nothing, Sendassian drew back another step and then turned. He studied his blistered hand once more, then clasped his hands behind his back—tenderly—and paced. "I have no use for these artifacts or magical follies."

"Your daughter believes they will turn the tide," Zaide said.

"I do not." The statement was bland, emotionless, as if it were a toy the king dismissed and not a weapon of legend. "Yet my daughter's stubbornness forces me to consider what they may be good for." That, on the other hand, was laden with suggestion.

Zaide shifted his weight from one foot to the other, a sudden discomfort that had nothing to do with strangulation lodging itself in his throat. "Your Majesty?"

Sendassian paused to regard the Spectrum Blade with a thoughtful eye. Zaide still held it, unsure what to do with the weapon, not instructed to sheath it or leave it anywhere for study, but that gaze left him unsettled enough that he returned the blade to his hip. The moment its swirling surface was out of sight, the king's eyes snapped to his face.

"My daughter wishes to go to Jadora."

"Yes, Your Majesty."

"You will take her."

Zaide blinked twice, unsure he'd heard correctly. "Sire?"

"Bidding her to stay put has done nothing. Time and time again, Dasienna has sought to put herself in harm's way. But Jadora is a fortress unlike any other, and the goborrin hordes have yet to find a way across the desert. If she wishes to see Jadora, there are few places where she could be kept safer."

"You're giving the trip your blessing?" Now he was sure he hadn't heard correctly.

The king paced back the other direction, shaking his head. "Understand the purpose of this trip, boy. I do not, and will not, believe magic is what will end this war. Her swords, her artifacts, they mean nothing. But if they are what lure her to safety, then we shall play along."

"You just want to put her away?" The question escaped before Zaide thought better of it.

"To protect her. Since she will not cooperate to be protected elsewhere."

The last thing Lark needed was someone to protect her, and he was the last person to be given such a task. The corners of Zaide's mouth quivered and drew down.

Sendassian lifted his chin. "You hesitate."

"I mean no offense, Your Majesty, but a moment ago, you tried to strangle me. You didn't even know who I was. Turning around and immediately entrusting me with the princess's wellbeing is a little unexpected." His hand lifted toward his throat, but he thought better of touching the marks there and forced it back down.

The king's attention slipped downward, to the sword now sheathed at Zaide's side. That was it; that was what had changed his attitude and demeanor. The moment the Spectrum Blade refused his touch. What thoughts or machinations had started within Sendassian's head were impossible to guess, but the shock was the moment he had grown cool.

"My daughter has chosen you as her champion," Sendassian said after a time. "So, too, did the Kolmari Elder. Either you have already proven your worth, or you have failed everyone who ever sought to trust you."

Zaide wasn't about to admit he felt closer to failure than the alternative. A champion? He hadn't even been able to recover the artifacts without assistance. He tried to think of something to say, something modest without being self-effacing, but the king raised a hand and waved him away before he found words.

"You are given your assignment. A ship shall be hired to carry you down the river to Chithal, and from there, you will sail to Jadora's port."

"Chithal?" Zaide repeated. "Going around the northern side of the continent could take weeks. When we visited Jadora before, the caravans—"

"The caravans cross land," Sendassian said, a hint of an edge in his tone. "And goborrins do not swim. By sea is the safest way to travel, and it is how you will go."

Getting Lark on that ship sounded impossible, but it was clear there was no room for argument. "Yes, Your Majesty." Zaide made himself bow, though he never removed his eyes from the king, lest he be caught off guard and throttled again.

Sendassian flicked his fingers toward the door. "Go."

Zaide spun to leave, opened the door, and tripped over the princess.

CHAPTER EIGHT

"THIS IS ABSURD." Lark jammed her fists against her hips, but a moment later, she went back to pacing and clenched them at her sides. "What of the weather? It could be months before we reach Jadora!"

Zaide followed after her, making soothing motions with both hands. "It would take weeks by caravan, too. No matter what we do, travel will take a while."

"There's a river south of Amrochan," Tula suggested, though she twisted the tip of her little finger, betraying her nerves at suggesting anything at all. Was it the idea of defying the king's order after his outburst in the throne room that made her nervous? Or had Lark's mood grown as dangerous as her father's? "It would take us as far as the fork to Tinith, and we could find a caravan there."

"But we don't know if there are caravans in Tinith." Zaide tried to sound factual instead of argumentative. When Lark dug in her heels, arguing only made things worse. "We don't know if the market stands, even. If Gadranus managed to get an army as far as Amrochan, he could have flattened Tinith, too. We'd be stuck on foot through the desert, and I know we aren't prepared for that."

Lark shook her head so hard, it looked as if she might make herself dizzy. "There has to be another way."

"Unless you can fly, I don't think there is. And the sooner we go, the better. We could get on a ship by this evening." Zaide hated to think of departing so soon, but he saw no better way to shave time from their journey. He had hoped to visit his foster parents again before the trip began, but he assumed they would understand.

Tula glanced between the two of them and cleared her throat. "May I make a suggestion?"

The fact she didn't offer it without asking first answered Zaide's previous question. Were Lark in better spirits, the librarian wouldn't likely have asked at all. The princess said nothing, so Zaide shrugged and tried to appear attentive.

"I think we should do it. For one, it's the easiest way for us to travel, the king is willing to sponsor the expedition, and we can take as many provisions as we need. I can transport a lot of books to the Great Library for examination and archival, too, which means my visit here will look a little more legitimate in the eyes of my superiors. Besides, the closer we get to summertime, the easier it'll be to visit the Desheni Shaman, right?" A flicker of a smile lit her face.

Zaide squared his shoulders. "Who told you we were going to see the Shaman?"

"You did, silly. You said the Paragons were needed to awaken the blade, and that the princess wants to see the Magister. You told the Kolmari someone named Resia is the new Elder and that she took the role while you were in Kolmar, which means you've already spoken to her. That leaves the Shaman." Tula grinned.

He gave her a blank look. She remembered all that just from what she'd overheard? Lark, too, regarded the librarian with an unreadable expression.

"We should take the rest of the day to prepare, though," Tula said, unbothered by their scrutiny. "I need time to go through the books to determine what needs to go back with me, and I suspect Her Highness would appreciate a bath."

The notion of Lark in a bath made the tips of Zaide's ears heat. He rubbed the blunted ear, then turned away, scratching as if it had only been an itch.

The princess's fists uncurled. "I suppose you're right. Both of you. We have no way of knowing a caravan is available, or whether it would be faster. If we encounter trouble on the road, it could take just as long as a ship."

Tula's grin widened. "That means we'll have time for study aboard the ship, too. You do remember your promise?"

Zaide had almost forgotten the two of them had spent time together after he'd left them in Jadora. There were plenty of things he would have missed. "What promise?"

"To allow her to study the Molten Dagger." Lark waved a hand as if it didn't matter. "She's a scholar and the artifact belongs to her home city. After her assistance in recovering it, it only seems fair." She turned as she spoke and led the way toward the palace entry. The waiting room they stood in remained empty, save the guards at the main door.

Zaide studied their bored faces as they exited to the courtyard. "Yeah, that does seem fair. Lark, is your father always without guards when he isn't holding audience?"

She arched a brow. "Did he strike you as the kind of man who needs guards at every waking moment?"

The bruises on his throat spoke loudly enough to answer that question on their own.

"I didn't think so," Lark murmured when he didn't reply. She stopped in the middle of the palace courtyard. "Very well, then. The three of us will go our separate ways for this evening. We'll set out tomorrow morning. Is that enough time to prepare your books, Tula?"

"I believe so." The librarian tapped her finger against her chin. "It will let me gather research materials to go along with the dagger, too."

"What about me?" Zaide asked.

The princess crossed her arms. "What about you? It's not like you have business to attend in Amrochan, and I haven't got anything for you to do. You're free to go have some of your foster mother's stew."

"So I have time to see family, ask after the soldiers I've befriended, and get a chance to clean up and shave." The dismissive tone she used also made him rather defensive, he noted with an internal wince.

She examined the sparse collection of white whiskers on his chin and was decidedly unimpressed.

Oblivious to his discomfort, Tula waved good-bye and trotted off toward some wing of the palace that must house the library. "I'll see the two of you in the morning, then."

Zaide watched her go. "She's going to make the trip interesting."

"She's excited. She's been petitioning her superiors to let her attend a research expedition for four years, but every application has been denied. This is her first chance to study something of her own accord. It's exciting when we get what we want, isn't it?" Instead of watching Tula, Lark watched him, a soft, knowing light in her blue eyes.

The sword on his hip gave him a sense of satisfaction that set his hair on end. An unpleasant reminder of all the questions he had yet to ask. "I suppose. Listen, I need to speak with you about some things, but I guess we can do that tomorrow."

"We'll have plenty of time on the ship," she agreed.

He offered a stiff nod. "Right. See you in the morning."

She did not bid him goodbye when he turned to leave.

The feeling from the sword faded as he walked, but the sheath bounced against his leg until he grasped the hilt and held it still. It was still too long, the weight uneven, and a stop by the armory before they departed would be wise. Instead of making for the part of the city where his family and neighbors took refuge, he altered his path and swung toward the barracks in the corner of the palace grounds. As he approached, soldiers slowed to watch him pass. The weight of their eyes was almost as stifling as the king's grasp.

"Decided to join us, have you? Don't think you'll find much improvement in here." One of the sentries by the armory door offered a sly smile.

Zaide paused. "I'm sorry?"

The man leaned against his spear. "There's not a blade anywhere in Amrochan that can match what you've got. Half the city's heard about it by now. Wasn't sure things like that were real, myself, but here you are. And there's a mountain of dead goborrins outside to prove it."

"Uh, thank you?" It was inevitable word of what they'd done would reach the city and make it around, but he hadn't expected it meant he would be recognized. Nor was he sure how that felt. "I don't need any weapons, though. Just a scabbard. Mine was for a guard-issue sword and it's too long."

"Well, we've probably got something. If not, one of the leatherworkers can see to it." The sentry scratched his eyebrow and motioned toward the door. "Go on, have a look. Nobody in there now, but at least you can try a few on for size, eh?"

"Thank you," Zaide said again.

"Don't mention it. After seeing what that thing can do, I'm just glad you're on our side." The man grinned and nudged the door open with the end of his spear.

Zaide slipped inside. The interior of the armory was lit by lantern, its glow cozy and inviting. It hit him like a wave of sleepiness and he breathed a sigh.

He was still beyond tired and wasn't sure he could find his feet again if he sat, so he remained standing while he shed the old scabbard and scouted the racks of weapons and armor to find something new. The short sword sheaths were too small, most of the rest the same size as the one he'd abandoned on the floor.

Eventually, a side door opened and a burly, bearded man in a leather apron cleared his throat. "Who sent you for what?"

Zaide spun toward him, alarm bells sounding in his head. The man was as big as Sendassian, though older and more grizzled. Was this a new fear to add to his collection of nightmares, then? Large men in doorways? It was certainly a change from howling ice wolves and the chittering feet of spiders.

"Princess Dasienna," he replied, though the urge to correct himself rose to the surface a moment later. "Or, I'm here to... Ah, King Sendassian is sending us... I need a sheath for this." He held out the Spectrum Blade by its hilt, point down, then drew it back and gripped it with both hands. He hadn't meant for that to look like an invitation. The king touching the blade had been bad enough.

The man made a soft hum under his breath. "Bit of an oddity, isn't it? Won't find anything over there. Come on back, lad. We'll get you something suitable." He beckoned him through the door, to a portico where a glowing hearth waited. "What's your name, boy?"

The acrid scent of hot metal greeted him as he stepped outside. "Zaide." It came out right this time, without someone trying to kill him.

"Hm. Thank you for that. No one here seems to know who you are, boy, though every soldier that's been back through has had something to say about what you've done." The man offered a grin. "I'm Portran. Portly, though, to the lads around here." There was a softness to his voice that didn't match his brawn, but it suited the warmth in his small brown eyes.

"The nicknames they give you in the army really aren't flattering, are they?" Zaide chanced a smile.

"Not a bit, but maybe that's why they do it. Wear the worst of you as your name, and everyone knows what to expect." Portran grinned behind his beard and crossed to a table. "Bring that pretty sword over here. We'll see if we can fix you up. How much time have I got?"

"I need to leave in the morning." Zaide joined him at the table as he unrolled a cut of pale leather.

Portran pulled a piece of graphite from his apron and patted the leather, simple instruction to lay the sword down. "Not much time, then. A proper scabbard ought to be wood or metal, but I'll see if I can make you something to hold you over for now."

The sword's colors were more blue, a sleepy shade that drifted across its surface like beads of water. Zaide couldn't help but run his fingers down its surface as he laid it down. "You're the leatherworker?"

"A blacksmith, but it's all the same to these folk here. We do what's needed, and that means a bit of everything. I might've even made what you've got on now."

The leather armor Zaide had borrowed from the palace had gone all but forgotten. He brushed his fingers over it. "It's nice. I've appreciated it."

Portran offered a low chuckle in return. "Flattery is nice, lad, but it won't make much of a difference in the goods you get from the army. Now, let's see." He spread a hand over the sword, comparing its width to the distance between his fingers.

"Don't touch it. It bites." There was probably a better way to describe the shocks it delivered to everyone but him, but Zaide wasn't sure. He'd never felt it himself and had only the reaction of those who'd made the mistake of touching it as an example.

"Aye, I feel that. Strong magic in there somewhere. Not quite like what I'm used to, though." Slowly, the smith traced the sword onto the smooth surface of the leather, leaving wide gaps all around it.

Zaide tilted his head. "You're a mage?"

"You're not?" Despite the question, the man didn't sound surprised. "I think we've all got a little something in us, whether we know it or not. Here, I've got it now. You can move it." He stepped back, and Zaide slipped in to retrieve the blade.

"Not me. No magic at all." He wouldn't elaborate, either, or acknowledge the wishful thinking he'd long since abandoned, himself. "How did you know I was the person people were talking about?"

Portran shrugged and drew a tiny but sharp knife from his apron's pockets, then set to work cutting out the piece he'd designed. "Weren't many others it could be. A white-haired boy with a shining sword? Don't get too many of those in Amrochan, either one. First of both I've seen in my lifetime, matter of fact."

Zaide rested the Spectrum Blade against his shoulder. "There aren't any broken-born in the army?"

"I'm sure there are, but not here. They join the garrisons, sometimes, places closer to the border so they don't have to travel so far or deal with so many people. But Amrochan's guard? No. Can't say I've ever seen that."

Whether or not he'd wanted information like that, it wasn't what he'd hoped to hear. Zaide's shoulders slumped.

The smith chuckled softly without looking at him. "Who've we been looking for, then?"

"My father." And for all the time he'd been on the road, this was the first time he'd had a chance to ask for solid information. "He left Kolmar when I was young. He was headed for Amrochan and meant to join the army."

"I see. I'm sorry, then, boy. I'm afraid he never made it quite this far." He cut out another piece and held up both. "Two layers ought to do it, don't you think? Won't be the same as a wooden sheath, but it'll be sturdy enough, and we can line it with some suede. Make sure your sword always shines."

"I don't think shining will be a problem."

Portran laughed at that. "No, lad, I don't think it will. Here, let me get you a punch. If you're here, you might as well work."

"Work it off, I hope, because I don't actually have a way to pay for this." Zaide accepted the oddly forked piece of metal with a nervous grin. Sendassian might have agreed to finance their trip, but his pockets were still empty.

The smith seemed unconcerned. "I'm sure you've already earned it, lad."

"How do you figure?"

"Because every soldier who's been through here talking about it wore a smile. Morale's important during a war, and this has been dragging without progress nearly since it started. The onslaught never seems to slow, and no matter how many we kill, more appear just as fast. Seeing you out there cutting them down faster than they can blink, well. That does a good bit to restore a man's faith the fighting's not all in vain." Portran shifted to one side and pointed as he spread the leather pieces atop a thick pad on the table. "Over here."

Zaide inched closer and inspected the object in his hand and the graphite lines marked along the edges of what would become his new scabbard. Assuming he would need both hands, he lowered the Spectrum Blade's tip to the ground and leaned it against the side of the building. "Everything the men saw was the sword's work, not mine."

"Ah, but the sword was in your hand. Here. Grab that hammer over there. You stick your stitch chisel in that beeswax there, then you line it up here. There are smaller chisels up here on the shelf for when you get to the end and only have space for a few more stitches." The smith pointed at each tool as he spoke, then settled to work. The line of holes he left behind was perfectly straight.

By contrast, Zaide's wobbled. He watched the man work and tried to match each action.

For a while, the steady tap of their hammers and chisels filled the air.

Then Portran made a soft, thoughtful sound. "They're all here, you know. Everyone who made it out of the garrison."

Zaide glanced up.

"Someone may know something," the man added. "You're what, eighteen?"

"I will be, in the fall."

Portran nodded. "Thought as much, by the look of you. You've still got a fresh face, not weary from war yet like the rest of us. Not many who've been in the army that long, but there are bound to be a few who may have heard something. Now would be a good time to ask."

And asking was something Zaide had intended to do when he had a chance to visit the garrison's men. "I have to leave tomorrow, though. I don't think I'll have time."

"Well, maybe when you're back, someone might have turned up a bit of news for you. I suppose you'll just have to come back and find out." The smith winked, then pointed. "If the spacing gives you trouble, put that last tooth of your chisel in the last hole you made. It'll keep everything tidy, it'll just take a moment longer to finish."

Zaide tried it. The result was much better than his wobbly, uneven attempts. "Thanks. That helps."

"Someone who's willing to take instruction is someone who'll go far. Keep that mindset, lad. It'll help you."

A silence fell after that, warm and comfortable while they worked. By the time Zaide punched the other side of the scabbard and moved on to his second piece, Portran was almost finished, but his work had grown neater and almost matched what the big man had done. The smith nodded his approval as he waxed thread and cut a soft lining for the inside. Then he lined up all the pieces and dragged a stool out from under the table, sat, and began to sew.

There was no second stool, so Zaide took the Spectrum Blade from where he'd leaned it against the wall and sat on the ground. Bits of sawdust and scrap leather littered the stone. He brushed some aside as he rested the sword across his crossed legs. The small smithy was a comforting place, he decided; had he more than a day to spend in Amrochan, he would have liked to spend more time there. Something about the older smith's manner made him easy to be around, and for a time, Zaide felt less of an outsider.

"No one comes back from the war, do they?" He traced the edge of his sword with a fingertip. It was a wonder the sword showed no wear, after everything he'd put it through that morning.

"Oh, they do. Not often, and not whole, but they do."

"Did you?" Perhaps the question was too forward, but it was the first thing that sprang to mind.

Portran didn't seem to be bothered. "Of course. My beard might be graying, but it's wear, not age. I served on the front lines. Out past Kolmar, in fact. Spent three years there before a goborrin's club snapped my leg like a twig. I was an apprentice smith before I went, though, and my wife was happy to have me back in my old profession."

"You still wanted to be part of the army after that?" In a place as big as the capital city, Zaide didn't doubt there were other roles for blacksmiths to pursue.

"Of course, lad. I still wanted to make a difference, any way I could. That's what we all want, isn't it? A chance to make the world a little bit better. Even if it's only for ourselves."

"I guess so." The sawdust and scraps on the ground weren't that interesting, but Zaide occupied himself with them anyway, pressing them into the gaps between stones. "After my father left, doing something to end the war was all I really cared about, even though it never touched us in Kolmar until this past Choosing."

The smith cut another length of heavy thread and scraped it over his block of wax. "It's a noble cause."

"It hasn't gone the way I thought it would."

"It never does."

Silence drifted again and Zaide closed his eyes. He rested until Portran's tools clinked and the man pushed himself back from the table. "There we are. A new scabbard, just the right size. Try it out."

Zaide pushed himself up. The leather was freshly burnished with oil, its color warmer and its surface bearing a soft sheen. He took it in one hand and fitted the Spectrum Blade to its opening. It slid inside, easy and almost soundless. "It's perfect. Thank you." He turned it over to inspect the other side and paused. An elaborately detailed Z had been tooled into its front, near the top.

"Glad you like it, lad. Now, get on, then. Sendassian's a hard man, and he won't abide dallying." The smith crossed to the hearth to check the coals.

"Thank you," Zaide repeated again, unsure what else to say. He gripped the sword in its sheath with both hands. "I'll be back. After everything's done."

Portran only grunted a soft confirmation.

Accepting that as dismissal, Zaide held the sword close to his chest and hurried from the armory. By now his stomach grumbled, and thoughts of Sarma's stew grew thick in his head.

Verlin wasn't there when he returned to the now-familiar house, though his foster mother was, and she was all too happy to feed him. She spooned three servings into his bowl before he'd had enough and retired to one of the side rooms to rest.

The moment he collapsed into one of the straw-filled mattresses, Zaide wasn't sure how he'd managed to stay on his feet. Fatigue swept over him, but he held the sword and its sheath above him for one more inspection in the soft light of an oil lamp. His fingers traced the initial in the leather's otherwise smooth surface. He'd found a friend, an ally, and knowing someone would be asking the questions he didn't have time to pursue should have been a comfort.

Instead, the thought left him burdened. He let the sword lay on his chest and one last question drifted through his mind before he sank into sleep.

Sooner or later, he'd know how his father's legacy ended.

What if he didn't like the answer?

CHAPTER NINE

BY NOON THE NEXT DAY, there was less smoke in the sky. Zaide leaned against the railing of the ship and watched as Amrochan slipped away behind them, the sounds of battle left behind but the burden of their task no lighter. When all was said and done, they would return, and the battle would be waiting.

If not outside Amrochan, then somewhere. He hadn't thought much about where the war could take them, aside from the field outside the capital or the garrison outside of Kolmar, where goborrins still waited to be purged.

Someone moved to his side. He didn't have to look to know who it was. "Can I ask you something?"

Lark leaned against the rail beside him. "I'm going to assume you mean something beyond what you just did."

He laced his fingers together and hunched his shoulders. "You and Tula brought a lot of books about the artifacts and the blade, right? Is there any way you could research something for me?"

"There's nothing stopping you from researching it yourself. Most of the books from the palace library are written in a language you can read." She turned her head as the ship slid toward the mouth of the river. Before long, the view of the city would be obscured by trees.

"I know, but you probably have a better idea of where to start than I do. And it'll go faster if there's more than just me reading about it, and it's not like there's going to be much else for us to do." At least the two of them. Tula had shut herself in the cabin she shared with Lark the moment the princess handed over the Molten Dagger. From the eagerness in her demeanor, it didn't strike him as likely they'd see her again soon.

Lark tucked a wisp of loose hair behind her ear. "I suppose that's true."

But that wasn't an invitation to offer more information. Zaide frowned and turned his eyes toward the water of the vast lake below.

After a moment, Lark sighed. "I suppose I could find a starting point for you. What do you want to know?"

"The sword," he said, knowing the rest of what he had to say would earn him more than a few strange looks. "It's not... It isn't alive, is it?"

Strange might have been an understatement. Lark braced her hands against the rail and pushed herself back, her face screwed up in consternation.

"I know that's a weird thing to say," he added. "Just hear me out. I told you that I felt something when I touched it, but we both know I can't sense any magic, so that's not it. It's happened several more times since Resia's ritual at the spring, though, and it feels like feelings. I don't know how else to explain it."

The perplexity never left her face. "I'm not sure I understand."

"Okay. Examples. Yesterday, when we were about to carve our way through the army and get to Amrochan's gates. I started to draw the sword, but it did... something. It feels like energy. But it also felt like it... like it wanted to fight. Like it was excited. Like I could sense emotions whenever I touched it. And sometimes even when I don't."

"That's absurd," Lark said.

"I know. I told you, I know it's weird. But it happened, and it keeps happening, and I just want to know if it's something I should know about." He almost wished he'd feel something from it now, as they drifted away from the city and the battle it had seemed to crave. He brushed a hand against the hilt, but he got nothing from the steel.

The princess shook her head. "I don't believe what you're asking is possible. Magic isn't sentient, it's just a force we touch. Something that exists in nature around us, that we tap into and use when the time comes. Even the artifacts don't bear any awareness. The magic is laid into them in a way that makes them react when it's needed, but it isn't as if they know. It's simply information, a force that responds when something pushes against it to trigger a response."

"Like the pressure plate in a hunter's trap," Zaide said.

She made a face. "You would manage to make the explanation woodsy, wouldn't you."

He tried not to be irritated. "I am a woodsy person. It's what I know. Either way, I feel something, and we already know it's not magic. Whatever it is, I'd like to know if your books say anything about what might be happening whenever I touch that sword."

Lark hesitated, but she'd already agreed, and they both knew there was little chance she could go back on their agreement with both of them trapped on the same ship. "Very well."

"Thank you." Again, he brushed his fingers across the hilt, but only the cold surface of the metal met his fingers.

"Don't make me regret it," she added as she pushed herself away from the railing and trudged across the deck.

Zaide returned his elbows to the rail and let his head hang. "No promises."

∾

The speed with which they approached and passed the city of Yithel left Zaide wishing he'd had money to travel by ship when he'd made the journey to Amrochan alone. As quickly as the city came into sight, it faded away, and they ventured down the river into unfamiliar territory.

As he'd expected, Tula spent most of her time studying, examining the Molten Dagger and comparing her findings to notes she copied from the books. Twice a day, she emerged from the cabin she shared with Lark long enough to eat. Aside from that, they didn't see her at all.

Lark was more present, though only slightly. Despite her insistence Zaide could research on his own, it wasn't hard to tell he was unwelcome in their cabin while they studied, and both girls had protested at the suggestion he could take a book with him back to his own quarters.

The end result was that he spent most of his time on the ship's deck, either watching the landscape slide by or practicing alone with the Spectrum Blade. None of the sailors appeared to be fighters, and if any of them were, they had no interest in sparring. They watched, though, and with time, Zaide began to suspect they were afraid. Of the sword, at least; it was the blade they watched with dubious frowns, never the hand that wielded it.

The ship made a stop in the port city of Chithal, then turned west. The ocean breeze was cool and grew cooler as they meandered past the familiar red-brick city of Beshnai and rounded the northern horn of the continent, where the frozen lake and the Desheni hid behind rocky mountains. He watched most of it alone, but now and then, the princess deigned to join him.

"Is it normal for people to be afraid of the artifacts?" Zaide asked Lark one afternoon, as the high crested ridge on the western side of Ganede's peninsula came into view. It was a sheer cliff, a straight drop to the sea, and the great bay on the other side remained effectively hidden.

"Who can say? They've been out of sight so long, all people know of them is legend."

"Aren't there other artifacts? Magic objects or weapons they might have heard of?" He couldn't fathom that he'd come into possession of all there were. Or, that Lark had. He carried the Spectrum Blade, but when Tula wasn't studying one, all three of the other artifacts found their home in the princess's bag.

"Not that I've heard of," Lark said. "That's why they're so precious, and why it was so important for Gadranus to keep them from our grasp."

He shrugged beneath his travel cloak, then drew up the hood. It was no longer necessary, the wind and water near Ganede comfortably warm this time of year, but it kept the sun off his face. He'd already sunburned his ears and cheeks more than once. "Does that mean we should be worried?"

Lark looked at him oddly. "About what?"

"The artifacts were what kept us from getting the blade. Now we're working on waking it, which means we need the Paragons. That puts the Paragons at risk, doesn't it?" He searched her eyes for confirmation, but they stayed cold and told him nothing. "Resia's probably safe, since her part's already done. No taking that back now. But we haven't seen the Magister or the Shaman yet."

"Hm." The simple sound she made was enough to set him on edge.

"Does that mean we should be worried?" he asked again.

"I suspect it's too early to say, but I can't say no. The power of the Paragons is constant, after all. A new one is elected shortly after the previous one passes, as you saw with the Elder. But..." Lark's eyes narrowed and she pressed a fist to her mouth as she thought. "Well, we saw what happened with the Elder, but still don't know much about how things work for the Magister or Shaman. I suppose it might be time."

"Time?" Zaide straightened as she turned on her heel and started off across the deck. "Time for what?"

Lark sighed. "Questions."

Tula had lost count of how many times she'd asked the princess to leave.

It wasn't that she didn't like Dasienna; she was quite fond of her, really, but there were distinct differences in their research and study approaches that made sharing a room difficult. Never mind that they had to share *materials*.

The princess was meticulous with notes and documentation. Tula felt haphazard by comparison, surrounded by a dozen books open to specific passages to be cross-referenced later, dozens more places within those books marked with scraps of paper or even other books to keep their spots from being lost. Her notes were a reflection of her state of mind, some in her notebook and the rest spread across the cabin floor, most pages half-filled and none of them bearing answers.

For the thousandth time since the voyage began, she raised the Molten Dagger and squinted at it against the light.

It wasn't obsidian. She was still convinced of that. It had the similar smoky translucency, but lacked the fragility. Nothing chipped the blade. Nothing even seemed capable of scratching it. Yet it had been carved somehow, knapped like one might shape any other type of stone, and that was just another thing that left her puzzled.

The Molten Dagger had been entrusted to Jadora's Magister because it had come from Jadora in the first place. The history texts weren't clear on how it had ended up in the royal family's hands or why, but Jadora had been its birthplace, so that was where it had returned. Yet Jadora's people had abandoned such primitive craftsmanship long before the first mention of the dagger appeared in history and legend. It told her nothing.

Worse still was that the dagger's first mention had been a simple statement that it existed, a reference to a thing so ordinary, it sounded as if everyone ought to know what it was. A weapon bestowed on their people to protect them. But bestowed by whom? Tula raked her hands through her hair and gripped her head with a groan. Everything she turned up indicated she needed more history books, more records. Things that could be found within the Great Library, for certain, but that was the last place she wanted to look.

"The first scholar to get a close look at this thing in who knows how many years, and I'm going to have to share the discovery," she muttered.

Not that it was hers to begin with.

Perhaps that was part of why she disliked sharing research space with the princess. She already had to share credit for the dagger's recovery with Zaide. She liked the young man fine—though she suspected the feeling was not mutual—but this was the archaeological discovery of the century. Of the *Age*, she corrected herself.

She'd always imagined that when her moment to shine came, she'd be shining alone.

A knock sounded on the cabin door. The interruption was wholly unwelcome, but Dasienna's manners were not.

"Just a second," Tula called, resisting the urge to grumble under her breath afterward. She scraped her papers into some semblance of order, snapped books closed, piled things out of the way, and hid the Molten Dagger in a pocket inside her coat. The princess hadn't asked to have the artifact back, but Tula lived in dread of the moment she did. She wasn't about to invite the request by having the dagger be visible.

"Can we come in?" Dasienna's voice was muffled, and Tula stopped and squinted, unsure she'd heard right.

We? Who was *we*?

"Hang on!" She chose one book at random and moved to her bunk to lay it down, pages open to a random point, implying the sort of peaceful, one-volume research the princess often did—

that the princess insisted others ought to use. Then she bounded over to open the door.

After all the times the princess had refused to allow Zaide in to use or borrow their books, seeing him on the other side of the door was a shock. Tula stared at him, and he stared at the jewel in her navel, until both their ears turned red.

"Oh, for mercy's sake," Dasienna said. She waved for Tula to move and dragged Zaide into their small cabin by his sleeve. "The two of you can ogle each other later. We need to speak."

"Ogle?" Tula repeated.

Zaide's cheeks took a reddish flush to match the color of his ears. He looked away.

"He has questions," the princess began matter-of-factly. "We're nearing the port, and there are a few things it would be wise for us to consider before it comes into view."

"We need a plan," Zaide said, his composure regained.

Tula appreciated his simple translation. "Oh. Of course." But her stack of books already teetered precariously, and if they sat to speak, something was sure to be knocked over. Or, even worse, someone would pick up one of the books and misplace one of her bookmarks. "The cabin's kind of small for the three of us, though. Mind if we speak on the deck? I could do with some fresh air, anyway."

This time, the flush that colored Zaide's peculiarly pale complexion was one of relief. "Good idea. There's a nice space on the... um, on the back."

"The stern deck?" Tula suggested.

"I don't know what that means, but I'm going to say yes." Zaide turned and motioned for her to follow.

Dasienna's expression was one of long suffering. "For being the former Elder's apprentice, he has a marked unwillingness to learn anything."

"Maybe he can't. Maybe his head's already full." Tula closed the door behind her.

"Full of ego, perhaps."

Zaide stopped and faced them. "You know I can still hear you, right? I'm six feet away."

"My apologies," the princess said dryly. "I thought the ocean was louder. I'll make sure to insult you more quietly next time."

His mouth twisted with displeasure.

"All right, come on, you two." Tula waved for both of them to walk. As they crossed the ship, she reconsidered her assumption that Zaide didn't like her. Maybe the problem was that he just didn't get along with anyone.

The aft of the ship was quiet, with only a small cluster of the crew present. They murmured amongst themselves about weather and wave patterns and docking plans and ignored their passengers as they took a spot in the farthest corner. The water was quieter in the ship's wake, promising an easy conversation, with no struggle to be heard.

Dasienna sat on the deck with her legs to one side, a ladylike figure Tula tried to emulate. Zaide crossed his arms and leaned against the railing.

"So, what's the question?" Tula asked with her best smile. For some reason, it always felt like she had a need to impress him— or at least, make a better impression than she had. Perhaps she was responsible for their difficulties in getting along. Their first adventure together had ended poorly, due in no small part to her own overeagerness to help. Correcting that mistake seemed to be a long road.

The princess was the one who spoke. "When we were in Kolmar, Resia, the new Elder, took us to a spring in a cavern underneath the forest's temple. The water was the source of her power, and from my understanding, it was necessary for her to rely on its power to bless the Spectrum Blade. Is there a similar source of power for the Magister?"

"Maybe? I think one of the Magister's guardswomen would be more familiar with any rituals he has to do." Tula kept her smile pasted on, though her cheeks had already begun to ache.

"We can speak to Elsanna once we make it into the city. She works most intimately with the Magister, you know."

Zaide pulled a face. "Intimately? Is that why—"

"Oh, hush," she interrupted. "I already explained the armor to you. I just mean she's the head of the guardswomen! Of course she spends a lot of time working with the Magister, she's the one who's in charge of his protection."

"Do you think Elsanna might help us gain audience with the Magister?" Dasienna asked.

"We can ask. There's usually a long wait list for appointments, but now that we're here at King Sendassian's behest..." Tula trailed off with a grin. That was something she could smile about easily. With the king's orders backing their work, she'd have more leverage against the senior librarians. More time off to complete her research, more access to volumes typically forbidden to apprentices. With luck, maybe one of those volumes would contain more information on the Molten Dagger. She was close to understanding it, she was sure. There were just a few important pieces of history and purpose she hadn't yet strung together.

"Have you met the Magister before?" This time, it was Zaide who asked.

Tula blinked at him. "No, of course not. It's not like he visits the library. Usually he sends one of his assistants to collect any materials he might need. He rarely leaves the palace, but it's not like I can blame him. If I had a palace like the Magister's palace, I wouldn't leave home, either."

"Is the palace safe?"

That question was even stranger. Her brows drew together. "Why do you ask?"

He started to speak but Dasienna raised a hand, a wordless order for him to be silent.

"Zaide posed a question earlier. I'm not sure how much merit it has, but you're obviously more familiar with the state of things in Jadora than we are," the princess said. "But the Molten

Dagger was locked away to keep it safe. Now we have need of the Paragons, and they're the only pivot point left between us and the power needed to strike down Gadranus. Is Jadora a safe place? Is it possible the Magister could be at risk?"

"Safe?" Tula almost laughed. "Are you serious? Jadora is the safest place in the world."

A cry went up from the ship's lookout and the crew turned. Zaide turned with them. "Are you sure?" he asked, the trepidation in his voice enough to shake her to her core.

Tula stood and turned to look as the great Jadoran plateau came into view.

Smoke rose from the city.

CHAPTER TEN

"Tʜᴇʀᴇ ᴍᴜsᴛ ʜᴀᴠᴇ ʙᴇᴇɴ ᴀɴ ᴀᴄᴄɪᴅᴇɴᴛ," Tula said as she leaned against the rail. The gray haze that billowed into the pale sky was smaller than it first appeared, wafting from only one side of the city. Before long, all of the ship's crew had gathered on the deck to look, low murmurs of speculation flowing between them.

Zaide wasn't sure what to think. Uneasiness stole up his spine and made his muscles tense. A similar sensation of unease entered his awareness and he hovered his hand over the sword at his hip. "It's doing it again."

Lark and Tula both tore their attention from the city to look at him instead.

"What's doing what?" Lark asked.

He started to answer, then thought better of it. For all that he'd asked Lark to research the issue, she'd never mentioned it again, and now didn't strike him as the best time to renew the subject. "Never mind. We need to figure out what we're doing. We should be ready for problems when we get to the city. Maybe we should try to hurry ahead." Traversing the stretch of desert between the city and the harbor built on the side of the cliff during daylight hours sounded like a nightmare, but the smoke put a lump of anxiety in the pit of his stomach. The sooner he knew what it was, the better he would feel.

"We can't leave the books." Tula squared her shoulders and planted her hands on her hips, as immovable a figure as she could possibly create. "And if the city is on accident alert, they may not be letting people through the gates. You won't get in without me."

Lark nodded her agreement. "She's right. We can't afford to leave our things behind. The city will still be there if we wait a few hours for the ship to properly unload, and it might give them time to solve whatever has happened."

"It looks like wood smoke," Tula added. "If that's the case, it's definitely an accident, because Jadora is largely built of stone and plaster. Our buildings don't burn easily."

Zaide remained unconvinced, but knew to accept he wouldn't win the disagreement. "If you say so." Still, he gripped his sword and couldn't help the tension that knotted between his shoulder blades.

They watched the smoke until the city disappeared, hidden by the ridge of the promontory. Dozens of ships clustered around the docks that jutted from the cliff face. More hovered in the sheltered expanse of the Ellean Sea.

Lark pursed her lips. "Looks like it may be a while before we can unload."

"More time to pack up and prepare, then." Tula waved a hand and made for the cabin.

"Do you need to pack anything?" Lark asked.

"I just need to get my armor." Zaide hadn't worn it since they'd left the waters near Desheni, where the extra insulation the hardened leather provided had been appreciated. "Other than that, I didn't bring anything."

"Easier for you than us, then." The princess offered a tight-lipped and insincere smile, then slipped away.

He twisted to search the sky one more time. From where they were, sheltered by the cliff, the smoke was no longer visible.

With nothing else to do, he returned to his own cramped sleeping quarters to gather his few things.

By sunset, their ship had been assigned a dock and they slid into the harbor. All three of them stood ready with their bags in hand, though a large crate of additional books from Amrochan's royal library waited behind Lark. A porter would move them, and they'd have to rent a wagon or other transport to get it to the city, which meant they'd be waiting in the entry line with the countless caravan wagons they'd been able to skip before.

"Are you sure we can't leave the books and let them be brought to the library?" Zaide asked as they shuffled down the gangplank to the saltwater-scoured mess of wooden walkways that composed Jadora's port.

"Absolutely positive." Lark planted herself near the cliff wall at the end of the dock and stood with her arms crossed. She wasn't even willing to let the crate be unloaded without supervision.

The porters were slow enough to be frustrating, though watching them lift cargo on a system of platforms affixed to rope pulleys proved interesting. Zaide kept an eye on the pulleys while they climbed the rickety stairs and ladders that led to the clifftop. "We should've asked if we could ride one of those."

Lark regarded the pulleys and then him with clear disdain, but Tula gave them a longer look and rubbed her mouth, intrigued by the idea.

"Maybe next time." Zaide assumed there would be one. He'd gone that way before on his way to Desheni, and there had been no ports or docks along the coast that made him think it would be easier to sail north again when it came time to visit the Shaman.

Though the cargo was offloaded at the top long before they made it up, they waited for some time before their crate of books was loaded on a small cart that looked more like a wheelbarrow than a wagon. The porters brought it to them, then departed.

Zaide stared at its wide, high wheels. They'd been designed

to roll on sand, he suspected, but the cart was missing one thing. "We have to pull it ourselves?"

"*You* have to pull it," Lark said.

He should have known.

"I'll help," Tula offered, but from how hard Zaide had to struggle to set it moving, he doubted the librarian would be able to do much.

Moonlight took the sky before they reached the rocky desert. The city glowed on the plateau above them, illuminating smoke that still churned from somewhere inside the high walls.

The last time Zaide had crossed that part of the world, it had been urgent but exciting, the first leg of his journey to be carried out alone. Making the same trip in reverse was unsettling. Instead of urgency, dread filled his chest. But neither Lark nor Tula shared his concerns, judging by the way the two of them took the lead and chattered while he wheeled the book crate along behind them, left to his own dismal thoughts.

He drew a breath and tried to shift his mind to something else. "You know, whoever started the rumors about Jadora must have been terrible at estimation."

Both girls looked back at him, puzzled.

"When we came before, you told me people said if you counted the plateau's cliffs and the walls together, Jadora's fortifications were a hundred feet high." Zaide skimmed the walls now, their rim backlit with an inviting golden glow. "That cliff's a lot higher than a hundred feet, and the walls are thirty on their own."

Tula almost beamed. "You're right. The mesa is nine hundred and seventeen feet high. The walls really are thirty feet tall, though. That's a good guess."

He stumbled in loose sand. "Nine hundred and—Maker's mercy, who measured that?"

"Some scholars, probably. It would be interesting to hear who started that rumor. I don't think a hundred feet would make for a very impressive plateau, and the whole point of building the city on top of the rock formation was making it defensible while letting its inhabitants see everything around it." She fell back and offered to take the cart's handles.

As much as he appreciated the offer, Zaide doubted she could move it alone. He let her take one handle and shifted over to grip the other. The cart rolled more easily with two of them pushing, so they let Lark lead the way alone.

"We'll rest when we get to the foot of the road to the gates," Lark said, but they stopped twice before they made it. Rounding the plateau took hours, and as they approached the entry side of the city, a haze of light hung on the sand in the distance.

"What's that?" Zaide squinted, but couldn't make it out. At first, he'd thought it was a reflection of the city, something like a mirage, but it grew too bright.

"It's... a camp?" Tula paused to swipe the back of her hand across her sweating forehead. The desert was cold at night, but moving the cart was hard. Her confusion made all of them stop.

"Isn't it normal for visitors to halt outside the city before traveling up the slope?" Lark asked.

Tula shook her head and smoothed her fiery ponytail. "Not really. Maybe they have the gates closed because of whatever accident happened up there. I can't say that's ever happened before, though. Usually, people stay on the trail so they don't lose their place."

"Maybe they are on the trail, and that's the overflow." Zaide hoped he was wrong, but lingering where they were wouldn't change anything. He hoisted the cart and started pushing again. It veered sideways before Tula caught her side and straightened it out.

They crept forward until the light resolved into numerous campfires and lanterns. Hundreds of wagons sat sprawled across the desert landscape, some in circles, others parked in orderly rows. The sloped, switchbacked trail that led up the side of the mesa was empty.

Lark continued toward it without saying a word.

"City's closed," a merchant called from a nearby wagon as they passed.

"Noted, thank you," Tula called back.

When they didn't stop, the man waved a hand and slumped before his fire.

They hadn't gone far before Zaide was grateful for how meticulously maintained the road was. The cart rolled smoothly, though going uphill was still a struggle. "Maybe you should run up ahead, Tula."

Lark made a cutting gesture, striking down the idea. "We stay together. I have no doubt they'll allow me in, but if they are refusing people entry, I cannot assist you in entering unless we arrive together."

"Mind helping with the cart, then?" He gritted his teeth as he heaved his side of the cart forward to round a bend.

"Why? You're doing fine."

"Thanks." He grunted and held back the words he really wanted to say.

By the time they reached the top, he was ready to collapse into bed and never climb out.

A cluster of guards stood before the portcullises, barring both the main entrance and the smaller entrance for foot traffic.

"City's closed to visitors," one of them barked, voice so weary it sounded like he'd been there for days.

Lark motioned for them to stop while she strode ahead. "I am not here for a pleasure visit. I am Princess Dasienna, escorted by one of Jadora's own librarians and my Bladebearer, and I am here by the order of King Sendassian." She produced a sealed letter from her bag and turned it to display the crest marked in the wax. "We've brought books from the royal library to add to the Great Library's collection. I am to seek refuge within Jadora's walls while Amrochan is under attack."

Pure bewilderment sprawled across the faces of the guards. "Amrochan under attack?"

The princess's expression grew cool. "Word of the siege was

sent weeks ago. Has this not become common knowledge in Jadora?"

"My apologies, Your Highness. It has not."

That gnawing sense of uneasiness boiled up in Zaide's middle again.

Lark sniffed. "I see. In that case, please notify whoever is necessary to authorize my entry. I'm certain this letter from my father is more than enough to clarify that my presence in Jadora is non-negotiable."

One of the guards stepped forward to take the letter when she offered it. He exchanged whispers with a few of the others, then called for the smaller entryway to be opened. When he disappeared inside, the rest of the guards rearranged themselves to ensure there were no gaps in their line.

Zaide leaned against the crate of books in its odd cart and willed himself not to fall asleep on his feet. Beside him, Tula gazed at the sky, the corners of her eyes pinched.

The scent of smoke was thick on the wind. The plumes glowed in the city's light, blotting out the stars.

"You okay?" he asked quietly.

"It's somewhere past the western gate," she whispered back. "That district is where my home's at."

The concern in her voice twanged something inside him. Sympathy, he thought. "I'm sure it's fine. An accident, like you said. They'll get it under control."

She said nothing, but he couldn't help feeling like he ought to fill the silence.

He fumbled for something to say. "When I was here before, I saw there were directions to different gates, but the only gate I saw was this one. The entry to the south of the city. Are there others?"

"Hm? Oh." Tula tore her eyes from the sky and mustered a smile, though it was nowhere near her usual cheer. "There's only one gate by which you can access the city, but the city's broken up into sections. Each district has a gate so it can be cordoned off in case there's a breach. Or an emergency." Her smile faded.

Wrong choice of subjects, it seemed. Maybe he could try another angle, work on fishing out the information they'd just begun to seek before the smoke had become visible. "Is the Magister's palace separated off into its own space?"

"Yes. Most folk aren't given authorization to enter. As far as I know, only the guardswomen are allowed to come and go from the Magister's district freely. It's on the other side of the north gate. Even the palace employees and usual guards have to stop for a gate check."

"Are there any other places that are forbidden like that? I know the city's legendary for its tight security, but it has to feel stifling sometimes if there are a bunch of places closed off." Zaide shifted, an unsettling prickle begging for his attention. The guards were looking at him. Maybe that was a bad subject, too.

"No, the palace is pretty much it. Everywhere else is open, and it's generally a wonderfully safe place to be. Even theft is exceptionally uncommon within the city walls." A hint more animation returned to Tula's demeanor.

He shifted the subject again, mindful of the guards and the way their eyes threatened to burn holes through his leather armor. "What's your favorite part of the city, then?"

"I'd say the library, but after that trip from the docks, I'm more inclined to say my bed."

Zaide managed a laugh without it sounding forced. "I think we can all agree on that."

Lark regarded him with a cold, thoughtful frown. She'd likely chastise him later for trying to wheedle out information. Her stare was enough to still his tongue, and when he grew quiet, Tula did, too.

After what seemed an eternity, a small cluster of guards appeared at the small gate, several bearing red streamers affixed to their pauldrons. "Your Highness?" one called.

Lark strode forward and beckoned for Zaide and Tula to

follow. They both grunted and strained to get the heavy cart rolling again.

"My apologies for your wait," the guard in the front said. He was the most decorated of the group, streamers reaching well past his waist. "Please, enter. The Magister has offered to host you in his palace and wishes for you to come right away."

The princess took in his armor and decorations. "Thank you, I would be happy to accept accommodations. To whom do I have the pleasure of speaking?"

"Jinohe, Chief Captain of the Magister's Mage-Guard."

"The Magister's what?" Tula asked as they passed through the gate.

The man's disposition cooled. "Your librarian may deliver your books to the Great Library now. We will see that she's settled for the night afterward." He led them through the reception area and the second gate, to where another group of guards waited. "Your escort, madam librarian."

Zaide glanced between them. "What—"

"My Bladebearer will assist my librarian in making her delivery," Lark said before he could finish. "Afterward, they will both join me in the Magister's palace."

"Of course, Your Highness." Jinohe pressed a fist over his heart and bowed.

The itch between Zaide's shoulders grew worse. Something new brushed his thoughts with the same uncomfortable sense he'd gotten before, that it spilled from the sword at his side instead of himself. Agitation. Distrust.

No, that feeling was definitely his. He regarded the Mage-Guard through narrowed eyes as he and Tula pushed their cart to join their assigned escort. "Be safe, Your Highness."

"The princess will be well protected by the Magister's guard," Jinohe said.

"I'm sure she will."

Lark shot him a glare that shut his mouth, then turned to the captain. They started off without another word, while their escort moved the opposite direction.

No one spoke as the guards led them to the Great Library. None of them offered to help with the cart, but at the leader's gesture, they carried the crate from the foot of the library's stairs to the door.

"I understand you sleep in the library?" the leader asked as Tula opened the door.

"I do when I'm on duty, but we'll be out shortly to join the princess, as she commanded." She smiled, but there was a steely glint in her eyes.

Zaide planted a shoulder against the crate and shoved it through the doorway into the library's lobby.

Tula all but slammed the door. "Magister's Mage-Guard?" she whispered angrily the moment it was closed. "Something is weird. I need to find Elsanna."

Across the library, a lamp flared to life at the reception desk.

They both jumped.

"Elsanna?" an old man in spectacles repeated, leaning across the desk to peer at them both. "Elsanna is gone."

CHAPTER ELEVEN

"You have company." The librarian rose with a surprising spryness and swept across the floor with equal grace. His weathered face screwed up in a scowl as he peered through a tiny glass set in the library's door.

Zaide had no doubt the guards remained outside, but their presence had become the least of his concerns.

"What do you mean, Elsanna is gone?" Tula demanded, an echo of the words that bounced around inside his head. He had planned to voice them himself, though likely with more volume than what she used.

Despite her harsh whisper, the librarian hushed her, a finger to his withered lips. "You won't be able to hide from them if they've set up camp on our steps. Are the houses in the west district still smoking?" The old librarian sniffed hard, then turned abruptly to point at the wooden crate in the middle of the floor. "What in mercy's name is this?"

"Books from the royal library," Tula said without missing a beat. "Master Arkosh, what's going on? Where is Elsanna?"

"What caused the fire?" Zaide asked.

"There's been fire daily since... oh, what does it matter? Come. We have to figure out how to extricate you from this."

Arkosh locked the door and beckoned them both toward the reception desk.

Tula hurried after him, a question forming on her lips, but the old librarian spoke before she got it out.

"I hardly know where to begin, and we haven't much time to work something out," Arkosh said. "Shortly after you departed to assist the princess in her research, it was discovered that the seal in the Magister's caverns had been broken, despite the guardswomen being responsible for watching over it. Elsanna insisted she knew nothing about it. The Magister fears the Molten Dagger may have fallen into Gadranus's hands."

Zaide met and returned Tula's worried glance. She still hadn't returned the dagger to Lark. All of a sudden, the fact they both carried artifacts seemed dangerous. His hand hovered above the Spectrum Blade's hilt. "Has the Magister blamed Elsanna for the dagger's disappearance?"

"I am not sure that he blamed her directly, but there was... a confrontation. As things stand now, the guardswomen stand behind Elsanna's claim she was not involved in the dagger being taken." The librarian drew a hand over his smooth-shaven scalp. "Of course, that led to the guardswomen being ejected from the Magister's palace, which led to the..." He trailed off and adjusted his spectacles as he peered at Zaide. "Who are you?"

"His name is Zaide," Tula answered for him. "He's the princess's, ah..."

"Beau?"

"No!" Zaide and Tula protested at the same time.

Arkosh sniffed again. "Hmm."

The thought was enough to make Zaide shudder. Lark was one of the coldest people he'd ever met. "I was the previous Kolmari Elder's apprentice, now I'm the princess's Bladebearer." Or so she had called him. He'd already decided he liked that title over the one Sendassian had used. Even after they'd sliced through more than a hundred goborrins, he wasn't fit to be anyone's champion.

The way Arkosh's eyes widened made him reconsider. "That cannot be."

Tula worried her hands and Zaide concluded he'd made a mistake.

He removed his hand from the sword. "What do you mean?"

"It means you cannot be! Who are you? The Kolmari Elder, you said? If you were an apprentice, the Vale Hymnflute, perhaps, but..." The old librarian's lips puckered and his eyes took a distant look. Then he shook his head. "No, that cannot be. Not with the Molten Dagger gone. All signs point to Sendassian, besides. But whether Elsanna stole the dagger or if Gadranus has it, either option would—"

Someone pounded on the library's front door.

Tula cleared her throat. "I mean no disrespect, Master Arkosh, but I get the feeling a dire mistake has been made."

"Yes, certainly. And that's precisely why we have to get you out of this." Arkosh nodded, his determination renewed. He bent to press something beneath the reception counter and a low thunk sounded in the floor. A moment later, a slab of stone shifted aside, revealing a dark opening.

Zaide snorted. "Oh, do all libraries have secret passages? Is that just something nobody ever thought I should know?"

"I get the feeling you don't intend that argument for me," Tula said. Arkosh disappeared down the hole and she sat to follow. When Zaide leaned over the counter, he saw the ladder in the opening's mouth.

No second knock came. Instead, the library doors shuddered beneath an impact.

"We need to go," Arkosh said from somewhere below, his voice a hollow echo in the dark below the floor.

Tula slipped down after him. "Master Arkosh, there's something I need to tell you."

"Yes, I'm sure there is. Hurry, there's not much time."

She clambered down a few rungs, then paused. "Zaide, come on."

The doors shuddered again and a deep crack echoed through the library.

He slid over the counter and the doors burst open. He froze as guards spilled in.

"Too late," Arkosh snarled in a whisper. The stone plate just beneath Zaide's feet slid closed with a rasp that was lost beneath the clack of guardsmen's boots.

Zaide could have cursed.

"Where are they?" A guard advanced on Zaide with his sword drawn.

Raising his hands in surrender seemed a sensible thing to do. "The librarians?" Zaide stepped to the side. If he could slip out from behind the counter, maybe he could keep them from finding the trap door. "They went to the back. Something about transfer records. They told me to wait here with the books." He nodded toward the crate, still untouched in the middle of the entryway.

The way the guard's lip peeled back from his teeth made his skepticism clear. "Search the back," he barked. "You stay right where you are."

Zaide stopped beside the reception desk and remained as still as he could, his hands still up and safely away from his weapon. Guards flowed past him in a march and disappeared somewhere into the darkness beyond the desk.

Their footsteps faded and silence hung in the air for a painful moment. Then they returned.

"They're gone!"

The lead guard snarled and lunged forward, caught Zaide by the shirt and slammed him backwards into the desk. "You helped them escape!"

Panic surged in his chest, but Zaide sucked in a deep breath and willed it to vanish. These people weren't his enemy. The Magister's guards were on their side. All he had to do was figure out how to clear the air and buy time for Tula to let the librarian—and the Magister—know the Molten

Dagger was safe. "I don't know what you're talking about," he managed.

"Liar." The guard caught his left hand and twisted hard, forcing Zaide to turn around. A moment later, something cold snapped shut around his wrist. "By the authority of Jadora's Magister, you are under arrest."

So much for clearing the air.

"Where are we going?" With the commotion upstairs, Tula didn't dare speak in more than a whisper. She couldn't see anything, but her fingers trailed along the walls to help her keep her bearings. Master Librarian Arkosh was just a few steps ahead, his sandals little more than a rasp against the stone.

"The librarians have done their best to remain neutral, but there are things you need to know, and the Magister's policy has been to pretend they haven't happened. If you are to assemble your own opinion, you deserve the right to hear from both biased and unbiased persons on every side of the situation."

"That doesn't answer the question." Tula's fingers crossed an edge and found a void. She paused.

"Turn right," Arkosh said.

She followed his voice.

"As for your question," the old man continued, "I am going to take you to see the guardswomen first. You'll have plenty of opportunities to speak to the Magister's Mage-Guard afterward, but if I don't take you to the guardswomen now, you'll have no way to reach them later."

"What about Zaide, though? What will the guards do to him?" And what would they do to her, after she reappeared? That she'd vanished in the library had to paint her with some sort of guilt, though what she was guilty of, she did not know.

Arkosh heaved a sigh. "My assumption is he will be taken to the palace and returned to the princess. They will probably detain him first, question him, perhaps confiscate anything on his person they deem suspicious."

Which meant they'd try to take the Spectrum Blade. Tula swallowed against an unpleasant thickness in her throat. "Will they do that to me?"

"Possibly. Now that you've disappeared from their watchful eye, you'll be treated with suspicion. The Librarians' Guild will offer some protection, but they won't be able to clear your name entirely. That will be up to the Magister."

She stopped. "Master Arkosh, I need to speak with you before we go any farther. Whatever is going on in the city, it's my fault."

The older librarian scoffed. "That's highly unlikely, my girl."

She plunged a hand into the interior pocket of her coat and unsheathed the Molten Dagger. Its soft, ruddy light flooded the hallway.

Arkosh stopped dead in his tracks and turned until the light reflected off his round spectacles.

"If they're fighting about this, it's a misunderstanding. Gadranus doesn't have it. Elsanna didn't take it. I did." Her fingers trembled with the admission. She gripped the dagger tighter.

"Maker's mercy," the old man breathed.

"You know the rumors about the Magister as well as I do. And you know they would have spirited the dagger away to where no one could have it. We didn't have time to wait. Princess Dasienna needed the dagger right then, and Elsanna said she would handle it. If something's happened to her, it's my fault!"

He removed his spectacles and wiped them clean on his shirt. "Then when you say that boy is Princess Dasienna's Bladebearer..."

The dagger's warmth was usually comforting. Now, it was stifling. Her fingers prickled, but she didn't dare put it away. "I mean exactly what I said."

His mouth tightened and he resumed walking. "Librarians are supposed to remain neutral." The gruffness in his tone hit like an accusation.

"The librarians serve the guild, but the guild answers to King Sendassian. That doesn't count as neutrality. It means we're allowed to see one side as correct, and that's whatever side the crown takes." Tula kept the dagger out, if only because she was grateful for what little light it provided. She still couldn't see where they were going, but she saw the outline of the walls around her.

"That is not my argument. But since you've already chosen a side, I am glad to see we have ended with the same conclusion."

A nervous flutter pinged in her chest. Master Librarian Arkosh was a perfect example of everything the guild sought to instill in its members. If he'd taken a side in one of the city's disputes, she dreaded what that might mean. Never mind that she hadn't a clue what that side *was*.

She decided to circle back to her original question. "If we're going to see the guardswomen, where are they?"

"In hiding, for the moment. We will have to make this brief." The passage ended at a door and Arkosh fiddled with a peculiar latch for a minute before it snapped open. They stepped out into a familiar basement and a half-dozen women sat up in surprise.

Tula lowered the dagger. "The basement of the guild headquarters? Master Arkosh, that does not seem neutral."

"The librarians are neutral," the old man said patiently. "I never said the guild was."

One of the women stood and Tula breathed a sigh of relief. If Elsanna wasn't there, Valla was the very next person she'd ask to see.

"Thank the Maker," Valla sighed. "How did you get back into the city? The gates were closed two days after you departed!"

Tula shuffled forward to wrap her cousin in a hug. "Princess Dasienna brought me. Zaide's here, too, but he didn't make it down the hole in time. We had to leave him behind."

The tall guardswoman took her by the shoulders and pushed her back a step. "The Magister had scouts visiting the cavern at regular intervals. He learned the door had been opened after just a few days and they saw the dagger was gone."

At mention of the blade, Tula tucked in her chin and returned it to its sheath in her pocket. From the sound of things, it would be wise to keep the artifact safely out of view. "How did they get down there? The guardswomen's house blocked the only entrance."

"We don't know. It doesn't seem possible that anyone could slip past us in our own home, but we investigated every inch of the tunnels and found no sign of any other entry. Whoever the Magister hired to search, they aren't to be underestimated."

"Speculation is it could have been one of the guardswomen," Arkosh said. "They all knew the Magister wanted the dagger as a tool to gain power for himself, but we don't know that all of them felt that stance represented corruption."

Tula shrugged away from her cousin's grasp and stepped back, giving herself space to worry her hands. "If that's the case, then they'd know about Elsanna volunteering to hide the fact the cavern opened. Is that why she disappeared?" It made little sense—if they knew about Elsanna, they'd know Princess Dasienna had been the one to take the artifact, and even the Magister couldn't stake a claim against the crown.

Unless that was part of the rumors of corruption. She twisted her fingertips and tried not to bite her lip.

"Maybe. We don't know." Valla sighed. "All we know is once the attacks started, Elsanna vanished. The Magister has blamed her for what's going on."

Attacks? Tula's breath caught. The smoke.

Before she could ask, another of the guardswomen appeared on the stairs. "Mage-Guards coming."

The women leaped to their feet and disappeared amid the shelves and storage crates that populated the basement.

Arkosh grasped Tula's arm and pulled her toward the stairs. "Hurry. Time to put you back in their good graces."

"Already? I've hardly begun to put together everything that's going on!" Despite her protest, Tula had no choice but to follow him, and they emerged into the back of the guild hall a moment later. The old librarian locked the basement door behind him and stacked random books from nearby carts in her arms.

They emerged into the front room of the guild hall as the Mage-Guards burst through the front door.

Arkosh blinked at them and adjusted his spectacles, his demeanor flipping in an instant from urgency to languor. "Good evening."

The lead guard pointed his sword at Tula's head. "You fled the library."

"Fled?" Arkosh scoffed. "What are you on about? Tula, dear, you can leave those on the counter. Give me a moment and I'll find that index for you." He posted himself between her and the guards.

She bowed her head and put the books where she was told.

The guard didn't lower his sword. "She was given instruction to check in and leave her books. Not to lock the door and vanish."

"And what do you suppose checking in involves? Are you an apprentice librarian? Lower your weapon and quit acting like a boor." The old librarian sniffed. "Honestly. My apprentice has just returned from an expedition requested by the crown, and this is how you treat her? Of course the library was locked, we had to cross the street to retrieve an index that was out for cross-referencing so we could ensure everything that's supposed to be in that crate is present, and I was the only member of staff there. You would have us leave the Great Library, the gem of Jadora, left unattended for all the masses to invade?"

A flush crept up the guard's neck. "You didn't tell us—"

"And why would I tell you anything? Are you a librarian?" Arkosh adjusted his spectacles again and leaned forward to squint straight into the man's face. "Ignore them, Tula, dear. If it wasn't in the back, that index must be upstairs. Let's go up and check the desks. Since these young men have barged in here, I'm sure they'll be more than happy to assist us in looking for it."

"Yes, Master Arkosh." Tula did her best to appear meek. She bowed her head and slipped around the corner to the stairs, gripping the open front of her coat. The dagger's presence in her pocket made her heart race now. What would the guardsmen do if they found it on her person? Would they steal her notebook and her research? Would they rush it to the Magister? Listen to her explanation? Or would she vanish like Elsanna? Valla hadn't said it, but Tula had grown up with the leader of the Magister's guardswomen. If Elsanna was missing, it wasn't because she'd run away.

Behind her, a handful of guards groaned and shuffled up the stairs to search for Arkosh's fictional index. She made a show of picking up books and inspecting their contents and the guards mimicked her, though their bewildered expressions made it clear they had no idea what they were supposed to be looking for.

"Honestly, the Magister's Mage-Guard should know better," Arkosh grumbled below. "Barging in on library business, flinging around accusations... It's almost like the lot of you don't want us to do our jobs. Why don't you just focus on yours, hmm?"

"Our job is seeing that she checks in and that she's returned to the princess in the Magister's palace," the lead guard said.

"Well, she's in the process of checking in, and you'll have to wait for all those books to be checked in before I am done with her. Ah! Tula, dear, I found it. It was down here. Come back, would you? We don't want to leave that boy waiting in the library for too long. Maker forbid he touch anything he oughtn't."

The way the lead guard coughed and cleared his throat was enough to make her smile. Tula wiped a hand over her mouth to shoo the expression away, though the corners of her mouth quivered when he spoke.

"Ah, the boy is on his way back to the palace now..."

"Already?" Arkosh exclaimed. "I told him to wait! No manners in you sword-bearing types. None at all."

She straightened her spine and did her best to stay calm as she trudged back down the stairs.

All she had to do was keep the dagger from being seen, return it to Dasienna, and let the princess sort things out.

Now that they were separated, whatever Zaide had gotten into, he was on his own.

CHAPTER TWELVE

THE COLD IRONS were less comfortable than the rope the Desheni used to bind his wrists. Zaide twisted one hand as the thought drifted through his mind. He wasn't sure comparing methods of arrest and imprisonment was the sort of thing normal people did, but there was little else he could do now. He didn't know where they were going or even where they were; the guards who led him took a convoluted path.

Maybe it was to confuse him, but another possibility was they had no more direct route to take. They'd passed what Zaide assumed was an interior wall in the city. Houses ran right up to it, some built with their walls pressed against it so there wasn't even a gap. It had arched over the wider roadway, and the gate was down. Guards stood on the other side of the gate, but their attention had been elsewhere. He wasn't sure they'd even noticed them walking past.

"Quit wiggling," one of the guards behind him said.

Zaide hadn't realized he was still twisting his wrist. "Sorry. Just trying to get feeling back in my fingers." The claw-like shape of the irons meant they overlapped themselves and scissored shut, closed tight on his wrists so there was no hope of wriggling a hand free.

Before long, the palace rose above them—or at least, its walls did. They were as tall as the city's exterior walls, without decoration and mortared perfectly smooth. The gates here were polished bronze instead of ugly iron, and finely wrought flourishes decorated every square in the grill. Something to make up for the plainness of the walls, Zaide supposed.

The procession stopped and one guard stepped ahead to request entry. Those who clustered around Zaide took the opportunity to give him a curious once-over.

"You aren't fighting much," one remarked.

"Why would I fight you? You aren't my enemy. We're all on the same side." Zaide couldn't help but wish they'd loosen the irons a bit, though. At least they were close.

The guard harrumphed as if he disagreed.

Remaining patient was difficult, but it wasn't as if anything could be changed. Zaide knew he had done no wrong, and Lark was waiting for him. He wished he knew where Tula had gone, but she'd been with one of the master librarians, and he doubted a scholar would put her in danger.

The gates creaked and a low clanking signaled their ascent. Both the exterior and interior portcullises began to rise.

"Dasienna will be expecting me." Zaide took care to ensure it didn't sound like boasting, but a calm, simple statement of fact. "I understand you're following orders and that there may have been some misunderstandings. I won't let her hold that against you."

The guards said nothing and shoved him through the gates.

An explosion boomed in the city behind them, rocking the ground on which they stood.

"Again?" one of the guards cried. The cluster of them spun to look for the new plume of smoke that rose into the sky as a chorus of screams and shouting rose into the night air. An alarm bell clanged above it all.

A few of the men started to go back through the gate, but one of the guards at the back spread his arms and herded them all into the palace's courtyard. "Stick to your orders!"

Zaide stayed rooted in place until two of the guards grasped him by the arms and made him move. He strained against his irons, but not their hands. "Someone could be hurt," he protested. "We have to go see what that was!"

"We know what it was," one of the guards said. "And what it was is no concern of yours. Move."

A retort leaped to the tip of Zaide's tongue, but he swallowed it back and made himself walk. Behind them, the gates closed with a bang.

The palace loomed ahead, a massive structure of sandstone carved in bold reliefs and glazed all over with red. Broad double doors dressed with gilt and more elaborate carvings sat at the end of the stone walkway, surrounded by glass lamps that burned with shimmering flames instead of the magic-infused stones that lit the rest of the city. It was a breathtaking sight, but one he didn't get to enjoy for long.

Instead of leading him to the doors so he might meet with Lark inside, the guards turned to a side path and ventured around a corner, to where there were no lamps or fancy carvings. A few shallow stairs descended into a recess in the side of the palace and when they reached the landing at the bottom, Zaide realized where they were.

"Wait a second." He pulled against the guards who led him for the first time as they opened a heavy, rivet-studded iron door. "What are you doing? This isn't—I'm supposed to meet with the princess, I'm not—"

A sharp cuff to his blunted ear cut him short.

"The princess can explain things to the Magister well enough on her own," one of the men said.

They dragged him into the forefront of the prison, where a hard man with a scarred face and shaved head sat beside a small, round table at the top of another flight of stairs. The man rose and crossed his arms.

"Pick a cell," one of the guards said. "We'll let Captain Jinohe know to come deal with him."

"Jinohe never deals with anything." The scarred man's voice was deep, booming, and made Zaide's heart skip a beat. The man paid him little mind, though, just swiped a ring of keys from the table and descended into the dimly lit row of cells below.

The guards pushed Zaide along until they reached the cell the scarred man held open.

"Strip him," that harsh bass voice ordered.

Zaide dug in his heels. "Wait—"

The guards didn't wait. Someone touched the hilt of the Spectrum Blade to remove it. The spark it emitted lit up the whole prison and the man reeled backwards with a shout. The sword clattered to the floor.

A moment later, someone else unfastened his belt and removed the empty scabbard. They unlatched his irons and unbuckled the straps of his armor, pulled his bags from his shoulders and took his travel cloak. His armor came off first, then his shirt and boots.

"What do we do with the weapon?" One of the guards raised the empty sheath as he stepped around the glowing sword on the ground. No one seemed eager to touch it.

"Leave it," the scarred man said. "It won't help him escape, if that's what you're afraid of. The Magister can send an artificer down to transport it elsewhere later."

"Maybe you should have the Magister send the princess instead," Zaide spat. They left his trousers, but probing hands checked thoroughly for hidden weapons before the guards finally retreated and the cell door slammed shut.

The big scarred man loomed in the hall on the other side, twirling the ring of keys around his finger. "The princess isn't going to save you, and neither is that pretty sword. But you behave, and I'll make sure your stay isn't miserable. Which is more than I can say for most."

Zaide glowered back at him as he knelt and took the Spectrum Blade in hand.

A wry smile twisted the man's mouth, but he didn't linger. The guards departed and he followed close behind them.

The cell was almost bare, but held a pile of straw and a hole-filled blanket. With the chill in the air, it seemed almost a kindness. Zaide settled cross-legged on the straw and dragged the blanket around his bare shoulders. Without its sheath, the Spectrum Blade filled the cell with an eerie glow. Zaide sat it across his lap and leaned back against the wall. The swirls of color shifted a little faster than usual, casting marbled shapes in greens and pinks across the ceiling. He watched, intrigued. Had it ever projected light that way before? It flowed and eddied like light distorted by rippling water.

When he hovered a hand over the blade, his fingers tingled. Agitation. "You and me both," he muttered. The feeling could have been his, yet when he sat alone with the sword like that, he was certain it was the blade and not himself.

"For all the good that does me." He let his head rest against the stone wall. Lark had never provided any answers. It was possible she'd learned something and simply didn't want to admit her initial response had been wrong. He knew it was absurd, but at this point, it wasn't the strangest thing he'd experienced. Maybe he just had to ask someone else.

His fingers slid down the length of the blade. An artificer, the prison guard said. Zaide had never heard that term before, but it wasn't hard to puzzle out what the job might be. Nothing he'd ever studied indicated magic-infused items were common, but he'd seen some aside from the artifacts. The lanterns they'd used for most of the journey were magic, as were the lights over most of the desert's fortress city.

"Maybe whoever they send down here will know a bit more about you, huh?"

But it was equally likely whoever arrived to deal with the sword on the Magister's behalf would find a way to take it from him, and the thought made his lip twist with a snarl. If the blade had chosen him, no one else had any right to it. And if the princess had decided he would use the sword to serve her, it seemed like the best thing he could do.

Zaide exhaled hard and raked his fingers through his hair. "And there you go, bending to the princess's will again, with no regard for what you really want." Or with any consideration for what she'd already put him through. He still hadn't sorted that out, though he'd stewed on it some during the long boat ride from Amrochan.

Not that he'd gotten far. Thinking on it at all made his nightmares worse and he hadn't determined how to chase the skittering feet of spiders or the creak of living ice from his dreams. Resia would have had intelligent words about what he was experiencing, but Resia wasn't there, nor did he know when he could discuss it with her.

After his foster sister, the next best choice was Lark.

A shiver ran up his arm and he paused. He'd kept one hand on the sword without thought, and that had been undeniable.

"Do you hear what I'm thinking?" he asked the blade quietly. "Or am I just going mad?"

The lack of answer offered no comfort.

He squeezed his eyes closed. "Right." Just mad, then. He pulled the shabby blanket closer around his shoulders and moved the sword from his lap to the straw beside him as he lay down.

Much like everything else, the trip had taken a sour turn, but there was no reason he couldn't allow himself a moment's rest.

The moment he closed his eyes, an explosion shuddered somewhere outside the prison.

CHAPTER THIRTEEN

Every time the Molten Dagger bumped against Tula's side, it felt like an accusation. Every footstep brought another wave of guilt.

This is your fault.

This wouldn't have happened if you knew your place.

You weren't authorized for archaeological pursuits.

You aren't even a proper librarian.

She swallowed hard and tried to combat each thought with something more reasonable.

This is because of the war.

Someone was going to find the dagger either way.

The princess ordered us to try.

I had her permission.

It didn't work. Awareness of the sheathed artifact in her pocket burned hotter than the heat that spilled off it, which was worrisome enough on its own. What if it set her coat on fire? How would she explain if her pocket suddenly burst into flames? They'd find her out then, find out she'd stolen the artifact after the Magister insisted any progress toward opening the sealed doors be reported to him.

No, she corrected herself, blinking fast, as if the flutter of her eyelids would dash the thoughts like wind might scatter the smoke above the city. She had acted on behalf of the crown, as any librarian ought. Jadora might answer to the Magister, but the Magister answered to the king.

The fact Sendassian didn't know his crown had been used to sanction the original expedition hardly mattered. Now Dasienna carried a stockpile of letters sealed with her father's crest, orders for everyone they would meet along their path.

The dagger bumped again, harder, and she set her jaw. The palace was just ahead. She couldn't let herself be distracted, couldn't become flustered and make a mistake. All she had to do was get Princess Dasienna somewhere alone, give her the dagger, and let her take care of it. The princess was the one raised and trained for diplomacy, the one who carried the king's orders, the one who could settle everything.

The guards that formed her escort herded her toward the door. As one of them reached out to open it, an ear-splitting blast made the whole city quiver.

Tula grabbed the nearest guard for support. "What was that?" she cried.

"Another?" The man's voice rasped in his throat, halfway between disbelief and fear. What could make the Magister's guards fearful? She wasn't sure she wanted to know.

The rest of the guards peeled off from the group. "Get her inside," the leader ordered, pointing toward the door they still hadn't opened. "Get her to the princess, then meet us at the gate."

The guard she clung to nodded, tense. He urged her forward, his touch gentle but firm. "Let's hope the princess is settled somewhere safe."

"Isn't the palace safe?" Then again, wasn't Jadora supposed to be safe? Until Dasienna and Zaide arrived, Tula had spent the entirety of her life within those walls, sheltered and confident. The way the guard shot her a worried frown and did not answer shook her as badly as that first sight of smoke.

Inside the palace, a cluster of mage-guards in streamer-covered armor gathered near the door. Jinohe stood among them, barking orders and pointing a dozen different directions. More guards came from hallways to either side of the entryway, replacing those who departed with each command. The chief captain spun to glower at them, though a flicker of surprise lit his eyes. "Where is the other one?"

Tula assumed he meant Zaide.

"He was already escorted this direction." The guard at Tula's side scanned the crowd. "I am to deliver her to the princess. Has Dasienna been sent to a safe location?"

Jinohe's face hardened again. "The princess is with the Magister in the receiving parlor. Take her there."

"Yes, sir." The guard thumped a fist against his breastplate and then turned Tula the way they were meant to go.

None of the faces they passed on the way were friendly, but she couldn't fault them. Whatever was happening, it was a first for the city. Strife between the Magister and his own guardswomen was unheard of, and she could not deny her resemblance to her kin.

Just return the dagger to the princess, she reminded herself. Then everything would be fine.

They rounded a corner into a new hallway and a massive, piglike monster swung a sword for their heads.

Tula shrieked and dropped to the carpeted floor. The blade missed the guard beside her by an inch.

"Maker's mercy!" he spat.

The monster swung again and the guard tried to parry. Metal screeched and a new wave of exclamations went up behind them.

"Breach!" someone screamed.

Tula rolled to the side and thrust herself to her feet. She didn't wait to see the fight. Instead, she sprinted down the hallway in search of the princess and the Magister.

Another tusked beast burst through a door, wood splintering

around its spiked club. She stumbled a step, but righted herself with a hand against the wall and kept running.

At the end of the hall, a door swung open and someone stepped out to see the commotion.

Dasienna.

"Goborrins!" Tula shouted. "Goborrins in the palace!" In the city. Inside Jadora's walls. This wasn't supposed to be possible.

The princess's eyes widened and she started forward, but a hand reached from behind the door to clasp her shoulder and stop her. She froze with her silver knives halfway drawn.

A low murmur, words that weren't quite audible to Tula's ears, made her pause.

Dasienna's stance tightened with frustration. She withdrew a step, then slipped back into the room she'd come from. The door started to close, but Tula bolted forward and caught it before it could.

On the other side, a man she could only assume was the Magister gaped in surprise.

"Your Highness," Tula said in a rush. She didn't know if she was supposed to bow, or if any acknowledgment of the Magister was appropriate in the princess's company, but the concern for her manners evaporated a breath later. The room behind them was empty. "Where is Zaide? Is he here? Is he okay?"

The princess blinked at her, taken aback. "He's not with you?"

The question made Tula's stomach lurch. "He stayed in the library while Master Librarian Arkosh and I—oh, what does it matter? Your Highness, we have to find somewhere safe!"

"I have a safe room. Come, both of you." The Magister turned them toward the far end of the parlor and coaxed them to move. He was calm despite the intrusion. Part of Tula was sure that was logical, a quality a leader should have. Another part screamed warnings in the back of her head. How could anyone be calm right now? Jadora's walls had been breached!

Dasienna showed no emotion either, though. She was calm,

serene, and walked with a steady pace. "My father will not be pleased with this turn of events, I'm sure."

"All the more reason to ferret out that traitor and recover the Molten Dagger, Your Highness." The Magister's words flowed like silk, well-practiced and smooth, but what he'd said stuck out like a thorn on a spindly stem.

The princess hadn't told him where the dagger was?

Uneasiness stirred in Tula's chest, spurring her heart to an anxious drum. She slowed, but still trailed along, following to wherever the Magister wanted them to go.

He remained unruffled, unbothered by her hesitance—or else unaware of it. She stole a glance at him from the corner of her eye.

The Magister did not associate with people outside his palace. The guardswomen—and the Mage-Guards now, Tula supposed—came and went freely in his place, acting as his eyes and ears throughout the city. Elsanna had described him several times, but somehow, the word *handsome* had never entered the description.

He bore graceful features, a rich bronze complexion, and thick, straight hair that was deeper black than anything Tula had ever seen. His beard had been trimmed to an elegant point and the depths of his dark, narrow eyes would have been enough to make most women swoon.

But you're not swooning, she reminded herself. And the fact she'd found herself caught up in the way he looked in the midst of all this was both strange and disconcerting.

The Magister noticed her attention and met her eye with a faint smile. "I am sorry. We have not been properly introduced. This way. We'll speak once we're settled."

He led them down a narrow hallway and stopped before an empty length of wall. The wood paneling here was lacquered the same red as the exterior of the palace, though a strip of wood painted gold ran along the middle of the wall. He grasped the golden accent trim between two seams and pulled. It slid outward and clicked, and a whole section of paneling swung outward. Shadows lurked on the other side, but he waved a hand and a number of mage-made lights sprang to life, suspended from the ceiling with delicate ropes.

"Hurry. I'll need a moment to secure the latch." He pushed them both toward the stairs behind the secret door.

Dasienna went first, her steps steady and sure as she descended into the depths of the palace. Tula was decidedly less sure as she followed. Halfway down the staircase, she paused and turned back.

The Magister twisted a handful of strange mechanisms to engage each one. She'd seen something similar before and it made her straighten where she stood. She and Zaide had solved the same sort of locks outside the chamber where the Molten Dagger had been sealed.

Her heart beat faster than before.

Below, Dasienna stopped at the foot of the stairs and stood with her hands on her hips. "You're extremely composed for a man whose palace has been invaded by goborrins, Magister."

He smiled in return and worked his way down the stairs at a sedate pace. "If I am to be honest, I was not positive that was what those creatures were. Jadora has always been so far from conflict. Such creatures have always been myths to my people."

"As they were to the Kolmari before the forest was razed, I am sure." The princess lifted her chin to peer down her nose at him.

Trapped between the two nobles, Tula pressed herself close to the wall and slunk down the steps. Hidden in her coat, the Molten Dagger shed more heat than ever, and beads of sweat she wasn't sure were solely the fault of the artifact trickled down her spine.

The Magister sobered as he joined them on level ground. He was tall, too; Tula was not short, but he towered above her. "I apologize. That must have sounded flippant. Let us continue to the end of the hall. The safe room is stocked with everything necessary to make tea, we may resume our conversation there."

Because tea was a priority during an invasion. Tula winced at her own thoughts. Perhaps it was a priority to nobles. She wasn't one of them, and now she was trapped with two. Without any idea what had already been discussed, or what would be before the night was out.

Maybe she should just draw the dagger from her coat now and get things over with.

And maybe you should just go ahead and tie a noose around your neck, because you've got the diplomatic skills of a rock. She'd proven that to herself with Zaide, and more than once. She'd never succeeded faster at getting someone to dislike her.

After everything he did to get the dagger, too. The archaeological discovery of a lifetime. A victory for her people, for the Librarians' Guild she was part of, that could put her name in history books. Right alongside his, maybe with a note of how she'd soured the expedition by almost losing the Vale Hymnflute in the ten seconds he'd trusted her with it.

Or maybe they'll just write about how you were responsible for stealing it, and how the unrest that caused resulted in the city you love being invaded for the first time in history.

"You ought to be walking too, you know," Dasienna called.

Tula gave herself a shake. The princess and the Magister were halfway down the hallway without her. She hurried to close the distance between them, holding the edges of her coat to keep it from flapping behind her. "Shouldn't we have guards with us?"

"They will join us. They know what to do and where they should be." The Magister smiled at her before he continued on.

The corridor was long and straight, hardly the sort of tactical tunnel Tula would have expected from a safe room. The library's tunnels were more convoluted than this, filled with dead ends and alternate exits to keep the unfamiliar from finding any destination with ease. But she'd never been in the tunnels under the library before, despite knowing they existed. Tonight had been a night of firsts, none of them pleasant.

At the end of the hall, a heavy stone door resembling those in the Molten Dagger's hiding place waited. Again, the Magister spun its dials and solved its puzzle with a practiced hand, but she supposed that made sense. The Magisters had always resided in the palace, including whichever Magister had been the one to build the catacombs where the dagger had been stowed for safekeeping. It was only the lock that required the Hymnflute to open that had kept the current Magister out. Perhaps the answers to the locks on the other doors had been passed down through the generations.

"Here we are," the Magister announced as the door swung open. He motioned for Dasienna and Tula to precede him. "I doubt any of those brutes can get past these doors, but the guards will be along to join us soon. My chief captain knows how to unseal the first door."

The room beyond was lavish, the sort of sitting room Tula might have expected to see upstairs, with low chairs and couches of dark-lacquered wood and rich red cushions. Thick curtains in red and gold hung the walls, with fine art and delicate pottery filling the spaces between.

Tula crept in and waited for Dasienna to take a seat before she settled nearby. "How will Zaide find us?" she whispered.

"I don't assume he will," the princess replied, as if his presence didn't matter. "If there are goborrins upstairs, that's where he'll want to be, too."

The Magister chuckled and closed the door. "He sounds like a savage. Although I suppose I can't be surprised, given what you've already shared about him. Still, I am sorry for the lack of your bodyguard. I will do my best to ensure the two of you are reunited once danger has passed."

Bodyguard? Tula raised a brow at the title. Had the princess not told him Zaide carried the Spectrum Blade? She raised her other brow as if to ask, but Dasienna regarded her in silence. Her face gave away nothing.

"I am sure he will be fine," Dasienna said, and the way she stared back at Tula while she addressed the Magister seemed as if it should mean more than it did. "Your guards are capable, my father wouldn't have sent me here for protection if they weren't."

"Yet I feel as if I have failed, because Amrochan has not been breached, but here we are. The great city of Jadora, invaded by pigs." The Magister sighed and smoothed his already sleek hair. "But we can continue. I apologize if I am distracted, I have great concern for my people and feel powerless to help them. Everything has collapsed so rapidly. Oh, I have been a dreadful host. Would the two of you like tea?"

Dasienna folded her hands in her lap. "Please."

Tula nodded numbly.

The Magister swept across the room to a tall counter nestled in the corner, where an arrangement of canisters and cups waited. The soft clink of porcelain and warm scent of spiced tea filled the air.

The princess watched for a time, then turned her eyes to Tula.

Was she supposed to say something? What had she missed? Her brow furrowed and she opened the front of her colorful coat to point at the pocket inside.

Dasienna's face twisted with alarm and she gave her head a vigorous shake.

So the dagger was a secret. Because Dasienna had not yet explained how they'd come to possess it? Or something else? Tula furrowed her brow and folded her coat closed as she settled into the cushions.

"Here," the Magister announced as he returned with a small silver tray hosting a tall teapot and handful of tiny cups. He sat it on a low table between the couches and chairs and rested his hands on his waist, clearly proud of his efforts. He only allowed himself a moment of pride, however. The next moment, he knelt beside the table to pour the tea.

The smile the princess plastered on was fake. "Thank you, Magister. Since we are the only ones present, I assume we can continue to speak freely?"

The man paused and glanced toward Tula. "If you feel that's wise, Your Highness."

Dasienna waved a hand. "Tula may as well be my personal librarian now. Whatever has happened in Jadora, she was not present when tensions arose, and her affiliation with the Great Library precludes her from any involvement with the guardswomen who have given you difficulty."

"As you say." He sounded doubtful, but offered Tula a cup of tea with a broad smile.

She did her best to return it as she took the tiny porcelain cup from his fingertips.

Now that they were settled, she allowed herself to evaluate him more closely. The fact he was handsome had been striking; now she thought it suspicious. This Magister had ruled over Jadora for longer than she'd been alive, yet the man before her was young, vital. By the timeline she had learned, he ought to have been seventy years old. Instead, she suspected he was half that.

There were also Elsanna's stories of the Magister being a man of sour disposition. A cranky old man who was more likely to loath someone who so closely resembled the guardswomen. Instead, his eyes twinkled as she sipped her tea, as if serving her and seeing her enjoy what he had brewed was a delight.

The Magister stood. "Truthfully, Your Highness, I regret that I was unable to act when I received word of what is happening in Amrochan. It has been an honor to lead Jadora on your father's behalf, and I am ashamed I have been unable to provide military support. I fear Jadora's guards have grown lax."

"The men upstairs hardly seemed lax." Dasienna accepted her tea with a murmured thanks, but she cradled the cup in both hands and did not drink. "I am stunned to think you trained them so quickly. Has it even been a month since the first attack?"

"A bit more, I believe, but I admit the days all run together in my mind." His face softened, touched by sadness. "I fear I have hardly slept since the first fire. Jadora is built to withstand flame, but nothing ever chases that fear from your mind, and nothing could have prepared us for the incendiary devices the goborrins use."

Tula lowered her cup. "I heard explosions as we entered. That was the goborrins?"

"I'm afraid so. I am unsure how they achieve it, but they carry glass bottles that contain some sort of explosive material. The librarians have inspected it, as have my personal scholars and alchemists, but it doesn't resemble any explosive powders we are yet familiar with."

"Before you arrived, Tula, we were discussing the smoke over the city." Dasienna raised her cup to inhale the steam. She closed her eyes and let that breath back out as a sigh. "There doesn't seem to be any way to predict the attacks, nor has the Magister been able to determine how the goborrins are getting into the city. They arrive suddenly, destroy buildings, and the guards rush to fight them off."

The Magister poured his own tea last and took a seat across from the princess. "There has been no indication of why they attack what they do, either. Sometimes it's shops. Sometimes residential areas. There are no connections between the different locations that have come under attack. At least, not that we've been able to discern."

"This is the largest attack that has taken place, is it not?" The princess tilted her head as if to listen. From the safe room, they heard nothing. No thundering of feet, clanking of armor, or shouts of combat. The room was well-insulated and buried well beneath the palace's main floor, but Tula hesitated to think of it as well-protected.

"It is," the Magister agreed. "I hardly know how to begin the investigation that will have to follow this attack. My guards have combed the palace grounds to ensure there is no way in or out, save the front gate and my own personal escape route, of which even Chief Captain Jinohe is not aware. There are locks along that escape route like the ones on this safe room. I am the only one who knows how they may be opened, so the chances of those monsters using that as a way in are nonexistent."

Tula was not sure she agreed. She'd seen the natural tunnels beneath the city and puzzled over the similar locks outside the chamber where the dagger had been hidden. She and Zaide had gotten past them, and they hadn't been alone. They had both seen the salamander in the tunnels, had seen the door it unlocked and passed through to clean dust and rubble behind the passage the Hymnflute unsealed.

Voices rose in the hallway outside their shelter and Dasienna made a thoughtful humming sound. "It seems we have guests."

The Magister put his tea on the low table and rose from his seat. "I hear Jinohe. If he's come so soon, it must be good news. Please, remain here. I will speak with the captain and determine if it is safe for us to return upstairs."

If it was, it would be the shortest uprising Tula had ever heard of. With how long the city was left to smolder, how was she to believe the Magister's Mage-Guard could dispatch the goborrins in the palace so quickly?

She remained silent as the Magister swept across the room to slip into the hallway beyond, where low voices greeted him and were then muted further by the door's closing at his back. The moment he was gone, she put down her cup. "Your Highness, that's not the Magister."

"No," Dasienna agreed after she finally took a drink. "The Magister is dead."

CHAPTER FOURTEEN

Zaide listened.

The prison was silent; as far as he could tell, he was the only person locked behind bars. His body ached from the cold, and the straw and ratty blanket offered little relief, so the discomfort chased away any hope of rest. Still, he tried to keep his eyes closed and willed himself to be patient.

Somehow, this felt more hopeless than when he'd been closed inside a wooden cell after being captured by the Desheni. It shouldn't have. He still had his sword, but how it was supposed to help him, he didn't know. Magic or not, the sword couldn't cut through iron. He'd seen enough combat with it already to know that much.

The silence that followed that explosion had been heavy. The weight never dissipated, either. It still sat on him, kept him from breathing easy, kept him focused on the uncomfortable lack of noise.

There should have been people shouting. Sounds of people pleading for help, sounds of battle, maybe even more explosions.

He shivered in the quiet and pried his eyes open.

Beside him, the sword brightened—or perhaps it only seemed brighter because he'd had his eyes closed. The ever-shifting colors on the blade looked no different, moved no faster, glowed no brighter.

He focused on the warmer hues and silently wished he'd thought to wrest the Molten Dagger from Tula's hands before they'd left the ship.

"I need my shirt back," he grumbled as he wiggled his shoulder deeper into the bed of straw. His toes were already numb. Maker's mercy, but why did the desert have to be so cold at night?

A click and rattle in the forefront of the prison made him regret having spoken. He grew still, listening until the sound of silence became a discomfort once again.

Except it wasn't silent. His brow furrowed and he strained to hear whatever it was that had brushed the edge of his senses.

Footsteps. Voices. Except they weren't right. The cadence, the weight was off.

He turned his good ear toward the front of the cell as his fingers curled around his sword.

The steady click of steps on stone.

Zaide pulled his sword beneath the tattered blanket and held it close.

The hair on the back of his neck stood as a hulking shadow moved into view, and he swore the Spectrum Blade grew hot.

The goborrin licked its snout as it turned beady black eyes his way.

Zaide stared back without a sound.

Its wide tongue flicked over its nose again, leaving a wet, slimy sheen behind. It snuffled, then continued on its way. Deep, soft grunts welled in its chest as it continued deeper into the dungeon.

Whatever it was looking for, Zaide wasn't it.

He scrambled to his feet. "Hey!" Calling after the monster wasn't the best idea he'd ever had, but either he was safe behind the bars of his cell, or that goborrin could get him out of there.

The monster continued on down the hall and descended

another set of stairs. It had to have heard him; it simply didn't care.

Zaide released a hissing breath through his teeth and moved closer to the bars, but the creature was already gone. His shoulders slumped, but his mind was already racing.

A goborrin in the dungeon of a city like Jadora was so discordant with what he thought he knew that it made his head spin. Where there was one, there had to be more, and he was willing to wager the shuddering explosions he'd heard were related to that thing.

But it knew where it was going. The certainty with which it strode through the prison, straight past his cell, made a wicked shiver that had nothing to do with the cold creep down his spine. He rested his free hand against the cell door and stared after it, unsure what to do next.

A clatter and squall sounded from the forefront of the prison. He spun and readied his sword, but he was unprepared for the group of monsters that spilled through the door.

Not just goborrins, either. A handful of the pig-faced beasts thundered down the steps, but something streaked between them to fling itself at the bars.

A salamander.

Zaide swiped at its head as it jammed it between the cell bars. It hissed, darted away and returned again to try and wriggle through. It lashed at him with its claws and he answered with his sword. The Spectrum Blade sliced through its spindly arm and the monster shrieked and retreated. Its severed hand flopped to the ground and was consumed by light. A spark and flash, and it was gone.

Howls of surprise and fright went up in half of the goborrins and they fled back the way they'd come. The other half surged toward him and slammed into the cell bars.

When he'd envisioned the cell being smashed open, it had been one goborrin, not three. The monsters gripped the bars and pulled. The iron groaned. Zaide backed up and braced for battle.

Something snapped and the cell door swung open.

A deep bellow rose from the prison's entryway and a man in armor collided with one of the beasts before it could dive into the cell.

Zaide was ready for the two that did. He lunged in and drove his sword into one's exposed stomach, but the monster had momentum, and when it went down, he was dragged with it. They landed hard and the second goborrin caught him by the leg. Zaide shouted as it swept him up and into the air to hold him upside down. The force tore the Spectrum Blade from his grasp.

The goborrin lurched as if it meant to slam him back to the floor. It only made it a step before a sword burst through its chest. The beast grew still as the armored man behind it withdrew his blade. Brown blood poured from the wound as the goborrin collapsed.

Zaide landed hard on the cold stone of the floor. A second later, a groan escaped him.

"One strike to the heart," the scarred man said. "That's all it takes." He stepped back from the cell and took off at a run, headed deeper into the prison.

Zaide jerked the Spectrum Blade free of the monster he'd killed and stepped into the hall. For a moment, he considered the front door. If the guards were distracted, he could find his way out and look for the princess, though appearing half naked before her sounded less than appealing. But if there were goborrins in the city, more guards would have been summoned, and it was unlikely he'd be able to walk free without being noticed.

"And if the goborrins are going deeper, there's another way out," he mused. That option meant there was only the scarred prison warden to contend with, rather than an entire city full of guards.

He clenched his jaw and made for the front of the prison. Escape that way wasn't likely, but getting far without his things wasn't likely, either. He found the Spectrum Blade's scabbard laying on the jailer's table, but his bags were gone.

For a moment, he couldn't fathom why they'd leave the scabbard and nothing else. His hand tingled and he glanced down at his sword. Of course. They'd left that with him; they'd need something to put it in when they tried to get it out of the cell when the artificer came. He tilted the sword, then laid it on the table long enough to belt the scabbard around his waist. He wasn't foolish enough to sheath his weapon with who knew how many goborrins around. And that salamander, too—maybe more of them. He hadn't seen where it had gone after he severed its hand, but it hadn't been with the dead goborrins in the hall.

"Hopefully we won't see it again." He took the sword and started after the scarred man, venturing into the deepest parts of the dungeon. The Spectrum Blade cast waves of colored light on the floor and into the cells around him. Every single one was empty.

"Which is good news or bad news, depending on what they were planning to do with me." Zaide hurried down another set of stairs. The stone was frigid beneath his bare feet. "Not that you care. You're a sword."

It didn't even have the decency to let him imagine a response.

The dungeon went deeper than he expected. After the fourth set of stairs in the straight-running hallway, the light from his sword reflected on something ahead.

"If you think you'll earn your freedom by killing me, you're more foolish than I realized," the scarred man's voice boomed in the dark.

Zaide slowed. "I'm not here to try and kill you, I'm here to try and help you."

The man grunted. "Noble." He stood beside another door, one identical to those around it, but different from the cells where Zaide had been. This was riveted iron, like the prison's main door, and the cells bore solid stone walls instead of bars. The guard jostled the door, then gritted his teeth.

"Locked?" There was space for a barricade bar on the outside, but there was none. Nor did it seem plausible that it could have been blocked from the inside. It was a cell, after all, intended for solitary confinement from what Zaide could see.

"I don't need your help, boy."

"Maybe you don't, but I need yours, and I'm not sure how else to win it."

The scarred man glanced at him, then his eyes slid to the sword in his hand. He said nothing, but he didn't move. Now was as good a time as any to try to convince him.

"Princess Dasienna was on her way to the palace." Zaide did his best to sound calm and confident. "She's a competent fighter, but King Sendassian expects me to be there to protect her. I can't do that from a dungeon, and I don't know how to get where I need to be. By now, the princess has to be here. Help me find her. At least point me in the right direction and tell me how to keep the Magister's Mage-Guard from throwing me back in that cell."

The man's lip curled back in a sneer. He straightened and Zaide realized how much he'd underestimated the man's size. He had to be as big as one of the goborrins, even without the plate armor he now wore. "What reason do I have to believe that? I'm supposed to think it's just a coincidence that you arrived tonight, with whatever that sword is in your hand? Artificed weapons are forbidden in Jadora."

"Then you should take that up with the guards at the gate who let me in with the princess." Zaide tightened his grip on the sword and fought the urge to take a step back when the man drew closer.

The stormy look in the man's eyes grew darker and he opened his mouth to speak.

A flash of movement behind him caught Zaide's eye. "Watch out!"

He darted forward as the salamander burst from the shadow, a twisted knife in its remaining hand. Zaide parried the strike and stabbed, but the Spectrum Blade only pierced the creature's side. It shrieked and a second later, it was silenced when the rake of the scarred man's sword ripped its head from its shoulders.

The lizard's body slumped to the stone.

"Fast as vipers, those rotten things," the man growled. He peered into the dark as if he expected something else to leap out at them, but nothing came. His mouth tightened and he returned his attention to Zaide. "One kill does nothing to prove whose side you're on."

"Then give me a chance to kill more. The princess and I took down more than a hundred outside Amrochan. I'll do the same thing here."

"Half naked?"

Heat rose in Zaide's ears, but he sucked in a sharp breath and straightened where he stood. "If that's the challenge, then yes." The goborrins outside Amrochan hadn't touched him. Then again, that had only been because of Lark and the Hymnflute. Fighting without any sort of protective gear here would be a different story.

"I don't make deals with prisoners."

"Well, I'm not actually in a cell right now, so maybe you can afford to just look the other way when it comes to that problem."

The scarred man snorted and stepped over the dead salamander to continue into the dark.

Zaide followed with the Spectrum Blade held out before him. "You're the prison warden, right?"

"I am."

"You keep logs of why everyone is arrested?" It was an assumption; he knew little of how such things might work.

"I do."

"What does mine say? Just for curiosity's sake, because I suspect the princess is going to spend the rest of our visit making fun of me for it." Zaide tilted his sword to the side to better illuminate the stairs the scarred man descended. He followed close behind.

"Just that Chief Captain Jinohe ordered it."

Zaide's brow furrowed. Jinohe hadn't been with the group involved in his arrest. The question of the log's accuracy sprang to the tip of his tongue, but he settled for something less likely to earn the warden's ire. "I thought you said the captain didn't take care of anything."

The warden stopped and turned toward him. He'd also told Zaide to behave. It was possible the questions were too antagonizing. Zaide wiped his face clean of any emotion, though his heart climbed into his throat. The way the man's eyes hardened until they glinted like honed steel made him wish he'd fought to escape instead of going calmly to his demise.

Then the big man turned away. "I am Moros." He continued down the stairs until they reached a flat stonework floor that was different from the others.

It was simple, terse, and the closest thing to an olive branch he was going to get. "I'm Zaide. Apprentice to the Kolmari Elder and Bladebearer for Princess Dasienna." Though he supposed he was no longer an Elder's apprentice. Resia had no reason to take him for apprenticeship, and it wasn't as if he was in Kolmar to continue that sort of education.

"Bladebearer," Moros repeated. His deep voice was so flat, it was an insult.

"Because of the shiny sword." There were no more cells here, only smooth stone walls.

"I assumed as much."

Zaide glanced over his shoulder once, but there was nothing behind them. No hint of light reached from elsewhere in the prison to where they stood. "Did the goborrins come this way?"

"I don't believe so."

"Then why are we going this way?"

"You ask many questions for a boy who could be executed in the morning, should the Magister be in a foul mood."

Zaide flashed him a nervous grin, though Moros never turned to see it. "No point in holding back, if that's the case. At least I'll die with answers. Are we working together now?"

The warden grunted. "We are working in the same general direction. What comes beyond that is not up to me."

Strange. Zaide turned that over in his head for a moment before he decided to ask. "What's that supposed to mean?"

Moros stepped to one side as they reached the end of the dungeon's walkway. A plain wooden door stood at the end, its iron fittings rusted. It bore no locks. He motioned to the door. "This will take you to the Magister."

"Just like that?" The door was so plain, so poorly secured.

"Just like that," the warden said.

Zaide gripped the ring and hauled the door open.

On the other side, a handful of goborrins squatted in the center of a dank room, gnawing human bones.

CHAPTER FIFTEEN

Zaide fell into a battle stance and held his sword ready. The goborrins squalled and shrank away from the Spectrum Blade as it sparked and its glow intensified. They couldn't go far. Heavy chains anchored them to the far wall, iron cuffs and collars around their wrists and necks keeping them securely bound.

The door thumped shut behind him and he spun to point the blade at the warden's throat.

Moros stared down at him, his face stony.

"You did this?" Zaide demanded. He dared not look at the bones the goborrins left behind. The thought alone turned his stomach, and that single glimpse he'd gotten was already burned into his brain.

"I have done only what you asked. You wished to see the Magister, because you said the princess had come to see him. Well, here he is." Moros spread a hand toward the bones.

A new wave of panic washed over him and Zaide spun to look after all. He didn't know how many bones a body contained.

"Calm yourself." For all that it was deep and intimidating, the scarred man's voice was soothing, too. "It is only the Magister. I am certain your princess is fine."

Whatever relief that gave was short lived, for nausea returned so swiftly, Zaide was compelled to empty his stomach right then. He planted a hand against his middle and squeezed his eyes closed as he fought the contraction of those muscles. He would not. "They... ate him?"

"At Chief Captain Jinohe's command." A pause. "I suppose I lied. Jinohe took care of one thing."

"Maker's mercy." Zaide inhaled, hoping to settle his stomach, and regretted it instantly. The stink of death might have faded, but the stench of goborrins was almost as bad. He moved his right hand from his middle to his mouth.

Moros said nothing.

Eventually, Zaide's heaving subsided and he turned away. The goborrins had grown quiet, but the soft rattle of their chains betrayed the way they trembled. These were nothing like the monsters he'd seen upstairs, yet somehow even those suddenly seemed preferable. "When did this happen?"

"It has been no more than a week since Jinohe ordered the corpse be brought down. I cannot say when the Magister died."

"The captain killed him?"

"I do not know, but it doesn't matter."

Opening his eyes again took strength. When he did, he saw Moros staring at the goborrins—or perhaps the Magister's bones —without any sign that either meant anything to him. "Why are you showing me this?"

He received no answer. Instead, the scarred man opened the door and stepped backwards into the hall. "Somewhere in the dungeon, there is a path through which the final goborrin escaped. None have passed through here before. You will help me find it."

"And kill it?"

"And kill it."

For all that Zaide wanted to be away from the sight in the dungeon's depths, he struggled to make himself move. "What are these goborrins here for?"

A hint of motion on the warden's face betrayed his surprise, though his brows hardly rose at all. "To consume the prisoners after they die."

"And Magisters when they're deposed, apparently."

Zaide hadn't meant it as a joke, but Moros gave a dark chuckle.

The warden began the climb back up through the dungeon, though at a slower pace. "I am uncertain who leads us now, but my job is watching over the cells. There are more corpses and fewer prisoners these days. Little for me to do."

"The dungeon is empty," Zaide said. "I was the only one here."

"Fortunate for you. Had there been others, you would not have been able to convince those monsters to break open your cell."

"And you wouldn't have let me out?"

Moros snorted. "No."

"I suppose I can't blame you for that." Zaide took the stairs two at a time until he walked at the warden's side. The man gave him a dark look, but he flashed a nervous smile in return. "Let's find that one that got away. You were looking for it."

"I heard one of the confinement cell doors close, but I did not see which one."

Zaide nodded and slipped ahead. If Moros was concerned about him trying to escape, he gave no indication of it, though he did walk faster.

The heavy iron doors were a short distance ahead. Zaide slowed as he approached them and tilted his good ear toward the hall. There was nothing to be heard. No more goborrins had entered the prison, either, from what he could tell. He knelt in front of one of the doors and held his hand a hair's breadth from the floor.

Moros observed as he moved from one door to another, zigzagging across the hall. "Vibration?"

"Air." Zaide lingered until he was sure he felt nothing.

"When I was with the princess in Kolmar's temple, we found a hidden passage because of a draft."

The warden made a small, doubtful sound, but continued past. "I will retrieve the keys."

"You don't carry them all the time?"

"I am not the only person who oversees the prison." For the briefest moment, Moros paused. Then he shook his head and continued onward. Realizing the possibility of interference? Or realizing who could have already interfered?

Zaide moved to the next door, then the next. There were only two possibilities left when he caught sight of movement.

Dust shifting across the floor.

He slid forward and lowered his hand before that one. The faintest stirring of warm air brushed his skin. The Spectrum Blade's colors collided and flashed. "You feel it too, huh?"

"I feel nothing." Moros loomed at the top of the stairs.

"I was talking to..." Zaide trailed off as the warden crossed his arms. "Uh, myself. Sorry. I've spent a lot of time traveling alone this year. It's this one. I can feel air flow beneath the door."

The scarred man grunted softly and descended to the door. The key he produced was oddly shaped, a cylinder with peculiar prongs that jutted from the end. He twisted it to fit the lock and jammed it in. A hollow thud sounded and the door swung open.

A breath of warm air flowed out, dry and stale, and Moros grunted again.

Where the back of the cell should have been, a rough hole had been opened in the stone wall.

"This is new," the warden remarked. The faint elevation in his tone was enough to sound shocked, compared to the flat way he relayed everything else.

Zaide stood. "I think we found where our goborrin went." The warm air was soothing after the cold of the dungeon and he savored it for a moment before he realized what it meant. "This goes to the tunnels under the city."

"To the crater," Moros agreed. "Which you should not know about."

A foolish slip-up. Zaide's mouth worked without producing sound, but the man's scarred face revealed nothing of what he thought.

Instead of questioning, Moros strode forward and ducked to enter the gap. "Bring the sword."

"I wasn't planning on leaving it." The light shifted. Warmer, redder, then to a cool blue. Did that mean something, or was he just ascribing more of his own feelings to the strange things the artifact did? Zaide pushed it out of mind and followed.

The rough stone underfoot was warm enough that it returned some feeling to his toes. Part of him was grateful, but it was an unpleasant reminder, too. He paused a short way down. "I can't go down there."

The warden paused, the slight turn of his head the only indication he was listening.

"The—the air down there. I can't. It makes me sick."

"You are not Jadoran."

"Kolmari."

"You are not Kolmari."

Zaide's jaw clenched.

Moros hummed something to himself, a noise of puzzlement, problem-solving. "We are acclimated to the world we live in. Some of us—Jadorans of noteworthy ability—are immune to the vapors that rise from the volcano. The same as the Kolmari who speak to growing things. Our world suits who we are." He turned, his dark eyes narrowed. "And you are an outsider, who should not know those vapors exist."

Zaide took a step back. "I haven't done anything wrong."

"I didn't say you did." The scarred man's eyes flicked to the Spectrum Blade. "But I am not a fool, and you have embroiled yourself in Jadoran politics beyond what you know. You will come to the tunnels. Fixing this is going to be your responsibility."

"And when I pass out because of the air down there?" Zaide stayed rooted in place.

A grim smile twisted the warden's mouth. "Then I will carry you."

A thousand different words of protest sprang to mind, but Zaide chose to put them aside. The man before him was more useful as an ally than an enemy. He'd already provided information and shared secrets, though Zaide hardly knew why, and he hadn't had time to consider the ramifications of the Magister's death or Chief Captain Jinohe's betrayal beyond knowing that wherever Lark was, the captain was probably there—and the Magister wasn't.

Maybe the tunnel they ventured down wouldn't pass too close to the crater. The outer tunnels and the rooms with the canopic jars had been fine. If warmth was all that flowed from the volcano's depths, it wouldn't affect him.

Zaide swallowed the rest of his protests and moved down the slope.

Satisfied, Moros pressed ahead into the darkness.

The tunnel was steep, roughly hewn and poorly finished, and it showed little sign of use. The farther they went, the wider it grew, until it seemed as if it could accommodate even the largest of goborrins. As large a man as the warden was, he appeared small against the looming darkness and smaller still when light began to form at the end of the passage. Its golden glow was a stark contrast to the cool shades the Spectrum Blade cast against the walls, and Zaide silently prayed it wasn't light from magma in the volcano's heart.

The ground leveled out and Moros stopped so abruptly that Zaide collided with his back.

"By the desert sun," the warden swore.

Zaide stepped around him to see what justified the oath and froze, himself.

Elsanna.

CHAPTER SIXTEEN

BURNING braziers and large goborrins surrounded the tangle of chains that held the guardswoman to the stone wall. Some jabbed poles at her and squealed in rhythms that sounded almost like laughter. Others had already noticed the new arrivals.

Moros bolted forward before Zaide could ready his sword. The warden met the first goborrin head-on, a cry of rage tearing from his throat as he struck.

Zaide advanced with more caution. The ground was uneven and littered with sharp stones, and he had no gear. Not that his borrowed leather armor would have protected him from much, but it was better than trousers alone. He darted sideways and lunged in for a stab when a goborrin brought down its heavy club. The Spectrum Blade flashed as it dug into the monster's side and streaks of light lanced across its bare stomach.

Elsanna strained against her chains and released a triumphant laugh.

There weren't as many of the monsters as Zaide first thought. Moros felled two by the time he'd taken three, and the remaining pair were armed only with wooden poles. One flung its pole at them and turned to flee, but the warden pursued it and struck it down.

Zaide took the last. It tried to defend itself, but the Spectrum Blade snapped its pole as if it were a twig, then buried deep in the monster's face.

"That's it!" Elsanna shouted as he twisted his sword free and let the goborrin fall. When he finally got a proper look at her, the sight made his stomach twist, too.

Her hair was still tied in its high ponytail and she wore her revealing armor, but her coppery skin was marred by bruises and scrapes, her lip and eyebrow split. The sheaths for her swords were empty and her eyes and cheeks were hollow, too, but her spirit remained unbroken.

Zaide stepped over a dead goborrin and slid his sword into its leather scabbard. "What are you doing down here? What happened?"

"Jinohe," she spat. "Vile snake."

Moros returned when his monster was dead. The corners of his mouth were tight and his eyes crinkled with distress, and he wasted no time in jamming a goborrin's rough knife into the links of one chain. He wedged the tip of the blade against the stone and strained. Iron creaked as the link twisted open and he pried the rest of the chain free.

Zaide doubted he had the strength necessary to break any others, so he let the warden work and offered Elsanna an arm for support, instead. She leaned heavily against him and closed her eyes, a split-second action that betrayed her deep weariness.

"The Magister is dead," he said.

"Replaced. I know." She sighed. "Scorch it all, but I've failed."

"You are alive," Moros said as he severed the last of her chains. "That is what matters right now." He cast the goborrin blade aside and joined them, but instead of offering support or addressing the collar and cuffs that dragged the chains behind her, he cradled Elsanna's face in one large hand and pressed a kiss to her brow.

Zaide flushed and turned away. *That* was certainly not something he'd expected.

"And you took too long to find me," she said. "Where have you been? What took you so long?"

"Can we talk later? Escape now?" Zaide wedged his shoulders under Elsanna's arm and tugged her toward the passage they'd descended from.

She nodded toward the opening. "Where does that lead?"

"The prison," Moros said.

Elsanna scoffed. "It took them digging a tunnel straight to you for you to find me? Maker's mercy, Moros, when we're out of here—"

Before she could finish, the familiar clatter of goborrin hooves echoed down the tunnel.

Zaide veered another direction.

"Where are you going?" Moros asked.

"I don't know. Up, eventually?" At least, he hoped there was another way up. That the light had come from fire and not volcanic activity had been a small relief, but he wasn't certain they'd escaped that fate just yet.

"Get me somewhere I can sit and rest for a moment," Elsanna said. "As soon as I catch my breath, we can move."

Moros shook his head. "You're in no condition to be fighting."

"And I cannot afford to wait. Zaide, where is the princess?"

He'd hoped she wouldn't ask. "I don't know for sure, but she was supposed to be going with Captain Jinohe to see the Magister."

A string of vile oaths escaped the guardswoman's mouth.

Moros cast a glance behind them and offered his assistance at Elsanna's other side, but the guardswoman batted him away. She pulled away from Zaide, too, but couldn't move fast with the heavy chains dragging. The warden scooped them from the ground so they could walk faster.

"Elsanna, you know this boy?" he asked.

"I do." She shot him a weary grin. "He is Princess Dasienna's chosen errand boy."

"I think she's calling me her Bladebearer now." Zaide turned them toward an opening that looked promising, another dark tunnel that was roughly manmade. Or goborrin-made.

The warden grunted. Zaide already knew that meant disapproval.

Elsanna shrugged. "I'm not surprised. How bad is it above? The city?"

"There were explosions when they were dragging me to the dungeon," Zaide said.

She missed a beat. "Why were you in the dungeon?"

"Jinohe's orders," Moros said.

"Obeying that man is the last thing you should be doing."

"Obeying that man is all that keeps some of us from sharing your fate, Cactus."

Zaide cringed hard. "Can we not do the weird pet names right now? We need to be figuring out how to get to the princess." And how to find Tula. With luck, she'd figured out somewhere safe to go. Maybe the old librarian who led her into the tunnels under the library had somewhere she could hide.

"They brought me down through a door in the palace," Elsanna said. "I don't know where it was, I don't remember all of it. They covered my head so I couldn't see where we were going or who dragged me there, but I'd recognize Jinohe's voice anywhere. The son of a viper."

The tunnel they hurried into was smaller than the one they'd emerged from. Elsanna had to go first, and Moros followed her so he could carry her chains. Zaide took the back by choice and positioned himself to draw his sword easily, should the need arise. "You have a grudge with him?"

"He coveted my position as the Magister's chief protector

and right hand. The Magister's chief guards are exclusively guardswomen by tradition, so he had no hope of replacing me."

"Well, he did," Zaide said. "The guardswomen have been replaced with the Magister's Mage-Guard. The librarian we spoke with said something happened? Something about you and the dagger?" He didn't doubt it, but hearing the story from Elsanna herself was important.

She scoffed. "The Magister found out fast. It was Jinohe's soldiers who discovered the cavern had been unsealed, though I don't know how."

"Alternate routes into the tunnels," Moros said. "It must be."

"I assume so. But he was outraged, and nothing I said could convince him what I had done was for the best."

"You told him I took the dagger?" Zaide asked.

Moros shot him a startled look.

"I told him everything, and the end result was—" Elsanna skidded to a stop as they spilled out into a shadowy room. "Maker's mercy!"

A pair of salamanders sat in the room's center, hunched over glass bottles, filling them with powder.

Explosives.

The lizards hissed and leaped to their feet, but Elsanna was already in motion. She whipped her arm forward hard to strike them with the chain bound to her wrist. One of the salamanders emitted an unbecoming squeak.

"Watch the bottles!" Moros roared as Zaide charged the other lizard.

The Spectrum Blade flashed free of its scabbard and missed the salamander by a hair. The lizard lashed at him with its tail and the strike was hard enough to slice the leg of Zaide's trousers open.

Right.

No armor.

He ignored the heat and pain that surged in his calf, certain that whiplike strike had drawn blood. He started to swing again as the creature darted toward him with a dagger in its claws. Some sense he didn't understand told him to aim wide. He slashed down hard and caught the monster in its shoulder.

The salamander screeched and flailed with its knives and claws and tail. It connected twice, raking skin from Zaide's thigh and shin before he stabbed again and it crumpled to a heap.

He spun to help Elsanna, but she didn't need it. She tightened one of her chains around her salamander's throat and gritted her teeth. Its gagging ended and its body went limp.

"I hate those things." She swiped the back of her hand across her forehead.

Zaide lowered his sword and checked his legs. None of the injuries were severe enough that they needed attention now. Instead of worrying about them, he scanned the room. There were three exits, all of them the same from where he stood. "What now?"

Elsanna looked at the doorways, then glanced down and smirked.

"You have an idea," Moros said. An observation, a note of dread.

She took one of the explosive bottles from the floor.

"Forgive me," the fraudulent Magister said as he returned to the hidden room where Tula and the princess waited. "It is not safe to emerge just yet. Chief Captain Jinohe assures me the goborrins are being pushed from the palace, but they are still in the city. I don't feel as if we can rest comfortably within the palace until we know where the breach occurred."

Tula had her own suspicions how they might have gotten into the palace, but she kept her tongue still and let the princess do the talking.

"It seems there is no safety to be had anywhere in Amroch."

Dasienna put her teacup aside. It was so full that Tula was uncertain she'd truly tasted a drop. With the newfound conclusion the Magister before them was not the Magister at all, she wondered at her own wisdom. Perhaps she shouldn't have sampled the drink.

"So it would seem. No matter where we go or how high we build our walls, that broken-born wretch hounds us." The Magister sighed and swept a hand over his black hair. One of his jeweled rings caught and he took a moment to right it and the hair it displaced.

Dasienna lounged in the cushions of her chair. "Gadranus can only reach so far on his own. I have often wondered about the armies he pushes toward us. They're largely composed of goborrins, I believe, though they sometimes contain other creatures. The brutes are strong, but they don't appear to be the most intelligent. With how great of numbers they boast, who do you suppose keeps the armies organized?"

"From what I understand, his generals are as human as you and I." He passed before Tula, a swirl of red and gold robes, and sank to sit closer to the princess.

"There have to be messengers, though." Tula pinched her lower lip as she thought. "Do you suppose they use average folk as couriers? There's little chance anything else could slip through."

"Perhaps," the Magister said. "The largest portion of his generals are others of the region from whence he hails, people who surrendered long ago. We have assumed their messengers would come from similar groups."

The princess sniffed, the most drawn out and disdainful thing Tula had ever heard. "If you mean to cast aspersions on my personal guard, Magister, I assure you he has more than proven his loyalty and worth. If he is trapped out there in the city, I hope your soldiers consider him with utmost care."

"My apologies, Your Highness. I mean nothing of the sort." The Magister bowed his head and touched the side of his index finger to his nose and brow, a gesture seeking forgiveness that made Tula straighten in her seat.

"Your family comes from Addare, Magister?" She pasted on a broad smile and her best look of scholarly curiosity.

His pleasant facade faltered. "I beg your pardon?"

"The sign for apology." She mimicked the gesture. "I've never seen that from anyone but visitors from Addare."

His face fell further. "I was born in Jadora. I've spent my entire life within these walls."

"I'm sorry, I didn't mean any offense. I am an apprentice librarian, you know. One of the things I'll have to do to graduate is write something new to contribute to the library." She tucked in her chin and tried to look coy. "I'm always watching for more subjects. A paper based on our own Magister might be worthy of consideration, and it's just you're the most mysterious Magister we've had in centuries."

The compliment seemed to work, for he settled back in his chair and his expression softened. "Ah. In that case, no apology necessary." He lifted his hand and tried the gesture again. "Hm. I hadn't realized I was doing that, to be frank. I must have picked it up from visiting dignitaries or merchants. Did you know that despite Ganede being so close, most of our trade takes place with Addare? The ports from Tinith and Parral primarily export things to the oasis city, and from there, they come to Jadora. There's a stretch of sea off our coast that's too rocky to..." He trailed off and glanced up.

Dasienna straightened. "Is everything all right, Magister?"

"Do you hear that?" He cocked his head.

Tula listened, too. A soft scrabble interrupted the silence. "A rat or mouse, perhaps?" No matter how well protected the safe room was, it was unlikely to keep vermin at bay.

"No," the Magister said slowly. "It almost reminds me of—"

The wall exploded inward with an ear-shattering boom.

Tula squealed and ducked, while Dasienna flew to her feet.

"Seize him!" Elsanna rushed forward with small blades in

both hands and chains dragging from her wrists. Behind her, a massive man with a scarred face and a smaller, more familiar figure climbed through the gap.

"Zaide!" Tula leaped out of her chair.

Dasienna spun at the sound of his name, surprise and then careful neutrality sweeping across her mien.

The fact the Bladebearer was only wearing torn trousers hadn't escaped Tula's notice, exactly, but she'd been more excited to see him than to see... everything she saw.

The Magister sprang from his seat with storm clouds in his eyes. "What is the meaning of this? Moros, apprehend her!"

The large, scarred man loomed behind Elsanna, his face twisted with disdain.

"Moros?" Tula whispered. She'd heard that name, but she'd never imagined it would be attached to someone like the hulking figure at Elsanna's back.

Dasienna unsheathed her knives, a challenge in her gaze, but Zaide darted around the guardswoman and her sweetheart to catch the princess by the arms and drag her to the floor. An instant later, Elsanna whipped a chain across where they'd been. It struck the Magister with enough force to wrap around him, and she pulled hard. He staggered and his face reddened as panic tensed his slender frame.

"I should have killed you the moment I first laid eyes on you," Elsanna snarled.

Tula scrambled over to help the princess to her feet, but Zaide already had her halfway up. He spared her the briefest of nervous smiles, then positioned himself between the two of them and the Magister. He drew his sword and the Magister went pale.

"That sword—" He cut off with a choke as Elsanna struck him with the chain from her other wrist and dragged him closer.

"That sword is too good of an ending for you." She drew back a dagger.

Moros caught her arm. "Peace." His voice was soft, despite how deep and powerful it was.

Tula held tight to Dasienna, afraid she might strike the same way. But who could stop her? She was the princess. If anyone had the authority to order a man dead, it was her.

Instead, Dasienna raised her head and squared her shoulders. "Bind him," she ordered.

A muscle twitched in Elsanna's jaw, but the tension in her arm eased.

Moros pulled a dagger from her hand and wrenched the blade into the chain affixed to the collar around the guardswoman's neck, but it would not sever.

Tula's hand went to the pocket of her coat. "I have an idea."

Beside her, the princess gave a nod of approval. With Dasienna's blessing, she drew the Molten Dagger and crossed to Elsanna's side. Mindful of the heat, she chose a spot several links down and rammed the artifact into the chain. It melted through in seconds.

The false Magister's eyes widened, then narrowed to slits as Moros used the severed chain to wrap him more securely.

Dasienna put her knives away and stalked toward them. "Now that my Bladebearer has returned, Magister, I have some questions."

"Yes," the Magister said, the single word laden with venom. "So do I."

CHAPTER SEVENTEEN

Zaide and Lark held Elsanna's remaining chains out straight so Tula could sever them with the Molten Dagger. The guardswoman held her tangled hair out of the way. Now and then, Moros glanced their way, but the warden hovered over the Magister—or whoever had taken his place—to ensure he did not move.

The chained man scowled at them, but kept his jaw clamped tightly shut.

"I don't think we'll be able to cut through these without burning you," Lark said as she slid a finger between Elsanna's iron collar and her skin.

"They don't matter." The guardswoman shook her head. "We'll get them off when everything is done."

Zaide flinched away from the heat as Tula snapped the last chain. The stench of hot iron was out of place in the luxuriously-furnished safe room, though the gaping hole Elsanna's stolen bomb left in the far wall did a little to lessen its prestige. "Lark, you have the Captured Spring?"

The princess paused. "Why?"

He motioned toward the guardswoman between them. "Is now a good time to use it? She's been through a lot."

Lark considered the suggestion, then shrugged and reached for her bag. The slender vial brimmed with pale, bluish liquid and Zaide wondered how many injuries that might treat. The spring regenerated the elixir inside on its own, and he'd only spared a drop for Andriun when the Desheni hunter helped him recover the artifact, but he hadn't stayed long enough to see how quickly it worked—or how well.

"Here." Lark uncorked the bottle and poured a single drop onto her finger, then offered it to Elsanna. "Drink this."

The guardswoman flashed her a grin. "A gift, or an experiment?" she asked, though the answer apparently mattered little, since she accepted the tiny taste. "Hm. I did not expect it to be sweet."

"Is it?" Zaide asked, surprised. Andriun hadn't commented on the flavor at all. "What does it taste like?"

"I don't know. Blue?"

Tula snorted a laugh. "Blue isn't a flavor."

"And none of you deserve that object," the Magister interjected. "What a waste. The power to save lives and you use it because one of you is tired."

Lark straightened and returned the stopper to the bottle, then strung the spring's chain around her neck. "I am surprised you know what it is, given that you aren't really Jadora's Magister."

The man's face crumpled back into a scowl and he clammed up again.

"Sure got quiet, for a man who said he had questions." Zaide eyed the man's robes with some jealousy. The false Magister had to be wearing three layers. Would anyone begrudge him if he took one for himself? Aside from one strange look he'd gotten from Tula when they first blew a hole in the wall, he hadn't received any acknowledgments for his state of dress, but he was self-conscious enough without it.

"He did," Lark agreed. "Do any of you know him?" She glanced from Elsanna to Moros, but they both shook their heads and she allowed herself a puzzled frown.

"I saw him in the palace before I was poisoned, but I did not know his intentions then," Elsanna said. "Only that he set me on edge. I should have trusted my instincts."

"Poison, Cactus?" Moros asked in a murmur.

The guardswoman waved a hand as if it didn't matter.

Tula returned the Molten Dagger to its sheath, but hesitated to put it back in her coat. After a moment's consideration, she offered it to the princess, instead. "Thank you for letting me study this, Your Highness. At this point, it may be safer in your hands."

The chained man wriggled in his seat, agitated again. "It never should have been in her hands to begin with. The dagger belongs to the Magister."

Lark plucked the artifact from Tula's hand and tucked it beneath her belt. "Which means it wouldn't be yours, would it? But maybe you'll surprise me. The position of Magister isn't purely political, and I'm willing to give you a chance. Zaide?"

He straightened when she addressed him, but she looked at the sword sheathed at his right hip, not him. He unsheathed the Spectrum Blade and held it vertically before himself.

The princess planted her hands on her hips. "This is why we've come here. Do you know what this is?"

The way the Magister shrank back showed that he did.

"Were it not for this, we wouldn't have returned to Jadora any time soon. I suspect you were likely counting on that, given that my father has been distracted with affairs in Amrochan." Lark shifted her weight from one foot to the other. "Now we find ourselves in need of the Magister's abilities, and instead of the Magister, we find you."

"Why should I assist you?" he sneered.

"What makes you assume you can?" the princess asked.

Zaide shifted the sword to the side to better see the man's face. Resia hadn't been able to help until after the spring of power accepted her. How power passed between Magisters, they hadn't yet determined. It was wholly possible there was no true Magister at all.

Whoever it was that sat before them, his face revealed nothing.

"More importantly," Elsanna said as she crossed her arms, "why wouldn't you want to?"

The Magister gritted his teeth and leaned forward to speak. "Sendassian has enough power in his grasp without stealing more from Jadora. When the Allied Kingdoms chose to unite under Amroch's banner, the royal family in Amrochan was only chosen to lead due to their proximity to the front lines. Jadora has always been a better seat of power. Better positioned, far enough away for safety, close enough to the sea to allow refugees to seek us with ease. What good is Amrochan? It's a fortress on a meadow peninsula in the middle of a stinking swamp. Its power comes from everywhere else. The city is a drain on the rest of the Allied Kingdoms. We're better off separate."

"Better off regaining power for Jadora," Moros said. "I've heard this sentiment often among the Magister's Mage-Guard of late."

Lark snorted. "Jadora is only safe because of the effort the rest of us put into holding the front lines where they are. If not for us, for Amrochan being a centralized point where the military can converge, prepare, and move swiftly to engage our enemy, this city would have been penetrated by enemy forces long ago."

"Even then, we're losing ground," Zaide said. "If Gadranus can get armies to Amrochan, he can get armies to Jadora, too. You might think this city can stand alone, but what's going on in the palace right now proves it can't."

Elsanna nodded as he spoke. "When the Magister found out the door below the city had been opened and the Molten Dagger retrieved, we thought one of the guardswomen had told him, but the tunnels beneath the city have been expanded and we did not know. That answers how he found out, and those same tunnels must have let the goborrins into the city, though I don't know how they found their way in."

"Are there ways into the tunnels from outside the city?" Zaide asked.

The Jadoran natives exchanged looks.

Lark was unimpressed. "The fact none of you know is as good as a no, but is as equally likely to mean yes."

Before anyone else could voice an opinion, the rattle of footsteps approached the heavy door on the far end of the room. "Magister, news," a muffled voice called from the other side.

A cold smile wreathed itself on the princess's face. She crossed to the door and pulled it open a hair.

A pause. Whoever it was, they hadn't expected her to be the one to answer.

"Jinohe," Elsanna mouthed silently as she readied the daggers she'd stolen from the salamanders they killed.

The false Magister stared.

The guardswoman made a hushing motion and pantomimed stabbing.

Undaunted, he screamed.

The door slammed open and Lark stumbled back. Zaide darted forward to catch her arm and block the captain's path.

Jinohe's eyes widened at the sight of Zaide and the glowing sword in his hand. "You!"

"And me," Elsanna called as she lunged forward and pressed the edge of a dagger to the false Magister's throat. "Maybe you know who this faker is, Jinohe? Certainly not the Magister you swore to serve."

The captain froze and grew pale. "Elsanna. I was told you were dead."

Her lip peeled back from her teeth. "By which of your lackeys? The ones that poisoned me and dragged me to the caverns? Or the goborrins sent to give me water while they tried to break me?"

Jinohe ignored the question. "How did you get past my men?"

Lark righted herself and pulled away from Zaide's support. "If you haven't noticed, Captain, there's a large secondary exit in the back of the room now." She waved a hand toward it. "But then, it was always there. A tunnel, and a patched section of plaster hidden behind a curtain. Which certainly makes things seem like our supposed Magister was involved in Elsanna's imprisonment."

A muscle twitched in his jaw until he opened his mouth to speak, but he worked a moment before he produced words. "He was not."

Lark arched a brow. "An admission of guilt?"

"It was the Magister," he blurted. "The old one, when he learned the dagger was missing. Everything pointed to Elsanna. He ordered her imprisoned, but knew Moros couldn't be trusted with her."

A twinkle lit the guardswoman's eyes.

Zaide cleared his throat. "He seems a very responsible warden to me."

Jinohe shook his head. "The Magister told us to take her below, to chain her there. I didn't know about the goborrins. If I had known the city would be attacked..."

"Spare me," Elsanna spat.

Belatedly, Zaide cast a look around the room. "Where's—" He stopped when he spotted Tula, sitting against the far wall, scribbling furiously in a tiny book.

Everyone grew quiet.

She glanced up. "Huh? Oh! No, no. Go ahead. I'm recording all of this for the library's history books."

Jinohe grimaced. "I don't wish to be on record."

"Maybe you should have considered that before becoming involved in all this," Lark said as she stalked toward the Magister. "I'll give you one last chance to answer. Who are you, how did you come to seize the position of Jadora's leader, and will you assist us with the blade or not?"

"You can burn in the crater," the man snapped back.

A moment later, a swarm of soldiers poured in through the door.

Elsanna and Moros cursed at the same time.

"Ooh, talking was a distraction." Tula wrote a little faster.

"Could you do that later?" Zaide snapped as he met the first soldier and the crash of their swords made his arms tremble.

The librarian snapped her book shut and leaped to her feet. The book disappeared into her robes somewhere and she drew a blade from her hip. "Now's the adventure part, right?"

"Maker's mercy, Tula, this is serious!" Elsanna rushed forward, but Jinohe stepped into her path. Her daggers should have been outmatched, but she was deft with them, and the chief captain's face contorted with distress when she parried every strike.

Lark and Moros flowed to Zaide's sides to try and drive back the soldiers, but they were fast, and it didn't take long for one to duck under a sword and slip into the room.

"I got him!" Tula cried as she intercepted the man.

Zaide could only hope she was competent enough to deal with the mage-guard on her own. As it was, the relentlessness of his own opponent was enough to make him second-guess his abilities. He'd slain hundreds of goborrins by now, what made this man different?

An opening in the man's defense gave him the answer. It would have been easy to take it, to stab deep and kill him. It would have been hard, if not impossible, to only wound.

He didn't *want* to kill the soldier. He didn't even want to hurt him. It took everything in his power to hold the fight without doing more than landing a few bruising blows, and it didn't take long for that to turn things sour.

He's not getting tired, a small, intuitive voice whispered in the back of his head. And it was right. The man's breathing didn't even seem labored, despite the flurry of blows Zaide was left to deflect. *Which should have been obvious. Mage-Guard means magic.* And he'd experienced Resia's restorative power on his own.

Despite his best effort, he lost ground. To his side, Lark fared worse. A hint of fear touched her eyes and he knew he couldn't hold back anymore. Zaide threw himself into the next opening he saw and squeezed his eyes closed as the Spectrum Blade pierced flesh and the sound of the man's death flooded his ears.

A single stroke of panic coursed through him, followed by a wave of cold.

Out of everything his quest had asked of him, he hadn't had to kill another human.

When he forced his eyes open a second later, Lark stared at him, her suntanned face gone pale.

He couldn't stop. The guard she'd been fighting lurched forward to strike while she was stunned and Zaide darted forward. Too late to parry, he severed the man's arm, instead. The guard went down screaming, his voice joined by others as Moros took the violence as permission. The warden tore through the men in front of him and blood spattered the walls and floor.

Still, the hallway beyond the door brimmed with soldiers. No matter how many they cut down, there would be more.

"Your Highness!" Elsanna shouted over the screams.

They spun toward the guardswoman. Her blades were locked against Jinohe's sword, and behind the captain, the Magister shook off his chains. Beyond them, Tula still struggled against her own opponent. Sweat caught loose strands of her red hair and splayed them across her face like wounds.

Zaide gripped Lark's arm. "We have to go!"

The corners of her eyes tightened and deep lines trenched between her brows. She looked from the Magister, to the hall, to the bodies now on the floor. Resignation made her shoulders slump, but she gave in when Zaide pulled.

They retreated.

Moros backed away from the hall until Tula could jump

behind him and join the princess in abandoning the fight. Only Elsanna clung to fighting, though her tiny, primitive daggers hindered her, and she gained no ground.

"Elsanna!" Zaide called.

The guardswoman bared her teeth at him, but when she caught Lark's distressed face, her anger lessened.

They reached the hole in the wall and Zaide pushed Lark and Tula through. The princess clung to his arm, but he lingered, his sword ready. Distracting droplets of crimson rolled down its multicolored surface.

Human blood. A first. And somehow, he knew it wouldn't be the last.

Elsanna abandoned her fight and rushed to herd them into the tunnel. "Go, go!" She urged them onward as Moros reached the gap, his large frame all but filling the hole they'd created.

The warden struck steel against the stone and something lit with the spark. Panicked shouts swelled in the room as he turned and ran with an urgency that pushed them all to move faster.

Behind him, the second bomb they'd stolen from the salamanders exploded, and the tunnel began to collapse.

CHAPTER EIGHTEEN

THE WHINE DIDN'T START until they were halfway down the tunnel. It was high, sharp, like a ringing in his ears but from somewhere deeper in his skull. Zaide shook his head once, as if to dispel the sound.

"Don't stop!" Moros almost roared behind them. That the man raised his voice at all was enough to encourage all of them to redouble their efforts. The crash of collapsing rock thundered down the passage and loose bits of gravel tumbled past their feet.

The whine grew louder. Zaide grimaced and tried hard to ignore it. The end of the tunnel was in sight, but Elsanna darted past him in the narrow space and seized Lark's arm to hurry her along, signaling the end of the tunnel wasn't good enough.

Neither were his efforts to ignore the sound in his head. A jolt of *something* traveled up his arm as it grew louder, shriller, increasing until it was more like a scream. He gritted his teeth and squinted against the sudden pain that split behind his eyes.

Elsanna and Lark spilled out from the tunnel and veered toward the right. Tula was close on their heels, her coats billowing behind her like wings. One coat, Zaide corrected himself. Now his vision was splitting, too.

He stumbled when his feet hit the smoother floor of the cavern and almost couldn't right himself. A moment later, a strong hand gripped his upper arm and dragged him along.

Another quivering jolt ran up his other arm—his sword arm—and he sucked in a sharp breath. This time, the sensation stung. "Stop it," he gasped.

"Don't stop," the warden repeated, less a shout and more a bark this time, but the noise coupled with the screaming in Zaide's head made him flinch.

"Not you," he replied, though his own voice sounded weak, dim, beneath the screaming and the growing sensation of wrongness that crawled up his arm and seeped into his head. They didn't make it far before he staggered.

Just ahead, Lark turned back as if to scold them, but her expression shifted when she saw the two of them stop in the middle of the cavern.

Zaide raised a hand to grip his forehead. Gritting his teeth did nothing to alleviate the growing pain. Panic, anger, and dismay swirled inside his mind, thoughts he wasn't certain were his own, all of them combined with the spiraling swell of noise that threatened to cleave his skull in two. His hand tightened on the sword he still carried. "Stop!"

"Sit him down," Lark ordered. She hurried back toward them as Zaide sank to the floor.

It wasn't until Moros removed his hands from Zaide's shoulders that he realized he'd had help. The stinging sensation in his arm had turned to something like fire. He panted and swept his other hand down his arm as if to extinguish the unseen flames.

The princess knelt beside him and gripped his left arm, just above the elbow. "Put down the sword."

"I can't!" he gasped. No matter how he tried, his fingers didn't respond.

Elsanna padded toward them with her hands on her hips. "We don't have time for this, get him moving!"

"We move when I say we move," Lark snapped back. She stroked his bare arm, her fingertips cool and gentle, her touch leaving streaks of soothing painlessness in its wake.

Zaide tried to focus on her face. "It's angry," he managed.

"The blade?"

It took great effort to nod. The fire began to creep up his shoulder and claw at the back of his neck. He squeezed his eyes closed and bit back a breath, lest it escape as a shout.

Her hand slipped down the length of his arm to rest on the back of his hand. "Don't simply punish him, tell him why!"

"Is she talking to the sword?" Tula asked in a whisper nearby, the question accompanied by the soft scratch of her writing something down.

Moros hushed her.

Lark's cool fingers closed around Zaide's hand on the hilt of the sword. A rush of sensation followed; complaint, despair, sorrow, and a strange sense of griminess. Then the anger swelled again. It was his fault everything was wrong.

A single moment of clarity lanced through the haze and Zaide pried his eyes open. "Cloth."

Beside him, the princess sat back on her heels and opened one of her bags. She jerked the Hymnflute free and removed its cloth wrapping.

Zaide all but snatched it from her hand. His arm trembled, but he turned the sword enough to sweep the cloth down its length. Dust-riddled blood smeared down its surface.

The whine in his head shifted until it gave him a sense of discomfort instead of anger. Wrongness still poured from the blade and traveled through his nerves, but the screeching abated until he grew aware of the pounding in his head. Determined, he scrubbed the surface until the drying blood began to flake away.

"It didn't clean itself," Lark murmured. "Whenever you kill goborrins, it..."

"It's angry," Zaide said as he turned the sword over to clean the other side. The whine faded to a buzz, a soft sense of discontentment. His arm still burned, but now it was with fatigue instead of whatever the Spectrum Blade had done. "I used it wrong."

The princess nodded, her brow furrowed. "The guards up there... It's not meant for killing people."

A thrum of assent coursed through his fingers. "I'm sorry," Zaide said, though he wasn't sure if he was apologizing to the sword or the princess.

"You have nothing to apologize for. You had no choice. If I hadn't been fighting beside you like that, or if I'd held my own better—" Lark's voice cracked.

"We need to move," Elsanna snapped before she could finish. "That tunnel is down, but there are a dozen others that lead into this system of caves and every moment we spend dallying is a moment for Jinohe and the Magister to rally soldiers and send more after us. Your magic sword is free to be angry at you for killing men, but unless it wants you to kill more, you'd better get on your feet."

Zaide scraped the cloth down the Spectrum Blade's surface one more time. A few orange-brown streaks still muddied its glowing colors, but it was the best he could do. "I'll clean you properly when we get out of here," he promised. "Oil and everything."

Moros touched his shoulder. "Move."

"We need to find somewhere safe to hide and recuperate," Lark said as she pushed herself back to her feet.

Zaide was slower to follow. His head still throbbed and his eyes ached, and a new sense of exhaustion weighted his limbs. He used the sword for leverage to help push himself to his feet, grateful it didn't object. In fact, the sword had gone quiet. No more hum, no more shrill. Not even a tingle in his hand when he experimentally lifted his fingers, one at a time. "I'd recommend somewhere other than the library." His head felt hazy, but he dared not let himself look weak after... whatever it was that just happened.

"I'd agree with that." Tula scratched out a few more notes before her tiny book disappeared into her coat, hidden away in some pocket where her observations would be safe. "But we can probably use the library's tunnels. Right now, getting Elsanna to the other guardswomen is the best thing we can do."

"Safety in numbers," Moros agreed.

"Doesn't that mean going back to the library, though?" Zaide asked. "Or do you know of other ways into those tunnels?"

Tula shrugged. "We're not likely to be noticed if we slip in the back door of the guild hall. That's where most librarians sleep when they're off duty, so there's a lot of coming and going."

"And the city is under attack," Lark added. "The rest of the city's guard is bound to be distracted."

"Unless they're in on it," Elsanna said.

"I don't know. The Magister's soldiers seemed as surprised to see goborrins as I was." Tula scratched the back of her neck, then gave her red ponytail a swish.

Zaide grunted softly and rolled his shoulders. Light as the sword was, it felt like a fifty pound weight in his hand. "Even if they're not surprised, they'll be distracted trying to keep the city from panicking, right?"

The princess nodded. "They won't be looking for us back on the city's surface so soon, either, I'd expect. Remember, the Magister is who we're after. They'll probably assume we'll be looking for another way back into the palace."

"Doubtful," Moros rumbled, but he herded them all in the direction of the prison's tunnel.

Tula and Elsanna led the way, but Lark hung back and walked close by Zaide's side. A hint of worry put lines between her brows, but she said nothing.

The narrow tunnel wasn't difficult to traverse, but the air grew cold as they walked. Zaide fought back a shiver as his exposed skin rose in gooseflesh. The first thing he was going to look for after they found a safe hiding place was something fresh to wear, with a good pair of boots.

Moros motioned the group aside when they reached the top of the tunnel. He squeezed to the front and rested a hand against the ring of keys that hung from his belt, but the door that sealed the confinement cell remained unlocked. The prison beyond was quiet.

"Isn't coming up through the dungeon a bad idea?" Tula asked in a whisper. "We're exactly where they'd want us, if we got caught."

"All the more reason they will not look for us here," Moros said. He led them up the stairs, to the chilly room where Zaide had first seen him.

Zaide glanced around in hopes of seeing some sign of his other belongings, but the room was empty.

His looking hadn't been subtle, it seemed, for Moros gave a single nod and answered the unspoken question in a low voice. "Artificers will be going through your things by now. It is unlikely much will be recovered."

"Resia will be very unhappy with me if I've lost the songbook she gave me," Zaide said.

"Then we'll have to defeat this false Magister quickly, so we can find your songbook and spare you." A hint of sparkle in Elsanna's eyes indicated her jest, but it sounded like a reasonable assessment of the situation.

Tula trotted ahead to peer out the door. "The courtyard is empty on this side," she whispered as she swiveled her head back and forth, checking both directions repeatedly, as if someone might appear.

Elsanna nodded. "The wall is right there. Can we go over it, or will we be forced to cross the courtyard?"

"Jadora's walls are impenetrable," Moros said. "You know this. The walls were not what failed today, but the tunnels under the palace."

"That would be a no, then." Lark joined Tula at the door and peered up the wall, as well. "It's too high to climb without rope, and there doesn't seem to be anything on top that we could use for anchoring a rope, anyway."

"So we go across the courtyard." Zaide stepped past them and turned. The space ahead was nothing but a shadowed alleyway that dead-ended at the wall. *Wrong direction.* He turned the other way, the way they'd come when he'd been arrested. The soft glow of lanterns was inviting in the night.

Moros reclaimed his place at the back of the group. "Be ready."

Together, they stalked along the side of the building until they could see the courtyard before the palace. The gates were closed, the yard empty.

"That's suspicious, right?" Tula asked in a whisper.

"Very," Elsanna murmured back. "Hurry to the gates. Moros, I'll open them, but you'll have to hold one."

The warden grunted. "I can hold only one."

"We have hands," Lark said. "I am sure we can manage the other."

With as weak as Zaide felt, he was disinclined to agree, but he held his tongue. They ran across the small courtyard together and Elsanna disappeared into the gatehouse. Even with as little experience as what Zaide had with the world outside of Kolmar, he knew the gates should not have been left unattended. That they were made the hair on the back of his neck prickle. He almost expected a sense of trepidation from the sword, but the Spectrum Blade emitted nothing.

Never talkative when I need reassurance, huh? he thought at the weapon. It yielded no response. Not that he'd expected it might.

The portcullises rattled and began a slow, creaking ascent. Moros positioned himself under the near gate and pointed for the others to take the second. Tula scurried forward with Lark right behind her. Zaide reluctantly returned his sword to its sheath. With the way his neck prickled, he didn't want to be caught unaware, but he couldn't help one-handed, either.

Instead of dropping, the two gates inched downward until

their full weight sat upon the people beneath them. Moros accepted his burden without so much as a flinch, but Lark and Tula both emitted small sounds of surprise at the weight. Zaide released a hissing breath as the heavy grille bore down on them and squared his shoulders a little better to try and take more weight off the girls, but sweat already speckled his brow. How much more could one person do without rest?

Elsanna reappeared a moment later and ducked past the gate with little ceremony. The instant she was past, Moros rolled his shoulders out from underneath his gate and let it drop with a bang. The noise made the rest of them jump, but no sound of alarm went up from the palace.

"Go," the warden ordered as he hunched beneath the second gate and pushed it upward, relieving the rest of them of its weight.

Zaide wasn't sorry to let go, but he glanced at the towering man with a new sense of respect for his strength. He'd been lucky to be spared a fight against Moros.

Lark and Tula dipped out behind Elsanna. Zaide went last, and Moros let the second gate fall with little more than a grunt to show his exertion.

"This way," Tula said before anyone could speak. She lit off at a sprint, leaving the rest of them no choice but to follow.

The streets were no less confusing to Zaide than the previous times he'd visited, but Tula led them through narrow back streets and thin gaps between buildings, where the stone pressed so close that Moros almost became stuck more than once. Eventually, they stopped beside a plain wooden door with iron hinges. "This goes into the kitchen," she whispered as she tugged it open. It wasn't locked, and warm firelight spilled out across the alleyway.

"Tula! Maker's mercy, what are you up to now?" a woman inside asked as they filtered in behind their librarian. A handful of what Zaide assumed were scholars stopped to stare at the group.

Tula lifted a finger to her lips. "I'm having an adventure!"

The woman huffed. "I swear, if you've been off to look at those tunnels again, I—" She stopped short as Elsanna stepped in and closed the door.

"Good evening," the guardswoman said, voice more cordial than Zaide had ever heard. "I understand you are in possession of secret tunnels?"

For a moment, the woman's mouth worked without producing words. A man nearby took over. "Forgive us, Elsanna," he almost stammered. "The librarians' guild never intentionally hid—"

"I don't care," Elsanna interrupted. "Show me where they are."

The man gulped, turned, and beckoned for them to follow. Tula and Elsanna went without hesitation, but when Zaide was slower to start, Lark stayed back to remain beside him.

"Are you all right?" she asked softly. Her fingers twisted in the hair that hung around her shoulders, a small betrayal of her thoughts. Her concern was genuine.

"Ah," Zaide sighed as he followed the others. Even Moros moved ahead, leaving the two of them a little space to themselves. Respectful, though he assumed it was more because the princess was speaking than because his words deserved any privacy. "I never thought I'd go to jail, but I think my foster mother will forgive me for leaving home and suddenly becoming a delinquent."

Lark's eyes darkened, unappreciative of his attempt at humor.

He sobered. "I'm the best I can be. It's not angry at me anymore, I don't think. It hasn't done anything else."

"Are you hurt, though? Did it cause you lasting harm?" Her voice lowered as she spoke; he assumed she didn't want the librarians to hear more than they ought.

"I don't think so. It made me tired, more than anything. I should be fine after a good night's rest. And once I get some clothes back. Sarma made me that tunic, and I think she'll be angry if those artificers don't give it back."

The soft sound the princess made indicated that was a satisfactory answer. "We'll dress you appropriately as soon as we find somewhere to rest. I don't believe Tula is impressed by your physique."

Zaide blinked, then frowned. "I don't look bad."

"You look like a snowman."

"Snowmen don't have visible abdominal muscles."

"They could, depending on the competence of their sculptor," Lark said breezily.

Both self-conscious and sullen, he crossed his arms over his bare chest and tucked in his chin. A hint of a smile fluttered at the corners of the princess's mouth, but she said nothing more, and the quickening of her pace coupled with his unwillingness to be left behind meant they closed the distance between themselves and the rest of the group a moment later.

In the corner of the guild hall's storage room, the man leading them knelt to move a slab from the floor. "I can't help you beyond this," he said as Lark and Zaide came close enough to hear, "I'm not familiar with where the tunnels actually go."

"That's all right, I am." Tula was the first to drop into the dark. Her voice echoed from below. "Besides, there are only so many places we can get to from here."

"A light would help," Elsanna muttered as she went next.

Zaide unsheathed a few inches of the Spectrum Blade. Its glow was muted, but it would be better than nothing.

"I have light," Lark said. She spared a glance for Zaide and his sword before she lowered herself to the floor and climbed cautiously over the edge. The others had descended rapidly, maybe even jumped, but there was a ladder inside that the princess used with extreme care.

Zaide turned to suggest Moros could go next and was met with a withering stare from the tall warden. He swallowed and nodded in response to the silent, gestureless order, then knelt and sought the ladder with his foot.

"We will not be followed," Moros said to the librarian. "We were not seen."

"Elsanna has been missing for weeks," the man replied. "No one would believe me even if I did say I'd seen her. Not that I would, of course."

A low, doubtful *hmm* was all Moros gave as response.

Zaide worked his way down the ladder until his bare feet found the floor. If the prison had been cold, the tunnel here was frigid, but the feeling was already gone from his toes.

A soft, warm glow filled the space around them. Lark held the Molten Dagger aloft. It cast strange shadows across her face, magnified by the worry that still drew her brows when she looked at him. Was what had happened with the blade that concerning? He'd already made it clear he believed the artifact was sentient, if unable to communicate in words. It had certainly made its displeasure clear enough without them, and after his questions, she shouldn't have been surprised by what it had done.

He frowned at her, and she turned away.

Either way, it was obvious she no longer doubted him, and perhaps that was what made her worried. Whatever it had done to him, he couldn't deny it had to be some sort of magic, and that raised new questions he'd have to ask and explore. Was it normal to sense a power he couldn't wield by himself? Or was the blade merely wielding that power against him to make its wishes known?

Moros crept down the tiny ladder as the librarian replaced the slab. The moment he reached the floor, Tula pointed into the darkness. "This way."

Elsanna took the lead, despite having no light, and Tula went right after her. Lark raised the dagger and started to move at the same time as Moros, but Zaide caught her arm.

"Let me," he said as he unsheathed the Spectrum Blade. Its

colors were cool, slow-moving, but its glow brightened as if it sensed its light was needed.

The princess looked down at it, her eyes traveling the length of the blade and lingering on the dark spots that still marred the surface of its glassy, iridescent steel. "I don't understand," she murmured, and somehow, he knew she didn't mean his insistence that he go first.

Slowly, she raised her head and met his eye. "It was made to kill Gadranus, yet it's not meant to kill humans."

The same thought had occurred to him, but it was hardly the time to discuss it. "There's still a lot we don't understand," he said. "But you're a scholar. You'll figure it out."

The lines between her brows deepened like never before and a new sense of ill ease washed through him.

"You'll figure it out," he repeated as he turned and raised the blade, its cool light flooding the tunnel ahead.

"Maybe," Lark whispered behind him, the uncertainty in the single word leaving him colder than ever before.

CHAPTER NINETEEN

THE TUNNELS all looked the same. Zaide glanced back the way they'd come now and then, unsure they'd traveled anywhere at all. The stones were all different sizes and shapes, but he could have sworn they'd passed that same patch of rock half a dozen times already.

Tula paused at each intersection and tilted her eyes toward the ceiling, as if recounting each twist and turn to herself. Zaide didn't know how she knew where they were supposed to go. At first, he thought she might be taking them back toward the library, but she'd pointed out the passage to the library when they passed it by, eliminating that theory.

When they paused at another turn, Elsanna pointed. "Left."

Tula flashed her a grin, her teeth bright white in the shadows. "Figured it out?"

"Only so many options in this part of the city. Besides, I've been through the tunnels before." The guardswoman stuck out her tongue in an uncharacteristically childish gesture, but she grew serious again a moment later. "What makes you think they'll be here?"

"Because when I saw them before, I could smell the kiln on Valla's clothes."

"Smart girl. That's why you're the scholar and librarian and the rest of us are brutes, eh?" A note of teasing touched Elsanna's words, so familiar in tone that Zaide squinted at their backs.

"Sisters?" he asked.

Both Elsanna and Tula stopped in their tracks. Instead of any of the jovial retorts he expected, he got a frosty glare from the guardswoman and a worried frown from Tula.

"Yes," the librarian said as she turned back to the tunnel.

Elsanna released a low hiss. "He doesn't need to know that."

"It doesn't hurt anything," Tula murmured back.

Zaide was inclined to agree. "I just thought... That is, Valla said all the guardswomen were related, and Tula looks so much like the rest of you. Was it supposed to be secret?"

The way Elsanna's shoulders squared at the same time Tula's slumped said yes.

Lark nudged his side. "Elsanna is in a position of power as the leader of the guardswomen, and right now, that position is precarious. Jadora's problems usually come from within the city, and the identities of family members or loved ones being known could put them at risk if someone in the city wishes to blackmail someone of authority. Do them a favor and keep that knowledge to yourself."

"Politics," Zaide grumbled.

Moros shared a grunt of agreement.

"That goes for you, too," Tula said. Her lower lip stuck out in a pout when she looked back at the scarred man. "I didn't know who you were, either, until tonight."

"You don't need to tell me. I am Jadoran. He is not." Moros let his eyes slide toward Lark. "But the princess's familiarity with our ways and customs is appreciated."

Whether or not that was intended to be an insult, it made Zaide's hackles rise. He smoothed a hand down the back of his neck and raised the Spectrum Blade higher when he realized he'd let it droop.

"Here," Tula said before any more insults—intended or otherwise—could be shared. She pointed toward a rough wooden ladder that ended at the base of a narrow stone slab.

Zaide examined its shape, then glanced to Moros, taking in the breadth of his shoulders. "We're going to need another way up."

"You will not be there long," the warden said. "I will guard from below."

Elsanna scaled the ladder and tapped the crude hilt of one of her salamander's daggers against the stone, a rhythmic knock that was answered by a soft rustle above. A moment later, a series of taps came from the other side. Elsanna replied with a series of her own, and the slab shifted aside.

Above, a guardswoman in plain clothes gasped. "Elsanna!"

A chorus of surprise went up in the room above. Hands reached down to pull Elsanna up, though she batted them away and climbed on her own. "Someone tell me you've got enough water drawn for a bath," she joked.

A few relieved laughs answered as Tula skittered up the ladder next.

Zaide watched her boots vanish into the room above, then motioned for Lark to go next.

The princess studied him for a time, but said nothing. Whatever information she'd been looking for, she'd reached the conclusion on her own. Deciding whether or not he was fit to climb, perhaps? He was tired and his entire body ached, but he considered himself unharmed. The blade in his hand remained silent, as swords were meant to be. He considered the weapon for a moment before he returned it to its sheath and waited for his turn to climb.

Lark turned back when she reached the top, but she didn't insult him by offering a hand. Zaide climbed on his own, crawled through the gap, and sat on the cool stone floor of a pottery shop.

The kiln, Tula said. A logical conclusion.

Across the room, Valla folded her arms over her chest and leaned back against a table. "No water for that here, but I agree with the bath. You smell like a goborrin."

"So will half the city, at this point." Elsanna sighed and wiped her forehead with the back of her hand. For the first time since they'd found her in chains, she looked weary.

Zaide sympathized. He climbed to his feet and glanced into the passage below. Moros raised a hand in a simple wave of acknowledgment, but he made no move toward the ladder.

The guardswoman beside the tunnel entrance peered down at him. "Is that the prison warden?"

"He helped find Elsanna," Zaide said.

Her head snapped up and she regarded him with narrowed eyes. "I recognize you."

"I wish I could say the same, but most of you were in your armor the last time I saw you, and I was trying not to look," he replied flatly.

The guardswoman blinked at him, then laughed.

"Forgive him," Elsanna said. "He's shy."

"Not that shy. He's as clothed as we are when we're on duty." The guardswoman grinned when a hint of color rose in Zaide's cheeks, but then she pushed herself up and left him alone. "And you, Your Highness. I recognize you, as well. I trust this isn't a pleasure visit."

"Certainly not." Lark stood straight and lifted her chin, imperious as ever.

Tula smoothed her coat and hair. "We need the Magister, but he—"

"Is not the Magister," Valla finished for her.

The librarian nodded.

Lark gestured toward Zaide. "The Magister's power is what's necessary. If whoever leads Jadora now has been accepted by whatever source of power Jadora hides, he will suffice, but our visit was interrupted and I was unable to discern whether or not he has inherited any sort of magical ability. I had hoped we could find more information about the root of the Magister's power at the library, but I doubt we'll have a chance to sit and study now."

Valla sighed. "Not something we can help you with, I'm afraid. Unless you want us to take the library by storm and hold it while you read."

"Tempting, but unlikely to work," Lark said.

Zaide fingered the Spectrum Blade's hilt. "Researching could take hours."

"So we need another way to find out where the Magister's power comes from," Tula concluded.

"What do you suggest, Elsanna?" Valla glanced toward her superior, a hopeful light in her eyes. "It would be unlike you to be without a plan already."

Elsanna's face scrunched into something that wasn't quite a grimace, but was equally unpleasant. "I wouldn't be generous enough to call it a plan yet. It's simple. We find a way to get the new Magister, we force him to help us."

"Kidnapping?" another guardswoman asked.

"I'd rather kill him, but that won't help with whatever the princess is after," Elsanna said.

Zaide backed up to lean against an enormous pot and drew his sword an inch. With goborrins in the city, he expected its glow would brighten if trouble came near, but its light remained soft. Something in the pot beside him glinted and he leaned forward to look. "Huh."

Lark cast him a questioning glance.

He pulled the small coin from the pot's depths and turned it between his fingers, then craned his neck to look into another and scanned the rest of the room. Dozens of pots sat on the floor and decorated shelves against the walls.

"Stay right where you are," Lark whispered.

He hadn't intended to move, but he settled against the massive pot behind him and rolled the coin between his fingers.

There was little he could contribute to the planning and it had grown too crowded to walk around, either way. Guardswomen had continued to filter in from the next room, all of them looking to their leader.

But Elsanna seemed short for words. She frowned at the floor, rubbing her chin.

Tula mirrored her behavior for a while, then lifted her head. "So we need to get his attention somehow. How are we supposed to do that?"

Zaide tilted his head as he rolled the coin a little farther, so the unfamiliar emblem on its face was right side up. "What about a bribe?"

Everyone glanced his way.

He held up the coin, as if it offered enough explanation on its own.

Lark paced toward him, her eyes fixed on its small shape. "That might have merit. We could try and lure him out to capture him, but I think he'll expect an attack. If we offer parley, though..."

"He might hear us out," Elsanna agreed. "Maybe even offer to help us. But what have we got that might draw him out?"

"The dagger?" Tula gripped the edges of her coat, a glitter in her eyes. "He believes it belongs to Jadora, and to the Magister specifically, right? If we offer him the Molten Dagger in return for assistance, he may be willing to meet."

"Are we willing to sacrifice the dagger, though?" Valla asked. "You took it for a reason, can you really spare it now?"

Zaide closed his hand around the coin and shifted to indicate the sword at his right hip. "We've already gotten what we needed the dagger for. It's been useful, and I'm sure we'd all be sad to see it go, but nobody's saying we're actually going to give it to him."

"If he's actually capable of helping us and is willing to do so, I am willing to release the dagger to the Magister's hands." Lark gripped the strap of her bag, where Zaide assumed she had the obsidian blade hidden. He no longer saw its sheath at her belt, though he wasn't sure when she would have put it away.

"Then that's a good start," Elsanna said. "Jadora's problems are its own, but we are here to help Her Highness first. If she deems the new Magister a suitable leader for the city, we'll have to accept that and sort out our issues with the situation on our own time."

Valla snorted. "He wants to disband the guardswomen and replace all of us with his Mage-Guard."

Elsanna gave her a hard look. "A problem for another day."

"What we need right now is a way to deliver the message," Lark said. "Tula is a librarian, and the librarians are still a neutral party."

Zaide shook his head. "She was with us, though. The Magister could just as easily arrest her instead of hearing her out."

"I would like to see him arrest someone with no warden," Moros called from the tunnel below. Several guardswomen started at the boom of his voice, but a few giggles rolled through the group afterward. Had they forgotten him already? The tunnel was still open.

The princess ran her fingers down her bag's strap. "I don't mean to send Tula to the Magister, but to the rest of the librarians. They are more than capable of delivering a message on our behalf, and Tula is the most likely of us to be able to reach the library and convince them to cooperate. I have no doubt the Magister's kindness toward me was merely show, and I have no reason to assume my title grants me any sort of protection here."

"So we send Tula to the librarians, they organize a meeting, and we go from there?" Zaide asked.

Elsanna gave a slow nod. "I think this is the best option we have. We can send an escort with Tula to ensure she reaches the library safely. While she arranges things, we'll have time to prepare for the meeting."

"Do it, then," Lark said.

The guardswomen straightened and Elsanna motioned for Valla to join her. The two of them conversed in a murmur too low to hear, then Valla bowed her head and disappeared to another room.

"I need six volunteers to escort our librarian," Elsanna said.

Every guardswoman present raised a hand. Zaide no longer knew how many there were. Their leader made her selections, and the women vanished to gather their weapons and scant armor, for all the good it would do them.

Lark straightened and dropped her hands to her sides, though they curled to fists and betrayed what had to be nerves. "I would like to request materials from the library, as well."

"Why not have Tula ask if we can wait in the library and hold our meeting there?" Zaide asked. "It's neutral territory. If the librarians don't want us to have the actual meeting there, we can always step outside so we'd be fighting on the steps."

"Having the high ground would be an advantage," Moros put in from below.

"I'm not sure a library counts as the high ground," Elsanna said.

Zaide shrugged. "Maybe morally."

Beside him, Lark gave the tiniest snort of a laugh. The hint of amusement that curled her lips gave him an unexpected sense of delight. She was always so stern, so stoic. The sound of her laugh, however small, was a refreshing contrast.

"I'll ask," Tula said with a grin. "It's for the best, I think. If nothing else, we can ask the master librarians about the Magister's power while we wait for a response. I can't imagine they'd forbid the princess of Amroch from entering the library, though."

"Are they even allowed to do that?" Zaide doubted they were. They'd already established Lark made the rules—or she would, once she took the crown. Judging by the strength King Sendassian still bore, that was likely some time from now. Unconsciously, Zaide's hand went to his throat. The bruises had healed on the long voyage by ship, but the memory of the king's crushing grip would never leave him.

"I don't think they can forbid it, but I understand if they aren't comfortable having me near something as precious as all those books, what with the current situation." Lark curled her fingers around the strap of her bag again, as if she didn't know what to do with her hands. Maybe she didn't. Or maybe the situation made her nervous. It was hard to imagine it didn't; the Magister's mage-guards had been ready to kill them, regardless of what it might have meant for Amroch if the princess were slain.

Tula nodded and started for the door, then paused. "I should probably take the tunnels, huh?"

"You should also wait for your escort," Elsanna said.

As if summoned, the handful of women she'd chosen for the job reappeared. "We're ready, Elsanna. We'll take her now."

"I will remain here," Moros called.

Zaide crept forward to look down into the tunnel. The man's face was impassive, like rock. Fitting, considering the size and shape of him. "You're not lonely down there, are you?"

"Your company would be the last I would ask for."

"We'll send Elsanna down before long," Lark said.

Moros did not reply, but Zaide thought he saw a hint of satisfaction on the warden's scarred face.

With Elsanna's permission, Tula scampered down the ladder into the tunnel, and her six guardswomen followed. "I'll be back as soon as I have an answer," she promised. "Or at least, I'll make sure an answer gets back to you. The librarians might not want me to come back, myself."

Lark gave a flick of her fingers, both acknowledgment and concession. "Do what you must."

"And what do we do, while we're here?" Zaide rolled the coin between his fingers again, then stuffed it into his pocket.

The princess turned to face him with her hands on her hips.

"Now, we see to you. Elsanna, will you have someone bring me medical supplies?"

The guardswoman repeated the request as an order to a woman nearby.

Lark pointed toward a stool beside a pottery wheel. "Sit."

"I'm fine," Zaide protested.

"You are certainly not, and the blood on your leg can attest to that. You may be the new Bladebearer, but you're as susceptible to infection as any man. Sit down." She pointed again.

He tucked in his chin and did as he was told. Strange, he thought, how fast he submitted to her commands, despite how often his will clashed with hers. His sense of duty overruled the rest of him, eager to answer every order the princess gave him.

As he sat, Lark rolled up his bloodied pant leg and made a sound of disgust. Most of what had run down his leg was dry, but the wound he'd received was still gooey, and the fabric stuck. "This is quite dirty. Did you really intend to keep walking around like this? This is large enough to poison your blood."

"I've had worse injuries from training." And he was sure he had, though he couldn't recall any now. Never mind that his foster mother had always seen to his injuries, and later, when he was older, he'd been tended by Resia. Now that he was thoroughly entangled in the war, her gift with healing would be sorely missed.

A guardswoman appeared beside them with a box of things and a bowl of steaming water. Lark murmured a thank-you as she took a cloth from the box and plunged it into the water, then wrung out the excess. The heat was soothing when she pressed the wet cloth to his leg, though he wouldn't admit it.

After a few swipes, a hint of a smile curved her lips.

Zaide's brow crinkled. "What?"

"Your leg hair is white."

"All my hair is white."

A twinkle lit in her deep blue eyes. "You'll look ancient by the time you're thirty."

Zaide snorted. "If I live that long."

"Well, as long as you don't ignore injuries like these, you might." She sat on her heels and refreshed the water as she cleaned the injury. It wasn't deep, nor did it hurt, exactly, but it stung when she laid the cloth over it to soften the dirt-crusted blood that hadn't quite dried.

He fought not to flinch. "I'd better. Maybe by the time I'm thirty, I'll be able to grow a beard."

Lark lifted her head to appraise the state of his jawline. "That may be wishful thinking."

"You never know," he said, resisting the urge to check how much stubble had grown. Little, he was sure; he'd shaved regularly on the ship, and it wasn't as if his whiskers grew fast enough to warrant a razor more than every few days. "I'd like one, anyway. I've got a distinguished title, and I should look distinguished, too."

"Are beards what make a man distinguished?" the princess asked.

Zaide opened his mouth to answer, then paused. A number of guardswomen had filtered out of the room, off to carry out whatever orders Elsanna had given them, but a handful remained. Elsanna herself still leaned against the table, her arms crossed, and she stared at him with a smirk that made his ears heat.

"Actually, I think it's clothes," he said as he met the guardswoman's eyes. "Can we do something about that?"

"Of course. I'll see to that myself." Elsanna pushed herself away from the table, but the way her smirk deepened as she left the room made things worse.

Having an injury tended by the princess was embarrassing enough without the teasing he now knew it would bring.

"I'm sure everyone will appreciate that," Lark said, though the humor faded from her words. "You don't think you'll limp while this is healing, do you?"

"I don't think so. I haven't been, so I don't think it'll hinder anything if we need to fight." His attention drifted to the box beside her as she rinsed her cloth again and finished cleaning the cut. He didn't recognize anything in it, but the dark bottles promised tinctures to stave off infection and promote healing.

"Good," she sighed. "Because I get the feeling the real fight is still ahead."

CHAPTER TWENTY

TULA PAUSED AT YET another branch in the tunnels and tried to retrace her steps. She had a good memory when it came to directions, yet now that it was meant for official business, she found herself turned around. The same thing had happened in Amrochan's palace, when her excitement got the better of her. Why did her senses abandon her every time it was important?

"We should be close," one of the guardswomen behind her said, though Tula was unsure if she was speaking to her or the other women at her back.

"Sorry." The urge to apologize had risen at every other stop, but this was the first time Tula voiced it. "I'm nervous, that's all."

"No need for apology," the woman replied.

Tula tried to find comfort in the response. Chances were they were nervous, too. With tensions high between the guardswomen and the Magister, showing themselves came with certain risks, even if they were only setting foot into the library. On a professional level, the librarians did their best to stay out of the city's politics, but that didn't mean the librarians held no opinions of their own. Harm was unlikely to befall them in the library itself, but the chances someone would report their whereabouts to the Magister's Mage-Guard were high.

Even if Master Arkosh said the librarians had chosen a side, she knew he couldn't mean all of them.

"I think it's this way." Tula pointed, though she suspected the gesture was lost in the shadow. The guardswomen were prepared enough that one had thought to bring a lantern, but she faced away from it, and the way ahead was not clear.

"Maybe they should put signs down here, like they do on the buildings at street corners," one of the women joked as they turned.

Tula cracked a smile. It was more the guardswomen she worried about than herself, but their relaxed confidence helped. She didn't know how they remained so calm in the face of everything they must have been through, but perhaps that was why they were guardswomen and she was not. The life of a soldier had never been a good fit for her, no matter what her mother wanted. Her mother had gotten Elsanna; that should have been enough.

Ahead, a wooden ladder like the one beneath the pottery shop owned by Valla's family leaned against the wall at the end of the tunnel. Tula breathed a quiet sigh of relief as she approached. That was definitely the ladder to the library. She remembered the way the second-to-last rung was nailed on crooked. "I'll go first. It's probably best if a librarian is the first one out of the secret passage."

"You're going to have to build new secret passages. I think too many people know about these to call them secret at this point," a woman said. A few giggles followed.

"I think you're right," Tula agreed. She climbed the ladder, ignoring the nervous clamminess of her hands. The stone at the top was heavy, but it had been mechanized when Arkosh brought her down before. She braced her feet firmly against the ladder's rungs and scouted around the stone's edges with both hands. Eventually, she located the switch, and it slid upward and to the side.

Late as it was, she'd expected the library would be quiet. Instead, every lantern on the main floor was alight, and a handful of librarians in their pale robes turned in surprise when she popped up out of the tunnel.

"Oh," Tula squeaked.

"Is that Tula?" Arkosh's voice came from the other side of the large circulation desk. The old man hurried into view, mingled confusion and relief plastered on his face. "Thank the Maker you're all right!"

She crawled out of the hole and pushed herself to her feet. "Master Arkosh, what's going on?" she asked before she looked around, though one glimpse of the library was enough to explain the situation on its own. The front doors had been barricaded, and every librarian and apprentice she'd ever met was present. Most near the doors stood with weapons in hand.

Arkosh's confusion deepened. "Weren't you headed to the palace? The city is under attack. Gadranus has breached the walls somehow, his goborrins are tearing Jadora to pieces."

"They hit the palace first," Tula said. "That's why we ran."

The old librarian leaned forward to squint into the hole. Weak as the lantern light was, he hadn't missed that someone lingered in the tunnels. "Who's down there?"

To answer the question, the guardswomen stepped forward. "Elsanna sent us as escort," the woman in the front said.

"Elsanna!" Arkosh cried. A low murmur rolled through the library. Was that good or bad?

One by one, the six guardswomen climbed out of the tunnel and formed a half-circle behind Tula. There was no escaping it; she'd have to explain herself in front of every last one of Jadora's librarians. Her heart fluttered in her throat and thundered in her ribcage at the same time and she found herself twisting her fingertips as she drew a breath to speak. Unwilling to let her nerves show, she curled her hands to fists and held them by her sides instead. "I met with Princess Dasienna in the Magister's palace. We saw the Magister together. We sought refuge, but the Magister's mage-guards attacked us. They tried to kill the princess. Elsanna helped us escape, and now the princess has requested a librarian carry a message to the Magister on her behalf to ask for parley."

Arkosh grew paler with each word. By the time she finished, his mouth hung open and he sucked in a rattling breath. "Maker's mercy," was all he said.

Maybe that hadn't been the best way to present the state of things. Tula clenched her fists tighter. "I would go, myself, but I was there when the Magister's guards beat down the door of the palace safe room. Even though I'm an apprentice librarian and should be considered a neutral party, I don't think the Magister will see it that way."

"Where is Elsanna? Is she with you?"

Tula didn't see who asked, but a subtle note of contempt in the question made her eyes narrow. "She's taken Princess Dasienna somewhere safe."

"Are we sure that *is* safe?" a librarian closer by asked, near enough that Tula saw the quiver of her chin and the nervous creases at the corners of her eyes.

"The princess has her Bladebearer with her," Tula said. "If anyone can keep her safe while there are goborrins in the city, he can."

A few confused faces were the only response that yielded. She gave herself a mental kick. She and Dasienna had uncovered the blade's existence in the library's books, but how many had explored the existence of the artifacts in their research? These librarians didn't know what she knew; the existence of the Spectrum Blade or what it could do was virtually unknown, even in the Great Library.

"Her personal guard," Arkosh supplied with a nod. "He seemed a competent youth when he escorted you to the library earlier this evening. If they're together, I trust they'll get by just fine."

A number of librarians relaxed. Arkosh was one of the librarian's elders, in addition to being a master librarian. A vote of confidence from him would be taken as sound judgment.

"I need to return to the princess to let her know if parley can be arranged," Tula said, deciding it best to continue on with her assignment. "Is it possible for someone to seek the Magister and find out?"

The old man's face fell. "With goborrins in the city, that's a big thing to ask."

One of the guardswomen stepped forward. "What if we escort the librarian in question?"

"I don't think that will help. The Magister isn't fond of the lot of you." Arkosh kept what he thought of that to himself, though after having spoken to him earlier that very night, Tula could see the spark of disapproval of the Magister's stance in his dark eyes.

Tula huffed. "There has to be some way!"

"You know she can't even leave the city without the Magister's approval," the guardswoman to her left said. "Either this gets solved, or tensions in the city will be worse than ever."

"And may the Maker have mercy on us all if anything ill befalls Sendassian's daughter while she's in Jadora," the old librarian muttered. "Gadranus and his armies are more than enough to deal with, without angering the king. The Magister thinks highly of our forces, but Amrochan could flatten us if it chose."

"Something which would never happen," Tula put in quickly. "Because someone's going to carry word to the Magister that the princess has called for negotiation in neutral territory. On that subject, she has also asked if she would be allowed to seek sanctuary in the library while she awaits an answer."

A request more troubling than the trouble already at hand,

judging by the way the master librarians who had clustered around them shifted on their feet.

"I don't believe we have the authority to tell her no," one of them said, the slow and formal statement making her desire clear. She did not want Dasienna there, but would not deny her.

Arkosh sighed. "The Great Library answers to Sendassian, so we are not as neutral in this as we would like to pretend. The princess may stay in the library. And I will carry her request to the Magister myself."

A wave of protest went up across the whole of the library.

"Oh, be quiet!" the old man snapped. "If anyone's to do it, it should be a master librarian, and one at the top of our hierarchy. I don't see any of you rushing to volunteer."

"You could be killed if you set foot outside the library," someone cried.

"Not if the Magister's guards are worth half as much as Elsanna's guardswomen," he said.

Tula resisted the urge to shrink. Delivering the request was a job, nothing more. She couldn't be blamed for this turn of events. "Are you certain, Master Arkosh?"

He sniffed. "Well, you certainly can't do it yourself. I'll find a contingent of the Magister's guard force and demand escort. There have to be hundreds of them in the city by now."

"The doors are heavily fortified at this point," one of the other master librarians said. "You'll have to take the tunnels out."

A guardswoman raised a hand. "One of us can help you through the tunnels."

Arkosh waved her off. "Oh, no need. I helped build them, I know where to go."

"Are you sure you don't want to take some guardswomen with you?" Tula asked.

"More than sure. I'm inviting enough trouble on myself already." He lowered himself to the floor to climb into the tunnel. "I expect I am to tell the Magister the meeting will happen here? And the princess will be present when we arrive?"

"Yes, Master Arkosh." Tula wasn't sure how long that would take, but if they ran, they would have more than enough time to deliver the news and make it back. There just wouldn't be time for research after the princess's arrival. She watched the old man lower himself into the passage beneath the library, then lifted her head. A number of librarians wore stormy expressions, while the rest had grown sober. Nearby, a few nosy apprentices who had gathered to listen gave her sympathetic frowns.

She blinked at them in response, pretending she didn't understand their concern, then followed Arkosh into the tunnels. "We'll be back with Princess Dasienna."

"And enough guardswomen to protect the library from the Magister's wrath, if you're smart," one of the master librarians grumbled.

Tula pretended she hadn't heard. Her soft boots muffled her landing, and she moved back to make space for the guardswomen to follow her. They hadn't been necessary, but their presence was a comfort, especially when one of the last things she saw through the hole in the library floor was a bitter glower in her direction.

"The library will be perfectly safe," a guardswoman said as their group descended into the tunnel.

At the end of the tunnel, Arkosh sniffed. "Optimist."

Tula turned to ask what he meant, but the old man was already gone.

A gentle hand on her shoulder notified her the guardswomen were all there. "Don't mind him," the woman said softly. "The Great Library is the jewel of Jadora. Even the Magister won't risk that."

Somewhere farther down a dark tunnel, Arkosh barked a laugh.

CHAPTER TWENTY-ONE

ZAIDE BRUSHED his hands down the front of his new coat as he stepped into the doorway. "It fits." The cut was strange compared to what he was used to, with its wide sleeves and open front, but it was comfortable. Elsanna had insisted on retying the cloth sash knotted around his waist the moment he'd stepped from the back room, where he'd hidden to change. He wasn't sure how she'd done it and had no hope of replicating the knot, but he had to admit it laid better that way. The belt supporting the Spectrum Blade's scabbard was certainly more comfortable without the big knot he'd tied riding up underneath it.

Lark stood and offered a slight smile. "Do you like it?"

"I like the pointy boots. They're neat." He cocked a foot out in front of him to show it off. He was less certain about the loose-fitting pants, but his own were too torn to use. As soon as he got his things back, he'd swap the outfit for something that suited him better, but anything was better than freezing.

"Red looks good on you. It's a nice contrast to your hair, without making you look cold." The princess planted her hands against her hips, early warning the conversation was about to shift. "Valla just sent a group of guardswomen outside. There's a fire nearby."

"I'm sure the city's full of goborrins by now," Zaide said. "They're probably looking for us." After seeing the tunnels beneath the palace and the goborrins feasting on the former Magister's bones, he had no doubt the city could be overrun. So much for the walls offering safety.

Lark gave a single nod. "Between goborrins and the Magister, I'm not sure it will be easy to avoid detection for long."

"Well, maybe Tula will bring us good news." He tried to smile.

As if she'd been summoned by the statement, Tula's head popped up from the hole in the middle of the floor. "Princess!"

Lark spat a rather unladylike exclamation. One of the guardswomen lounging nearby snorted a laugh.

"Your messenger has returned," Moros called from the tunnel with a note of dry humor.

"Yes, I see that," Lark replied as Tula scrabbled out of the hole.

The librarian straightened her coat and fiery hair as she got to her feet. "Your Highness, Master Arkosh said you can come to the library. He's going to speak to the Magister himself and will —oh, Zaide, you look nice. Red's a good color for you."

He blinked and smoothed his hands over the fabric again. "Um, thanks."

Tula went on as if she hadn't interrupted herself. "Master Arkosh is going to arrange for the Magister to meet you at the library. I'm not sure how he's going to get in, I guess through the tunnels? The whole library is barricaded, and all the librarians are there! I've never seen anything like it, it's so bright and full of people. We have to go, though, I don't know how long it will be. They want as many of the guardswomen there as possible, too. The whole city is full of goborrins and they're worried about the safety of the books. Where's Elsanna?"

Zaide held out both hands in a gesture for her to settle. "Slow down."

A hint of pink touched her coppery cheeks. "Sorry. It's just—"

"Adventure," Elsanna put in as she planted a hand against the middle of Zaide's back and shoved him out of the doorway. "Move, you're right in the path. Tula gets excited any time something out of the ordinary happens, Your Highness."

"Well, this certainly has been out of the ordinary." Lark tried to smile, but couldn't hold it. "Did you hear all that?"

Elsanna nodded. "I'll gather all the guardswomen I can and we'll follow you to the library. I'll send someone to let Valla and her group know what's going on, so they can meet us there."

"We have to go through the tunnels," Tula said. "The library doors are nailed shut and there are great big bookshelves stacked behind them so nobody can get in."

Zaide tilted his head to one side. "Have they got supplies in there?"

"Who knows. Maybe knowledge is the only sustenance we need. I hope we don't run into the Magister in the tunnels, though. That would be awkward." Tula grinned and turned in a circle before she seemed to realize the hole was still right beside her. "Oh, um, I guess I'll go back down. Moros, are you coming with us?"

The scarred man grunted. "There is little reason for me to stay behind. I trust the entrance to the library is slightly larger than this?"

Tula touched a finger to her chin. "Oh, yeah, you can probably get through. Well, maybe. Step back, I'm coming down."

Lark gave a rueful smile and shook her head as the librarian disappeared just as quickly as she'd emerged.

Zaide glanced around the pottery studio, but he had no need to prepare. Everything he had left was already on him, and Lark still held her bags. "Ready to go, Your Highness?"

"No," Lark admitted.

He posted himself at her side. "Yeah, I'm not sure about this, either. The library's supposed to be neutral, but meeting anywhere that's barricaded so we can't get out easily is..."

"Concerning?" she asked.

"Not a problem." Elsanna flicked her fingers as if to dismiss the whole situation. "Remember, Your Highness, we'll be there with you. It's as dangerous for the Magister as it is for you, but you'll have an advantage. We're better fighters than what the Magister's Mage-Guard holds, and you're the one with all the artifacts."

"And the sword," Zaide added with a tap to the Spectrum Blade's hilt.

"Which can't be used against people," Lark said.

He shrugged. "It can be. It just doesn't like it." When he had the chance, he'd add a second blade to his belt. He regretted leaving his guard-issue sword behind, but how was he to know the Spectrum Blade would react that way to fighting humans? Never mind that he hadn't stopped to consider humans would be part of the fight. Until now, they'd only faced monsters, but he'd known monsters didn't comprise the entirety of Gadranus's forces. There were people there, too, he'd been told. Broken-born like him, who he'd have to fight eventually. The thought of finally meeting one of his own people on the battlefield, instead of over a hearty meal, was an odd one to grapple with.

Lark cast him a doubtful look. "When you did before—"

"If it comes to it, I'll deal with it," Zaide said. "Protecting you is part of my job now, right?"

"We'll just hope it doesn't come to that." Elsanna pointed toward the hole in the floor. "Go. Moros, go with them. The rest of us will be just behind."

"Be cautious, Cactus." The warden stepped back when Lark moved to the ladder.

"Never," Elsanna said with a laugh.

As soon as the princess was on the ground, Zaide followed.

Somehow, he'd expected the curled toes on his pointed boots would be awkward or get in the way. They didn't, and he sighed contentedly when his feet touched the floor and he couldn't feel the chill. "Before we go see the Desheni, we're going to need real heavy clothing. It's nice to be warm again, and I don't think I'm ready to give that up."

"Before we go see the Desheni, we need to take care of our problems in Jadora," Lark said.

Moros excused himself from the conversation and started down the tunnel. "This way."

They followed. Before long, the guardswomen began to file into the passage behind them. Several carried lanterns, so Zaide left the Spectrum Blade sheathed and rested his right hand against it.

Every time he touched the sword, he expected it to react, but it had remained quiet. He supposed he should be grateful.

Tula wasn't far ahead, and they caught up with her before long. She walked with a hop in her step, her ponytail swinging behind her like a pendulum. "This is exciting, right? This will definitely go in the history books. Do you think they'll let me help write them, since I've been part of it? I'm still going to give the elders my presentation on the Molten Dagger, but maybe this is part of it. That means it's part of my studies, right? So my name will be on it?"

"You talk a great deal," Moros observed.

"Only when she's not studying," Lark said. "When she's doing research, it's impossible to get anything out of her."

Zaide grinned. "Yeah, she wouldn't even let me look at the books on the ship. Is it going to be like that in the library?"

"She probably won't let you touch them," Elsanna put in from somewhere farther back in the tunnel. "She'll make you stand back while she puts on dainty white gloves and turns the pages for you."

"That's not a thing librarians do," Zaide said.

Tula squinted over her shoulder. "Yeah, what? We don't use gloves."

"You don't?" Elsanna asked, surprised.

"No, they don't. The books have survived countless ages and hundreds of hands, there's really no necessity for gloves when working with them. If they've lasted this long, there's no harm in a few more fingerprints." Lark hefted her bag a little higher on her shoulder. Zaide paused to offer his hand, silent suggestion he could carry it for her, but she ignored him and kept walking.

"Yeah. As long as there's no food on your fingers or anything." Tula's nose crinkled. "You wouldn't believe how many people try to bring food into the library. Oh. Maybe that means there won't be provisions in there. Hmm."

"A problem for when we get there," Lark said.

Zaide nodded. "If it goes well, we won't need provisions at all." The librarians still might, but he suspected once they had a chance to give the Spectrum Blade the Magister's blessing, everything would change.

Something skimmed against his senses at the thought, a soft buzz that gave him the impression of agreement.

Awake now, are you? he thought at the sword. As he expected, the sensation faded, and no further response came. He tempered his frustration. He didn't know how the blade communicated, or how sentient it was, but he supposed Lark would ferret out information on that subject after everything was settled. He brushed a fingertip down the hilt. *Maybe after we get the Magister's power infused in you and take care of the goborrins in the city.*

Which he hoped would come after a night's rest. Or a day's rest, depending on when it happened. He'd skipped far too many nights of sleep. His eyes burned with fatigue, but if a librarian was already off to retrieve the Magister, there wouldn't be time for a nap.

"Here it is, this next one on the left," Tula said. She rounded the corner with a hop.

"She is delightful," Moros said.

"She's something," Zaide muttered.

Lark dug an elbow into his side.

He rubbed it and gave her a dirty look. He hadn't meant it in a bad way, but there was no time for complaining. At the end of the passage, Tula was already up the ladder, pushing the switch to move the slab in the library's floor aside. She disappeared into the bright room beyond.

"Princesses first?" Zaide motioned for her to take the lead, but Moros grasped both of them by their shoulders and pulled them out of the way. Elsanna led half her guardswomen straight up the ladder. Murmurs filled the library above, too many voices in too low of tones to pick out anything they said.

"Princesses should wait until the way is clear," the warden said.

Lark remained still and silent until the scarred man put out an arm to halt the procession.

"Now." Moros turned them toward the ladder. "Half your force first. Half your force last."

Zaide looked up into the library, then stepped back to let Lark take the lead. "It sounds peaceful upstairs." Some cheerful conversation reached his ears, but who knew how long it would last.

Lark climbed, and he politely averted his eyes, rather than watching her backside. Instead, he ended up facing Moros, who stared down at him with his brick-like expression and made the moment far more uncomfortable.

The scarred man pointed. "You're next."

"You're not going to fit," Zaide said.

"Then I will remove some of the stones."

Maybe the Molten Dagger would help with that. Zaide contemplated asking to borrow it as he scaled the ladder, then quickly discarded the idea. They were supposed to be holding a diplomatic meeting. How would it look if the Magister arrived at the foot of the ladder while Zaide used the precious artifact they sought to barter with to chip mortar out of the floor?

Despite how fast he climbed, Zaide emerged to find Lark had already rounded the large desk and positioned herself in the middle of a group of librarians near the corner where they'd stood with Tula on their first visit, gathering books and formulating a plan.

"I realize we are short on time," the princess said, "but it is imperative that I know whether or not he will have the power necessary to help us. The Magister appears to harbor animosity toward the crown, which makes it clear his word alone cannot be trusted. I need some way to demand he prove his power and his willingness to aid us before I give him the dagger."

One of the old librarians shook her head. "I understand, Your Highness, but we simply can't help. We've sought information on the history of the Magister's power for years, but it's as close-kept a secret as... well, as the Molten Dagger's protection."

Zaide made his way toward them. "But you know what he's capable of, right? Even if you don't know where the magic comes from, you have to have seen the Magister do something at some point to show he has it."

The librarians exchanged frowns, and the tiniest hint of worry drew creases between Lark's delicate brows.

"You've never seen the Magister wield magic?" The question came out calmly, but disbelief shone in her eyes.

The old woman shook her head again.

"You've never seen *any* of the Magisters wield magic?" Zaide asked.

"The Magister is immensely secretive. Not only this Magister, but every Magister before him. You'd have better luck asking his guards."

Zaide turned to scan the library in hopes of finding Elsanna, but she had disappeared from view. With all the nooks and crannies between shelves, he could only assume she was scouting, or else setting up some sort of ambush in case something went wrong.

"Very well." Lark lifted her chin and spun on her boot heel to march across the library. Zaide trailed along behind her. He expected her to stop near one of the groups of guardswomen, but she passed them without a glance. Near the back of the library, behind one of the staircases, Tula stood with a cluster of apprentices, and the whole group went silent when the princess approached. Most stared at Lark in awe, but Tula's face brightened with curiosity.

"You've heard stories about the Magister." It wasn't a question. Lark planted her hands on her hips. She expected results.

"Yes," Tula said slowly. Her eyes flicked to the apprentices around her as her expression softened into something more cautious. How she'd heard them was supposed to be a secret, Zaide concluded. Which meant even the librarians were unaware of Tula's familial connections.

Lark hitched her shoulders in something that wasn't quite a shrug, but made it clear she awaited a more detailed answer.

Tula stepped away from the group and pointed toward the stairs. "Come upstairs, I'll show you what I can."

Again, Zaide trailed behind them. Part of him felt he should try and find somewhere to sit and rest while he could, but uneasiness prickled up and down his spine and made it impossible to consider rest an option.

They climbed to the second level and Tula's good cheer returned along the way. "What sort of stories were you interested in?"

"Any about his power," Lark said. "Examples of what he can do, what to expect, what would indicate he's inherited capability from his predecessor. I know you don't know anything about the source of his power, but surely you've heard about his magic."

Tula grimaced. "Oh. Well, I'm not sure you'll like what I have heard, then."

"The Magister does have magic, right? It's in his name." Zaide paused. "Title. I guess Magister isn't his name."

"It may as well be," Tula said. "Once they take the title of Magister, who they were before sort of disappears. They're the Magister, nothing else. The names of some go on record, but just as footnotes. Who they were before rarely matters."

"But he has magic," Lark pressed.

"Well, yes. Supposedly. The thing is, when it came to the previous Magister, the one Elsanna served? He... uh, he never actually used any."

They stopped between the shelves, safely away from prying eyes, though they couldn't rule out ears. The library was crowded, though from what they saw, most of the librarians clustered near the doors in anticipation of an attack.

The princess gave her head a twitch of a shake. "He never used it? At all?"

"Not that any of the guardswomen ever saw." Tula spread her hands and gave a wide shrug. "Who knows what he could do? He was sworn in as Magister in private, and after that—"

Zaide raised a finger. "Wait, sworn in?"

Tula's nose crinkled. "Well, of course. They all are. After the next Magister is identified, they're taken somewhere private and sworn in, so they can begin their oversight of the city."

"And this happens when the old Magister passes?" Lark asked.

The librarian cocked her head to the side. "No, just when he chooses to step down. Why?"

Lark buried her face in her hands and Zaide winced.

"Tula, ah..." He scratched behind his better ear. "I'm sure there's a lot more to how things are managed, but it sounds like..."

"Like you don't have a Magister," the princess groaned.

"What? Of course we do!" Tula tucked in her chin and drew back a step, offended. "He's probably on his way right now. I mean, sure, he's a fake usurper kind of Magister, but he—"

"He doesn't have any power, Tula," Zaide interrupted. "I was there when Resia took the mantle of Kolmari Elder. I saw how this is supposed to work. The Elder, Magister, and Shaman are supposed to be the same. When one dies, another is chosen by the power and takes its place. You can't just retire from being the Maker's chosen representative of magic!"

"But he's supposed to help us! That's why we're here, isn't it?" Tula's voice cracked. "He has to, right?"

"Your Highness!" Elsanna shouted from somewhere below. "He's here!"

Lark gritted her teeth and squeezed her eyes closed.

Zaide inched closer. "What do you want to do?" He kept his voice low, sure no one else would hear.

"We've already called for him. We have to deal with him now."

"He'll demand the dagger," Tula whispered. She worried her hands in front of her jeweled navel, the twisting motion reflective of the knots that had to be in her stomach.

"The idea was we'd give him the dagger if he could help us," Zaide said. "He can't, so he doesn't get anything."

Lark rubbed her brow. "I guess we know now why the Magisters are all so secretive."

Zaide squeezed her shoulder in gentle reassurance. "Maybe he can point us in the right direction."

"Maybe." The princess straightened and her usual mask of calm composure returned as she strode back to the top of the stairs. "We'll stand here."

"Take the high ground?" Zaide shifted so his right hip was forward, scabbard prominently displayed. He curled the fingers of his left hand around the hilt of his sword and a thrum answered him. He scoffed. "Don't you go getting excited. It's people again."

Tula squinted at him. "Who are you talking to?"

"The—never mind. Look." He nodded toward the room below.

Armored guards worked their way up through the hole in the floor, one at a time. They formed a protective ring around it, while the guardswomen formed a larger ring around them.

"I have a plan." Lark lifted her chin, imperious as ever.

"Good, because there he is." Zaide resisted the urge to draw the Spectrum Blade when the Magister's head poked through the hole. A guard helped him through the gap and assisted in smoothing his robes. "But you know who I don't see?"

Tula scuffled around Lark's back to position herself at the princess's other side. "Captain Jinohe isn't down there."

"Trying to get the city under control, maybe?" It was the most generous assumption Zaide could give him. The looks he got from the girls beside him said it was wishful thinking.

Lark stepped forward. "Magister," she called. "It seems we are both in possession of something the other would like to have."

"Something that never should have been yours," the man replied with a scowl.

"Indeed." Lark shared the word so softly, no one below would hear. She clutched the strap of her bag before she spoke again. "Contrary to what you may believe, I am not here to interfere in Jadoran politics. Our purpose here is merely to have one of the Magister's duties fulfilled. If you will do your part in awakening the sleeping power of the Spectrum Blade, then I will gladly leave the Molten Dagger in your hands. Any disputes with the crown are with my father, not me."

The ring of guardswomen rotated so Elsanna was nearest the foot of the staircase, directly between the Magister and the princess.

"Come down then, child." The Magister strode forward as if they weren't there. "Let's make a deal."

The princess released her bag and took the first step.

CHAPTER TWENTY-TWO

THE MAGISTER SPREAD his arms in invitation as he made for the foot of the stairs. Zaide fought back the notion it was inviting to his sword, too. He'd do anything necessary to keep Lark safe, but he wasn't eager to repeat the brain-searing headache the sword had given him only hours before. Still, he kept his hand on the Spectrum Blade as he followed Lark down the stairs.

He wasn't as intimidating a figure as the guardswomen, but he was the one the Magister studied, not them.

"You see my Bladebearer," Lark said as she walked. She took each step with a languid grace, but paused halfway down the steps. "And you've seen his sword, so am I to assume you have some idea of what I'm after?"

"The princess seeks power." The Magister's eyes narrowed with his smile, but they were anything but kind. "Don't we all."

"Not really," Zaide said before Lark raised a hand to silence him.

Tula fought back a grin as she stopped to Lark's left.

At least someone appreciated his input.

The princess slid a familiar sheath from her bag. "The Molten Dagger was a vital key toward unlocking my Bladebearer's potential. The artifact remains useful, but I am willing to release it back into the hands of Jadora's Magister if the next key can be offered in return. Have you the ability to bless his blade?"

The circle of guardswomen tightened and the Magister halted with a snort. "To barge into my city and question my power is an insult."

"And to set your Mage-Guard upon the crown princess of Amroch is an act of treason. My father would have your head."

"Your father isn't here," the Magister sneered.

Luckily, Zaide thought. He had no doubt Sendassian would have struck the man down already.

"And you are not answering my question," Lark said. "Can you bless the blade, or was that power lost with the Magister you had slain when the dagger slipped into my grasp?"

A few small gasps went up among the librarians. They had formed a ring of their own around the guardswomen, another barrier between the false Magister and the princess, but Zaide doubted it was for Lark's safety. More than one of the master librarians sent furtive glances toward the bookshelves. The books, the knowledge, were all they cared to protect.

The Magister scoffed. "There is no evidence for this accusation."

"Probably because you fed it to the goborrins you've got chained in the palace dungeon." Zaide said.

From the ring of guardswomen, Moros nodded with a grunt of agreement. When had he joined the lineup? He was comically out of place, a towering beast of a man surrounded by golden-skinned women with swords in their hands. The warden had yet to draw his blade.

"This is indeed a serious accusation," one of the librarians interjected. Several in their ring had turned toward the stairs. "You mean to say—"

Elsanna tossed her head. "That the old Magister was torn to pieces and fed to the pigs." She remained rooted in place, her back turned to the scholars, her blade pointed toward the red-robed man before her. "I would have cut you in half, you viper. But that's why you and Jinohe had me chained, isn't it?"

More murmurs.

"Answer the question," Lark snapped, a fiery glint in her eyes.

The Magister paused within reach of Elsanna's sword. "Of course I can bless his blade. Why else would you have come? It's my power you need. My authority, my grasp of magic. You know this, Your Highness."

Lark motioned toward Zaide's scabbard. "Then bless it."

The man's brows rose. "Here?"

"Now."

Zaide drew a few inches of steel from his scabbard, the sword soundless against the soft leather.

"Your Highness, I don't think you understand what you're asking for." The Magister's wide sleeves swished as he spread his arms wide. "The source of my power cannot be reached here, as I am."

Lark gave her chin a subtle tilt. "As you are?"

"When you took the Molten Dagger from Jadora, you took more than you realize, Your Highness. When it was locked away, so was the Magister's power. Do you understand?"

Her fingers tightened around the dagger's sheath. "This?"

He nodded.

"The *dagger* is the source of power?" Tula peered at it, but the princess tucked her wrist under to hide the blade from sight.

Zaide unsheathed the rest of his sword. "That sounds like an excuse. You accuse us of lacking evidence, but I don't see anything supporting your claims, either."

"I don't know." Tula rubbed her chin. "It would make sense. If we haven't seen any visible signs of a Magister with power since the dagger was put away behind that wall, then..."

"It's possible it's true." Lark's grip tightened further and her knuckles grew pale. "Do the librarians have any information to uphold this claim?"

Every librarian in the city huddled within the Great Library, yet no one spoke.

"Not promising, Magister."

"But lying to you gains me little, Your Highness."

"And killing me does?"

His mouth twisted with displeasure. "It would have gained me the dagger."

"Without having to offer anything in return," Lark mused. "Short-sighted, considering what it would have cost you in the long run. Zaide, go down."

A shiver coursed up his arm as he swept the Spectrum Blade to the forefront and began his descent. *Steady*, he cautioned, as if it meant anything.

Behind him, Lark's boots clicked on the stairs as she followed. "Elsanna, allow him to meet us."

The guardswoman stepped aside and let the Magister pass. His guards started after him and she held out her sword to block the way.

"Your guard retinue and mine will both stand aside," Lark said.

"But they haven't," the Magister sneered. "You have two, and I have none."

The princess paused on the stairs. "Tula, join the other librarians."

"Yes, Your Highness." Tula curtsied and slipped down the stairs, holding both hands where they could be seen as she gave the Magister a wide berth. The man watched her go with a curl to his lip.

"Zaide." The way Lark's eyes fell on him were early warning he wouldn't like the order that followed. "Lay the sword on the floor."

"But—" he started. Her hand snapped up to command silence.

"He can't touch it," she whispered. "None of us can."

"I'm not worried about the sword. I'm worried about you."

She quirked a brow. "I am more than capable of defending myself."

He couldn't argue with that, but it still didn't sit well. "Give me the Hymnflute, then."

Lark pointed at the floor.

Not until he cooperated, then. He set his jaw and descended to lay the Spectrum Blade at the foot of the stairs. His fingertips tingled as they left the hilt. When he straightened and turned toward her, she took her bag from her shoulder and held it out for him to take.

"Better?" Lark asked as Zaide took the bag and retreated to stand with the guardswomen.

"Infinitely." The Magister stared at the sword on the floor the way one might watch a snake.

The princess continued down the staircase to meet him. "The moment the dagger is in your grasp, you will bless the blade. We will consider our business here complete, and we will leave the city to continue our expedition. Do we have a deal?"

"As fair an offer as I could ever ask, Your Highness."

"That's not what I asked."

The Magister chuckled. "Your father has made a sound politician out of you. I agree to your terms."

Lark descended the last step and held out the dagger by its sheath.

His hand closed around the hilt. Ever so slowly, he moved backwards with the Molten Dagger in his grasp.

Zaide rooted in Lark's bag until he found the Hymnflute, his pulse quick in his throat.

"I thank you for your flexibility in this matter," the Magister said as he bowed his head in respect. He lifted his robes a shade as he knelt beside the Spectrum Blade. "I must admit, there were times I was not sure this was real."

"Which?" Lark lifted her chin. "The dagger, or the sword?"

"Both, I suppose. I feel an immense level of relief to know for certain what is now within reach."

Zaide drew the Hymnflute to the top of the bag.

"You will now bless the sword," Lark ordered.

"Of course, Your Highness." The Magister unsheathed the Molten Dagger and curved his hand around its glassy blade, as if to savor the warmth that radiated from it. He tucked in his chin and closed his eyes as his lips twitched with silent words—a prayer, maybe. Or a curse.

Lark remained still, her toes beside the Spectrum Blade. Its surface shimmered in a pattern that struck Zaide as anticipation, but without the blade in his hand, he couldn't be sure. Or at least, he didn't think he could feel it from there. Now that he thought about it, he wasn't always touching the sword when it sent those waves of feeling through his system. As long as it was strapped to his side, that was enough. Was it proximity, then? Or did something else constitute the bond that seemed to have come with the blade choosing him?

The librarians still ringed them, though they had split into two groups. The Magister's guards and the guardswomen glowered at each other like alley cats, neither side happy about their containment, but the librarians outnumbered them all and showed no sign they were about to let a fight erupt among the books. Only Zaide and Tula were left unhindered. That she could move as she pleased made sense; she was one of them. But as Zaide slipped the Hymnflute from the princess's bag and held it ready in both hands, the librarians flowed around him like smoke, clearing the way for him to move forward and rejoin the princess, or retreat and take refuge with the guardswomen, where he was supposed to be.

"By the Maker's blessing, Jadora will have a true Magister again." A smile twisted the Magister's lips and his eyes narrowed as he held the Molten Dagger before him and blew across the blade. Its glowing veins brightened, like coals given new life, and embers drifted through the air. They swirled and sank to settle on the Spectrum Blade's surface and the sword reacted, sparks of red flashing on each contact.

Zaide tensed, but remained still. That wasn't it. That was nothing like the flow of Resia's power as it coursed through the blade. He tried to catch Lark's eye, to silently ask if she knew, but she remained focused on the Magister and the blade at her feet. If she suspected anything, she didn't show it, and her motionless features told him nothing of her thoughts.

The Magister turned the dagger downward and gripped its small hilt with both hands. He drew a deep, triumphant breath, and plunged the Molten Dagger into the stone floor.

A few startled shouts rose as the glowing blade sank into the rock and an acrid stench flooded the library. Smoke poured from the stone and angry protests went up from a dozen master librarians.

The smoke stung Zaide's eyes and he lifted the Hymnflute to blow it away, but Lark's hand twitched, a single finger raised in signal to wait.

Light radiated outward from the Molten Dagger, illuminating one stone at a time in the library floor. It swelled past Lark's feet and the kneeling Magister, a wide circle of power with the Molten Dagger and the Spectrum Blade in the center.

Reflexively, everyone else stepped back, leaving Zaide alone. He stood, steadfast, as the circle of light swept under his feet. A breath of wind that hadn't come from the Hymnflute stirred the air as a deep sense of wrongness clawed the edges of his mind.

"Rise," the Magister whispered.

The ground beneath them trembled.

CHAPTER TWENTY-THREE

"WHAT HAVE YOU DONE?" Arkosh cried.

The circle of light streaked outward and dissipated as the ground quaked beneath them. The Spectrum Blade rattled against the floor.

Crimson flashes and sparks flew from the Molten Dagger as the stone it was embedded in split. Smoke billowed from the cracks.

Zaide raised the Hymnflute to play. Wind rushed outward with the first note, pushing the smoke to the far reaches of the library. Guardswomen rushed toward the Magister and the Magister's guards intercepted them. Swords clashed and screams rose, and below it all, the earth groaned.

Silver flashed in Lark's hands and she descended on the Magister with fire in her eyes. "What is this? What did you do?" she demanded. Her knives pressed to the man's throat, but he toppled backwards onto the shattering floor and laughed.

"Jadora's might will rise!" he crowed. "Let's see your father hold us under his thumb now."

New smoke gushed from the expanding cracks. The Molten Dagger's light intensified against the black clouds.

A chorus of coughs went up from those nearby.

Arkosh waved his arms. "The books! Move the books!"

But the clusters of librarians had already begun to scatter. Masters and apprentices both scrambled about like frenzied ants, arms filled with precious knowledge. Some tore at the barricade that blocked the front door.

Zaide tried again to clear the air, but there was nowhere for the smoke to go. The Hymnflute's gust chased the clouds away, only for them to creep back each time he drew breath to continue.

"The blade!" Lark snapped as she planted a foot on the Magister's chest. The tips of her knives drew blood.

The Spectrum Blade flashed as if to emphasize the order. Zaide darted forward to sweep it into his grasp and almost collided with Tula as she arrived to jerk the Molten Dagger from the stone.

"It's too late to stop it." The Magister grinned. "My power will awaken, and nothing will save you now."

Lark bared her teeth. "I should have let Elsanna kill you!"

The library's front doors exploded inward and a new round of screams filled the smoky air. The squalling cries of goborrins joined the frightened voices and the peals of steel.

Something twanged.

Lark gasped and stumbled backwards with a crossbow bolt in her chest.

Zaide dropped both artifacts to catch her. "Lark!"

She grimaced, but her eyes went to the door as goborrins poured in with Jinohe at the lead.

The captain tossed the crossbow aside. Before it hit the ground, Elsanna launched herself at him with blades in either hand. Goborrins spilled in around them and armed librarians and guardswomen met them head-on.

"Princess!" Tula helped Zaide lower her to the floor.

"Kill him!" Lark snarled through clenched teeth.

Zaide caught the Spectrum Blade's hilt and a surge of anger

that matched his own flared up his arm. "Tula, get the spring." He went for the captain in the swarm of goborrins.

Elsanna battered him with strikes, but he parried every blow. Zaide came in from the side and struck hard. The Spectrum Blade sparked as it hit the man's armor and drove him to the ground, and Elsanna's next swipe tore into a gap between metal plates.

Zaide didn't linger to watch him die.

The Magister had scrambled backwards and found his feet. He surrounded himself with guards, but a handful of guardswomen chipped at their defenses. A goborrin loomed above them and Moros intercepted it. Zaide ducked past their brawl and slipped between guards to launch himself at the Magister.

A pulse of something repelled him with a shock.

Magic.

Zaide hissed as he hit the floor. He shoved himself back to his feet the moment he landed, but the floor buckled and rolled when he stood.

"The books!" a librarian howled.

"The princess!" cried another.

Above them both, Tula's shriek caught Zaide's attention.

He spun toward her as a chasm opened in the middle of the library's floor and an enormous clawed foot reached forth to slam against the stone.

"Maker's mercy," he breathed.

A second foot followed. Massive talons gouged furrows in the floor as the creature pulled itself upward, and a crown of horns rose from the fissure. Its scales glowed like hot iron and smoke poured from the beast's maw.

"Zaide!" Tula screamed.

The monster's head turned first toward the sound, then swung back the other direction. Bright golden eyes fixed on the Spectrum Blade and it snorted. Steam rose from its nostrils.

In response, the Spectrum Blade flared.

Wings spread from the monster's back, shedding ash and embers across the library.

"What *is* that?" Elsanna cried as it rose from the earth.

"*That*," Arkosh said glumly, "is the fall of Jadora."

Its tail lashed behind it as it pulled its body from the pit and lowered its head toward Zaide.

His heart crashed against his ribs with such force, he wondered how they didn't crack. Slowly, he shifted to grip the Spectrum Blade with both hands and held the blade poised between them.

A soft snort sent a cascade of smoke and scorching steam across him and he flinched, but did not move.

All around him, people ran. Librarians with arms full of books fled past goborrins at the door. Even the monsters stared, their little black eyes glazed with awe—or maybe fear. Fighting stilled and mage-guards and guardswomen gaped at the beast.

Its reptilian jaw opened, embers bubbling in its throat.

"Dragon!" the Magister shouted.

The beast's mouth snapped shut, its head whipping around to face the man who dared address it.

The Magister stood with his arms open and his hands spread in welcome. "I've summoned you to receive your power. Bless me now, so that Jadora might have a true Magister at last!"

Zaide started forward, but Elsanna slipped between him and the dragon.

"We have to go," she insisted.

Every inch of the library shuddered when the dragon took a step. Zaide's eyes darted to the Magister again, but the guardswoman moved to block his line of sight.

"The ceiling is cracking. The library is going to collapse. We have to take the princess and leave!"

The princess. Zaide spat a curse and spun to look for her.

Tula and Lark sat at the bottom of the stairs, the latter slumped forward with her head hanging.

He sprinted toward them, passing under the dragon's wing and its rain of embers. The glowing motes singed his skin.

Tula shot him a worried look when he arrived. "The spring helps, but it's not instant."

"I'll be fine," Lark wheezed, though when she lifted her head, Zaide saw the blood that soaked her shirt.

He rammed the Spectrum Blade into its sheath and crouched to slide an arm under her knees.

Her whole body went stiff. "What are you—"

"Yell at me later." He slid his other arm around Lark's back and lifted her from the stairs.

"Ooh, you're strong, snow boy," Tula said.

Zaide scowled. "Okay, you're not going to call me that again, or I'm going to... think of some kind of witty but insulting Jadoran nickname for you as soon as we're out of here. Go!"

The dragon's tail swung mere inches over the top of his head and Lark huddled against him. Despite her initial protest, she said nothing more and let him carry her without complaint.

Tula ran alongside them, the Molten Dagger in one hand and the Vale Hymnflute in the other.

"Where's the spring?" he shouted over the screams and the scrape of claws against stone.

Lark touched her bloodstained shirt. "Here."

Guardswomen clustered by the doors, pressing goborrins back from the stairs as the librarians escaped with what books they could save. Valla and Moros were among them, both distracted. Instead of joining the fray, Zaide hurried down the steps and darted around the library's corner.

"We need somewhere to hide." He glanced to Tula for ideas.

She nodded. "Head for the west gate."

"Which way is west? It's dark outside!" Even if it weren't, plumes of smoke rose from a dozen places in the city to blot out the sky, hiding the stars and any hope he had of orienting himself.

Tula turned to lead the way.

Lark wasn't as heavy as he'd expected, but Zaide's back ached and his shoulders burned by the time they reached a small plaza beyond a narrow portcullis. A fountain sat in the plaza's center, illuminated by lanterns strung overhead, but no water flowed.

"This isn't really hiding," Zaide said slowly, masking that he'd grown short of breath, "but it'll do for now."

He crossed to the fountain to lower Lark to its wall. Her golden skin had grown ashen and her lips pale, and when she slid from his arms to sit by herself, she was so weak it put a chill in his middle.

Tula sat beside her, subdued. "I don't think your plan worked, Your Highness."

"Offering myself the spirit of fairness, my plan never involved a dragon." Lark grunted softly and pressed a hand over her wounded shoulder. It no longer bled, but how long it would take the Captured Spring's liquid to heal it fully, Zaide didn't know.

He slid an arm behind Lark to help support her and turned his eyes to Tula. "I thought you said projectiles are illegal in Jadora."

The librarian snorted. "Murdering the Magister to steal his place is also illegal, but that didn't stop anyone, did it? Jinohe's the chief captain of the new Magister's Mage-Guard, right? He's got authority over the city's gatekeepers. He's probably the only person who could smuggle them in."

"He was the chief captain of the Mage-Guard," Zaide said. "He's dead."

Lark released a soft hiss. "Did you—"

He guessed at the question before she finished. "Elsanna killed him. I'm fine."

The princess relaxed a shade. "I was hasty. That was probably a mistake."

"I don't know about that," Tula said. "He did try to kill you."

"But in killing him, we've also lost a valuable source of information." Lark probed her shoulder with two fingers and winced.

Zaide caught her hand and forced it down. "I don't think we need information at this point. And you don't need to be poking at that, you need to wait a minute for the spring to heal you."

She huffed, but a vague smile touched her lips. "Your turn to play healer, hmm?"

"I thought I was the healer." Tula sat with her hands against her knees. "I gave you the magic potion stuff."

"That you did. And pulled the bolt from my shoulder." Despite Zaide's effort to stop her, she lifted her hand and poked around the injury again. "I don't think he hit anything important, at least. I doubt he had much time for practice before shooting that thing at me."

Zaide tried to be patient as he took her hand and moved it again. This time, he gripped her fingers tight so she couldn't continue. "It introduces problems, though. If there's one of those in the city, there are probably more. He was probably planning to use them against the guardswomen."

"Huh." Tula drummed her fingertips against her chin. "Maybe the guardswomen wearing so little armor isn't a good idea."

He quirked a brow. "You're just *now* thinking that?"

"Hey, excuse me. You saw them fighting in there, right? Jinohe's guards didn't even touch them. Not a single one. That's why it's scary that they show so much skin. It's to show that they're fearless, and that they don't have any scars. They're untouchable."

"Until they aren't," Lark sighed. She tried to pry her hand from Zaide's grasp, so he held tighter. After a moment of effort, she relented. "I understand the capability of the guardswomen is a point of pride for Jadora, but it's obviously created a clear weakness, too."

"And the guardswomen aren't experienced fighting in

heavier armor," Zaide added. "Even if it weren't for Jinohe and crossbows, we don't know what kind of weapons the goborrins in the city might have."

Tula considered that, then let her head drop. "So we're at a disadvantage no matter what we do, now."

A rattle started farther up the street. Zaide's hand went for the Spectrum Blade, but the small squad of armored men that hustled by paid them no mind.

"Standard guard," Tula said.

Lark squinted at their backs as they rushed to answer whatever order they'd been given. "How can you tell?"

"No red streamers or crests on their armor." Zaide tapped his chest to mark the places he'd seen them affixed, and Tula nodded in agreement.

The princess watched them for a time, then moved to stand.

Zaide all but leaped from his seat to help her.

To his surprise, she grabbed his wrist to stabilize herself. "If the city's guard is still about and Jinohe is dead, they'll answer to Elsanna again, won't they?"

"Maybe? I don't really know how the guard hierarchy works," Tula said. "Though they all know Elsanna, and I think they're all scared of her. They'd probably listen to her no matter what, just because of that."

"I don't know why they're scared. She seems perfectly nice." Zaide rested his other hand against Lark's back to steady her when she swayed.

"To you," Tula said with a smirk. "You haven't made her angry."

"Then I hope I never do. Lark, where are you going?" Zaide followed along as she started toward the south, but he tried to restrict her pace.

The princess had so little fight in her, it was concerning. "The south gate has all sorts of highly defensible rooms. It's a good place to hole up for now."

Tula bounded ahead to stand in their path. "There are fires to the south. That means goborrins. That's why I brought you west. The fires that were here are under control now."

"Then you walk with me, and Zaide will kill the goborrins." Lark pushed him away and held a hand out to the librarian.

Zaide caught her arm. "Let me carry you."

Her eyes flashed anger. "I am not some doll to be toted about as you please. Tula and I will walk. You will fight. Do I make myself clear?"

Instead of replying, Tula took her hand and slid close to aid her in walking.

Zaide sighed. No sense in arguing with her once she made up her mind. "I'll lead."

The princess gave no confirmation, so he drew his sword and moved ahead.

Bands of guards were scattered throughout the city. Some stopped long enough to look at them as they worked their way back to the south gate, but no one recognized the princess, for no one stopped to offer assistance. They passed no packs of goborrins, which was promising for the state of the city, but the thick smoke that flooded the sky never let up.

"The palace is burning," Tula whispered after a time.

"Let's hope the library's not." Zaide glanced to the sky now and then, afraid he might see burning wings in the smoke overhead, but nothing came. Would the blade in his hand react to the dragon? It had glowed in the library, but there had been goborrins there, too.

Near the south gate, people swarmed. Gate guards held them back and forced them into orderly lines. The line that filed out through the man-sized gate moved slower than the tricen Zaide faced in the north.

"So many fleeing," Lark murmured.

"Can you blame them?" Zaide kept his sword ready, but fell back to help her walk. With Lark supported between his shoulder and Tula's, the going was a little faster.

They didn't make it far before a guard stopped them.

"Departures must stay in line." The rasp in the man's throat indicated he'd said it a hundred times already.

Lark slid free to stand on her own. "No departure. I am Princess Dasienna, heir to the throne of Amroch. We've come from the library. Let us rest in your facilities here."

The man blinked at her before recognition sparked. "Your Highness!" He thumped a fist over his heart and offered a deep bow. "You're injured. Please, let me escort you inside."

She acquiesced with a wave and followed him into the poorly-lit hall where the individual questioning rooms sat.

"I thought he looked familiar," Tula said.

Zaide scanned the guards at the gate as they entered. "They're all the same to me. Guards in armor."

"Really? His eyes are so bright, I thought he stood out."

"If you say so. I wasn't looking at his eyes." Zaide had been more concerned with the weapons at the man's belt. They had no way of knowing who among the guard force was trustworthy. One of the questioning rooms could be a refuge, or it could become a prison.

Unaware or else uninterested in their conversation, the man stopped at the end of the hall. "Here, Your Highness. Have you need of a medic?"

"I've been seen. I'll be fine." Lark was still unsteady on her feet, but she retained her composure. She always did. She slipped into the room without ceremony. By the time Zaide reached the door, she had already crossed to the desk and taken the chair. Her eyes were heavy and he thought she'd grown more pale.

"Bring water, please," he said to the guard beside the door. "And something to eat."

The guard bowed and hurried back down the hallway as Zaide and Tula slipped in to join the princess. Once they were alone, Lark leaned against the desk.

Zaide strode toward her, but she raised a hand, palm out.

"I'm fine. I just need to rest." She crossed her arms atop the desk and rested her head against them.

"We should look at your injury, Your Highness," Tula said. "I know you said what you drank from the spring would be enough, but we haven't had time to test how much is required, or how fast it works."

"I'm fine," Lark repeated, sharper.

Zaide remained standing in the center of the room, unsure what to do.

After a time, the guard returned with a pitcher of water and a handful of earthenware mugs in one hand, and a tray of fruit in the other.

"Leave it on the desk," the princess ordered.

The man did as he was told. "You said you came from the library, Your Highness?" A hint of caution laced his words.

Lark lifted her head long enough to give him a bleary-eyed stare. "Why?"

"There are rumors—" the guard started, but he stopped short when Zaide crossed between him and the desk to fill a mug.

Zaide stared straight at him as he lifted the drink and sipped from the top, then placed it in front of the princess. "Wait to drink that. Make sure I don't keel over, first."

Pure dismay sprawled across the guard's face. "I would never—"

"I'm sure you wouldn't." Tula made a soothing motion. "But it's been a long night, and we can't be too careful. You can see as plainly as anyone else that the princess was attacked."

"For weeks, they've acted like the goborrins weren't a real problem." The man's face crumpled into a scowl. "We've petitioned the Magister to recruit more guards, so we can ferret out the nest of them and stamp them out, but they seem as numerous as camel crickets in a grain bin."

"You should see the armies outside Amrochan," Zaide muttered. When he became confident the water was nothing but water, he nudged the mug across the desk. "Drink."

Lark took the mug in both hands. "Whatever rumors you've heard from the library, be aware they're probably true. The city's guard force needs to find shelter for everyone in Jadora. Allow people to evacuate. Open the gates and allow them to flee without interference if necessary." She took a long drink. A hint of color had begun to return to her face.

"We can't just open the gates," the guard argued. "Jadora prides itself on its security, and—"

"And you could have thousands of goborrins hiding under the city," Tula put in. "The princess is giving you an order!"

Doubt lurked in his eyes. "The Magister gave different orders."

Zaide fought back the urge to touch his sword. This guard wasn't an enemy; threatening him gained them nothing. "Well, your Magister is a traitor. His orders are what led to this." He jabbed a finger at the princess, who glared at it and then transferred her glower to Zaide's face.

The guard opened his mouth and then closed it, at a loss for words.

"A great deal of upheaval has occurred within Jadora's ruling power. It's not the fault of the city's people. I don't even blame the Magister's Mage-Guard. They're merely following orders." Lark drank slowly, but a bit of light came back to her eyes. While she drank her water, Tula inspected the fruits on the tray. Nothing had been cut or prepared. With everything happening within the city's walls, slicing fruit was the last of anyone's concerns.

Zaide snorted in disagreement. "Every man in that red-marked armor has a chance to refuse his orders. Every one of them accepted what they were told to do, regardless of whether or not it was treason."

Lark fixed him with a stare. "Sit down."

"I'm not—"

"Sit," she snapped. "I will not tell you again."

He didn't want to sit. He wanted to argue. But his fight

wasn't with her, and he stared back at her for a long time before he admitted that to himself. Lark was his ally. His friend. He was in the thick of all this because of her, because she'd asked him to carry the blade on her behalf and he'd accepted. And above all else, she was the princess. How could he berate the guards who refused to follow her, while refusing to heed her command?

He tucked in his chin, sullen, and sat on the floor.

After a time, the guard before them swallowed and spoke again. "Your Highness, please understand I mean no offense by questioning."

Lark did not smile, but the sternness of her face softened. "None taken. You represent Jadora and care for the city's safety. You've never had any reason to question the Magister's orders, and I don't expect you to begin now."

"You don't?" Tula blinked in surprise.

"Of course not. The man's after power and wants Jadora to secede from my father's rule. He has no reason to harm the city or its occupants. Without its people, the city is nothing. The Magister will protect them."

Zaide snorted again.

The princess raised a brow. "You disagree?"

"The man just summoned a giant dragon in the middle of the Great Library. That doesn't sound like the city's best interests to me." And any minute, that dragon would be departing from the library to do who knew what to the city and its inhabitants. His fingertips traced the cross guard of his sword, a soft hum gracing his skin. It was thoughtful, troubled. Even the sword didn't know what to make of the situation.

As if swords are supposed to know anything at all, he grumbled to himself.

"A dragon," the guard said. "So they aren't just rumors."

"I'm afraid not." Lark plucked a few grapes from the vine on the tray. Though Tula had looked them over, she inspected them herself, too. Satisfied, she ate.

"Worse than rumors, I'd say," Tula whispered. "Do you hear

that?"

Zaide tilted his better ear toward the ceiling.

A low, rumbling roar shook the building.

CHAPTER TWENTY-FOUR

"Where are you going?" Tula's voice went high and squeaky as she ran down the hall.

Zaide shook his head to himself and kept going. "Where do you think?"

"You don't know how to fight a dragon!"

"Well, I'm going to have to figure it out." He had artifacts, at least; Lark still had the Captured Spring on its chain around her neck, but he carried the Spectrum Blade in one hand and the Hymnflute in the other. He'd left the Molten Dagger on the desk. Lark wasn't defenseless, but some sort of weapon with power would help her more than her knives.

Tula huffed and worked her legs faster to close the distance between them. "You're going to get yourself killed! What if the Magister's out there? What about Jinohe's guards?"

"Half his guards ran when Elsanna killed him." The guardswoman hadn't been far behind them in fleeing, as far as he knew. There was just as great a chance Elsanna and her crew could be waiting outside. He'd be happy to have the guardswomen to fight alongside them. And Moros. If anyone was strong enough to split a dragon's hide, it was the warden.

"And what if the other half have crossbows? They'll shoot you like they did the princess, and—"

"Look, Tula, I appreciate your concern, but I'm supposed to be protecting the princess, and I can't do that from inside these stone walls. We're not leaving Jadora until we get the Magister to infuse the Spectrum Blade with his power, and if I've got to kill a dragon to get him to cooperate, that's just what I'll have to do." He stopped at the space between the gates. Beyond the portcullis to his right, a long line of people fled into the camp of waiting wagons on the desert. Lights glittered and glowed against the sand, and speckles of light across the desert's expanse revealed countless wagons making an escape.

Addare was a long way off, but at least Addare didn't have dragons.

"But the dragon *is* the power, Zaide!" Tula cried.

He turned to face her.

She stopped a few strides away and panted for breath. "Didn't you hear the Magister? We were looking for the source of power. So was he. The dragon is the power. If you kill it, how are we supposed to bless the sword?"

Zaide stared. He hadn't considered that. "So what I actually need to do is kill the Magister and appoint a new Magister who will be willing to help." Maybe he ought to take the Molten Dagger after all. It certainly hadn't screamed in anyone's head after slaying the guards who attacked them.

"What you need to do is rely on diplomacy," Tula said. "You can't just replace someone like the Magister!"

"You know he killed the old one and just put himself in place as the new one, right?" He stepped back and knocked on the inner portcullis. "Open up!"

A moment later, the guard who had escorted them to their requested shelter caught up. "Maker's mercy, I didn't think you'd walk that fast," the man wheezed as he braced his hands against his knees.

The rumble and scrape of the portcullis rising was drowned

by the dragon's cry. The people clustered just inside the gate clamped hands over their ears, screamed, or ducked. Some did all three.

"Don't open up!" Tula hopped forward and waved her arms. "Stop! Stop that, don't encourage him!"

The guard drew a deep breath and let it back out with a whoosh. "We need someone to organize the guard. If we can't rely on the Magister, we need—"

"Elsanna!" Zaide shouted. The glint of firelight off the woman's hair had just caught his attention.

The fact it was *firelight* should have caught his eye, first.

Flames licked up the sides of stone buildings, a problem that escaped him at first glance and made him blink twice when he looked again. "How in the..."

"Get down!" Tula slammed into his back and bowled him to the floor.

The roar that split the air rivaled the Spectrum Blade's screaming in the way it bounced inside his skull. With his sword and the Hymnflute still in his hands, he couldn't shield his ears. He tried anyway and stifled a shout.

He expected a gout of fire, but instead, a hot wind filled with ash and soot and swirling embers rushed in through the open gate. He shoved Tula aside and scrambled to his feet.

By the time he stood, Elsanna had found them. The guardswoman grabbed him by the open collar of his coat. "Where is the princess?"

"Inside," Zaide said. "She's all right."

"You left her alone?"

"There's no one else back there. It was just me, Tula, and—" Zaide paused to point to the guard, but the man surged forward on his own.

"Elsanna! You're alive!" He laid a hand over his heart and dropped to one knee.

The words were enough to snag nearby attention. Civilians and guards all spun to face them.

"Get up," the guardswoman snarled. "Call all the gate guards together. Leave the gates open, let the people go where they will. No one in their right mind would try to enter Jadora right now."

"Yes, Guardswoman," the man blurted as he scrambled back to his feet.

Zaide looked back to the desert. Part of him envied those who fled. "Any chance you know how to fight dragons?"

Elsanna offered a wry smile in return. "It's going to be a learning experience for all of us."

He shouldn't have hoped.

"Tula, go get Valla." The guardswoman pointed into the crowd. More reddish ponytails bobbed here and there among the people. "She'll stay here and guard the princess. You'll be with me. You too, broken-born."

Zaide stood straighter. "Tula says we can't kill the dragon." He spared the librarian a glance as she ducked out into the crowd to search for the guardswomen's second-in-command.

"If that man wasn't lying, and it's true that it's the Magister's source of power, killing it is the last thing we should do," Elsanna agreed.

"Should we kill the Magister?"

"We should probably refrain from killing anything but goborrins at this point. We go for the Magister. We capture him and do what we must. We're assembling the guard right now. The Magister may have a few on his side, but most are more interested in the well-being of the city." She stepped out from behind the gate.

Zaide followed. "Tell me what to do."

"What good will that do? You were supposed to be guarding the princess."

"I'm also supposed to be getting power put in this thing so I can save the world or something." He shook the Spectrum Blade and its colors flashed.

The guardswoman shot it a frown.

He frowned back, since the sword couldn't. "Did you know about this before? The dragon? The source of power?"

"I wish I had. I would have ensured that dagger stayed locked away. But now it makes sense. Why the Magister I served was so determined to get his hands on it." She gripped the sword sheathed at her hip until her coppery knuckles turned white. "I've sent a portion of the guardswomen with Moros to reclaim the armory in the palace. We'll need better armor."

"The crossbow?" Zaide asked.

"And that thing."

Overhead, the dragon's glowing form slipped between clouds of smoke. The whoosh of its wings sent more cinders flying.

"You probably should have opted for better armor to begin with." It was kicking the hornet's nest at this point, but Elsanna only gave him a flat look.

"Do you want to know a secret?"

Did he? He blinked at her.

"Why we wear the armor we do. It's because it's hot."

He gave her a quick once-over. "Uh, I guess."

Her lip curled under his scrutiny, but she returned her attention to the sky a moment later. "You've been here before. Do you know how hot it gets in this city? Unbearable. Imagine being in the sun with plate armor on. We'd bake alive. We aren't like the other guards. The guardswomen patrol. We're there to be seen, to make people aware the city's under our protection."

"Maybe it should be," Zaide said.

Elsanna didn't move, but a wrinkle in her brow spoke on its own.

"We need a Magister who can help us. Someone the people would be willing to follow, too. Someone strong enough to face a dragon and walk away with power so the Spectrum Blade can be infused with it. Have you got any better suggestions than you?"

The guardswoman chuckled. "You're bold, boy."

"Everyone I've met would be happy to see you take it." He paused. "Well, maybe not the current Magister."

"Enough. Curb your silver tongue, the monster's coming back." She drew her sword and stood ready, but even the fighting stance she adopted seemed small when the dragon swept into view once more.

It had seemed big in the library. Now, with its wings spread, it was immense. As big as the ice titan in the cavern north of Desheni.

"And you fought that, so maybe you can fight this," he murmured to himself.

Except the goal had been to destroy the massive trice, not convince it to aid them on their journey. He flexed his fingers on the Hymnflute. "I've got an idea for how to get it to land."

"Do we want it to land?" Elsanna flinched as a rain of ash and embers spilled over them. The dragon doubled back into the smoke.

Maybe not. "Let's find the Magister. Then we can decide if we want it to land."

"Too late." She pointed across the city, to where the dragon dipped from the sky to disappear behind the roofs of buildings.

Zaide turned in a circle and tried to orient himself. "The south gate's here, so the library is that direction, and that way..."

Tula and Valla appeared in front of him before he had it sorted out. A cluster of guardswomen followed at their backs.

Valla pushed a spear into Elsanna's hands. "The dragon's landed near the palace. The palace district is swarming with goborrins. You'll need this."

"Do I need one?" Zaide asked.

Both guardswomen appeared unimpressed.

"Your hands are already full," Valla said. "I'll see to the princess. You do what you must."

Zaide nodded, though he suspected she was speaking to Elsanna. She slipped past them and into the corridor between the gates. Her retinue followed, but Tula stayed behind, her head twisting back and forth as if she didn't know who to follow. Elsanna offered no direction as she started off toward the palace.

"Come on." Zaide jerked his head in invitation for her to come, though he wasn't sure she was welcome. He wasn't that sure *he* was welcome.

Tula's eyes brightened and they hurried after the guardswoman together.

Most of the city they passed through was ablaze, but he saw nothing to explain how the fires started. If it had been the dragon, it seemed as if large swaths of blackened stone would have heralded the point of ignition. He tried to study the buildings as they hustled along, but the flames were too bright and eventually, he just tucked in his chin and focused on his steps.

"You ever feel like we spend a lot of time just running back and forth without accomplishing much?" he asked as they ran.

"What, like how we just ran away from the palace, and now we're running back to it?" Tula kept pace with him easily, though her cheeks grew flushed.

"Yeah, exactly like that." It had been the same way in retrieving the Spectrum Blade from the forest's temple. He couldn't think of other examples while running, but he was sure there were more.

The librarian shrugged. "I think that's just sort of life. You take the books to the guild hall, you take the books back to the library. You take the books to the capital with the princess, then you bring the books back with the princess! And, well, the books are probably on fire now, so maybe that's not a good comparison. Most things don't burn up as part of it." Her voice cracked.

He couldn't help but grimace. "Sorry." It wasn't his fault; the library was supposed to be neutral ground. The Magister had been the one to strike first. Yet guilt clawed at him. He'd visited two libraries in his life, the Elder's library in Kolmar and Jadora's Great Library, and both had burned.

Maybe fire followed him.

Or maybe forcing him into the role of scholar had never been a good idea, and the Maker was punishing them all for urging Zaide to resist his nature.

Or maybe you just have really terrible luck, and should avoid libraries in the future, he scolded himself. The palace in Amrochan had a library, too. He'd be sure to stay far away from that one.

Elsanna skidded to a halt in front of them and they almost collided with her back. "Maker's mercy!"

Zaide sidestepped so they wouldn't crash and slowed to a stop. A wave of goborrins poured from the palace gates and flooded into the street. A shock of anticipation traveled up his arm as the Spectrum Blade reacted. Its surface flashed and glowed, the iridescent colors churning fast.

He swept forward to meet a monster.

Instead of fighting, the wave of pig-like beasts broke and split around them. Not attacking. Fleeing.

Zaide's stance faltered, but his question was answered before he had a chance to ask. A shrill squeal overhead pulled his gaze skyward as a goborrin sailed over the palace walls and crashed against a building's flat roof.

Beyond the palace gates, the dragon's sleek, glowing body slid by. Its massive claws and lashing tail pitched monsters into the sky. A howling roar tore from the dragon's throat with a burst of flame, and the stink of charred goborrins—all too reminiscent of scorched pork—filled the air.

"Whose side is it on?" Tula cried.

"The Magister's side." Zaide started forward, then paused, awaiting direction from Elsanna. Impulsiveness never ended well for him. As bad as everything he'd dealt with before had been, it hadn't been a dragon.

The guardswoman gritted her teeth and watched the goborrins flee. "We've got to push in and get to the Magister. He must be trying to reclaim the palace."

"And you think we can do what an army of goborrins can't?"

Tula didn't cower behind her sister, exactly, but she did shrink back to stand behind Elsanna and her spear.

"We've got to." Zaide strode toward the gates with his sword ready, but the goborrins didn't stop to fight. They parted as he progressed into the courtyard and he raised the blade skyward. It flashed, and the dragon turned toward him with flames flickering behind its teeth.

Slowly, with the sword still raised, he lifted the Hymnflute to his lips.

"Now!" someone screamed nearby.

Guards in red-streamered armor surged from the palace to strike the dragon's legs and underbelly. The beast roared and reared onto its back legs, clawing at the sky.

Tula gasped. "What are they doing? They'll kill him!" She ducked under Elsanna's spear and bolted past Zaide, digging something out of the pocket of her coat as she ran. It flashed red in her hand.

The Molten Dagger.

"Tula!" Elsanna ran after her, but the tide of goborrins turned. Hundreds of the monsters swarmed back through the gates to join the attack on the dragon.

Zaide pushed back against the surge. His sword flared as he skewered one goborrin after another, but their deaths made no difference. "Where are they all coming from?"

"The tunnels must be open! Scorch me, how many are there?" Elsanna twirled her spear instead of striking, the spinning shaft opening a path where she could walk. "Tula!"

The librarian reemerged on the other side of the swarm. She swiped at one of the mage-guards with the dagger, leaving a trail of embers in the air.

Zaide turned to fight forward. The path Elsanna carved made going easier, but death had caught the attention of the goborrins around them, and some had begun to fight back. Ahead, beyond the dragon's lashing tail, a streak of red caught his eye. "There! The Magister's in the palace!"

"Great. On the other side of a dragon. Should be perfectly easy to reach!" Elsanna grunted.

The dragon's wings spread wide and a rush of flame spilled from its jaws to rake across the masses. Zaide snapped the Hymnflute back to his mouth and summoned the notes they'd used in the fields outside Amrochan. Wind rushed around them and swirled into a barrier, forcing the goborrins back and turning the flames away.

Elsanna gave a triumphant laugh. "Now that's a trick! Keep that up!"

He kept his breathing steady and focused on the song. The magic parted the way with such ease, he could have kicked himself. He should have done that first. Why were defensive tactics always the last ones on his mind?

The dragon dropped back to all fours and Tula shrieked, but it ignored her beneath it. One great paw swung at the guards. It struck with enough force to kill the man it hit first.

"Get to her," Elsanna shouted. "Get her out of there!"

Zaide pressed forward on his own. The going was easy with the shield up, but he couldn't play forever. His chest had already begun to feel tight. He tried to get a deeper lungful of air between notes.

Tula didn't seem to notice. She regained her footing and resumed the fight, chasing the mage-guards away from the dragon's underbelly, one by one. Her mouth moved, but the noise of goborrins and guards was too great.

The dragon saw his movement. It arched its neck and spewed fire downward, directly toward him. The flames rolled against the Hymnflute's barrier in blinding waves and Zaide screwed his eyes shut. Heat spilled through the barrier, intense, but not unbearable, and the dragon ran out of breath before the magic faltered.

Zaide, too, was almost out of breath. "Tula!" he gasped. The barrier quivered and he renewed his efforts. He was close; she was just ahead, a handful of mage-guards around her.

She twirled and kicked, holding her own, but sweat plastered her fiery hair to her face and her chest heaved with exertion.

He chanced another call. "Tula, we have to move!"

"No! They'll kill him! He's the source of power, we need him!"

A mage-guard darted in from behind one of the dragon's legs and lunged for Tula, his sword upraised.

Zaide surged ahead to meet him. The Spectrum Blade sparked as he deflected the strike. "We need the Magister. Find him!"

The dragon drew back, its head twisted to glower down at them.

Zaide bit back an oath and sucked in a breath instead. He raised the Hymnflute, but the dragon didn't flame.

Magister? The word exploded into Zaide's head with the force of a hammer, a voice too big to comfortably grace his mind.

The dragon reared onto its hind legs and spread its massive wings as a noise like laughter threatened to cleave Zaide's skull in two.

Tula gripped her head in both hands. She didn't see its paw swing toward her until too late.

"Tula!" Zaide lunged forward as the dragon's claws wrapped around her and lifted her from the ground.

It raised its maw to the sky and roared.

I am the Magister!

CHAPTER TWENTY-FIVE

THE DRAGON'S wings thrust down so forcefully, Tula's head snapped down against the beast's clawed digit. The ground retreated at an alarming pace, the rushing wind cold against her face, and it took a moment to realize the city wasn't shrinking; she was climbing.

Not climbing.

Flying.

She tried to say something, but her voice failed and her breath escaped as the tiniest squeak.

The dragon—the *Magister*—spiraled upward over the city with her in its grasp. The first few wingbeats were rough, jarring, and made her stomach lurch. She twisted to see the dragon's other paws, but they were empty. It had picked her up, and only her. For a moment, she couldn't fathom why. Then something pricked at her stomach.

The Molten Dagger. She held it in a death grip, but her arm had been flattened against her body mid-swing. She struggled to adjust it, its heat unpleasant, but not unbearable.

The dagger had been the key, the power that released the dragon from... wherever it had been held. And she'd brought it straight to the beast, like an idiot.

Why had she picked it up?

Why had Dasienna encouraged it? They'd meant to leave the dagger for the princess to protect herself, but she'd been quick to give approval when Zaide took off and Tula looked its way.

They twisted in midair and the dragon's path leveled out. Smoke billowed from the city, but it was thickest near the palace, where a churning mass of goborrins still seethed in the courtyard.

Vile things, the dragon's voice rumbled inside her head. *Worthless beasts. Not even fit to eat. The filth taints even the taste.*

A throbbing headache bloomed in the sudden absence of his words, muddying her thoughts. She would have rubbed her temples, had she been able to move. She blinked hard and shook her head to try to right it.

A deep rumble sounded in the dragon's chest, accompanied by a whisper of laughter in her mind. When the dragon spoke again, though, it was anything but a whisper. *Too powerful for you, am I? Little surprise. Even your most competent scholars shudder in the face of my might.*

Her ears rang when he finished. Tula shook her head again and tried to focus. "Magister," she gasped. Her voice was feeble in the rushing wind and she struggled to make herself heard. "We came seeking you! We need your help."

My help, he sneered as he banked, continuing his circuit over the city. *Look what you've done to my plateau! My great city!*

"And what you've done to our library!" she shouted back, unable to help herself.

The dragon's head tilted, one great, golden eye fixed on her.

Maybe shouting at a dragon wasn't the wisest decision.

A moment passed, and he rumbled a laugh again. *Your library. Your little records for your pitiful little lifespans. Such simple things your kind always prize.* They turned again, and this time they swept out across the desert. The cool expanse of sand shone blue in the moonlight.

Away from the city, the night air was cold as ice. "Where are you taking me?" The wind tried to steal her breath. She wiggled in the dragon's claws, trying to make room to inhale more deeply.

As if to answer, the dragon dove. Ashes swirled on the drafts made by his wings as he settled on the sand, his glowing scales washing the desert with orange light. He sat her on the sand and let go, though the movement was so abrupt it made her stagger.

You have something that belongs to me, the dragon rumbled. *Give it here.*

His massive forefoot unfurled before her, demanding.

Tula rocked on her feet. She glanced at the dagger in her hand.

The dragon huffed, a plume of smoke curling from each nostril.

She jabbed his palm with the blade.

His claws snapped shut and he bellowed, though the sound faded to a mental cackle. *You are a spirited one. Have you no respect for fear?*

"I don't have any reason to fear you." Her heart was racing, though, and she'd chosen her words carefully to ensure she didn't lie. She was more than afraid. The dragon before her could have smashed her like a bug. Or bitten her in half, or incinerated her with little more than a puff, or... She shook her head before her mind could race off to any other horrible possibilities. "If you're the Magister, then you're the one we need, not whoever is in the palace. We brought the Spectrum Blade to Jadora to seek your help in reawakening its power."

Yes, I saw the new Bladebearer. I cannot say I am impressed by the choice. Disdain dripped thick from the dragon's tone, but his voice no longer left her head feeling like a bell after it finished clanging around inside her thoughts. *He lacks your foresight. But that hardly matters. What matters is that you give me that dagger, so I can put it back where it belongs.*

Tula stepped back and held the Molten Dagger deliberately

out of reach. "Why, so nobody can use it to summon you? Or so you can do something to it?"

Because the man who summoned me has proven unworthy. It belongs in the cavern where I first hid it.

"It belongs in the city of Jadora, so the Magister—I mean, our acting Magister—can bring peace to the city," she protested.

The dragon scoffed, a noise like grating stone. *I hid it for a reason, and I am being far kinder than you deserve, for I still bear a fondness for Jadora's librarians, petty as their modern pursuits may be. I ask but once more. Give me the dagger.*

She held it farther away. "Promise to help us, first."

I owe you nothing.

"Without the blade's power, we won't be able to chase the goborrins out of the city. Out of *your* city, Magister."

His claws unfurled before her again. *I am capable of ridding my own city of those pests.*

Tula's heart sank. Slowly, she lowered the Molten Dagger to his scaly palm. This time, she laid it flat.

The dragon closed his paw around the tiny obsidian blade. *A wise choice. You are free to return to the city, human.*

"Wait," she called as he spread his wings. "One question, before you go. Please."

He grew still, poised to launch himself skyward.

Tula swallowed hard. "You said you were the one who hid the dagger. That means you're Magister Vorkaris, so you should know, right? What's the name of the song?"

His golden eyes narrowed. *What?*

"The song. The one that was etched on the doorway that hid the dagger, the one that took the Vale Hymnflute to unlock." She twisted her fingertips. "What's the name of the song?"

The dragon stared down at her for a long time. Then, slowly, he eased his forepaws back to the cool sand. *Well, well,* he mused as he folded his wings. *Now that's a very interesting question, indeed.*

The wind from the dragon's wings bowled Zaide over as it launched itself upward. He hit the ground hard, the Hymnflute cradled to his chest. The landing was enough to knock the wind out of him, but not enough to knock the Spectrum Blade from his hand.

A shadow crossed him and he snapped his sword up to deflect a mage-guard's strike. He had to get off the ground; turtled on his back like that, a second attacker would kill him. He shoved hard and spun to kick the man's legs out from underneath him. The mage-guard toppled and Zaide scrambled to his feet.

The next instant, a handful of guards were on him—and just behind them, the goborrin horde pressed close.

"Destroy them!" the Magister snarled from the palace doorway.

A spear hurtled past the man's head and he backpedaled with an unbecoming squeal.

Elsanna had her swords in both hands when she reached Zaide's side, but she spared him little more than a glance before she advanced toward the stairs. "You desert-blighted sea slug!" she spat. A pair of mage-guards tried to stop her. She killed them both unceremoniously, their blood leaving dark spatters across the bronzed skin of her exposed midriff. "Which way did it go?"

A familiar keen made Zaide spin back. Behind him, a wave of goborrins fell as the guardswomen arrived. Their new armor glinted in the lantern light, shielding most of their bodies, but there was no hiding the long ponytails that cascaded down their backs.

All across the courtyard, goborrins fell into ranks. They bore weapons and shields of all sorts, hardly an army that had been thrown together, nor one that could have traversed the desert easily.

One of the monsters thudded its crude blade against its

shield. More picked up the beat. The steady rhythm they drummed out sent Zaide's thoughts reeling back to the river when he'd first left Kolmar. What he wouldn't have done for a bridge now.

A tingle coursed up his arm, snapping Zaide back to attention as Elsanna gave a shout. His chest tightened, but she needed no help. She launched herself past a second pair of mage-guards to strike at the Magister.

Zaide could have cursed. If anything, she needed to be restrained. He spun after her and bolted up the palace stairs. "Stop!"

They'd come this far to see the Magister, skirted death and escaped the goborrin siege. To see the man killed now could only make things worse.

Elsanna did not stop. She bore down on the Magister with her blades crossed, until the man collapsed to the stone and she pressed them close to his throat. "Where has it taken her?"

"Straight to the pit," the Magister spat.

She gritted her teeth, but the moment her arms tensed, Zaide dropped his sword and caught hold of her.

"Elsanna, stop! That's not going to save her! We need him, remember?" The guardswoman's arm was like iron beneath his fingers. Even if he dropped the Hymnflute and used both hands, he doubted he could stop her.

But her self-restraint won out, and the blades eased away from the Magister's throat by a hair.

Evidently, it made no difference. The Magister sneered at them, his lip curled back from teeth that struck Zaide as too white. "I'll die before helping you."

The guardswoman shifted her weight again. "That can certainly be arranged."

It took all of Zaide's strength to hold her back. "We need him," he repeated. "Take him prisoner. Moros can hold him."

"Moros should stuff him in that cell where the old Magister's bones lie." Elsanna planted a foot on the man's chest to hold him down. "Tell me now, or you'll be alive when they feast on your flesh. Where has the dragon gone?"

"Any guess is as good as mine. The beast is useless. Mindless. Impossible to use or control." The Magister wriggled, but he couldn't escape from underneath Elsanna's boot.

"He sounded pretty collected and intelligent to me," Zaide said.

A pair of guards rushed toward them from somewhere deeper in the palace, but the Magister lifted a hand to halt them before Zaide had a chance to retrieve the Spectrum Blade from the floor.

"Hold," the Magister ordered. "He... what do you mean, boy?"

Elsanna, too, gave Zaide a look of curious befuddlement.

His gaze flicked between them. "You didn't hear the dragon?"

They both shook their heads.

Zaide released Elsanna's arm and crouched to reclaim his sword without removing his eyes from the guards. The Magister's patience wouldn't last long, and he wouldn't be left unarmed. Battle still roared in the palace yard just beyond the open doors, too. Any moment, they'd be pulled back into it.

"It was so loud. I was sure everyone would hear it," he said as he grasped the glowing blade and stood. A fizz of sensation gave the impression the sword was unhappy about having been dropped. He chose to ignore it.

The Magister wriggled again and his face brightened. "What did it say? It acknowledged my power?"

Zaide hesitated.

"Could you understand it?" Elsanna asked.

"Oh, yeah. He, uh, made himself very clear." He drew back a step.

The guardswoman's mouth tightened. "Well?" she asked when he didn't continue.

He cleared his throat and fixed his gaze on the Magister's face. "He said he is the Magister, and not you."

The man on the floor almost roared. He whipped a blade from his robes and slashed at Elsanna's leg, but she was too fast for him to make contact. She whirled away, raking a sword across his chest and leaving him howling in pain. His guards rushed her and she feinted, then pivoted to strike.

Zaide took on the other guard as a knot pulled itself tight in his stomach. He didn't want to fight, not against the Magister's men. Not when he knew how his sword would react. He had no other weapon.

He also had no choice.

His sword sparked as he intercepted the mage-guard's blade, but he opted to remain defensive. It wouldn't take long for Elsanna to dispatch the guard she fought. Then she could sweep in and take over.

Except when the guard she battled fell a moment later, she didn't turn to help. Instead, she returned to the Magister and pressed the tip of one blade to his throat. "You begged the dragon for power and he gave you nothing. You killed my liege and threw my city into turmoil. The leader of your Mage-Guard is dead. Do you care to join him, or shall I have Moros toss you behind bars and wait for you to squeal like the pigs in the yard?"

The Magister spread his hands across his wounded chest, as if to stop the bleeding, or perhaps protect himself. His mouth worked without producing words.

Zaide tried to watch, but a renewed assault from the guard he fought took all his attention. "Elsanna!" he called through gritted teeth. "A little help?"

The guardswoman's nose crinkled and her lip curled. For an instant, he expected scolding. Instead, she raised her second sword and flung it. The blade struck the gap between the guard's helmet and gorget and the man fell, dead.

Seeing the opportunity, Zaide sheathed the Spectrum Blade, seized the hilt of Elsanna's sword, and jerked it free. "I need more hands," he muttered as he glanced between the sword and the Hymnflute in his right hand. Another scabbard would help. Or a bag for the Hymnflute. He hadn't considered that before running off with the artifact in his hand. Where was he supposed to put it now?

"Go get Moros," Elsanna said, indifferent to the loss of her second weapon. "He should be in the fray by now."

"Right." Zaide hurried back into the palace yard and stopped on the stone walkway. Smoke hung heavy in the air. The upper levels of the palace were aflame, casting bold orange light across the fight scene below. Brawling mage-guards and goborrins and guardswomen occupied every bit of the palace grounds, but even among them, the prison warden wasn't hard to spot. His bald head rose above the human fighters, his dark skin a stark contrast to the fleshy pink sea of goborrin faces.

The sword at his side would have been more useful for parting that particular sea, but Zaide clung to Elsanna's ordinary sword instead and pushed toward the scarred man. More than once, a mage-guard or goborrin struck at him, but he ducked their weapons and wove his way between the monsters and men to spill out into an empty space before Moros.

The warden turned with his mace ready. His hand stayed when he saw who it was.

"Moros," Zaide panted. "Elsanna wants you."

"I am aware," the big man said.

Zaide stared for a heartbeat before the warden's facade cracked and the tiniest hint of a smile tugged the corner of his mouth. Zaide blinked, understood, and would have clapped a hand to his face, had they not both been occupied. "Augh, why would you say that?"

"Lest you think I am a man with no humor. Where is she?"

Grimacing, Zaide turned to point toward the palace.

Moros hefted his mace and started off in that direction. The guardswomen and mage-guards knew to steer clear of him; the moment he appeared, they scattered. One sweep of his arm was enough to send a large goborrin crashing to the ground, and he demonstrated repeatedly as he cleared a path to the palace stairs.

Zaide trailed along in his wake, unsure if he should be helping or rejoining the fight. For every goborrin that fell, one appeared to take its place. Nothing made a difference, and the bodies of mage-guards and guardswomen littered the courtyard alongside the swine.

By the time they reached the palace doors, Elsanna had the Magister tied with strips of cloth cut from his own ornate robes. His black hair fell about his scowling face and sagging shoulders in loose tangles, but his eyes burned with a hateful intensity.

"Take him to the prison," Elsanna ordered without looking up.

Moros stopped at the threshold. "Now, or after the next problem is dealt with?"

Next problem? Zaide started to ask, but the warden held up a fist and tilted his head.

First came the sound of wingbeats, then came the screams.

CHAPTER TWENTY-SIX

Battle in the palace yard halted as both goborrins and humans looked skyward. Beyond the palace gates, sounds of terror rose from the city. Zaide stared as wings parted the clouds of smoke and the dragon crossed overhead.

"It'll bank on the far side and come back," Elsanna shouted. She followed it with a string of orders, but Zaide didn't catch them all. Instead, he slipped past the guardswoman to aid Moros.

The warden hauled the Magister to his feet and Zaide stepped forward to tighten the strips of cloth that held his arms. The robed man tried to kick him, but Moros gave him such a shake that his head rocked.

"Get his legs," the scarred man said.

Zaide used his borrowed sword to cut another piece of fabric from the Magister's robes. A slippered foot struck at him and missed by a hair. Zaide considered the footwear for a moment as he caught the Magister's legs and bound his ankles, then flicked both slippers from the man's feet.

Moros stared at him with an unchanging expression, but the few hours they'd spent together had been enough to learn the man's silent method of questioning.

"Being barefoot was the worst part," Zaide said. "The floor down there is as cold as the ice on the Desheni lakes."

"Simple discomfort is sometimes the most miserable part of imprisonment." The warden dragged the Magister forward until the man was forced to hop. The movement was awkward. Judging by the way color bloomed in the Magister's face, it was embarrassing, too.

Zaide offered an awkward grin. "The blankets are horrible."

"I would not know," Moros said, though the tiniest hint of amusement touched his words. "But they are cast-offs from the palace dogs, so I can assume."

The Magister made a pitiful noise.

"Here it comes!" Elsanna called.

Zaide spun to watch as the guardswomen across the yard ducked.

A rain of ash preceded the dragon's appearance, but the beast wasn't far behind. It swept low over the yard and plucked two unlucky souls from the earth. The frenzied squeals that followed as the dragon pulled back into the sky said they were lucky. Both goborrins, this time.

"I will take the false Magister to the dungeon," Moros said as he hauled the man toward the open door. "Am I to wait there?"

"We can't spare you now," Elsanna said. "Put him in one of your confinement cells, opposite the side where they've tunneled through, and leave one of the city guards to keep watch. Even the worst of Gadranus's army can't tunnel through rock fast enough to find him."

"Should I come?" Zaide asked. He tracked the dragon until it disappeared into the clouds of smoke, then glanced down to his hands. The Hymnflute. He'd just had it, where did he put it down? It sat on the floor behind him, where he'd knelt to tie the Magister.

Elsanna shook her head. "Stay here. We're going to need that shiny sword of yours."

He tilted the borrowed blade in his hand. "This, uh—"

"Incoming!" the guardswoman shouted.

Despite the warning, Moros pulled the Magister from the palace and down the stairs. The man's knees buckled as the dragon came back into view. The warden dragged him along the earth, instead.

The dragon's sweep was the same as before. A fast rake across the courtyard, enemies seized in its claws, an upward swoop that kept its belly from brushing the palace walls.

"Maker's mercy," Elsanna groaned. "How are we supposed to fight that?"

Zaide squinted against the churn of smoke that muddied the air. "Why isn't it using flame?" It had before, and it would have been a faster solution than darting back and forth, taking out two at a time. There had to be two hundred people—well, people and goborrins—clustered in the palace grounds.

The smoke in the sky was thinner now, the dragon's body a blob of golden light in the haze. The more it swung back and forth across the city, the more its wings destroyed its own cover.

His cover? The dragon had identified itself as Magister, and its mind-shattering voice had been male. But it was a monster, too, and like the goborrins in the yard below, he hesitated to give it too much thought. He couldn't afford to humanize it, couldn't risk anything that might stay his hand.

"Thank the Maker it's not. My guardswomen would bake in that armor with any additional heat, even if the beast didn't flame them." Elsanna held out her hand, the flex of her fingers toward her open palm demanding her sword.

Reluctantly, Zaide pressed the hilt into her grasp.

She curled her fingers around it and readied her other blade at the same time. "Get that shiny sword out, boy. The dragon's coming and I've got an idea for how to strike."

"The fact you want my sword makes me think you have an idea for how you want *me* to strike." He drew the Spectrum Blade anyway, though its hilt sent an uncomfortable prickle through his hand. The sensation put a lump of dread in his throat. *Not people,* he thought at the sword. *We won't do that.*

The lack of response from the weapon left him with little comfort, which made him scold himself in turn. Why did he keep expecting something from the blade? Why did he keep thinking at it, like it was capable of responding?

"Maybe it just makes you feel better," he muttered.

Elsanna glanced back. "What was that?"

"Nothing." He talked to himself less since he'd returned from Desheni, but it still slipped free now and then.

The guardswoman pointed with her sword as if it didn't matter. "Scare the goborrins so they go that direction."

"Scare them?" Zaide tilted the Hymnflute in his hands. "Shouldn't I just push—"

"Just swing your sword around, encourage them to move. We need a hole in the crowd."

"Then pushing is better." He sprinted down the steps and pushed into the fray. More than one goborrin swung at him, but he ducked and darted between their heavily muscled bodies, taking advantage of their size to lose himself between them. Then he raised the Hymnflute and with the first soft notes, a barrier formed around him. Small, at first, proportional to the intensity of the music. He hadn't realized he'd absorbed that information until he blew harder and the notes strengthened.

The barrier expanded, forcing goborrins and mage-guards away from him.

The dragon came back around and when its golden eyes fixed on his face, the realization of just what Elsanna's plan was made his heart drop into his stomach.

Fire glowed behind its teeth and Zaide didn't know whether to keep the barrier up or focus on bearing his sword. The Hymnflute was powerful and had proven invaluable against the dragon's flames once before, but was the barrier strong enough to deter the dragon itself? He locked gazes with the creature as it rushed down toward him and its jaws began to open.

An arm waved beside the dragon's neck, begging for attention, and Zaide's playing faltered.

For a single second, he saw Tula's beaming face.

Then the dragon's wings leveled out and its maw opened wide, but the flames spewed from behind its teeth swept across the top of the barrier and crashed into the swarm of monsters behind him.

Squeals filled the air, deafening above the sound of the Hymnflute in his hand. The dragon's tail tip bounced off Zaide's magical shield as the creature veered skyward again, and air rushed outward as the impact made the barrier shatter.

A split second later, Elsanna was at his side. "You were supposed to stab it, not stand there!"

Zaide spun to point after its form with his sword. "Tula's on that thing!"

The guardswoman blinked.

"And I am not dragon bait!" He would have shaken a fist at her if he'd had a hand free. Instead, all he could do was stamp his foot and hope the way he glowered was enough.

It wasn't, for Elsanna grabbed him by the shoulders. "What do you mean, Tula's on it?"

He half expected her to shake him, but she did no such thing, so he twisted his shoulders out of her grasp and retreated a step. "On its back. It looked like she was saying something, but I couldn't hear over—" He raised the Hymnflute, but she spoke before he could finish.

"Was she all right? Did she look frightened?"

"She looked excited. Her cheeks were pink." That could have been from the rushing wind, too, Zaide supposed, but her grin had been unmistakable.

Elsanna hung her head for a moment, her palm against her forehead, but their respite was short-lived. An instant later, a mage-guard rushed her, and she spun into combat.

Zaide started after her, but a hand closed on his shoulder and jerked him backwards. He stifled his yelp and rounded on his opponent. The Spectrum Blade almost made contact and he stayed his strike at the last instant.

Valla drew back with her hands up in both apology and surrender. "There's a situation. You must come with me."

"Why—"

"Just come!" the guardswoman spat as she wheeled and ran for the gates.

The dragon's wingbeats stirred the goborrins around them into a new frenzy. The Spectrum Blade hummed as if ready to fight, and part of him wished he could. Killing goborrins was simple. All this was more than he'd asked for.

Just beyond the gates, Valla stood with a small group of guardswomen. Nearby, more of the women herded groups of Jadoran citizens down the streets. Bodies of goborrins littered the roadways, most of them charred. It seemed the dragon's passes back and forth hadn't been limited to the palace.

When Zaide joined Valla's group, the guardswoman's mouth was pinched. Whatever words had passed between her and her subordinates, they hadn't been good.

"There's a new hole in the city, right in the middle of the streets. Goborrins are pouring out in numbers like never before." Valla flinched at the sound of wings. "The dragon—"

"Don't worry about the dragon," Zaide interrupted. "The hole, where is it?"

"Near the south gate. The guardswomen have evacuated everyone present, or at least gotten them inside the wall's fortifications, but if they can't hold—"

Zaide's breath caught. "Lark." He turned south.

Valla made no move to stop him. He ran, gripping both the Hymnflute and the Spectrum Blade so tight, his knuckles ached.

The streets were all but empty. Scattered bands of city guards in plain armor battled with squads of goborrins or rattled their way toward the south gate, the same as Zaide. He moved faster, unhindered by a group or the heavy plate armor they wore.

Injured guards lingered at the sides of streets. Strings of

lanterns hung low or had been snapped, forcing him to duck or sidestep, lest he be tangled. Blackened buildings marked sites the goborrins had attacked, and flakes of ash still rained from the sky. It sullied his hair and borrowed robes, made his skin itch and made his dread that much worse.

Fires still glowed around the city, and a large splash of red waited due south.

Had they moved the princess? Taken her outside the city?

"I shouldn't have left her behind," he breathed as he ran.

He should have moved her along with them, or else stayed to defend her. He'd done little to help at the palace, spurred there by the mere need to do *something* while the city was under attack. Kolmar had burned. Now Jadora burned. He was supposed to make a difference. Why couldn't he?

The south wall came into view first, its face licked with tongues of fire.

The wall of goborrins below it caught his attention next.

They packed the street from wall to wall in dense formation, like the armies outside Amrochan. Except their backs were turned. Save a thick cluster of goborrins around what had to be the hole Valla meant, the whole force was focused on the south gate.

Guards ran back and forth atop the high wall, flinging stones and dumping cauldrons of oil. The oil was what burned; splashes of it clung to the face of the wall, spitting flames and oozing downward.

Zaide was almost to the goborrins when hurried footsteps rushed up from behind.

"Scorch the sand, but you're fast on those legs when you want to be," Valla wheezed. "Where was that speed when you were supposed to meet me north of the city?"

"There weren't any goborrins threatening the princess then." He set his jaw and made himself still.

The monsters didn't seem to hear them. They continued to

press toward the gates, but Zaide doubted they could stand in the middle of the street without notice for long.

"And those goborrins mean you can't just throw yourself in there without a plan."

"All right, then here's a plan. You go left, I'll go right." He shoved the Hymnflute into her hands and sprinted ahead.

"Zaide!" Valla shouted, her voice small and distant as he cut into the first beast.

It took a second for the goborrins to realize what happened, and longer for them to react. He'd taken them by surprise and tore into their army with the Spectrum Blade flashing and sparking in his hand.

Zaide was exhausted, but angry. The trip to Jadora was supposed to be an easy visit. Why couldn't it be an easy visit?

Why couldn't *anything* be easy?

He spun his sword in hand, deft and aggressive, fueled by frustration and a sense of desperation that clawed at the inside of his chest.

Lark had to be safe. He had to ensure it. He had to get there, even if he cut down the whole army by himself.

Valla and a contingent of guardswomen struck the goborrin ranks behind him. They were fast, skilled, and the swath of death they left behind made more than one of the monsters ahead turn to flee.

But more spilled from the hole in the earth. A tunnel they'd carved while everyone slept, while the Magister let them believe they were safe.

Goborrins flung crude wooden ladders against the south gate's walls in increasing numbers. The guards wouldn't be able to pour burning oil on them all. They had to get to the tunnel, close the entrance somehow. Yet the goborrin swarm was thickest around the massive hole in the center of an intersection, and Zaide didn't know if he could pierce it.

But you have to, he told himself.

"Stay with him!" Valla shouted somewhere nearby, her voice

distant despite her proximity, dulled by the rush of blood in his veins. He didn't see who received her orders and did not turn to find out. All that mattered was moving forward, and as he let the Spectrum Blade carve its way through another monster, the artifact *sang*.

The note it called as it sliced through the air. The resonance of the blade as the steel struck its goal. The soft whistle when he pulled it free. The sounds converged into a battle hymn in his head, as a warmth of invigoration that didn't stem from his own tired muscles flowed through his arms.

A goal. A purpose. What it was made for. The colors on the sword whirled faster with the harder he fought.

Without warning, the melody screeched to a halt.

The sea of goborrins had parted before him, the cluster split to the jeering of beasts as something new rose from the depths of the earth.

Zaide stopped in the street, heart thudding and lungs burning, as the giant glass sphere reflected fire from every direction.

The monsters howled.

Zaide took a half step back. He knew what it was, had held a smaller device only scant hours before, but this sphere was so large, it took half a dozen goborrins to lift it. His eyes flicked past the army, toward the gate, where the guards still struggled to hold on.

A bomb.

The goborrins had a bomb.

CHAPTER TWENTY-SEVEN

"Incoming!" The guardswoman's voice scarcely cut through the sounds of battle.

Zaide pivoted on his heel and scanned the sky. Not far off, the glowing shape of the dragon's body loomed in the haze of smoke. It turned their way and came in from the side with embers spilling from its jaws.

His heart skipped a beat. "Valla!" Where was she? He'd moved ahead so fast, he hadn't seen where the woman ended up. Cries of panic went up from the gate guards.

A second later, the dragon swept by, pouring flame across the mass of goborrins that pressed close to the south gate, and the sounds of distress morphed to cheers.

As quickly as a gap in the army had opened around Zaide, it closed again. He whirled and fought, his breath ragged with the choking smog that rose in the dragon's wake.

Valla emerged as if from nowhere. She still held the Hymnflute, but it was in her off hand, and her blade flashed with more dexterity and skill than his.

Zaide darted toward her without explanation and seized the artifact from her hand. The guardswoman made a small sound that could have been confusion or surprise, but the moment he blew a note and wind kicked up to clear the air around them, her face lit with delight.

The smog was the least of his worries.

"The dragon—" Valla started, giving voice to his primary concern.

"Tula's with it," he answered before she could finish. "I think it's on our side." But the great beast hadn't seen what he'd seen emerging from the hole in the earth.

Valla blinked in surprise and looked skyward again, perhaps searching for the librarian, but the dragon was too far off for the girl to be visible now.

"Listen to me." Zaide paused to defend when a goborrin rushed him, their skirmish fast and fleeting with the way the Spectrum Blade sliced through its armor and flesh. He tried to get a good breath before speaking again. "You have to evacuate this part of the city. Abandon the south gate, get everyone out on the desert. Anyone who's left stuck inside needs to get to the far side of the city."

"Abandon the gate?" Valla cried.

"Just get everyone out of here!" He couldn't explain further. The dragon was on its way back.

Zaide ran for the open tunnel, ducking and weaving between goborrins. A harsh note on the Hymnflute churned a gust that sent the monsters toppling over as the dragon returned. A hasty song spun the artifact's barrier over himself, the bomb, and all the goborrins around it.

Blistering flame splashed against the barrier and flowed across its top, but the dragon didn't strike the barrier this time, and it remained intact. Overhead, an obvious roar of displeasure split the air.

Zaide bit back an oath. Would the dragon hear if he tried to explain? Would Tula figure out that something had gone wrong and explain it on his behalf?

The goborrins around him climbed back to their feet and robbed him of the chance to consider.

He let the barrier fall. The moment it did, the stench of charred corpses made his stomach lurch and brought tears to his eyes. He spun to look for Valla and the other guardswomen, dreading he might find them among the wide swath of the dead, but they were up and moving, cutting through the enemy to reach the south gate.

Of course they were. Tula wouldn't have allowed the dragon to incinerate the guardswomen along with the rabble.

Assuming she has any say at all, he reminded himself. She'd been on the dragon. That didn't mean she controlled it.

He tore his attention from the guardswomen and focused it behind the next drive of his blade.

The team of goborrins with the glass bomb were just ahead, but he never seemed to get any closer. Goborrins streamed from the hole in the earth in never-ending numbers. Zaide's sword arm ached and his shoulder burned, but he was too close to stop.

A handful of guardswomen broke through the line and reached the gates. New sounds of commands and confusion rose from the gate guards, the smallest reassurance that the people there—that Lark—would be taken somewhere safe. Whether or not the guardswomen had begun to evacuate the rest of the city, he had no way of knowing.

Forced to trust his order would be taken seriously, to hope the guardswomen would move everyone fast enough. With nothing else to offer, he shifted his efforts to one side of the hole. The bomb was free of the tunnel now, and the goborrins that toted the litter on which it rode pushed toward the gate.

Your Bladebearer seeks to foil me, the dragon snarled into Tula's mind.

She'd grown used to the forcefulness of his mental voice, but the intensity of anger that flowed into her alongside it left her shaking with unbidden fear.

As if he sensed what his words had done, he released a long, smoky breath through his nostrils and quieted his voice. *He shelters the monsters against my flame. Has he betrayed your princess so easily?*

"He has to have a reason." Tula spread her fingers wide and smoothed her hand over the glowing scales of his neck. She'd expected them to burn, but the sensation of touching him had proven pleasant. His scales radiated heat like a hearth fire, or a cup of hot tea cradled in hand. Soothing, reassuring. The kind of heat that brought comfort, not pain.

Vorkaris snorted his disagreement.

She leaned close, until her stomach flattened against the base of his neck. "Give him a chance, Magister. He'll prove himself."

If he continues to interfere with that artifact, I will burn him alive and take the Hymnflute for myself. They swept past the city and banked on the wind in preparation for another pass. *And I still say it would be more efficient to flame from the ground.*

"Maybe, but you can't see everyone you're breathing fire on from down there. Look! There are guardswomen at the gate!" Tula strained to point, knowing the dragon wouldn't see her hand, but hoping whatever power let him speak to her mind let him read her actions, too.

His head tilted the right direction. *They are in the way.*

"They're your people. They're your servants. The guardswomen answer to you, don't they?"

Jadora has forgotten its ways. The words came with a sour sense of sullenness.

"But you haven't forgotten." She stroked his neck again.

The gentle touch soothed some of his agitation, for his grumblings and dour attitude abated as they went in low again. Instead of the avenue nearest the gate, Vorkaris flew in farther north and breathed flame across a straggler group. From up in the air, the goborrins looked and sounded more like pigs than ever before. Tula shut her eyes and clung to the dragon's neck, trying to convince herself the sounds of death came from wild boar instead of monsters destroying her home.

The destruction has been extensive, he murmured into her thoughts. *My caverns are ruined by their tunneling.*

"I guess you'll just have to live in the palace now." They passed over a group of guardswomen and civilians who hurried northward through the streets. Tula sat a little straighter and gave a squeeze with her knees, alerting the Magister.

They flee to the palace? The palace is still under siege.

"Something must be wrong. Take us back over the south gate." Maybe they could land and find someone to explain the situation.

You will remain on my back, where I have put you, Vorkaris said flatly.

Tula snorted. "You're not the boss of me."

I'm the Magister, he replied. *I am the boss of everyone.* Still, he obliged, and their next pass over the south gate was slower and without flame.

"There's so many of them, they'll never get through. Look! There's Zaide." Tula leaned as far to the left as she dared without falling.

I am aware of where your puny Bladebearer is. I do not need him pointed out, nor would I like to see him.

Tula batted her hand against the ridge of his neck. "Stop it, you're being mean. Zaide's a good person. Look, the goborrins are all coming out of that hole, can you do something about that?"

The dragon's rumble vibrated beneath her. *With pleasure.*

A hard stroke of his wings sent them spiraling upward. Tula squealed and clung to his neck as the city rushed away beneath them. Their ascent slowed and he angled his wings in a new direction. The flight crested and they dove toward the desert.

Tula screwed her eyes shut tight and bit her tongue to keep from screaming. The wind sucked all the breath out of her, and when they leveled out again, she gasped for air.

Hold tight, Vorkaris said. *We're going up.* His claws latched onto the top of a boulder and he tore it from the desert sands. It crunched in his grasp as his wings pumped furiously, dragging the boulder skyward.

Tula wrapped her arms as far around his neck as she could manage and gaped at his strength.

A new wave of people flowed from the south gate to work their way down the switchbacked trail to the desert. The dragon arced high over the top, so the people were little more than shadowy dots accompanied by an occasional splash of light.

Tula patted the dragon's scales. "Do you think the princess is down there? Can you let me down so I can see?"

I am unimpressed by your listening skills, little human, he rumbled.

"You're unimpressed by a lot of things. Maybe it's just because you're old." She twitched her heels against his shoulders with the playful jab.

I am ancient, but that does not mean I am not fun. Watch this. Vorkaris passed the south gate and the goborrin army, then veered hard to one side and dove for the city. Not a moment too soon, he snapped his wings wide and pitched the massive boulder toward the street with the force of all four legs.

It slammed into the street and shattered the pavement, but its momentum was too great for it to stop there. The boulder bounced over a tier of stairs and tumbled down the road to strike the army of goborrins like a bowling ball. It hit the mob with a crack and the dragon cackled in the back of Tula's mind.

He flapped hard and they pulled upward as the boulder crashed through the swarm. It wasn't until they passed the hole in the street that Tula realized the path wasn't clear.

Each time the dragon passed overhead, Zaide grew more nervous. Was it angry? Would it strike him? Would Tula keep the creature from burning him to a crisp? He didn't have time to worry about it, but it sprang to mind every time he saw the dragon coming.

He alternated between fighting and chasing smoke away with the Hymnflute, both tasks that left him breathless. The moment he'd decided to focus on getting past the pit, the goborrins had redoubled their efforts to hold him back. And doubled their numbers, he thought grimly as he slammed his sword through another enemy. Pulling it free again took more strength than he thought he could muster.

But you have to. He tried to steel himself with the unspoken words, though he feared his arm would turn to jelly the moment he drew the sword back. By some miracle, it didn't.

Something like a thunderclap cracked over the city, but instead of fading, the rumble grew. Zaide looked skyward first, praying for rain to combat the fire and smoke. Instead, the dragon swept past and soared southward. He turned back the way it had come and his heart dropped so hard, it could have shattered on the stone.

The boulder barely slowed its roll as it flattened goborrins in its path.

Zaide backed up a step, then turned and ran.

The goborrins around the hole squalled and ran alongside him, strife momentarily forgotten. They rounded the pit and as they made for the south gate, Zaide looked back.

The boulder hit the hole and bounced right over it.

He spat a curse his foster mother would have slapped him for and ran harder. The intersection before the gate wasn't far ahead when Valla suddenly appeared in the crowd.

"What in the—" was all she got out before Zaide slammed into her and rerouted her with his arms.

"Go sideways, go sideways!"

He shoved her in that direction and lit off toward the side street. The boulder tumbled past as they darted out of the way. It crashed into the gate, shattered the portcullises and tore through the wall.

Zaide staggered, then collapsed onto the road. It was blessedly solid underneath him, and he sprawled out on his back to gasp for breath. Every inch of him felt as if it would melt into the pavement.

Valla scrubbed the back of her neck with her hand. "Where the blazes did that come from?"

"I... don't know," he got out between lungfuls of air.

She glanced down at him. "Get up. We need to check the damage."

He closed his eyes instead. "I'm... going... to die." It certainly felt like he might, with his heart knocking around in his chest hard enough that he felt his pulse in every fingertip.

A soft snort above him came followed by a nudge to his boot. "You'd better not, we've still got work to do."

His eyes snapped open. "Lark! You're—"

Her face twisted. "If the next word out of your mouth is 'alive,' I'm going to kick you."

"What if I was going to say pretty?"

She kicked him anyway.

Zaide grunted. "Pretty alive, anyway."

She kicked him again.

"Ow! Would you stop that?" Whatever relief he'd felt at her apparent wellness had already diffused. He tried to sit up, but his hands were still full. He extended the Hymnflute toward the princess.

Lark plucked it from his fingertips and stuffed it into her bag. "That boulder just went through the south wall. Someone needs to check to ensure none of the evacuees were harmed."

"Valla?" Zaide asked.

"On it," the guardswoman said before he had a chance to face her.

He dragged himself to his feet. "We need to move. There was no explosion, I don't know where the bomb went."

Lark shook her head. "Excuse me, the what?"

"The bomb! The goborrins brought it through that tunnel, we've got to find it." His knees threatened to buckle beneath him and he willed them to steady. A tingle brushed his left hand and he glanced down at the Spectrum Blade. It almost felt like a question. "I'm fine," he spat.

"I didn't ask."

"Not you, the—oh, just come on. They were taking it toward the wall. If the wall's got a hole blown in it already because of that boulder, then they'll use it somewhere else." The first place that came to mind was the palace. Zaide stumbled and Lark caught his arm to steady him.

"You need to sit down." The order was gentle, un-Lark-like, but there was nothing gentle about the way she gripped his arm when he tried to pull away.

He pulled harder. "I *need* to find where they took that thing! I just had Valla send everyone left in this part of the city toward the palace. If the goborrins are going that way, they'll be in danger and it'll be my fault!"

"Sit down," Lark snapped. This time, she pushed so forcefully, he had no choice but to cooperate.

He sank to the street and pressed a hand to his head. He was dizzy, weak, and so tired he didn't know if he could stand again. The princess stood over him with her stance wide. She pulled the Captured Spring out from beneath her shirt.

Zaide started to protest, but she raised a hand.

"This should help, though I don't know how much, since you aren't really injured. At least, you don't seem to be." She leaned forward to hold the open vial before his mouth.

He gave it a dubious frown. "You drank straight out of that." So had Andriun, for that matter.

Lark scowled and shoved it against his lips. "Drink!"

He made a sour face, but allowed the tiniest drop of liquid to pass his lips. It was cold, refreshing, and left a sweet tingle on the tip of his tongue. He swallowed and smacked his mouth. "Huh."

"What?"

"That does taste blue."

The faintest smile curled her lips. "Doesn't it?"

A cool sensation swept through his burning limbs a moment later. Zaide fought back a groan of relief. His breath came easier and the ache in his chest abated. It was subtle, but within moments, his strength began to return. He planted the Spectrum Blade's tip against the ground and used it to push himself to his feet.

Lark capped the vial and hid it beneath her shirt again. "The guards have all departed to the desert. The gate is ruined."

"Then we start there." He glanced to the sky, half expecting the dragon to make another pass, but he saw nothing. Where had it gone?

The princess nodded and led the way. She drew her knives, but the streets were almost empty and her stance was relaxed. The few goborrins that remained nearby were dead or dying, and a handful of guardswomen ranged between them to end their misery.

"Whatever the goal of those monsters was, it wasn't pursuing those who fled to the desert," Lark said. "I was on my way out when the boulder crashed through the wall, but the goborrins were already moving in other directions."

"Toward the palace," Zaide concluded with a sigh. Everything he'd done seemed to have become the wrong choice.

Lark ignored him and trotted toward a cluster of guardswomen. "Where are the goborrins?"

One of the women pointed toward the hole in the street. "They retreated. We're organizing a force to go in after them."

The princess's arm snapped out in front of Zaide.

He exhaled hard. "I didn't do anything!"

"Your sword turned. You point with that thing before you go anywhere. You are not going into that tunnel alone, do you understand me?"

"Which means you're going with me." He grasped her arm and pulled her toward the pit.

She dug in her heels. "Unhand me this instant!"

"If I do, you're probably going to hit me."

Lark glared.

Zaide pulled harder, to the amusement of the guardswomen, who stood back and watched.

Unable to match his strength, Lark stumbled forward a step. "I didn't give you that potion so you could immediately run off and get yourself hurt."

"And I can't let them sneak that bomb off in some other direction while I might be able to do something about it," he said.

Lark planted her feet again. "Zaide—"

"I'm not going to argue about this with you! What about the guardswomen? What about Elsanna? They're people who will die if we don't do anything!"

"Zaide!" She jabbed a finger past him and he spun to look.

A giant glass sphere rolled toward them.

CHAPTER TWENTY-EIGHT

"Is that…?" Lark squinted at the orb as it gained momentum.

Zaide leaped forward. "It's going for the hole!"

"Is that bad?" She sprinted along behind him.

"Is a giant bomb blowing up bad?" He leaped the charred corpses of goborrins and rounded the pit in the center of the intersection. The hole was dark; he had no idea how far down it went, but it was rough, and the bottle bombs they'd stolen from the salamanders had all exploded the moment they broke.

Lark shut her mouth and hurried.

How they were going to catch it, Zaide didn't know. The closer he got, the more he realized he'd had no concept of how large the bomb was. It was big enough to be level with the middle of his chest, were he standing beside it. But he wasn't standing beside it, and it was rolling with enough force that something that size would flatten him. The fleeting notion he'd just scoop it into his arms and take it somewhere else evaporated.

The bomb wobbled over a mass of dead goborrins and slowed as it reached the ridge beside the hole.

Lark gave a laugh.

It hung at the rim for an instant long enough to make Zaide hold his breath.

Then it slipped over the hole's edge.

"No!" He reached it a second too late. The glass slipped against his fingertips and the orb rolled past him.

Lark tossed up her hands. "You missed!"

"I'm trying, okay?" Zaide slid over the edge of the hole and spread his arms to regain his balance. The tunnel ahead was dark, but the sword in his hand brightened its glow. "Thank you. At least someone's helping."

The princess scoffed as she followed. "I am helping! What do you think giving you the spring's potion was?"

"Weird because you had your lips on it?" He held the sword out in front of him. The bomb wasn't far ahead. Its roll had slowed considerably and it teetered back and forth across the rocks and ridges in the uneven tunnel, which was far less steep than Zaide expected. He scuffed his way down toward it, mindful of his footing, and winced when the sphere rolled enough for him to make out the crack in one side.

"Oh, Maker forbid you ever touch a girl's lips," Lark said. "You'll be lucky if you—look out, ahead!"

The Spectrum Blade had already alerted him to the goborrins ahead. A spark shimmered down its blade. "I see them!" There weren't many, but quarters were tight.

Stones shifted under his feet and he slipped.

His foot shot forward and the rest of him followed, skidding down to the next ridge of the incline just as the bomb rolled up against it and slowed. He glanced between the sphere and the goborrins charging up the tunnel.

"Zaide, the bomb!"

"I know!" he shouted. His back was skinned raw from the rock and anything touching it was the last thing he wanted, but he slid ahead of the glass ball and braced his feet against the most solid piece of stone he could find. The bomb rolled up against his back and stopped. He winced as it pressed the fabric of his robe into the scrapes in his skin.

The two goborrins were just a step ahead. He shimmied to the right side of the tunnel to give himself room to try and fight, but Lark skimmed past him with her knives drawn.

He gritted his teeth and scanned the ground for a rock to wedge beneath the front of the bomb. He pinned it against the wall just as the princess drove a blade into the first goborrin's gut.

"Move!" Zaide darted in beside her and brought his sword down hard and fast. It flared when it hit the monster and Lark jerked her blade free.

She dispatched the next on her own as pebbles skipped down the tunnel.

Zaide hardly had a chance to turn before the sphere bore down on them. He grabbed Lark by the wrist and slammed her against the wall to shelter her with his form. The bomb rocked past them and clattered down the incline.

Lark met his eye for a panicked moment. "We have to stop it!"

"How?" He'd thought the rock would hold it. All he could figure was the sphere's weight was too great, the area of the tunnel where it stopped too sloped.

She huffed in exasperation and shoved him away. He almost slipped in the loose stone again, but caught himself at the last second. She was twenty paces down the corridor by the time he found his footing and rushed after her. The light from the Spectrum Blade was all they had, and its glow glinted off the sphere as it raced down into oblivion.

Zaide panted as he tried to close the distance. "If it breaks—"

"I know," Lark said.

He jumped a drop-off and took the lead. Running with his sword out was dangerous enough without having the princess directly in front of him. Far ahead, the sphere glittered, light refracted in its multitude of growing cracks. Beyond it, a soft glow lit the tunnel.

"Oh, no," Zaide groaned.

Heat swelled around them as the tunnel widened and the ground leveled off. He dropped the sword and ran with all his might.

He emerged onto the flat platform overlooking the volcano's heart just a step behind the bomb. Three more strides and he was beside it. He slammed his hands into the sphere to reroute it and it veered sideways, toward the cliff.

"No, no no!" Zaide almost tripped over his own feet in his haste. A second shove made it careen back toward the wall, but the ground was sloped, and its roll slowed as it went uphill. He caught up with it and dug his toes against the soles of his pointed boots as he planted himself in its path and put up his arms.

The whole weight of the bomb sagged against him until he thought his body would break, and ever so slowly, its roll came to a halt.

Lark burst from the tunnel a second later. "Zaide!" She stumbled to a halt and her shoulders sagged with relief when she saw him before the sphere, both hands still against it.

Zaide's head swam. He sucked in a deeper breath to try to clear his thoughts before he remembered where they were. His gaze swung toward the far end of the platform, where the cracked crystal case that once held the Molten Dagger still lay. "Huh." The single word came out sleepy, weak.

"Zaide, what's wrong?" She held out a hand as she advanced, her posture reminding him of the way one might approach a wild animal.

"This is where that other tunnel leads," he remarked, as if it would mean anything to her.

Lark stared at him as if she hadn't understood. "What?"

He swallowed and pressed a hand to his head. "I just remembered."

"Remembered what?"

He didn't have a chance to answer before the volcanic gases took their effect.

A calm morning light graced the room when Zaide woke. He blinked at the distant ceiling for a long time, unsure where he was or what had happened. There had been the bomb; he remembered that much. But the last thing he'd known, he'd had his hands against its crack-riddled surface. Now he lay in a plush bed in a room with a soaring ceiling and tall windows, where fresh air and sunlight were plentiful.

Delightfully fresh air, he decided. No smoke lingered to clog his lungs, and the acrid stench of the volcano was gone. Ah, that was it. The volcano. He grunted softly and rubbed his face.

"Ah!" Lark exclaimed nearby. "You're—"

"If the next word out of your mouth is 'pretty,' I'm going to kick you," he interrupted.

A pause came, followed by Tula's questioning voice. "Pretty?"

The princess snorted. "Nobody in their right mind would call you that. How do you feel? Vorkaris said you would be fine."

"Vorkaris?" Zaide turned to seek her face. Instead of Lark, he found his attention fixated on the massive dragon that reclined behind her chair like a great cat, his forepaws crossed and his tail swishing.

Magister Vorkaris, if you please. The dragon's voice was softer than it had been, though the way it crawled across his brain was still unpleasant.

"Oh. Right." Zaide ran his fingers through his soot-stained hair as he sat up. He was still woozy and his muscles ached after everything he'd put himself through, but it was better than he'd felt when he'd laid on the street outside the south gate. "The bomb?"

"Safely detonated in the desert outside the city, thanks to the Magister," Elsanna said. She stood beside the door with her arms crossed, and Moros stood with her. "And you, since you were the one who kept it from falling into the crater."

A momentary sense of discomfort gave him the urge to draw the blankets to his chin, but he resisted. "Why is everyone in my room?"

"Technically, it's his room." Tula jerked a thumb toward the dragon, who twitched his head upward in a motion Zaide dared say was amusement.

"The Spectrum Blade is on the table," Lark said, a gentle flick of her fingers pointing the way.

Tula grinned. "Moros got shocked five times before he got it into its scabbard."

"I have experienced worse things," the warden said.

Zaide didn't dare ask what. "How'd we get out of the tunnel?"

"Well, you did give me the Hymnflute." The princess cracked a smile. "It proved quite useful for chasing away the toxic vapors, and Valla found us shortly after."

"You woke up while the guardswomen were dragging you out of the underground tunnels, but you were so tired you fell asleep right after," Tula added.

Lark nodded her agreement. "The Magister offered his palace so we could rest. It's only been a few hours, though."

Zaide straightened his robes and pushed himself from the bed. "How bad are things at the gate?"

Elsanna fluttered a hand. "Eh, we will rebuild. Our people are safe. There were few civilian casualties, and the goborrins are gone."

"All of them?" He had trouble believing that, but the troubled looks that crossed the faces in the room made him more uncomfortable than a simple no.

The dragon was the one who spoke, his mental voice subdued. *The goborrins fled back into the underground. I suspect they will not show their faces again, now that I am here. Where they went, I cannot be sure, but the salamanders will keep watch.*

"Salamanders? Those lizard things that kept trying to kill us?" Zaide asked, incredulous.

A short-sighted mistake on their part. Forgive them. They are not that intelligent. Vorkaris released a soft whuff. Plumes of smoke drifted from his nostrils. *The salamanders answer to me. They were meant to be guardians of the tunnels, and I suspect they may have taken that job too seriously. Some were swayed by the forces Gadranus sent to claim my city, but they have been dealt with.*

"You will note that there were no salamanders in the army that filled the city," Lark said.

Elsanna nodded. "There were some in the palace, and in the tunnels, but they did not seem to know who they were meant to attack. As we cleared the palace, we found a handful of them fighting with goborrins on their own."

They made an effort, the dragon sighed.

"When we came for the Molten Dagger, a salamander was trying to bust its case open to get it out," Zaide said. "They'd attacked us, so I assumed they followed Gadranus. I killed them."

I am aware. A hint of annoyance brushed Zaide's mind, bleeding over from the dragon's voice. *My salamanders told me what you had done. They sought to wake me on their own when they sensed the city needed help. You foiled their efforts. Jadora would not have fallen if they had been able to recover the dagger on their own and wake me in a more timely fashion.*

A heavy silence fell across those gathered.

"So... this was our fault," Tula concluded.

Vorkaris bobbed his head. *Yes. And no. I do not like how events have unfolded in my city, but I do not condemn you for actions Gadranus has forced you to take. And despite your Bladebearer's folly, I concede that he risked himself to aid Jadora.*

"So you're not mad at me?" Zaide wasn't sure if smiling at a dragon was appropriate, so he kept his face still.

This time, when the dragon snorted, embers joined the curls of smoke.

Zaide ducked his head. "Understood."

But as I said, I concede that you put yourself in harm's way to right what happened in my city. I do not reward ignorance, but your courage, at least, is commendable. Vorkaris tilted his head to one side. *Had that sphere fallen into the magma, I doubt things would have ended as well for my city.*

Tula rounded on the dragon with her hands against her hips. "And if you'd blocked the hole, Zaide wouldn't have had to chase it down into the cavern to begin with."

The boulder was supposed to seal it.

"You missed!" Tula cried.

I am rusty, Vorkaris replied, unusually sheepish for a dragon.

"Wait!" Elsanna stood up straight. "*You* threw the boulder?"

The dragon craned his neck to avoid looking at her.

"It will take us months to rebuild the wall!" The guardswoman pressed fingers to her temples and gritted her teeth. From the look of it, she struggled not to scream.

"What about the city's defenses?" Zaide directed his question to Elsanna and Moros, lest he risk the dragon's ire again, but Vorkaris was the one who answered.

I have long prized Jadora's safety. You can rest assured my people will be safe.

"The city's defenses are imperiled by the gap, but I suppose having a dragon present as Magister will deter most attacks." Lark rose from her chair to pace the room, but she only made it as far as the table. She stopped there and touched the Spectrum Blade's scabbard, her face drawn with longing.

A hint of guilt quivered in Zaide's chest. How much smoother would things have gone if she wielded the blade, instead of him?

Her spine straightened a moment later and she turned to face the dragon. He towered over all of them, but as she strode toward him, he appeared larger than ever. She was tiny, small enough to fit in the claws of one of his forepaws, yet she stared up at the creature without fear.

"Should you require assistance in Jadora's defense, my father's soldiers will answer," she said.

The way the dragon tilted his head implied a smile, though his reptilian face was less than expressive. *Such an offer is appreciated, Your Highness, but not necessary.*

Lark sighed. "Then I fear I shall have to ask a favor with no way to repay it."

Ah. Zaide brushed his fingers across his forehead. How had he forgotten? Seeking the Magister's assistance was their sole purpose in visiting the desert city. He slipped from the bed and padded over to the table to reclaim his sword.

Vorkaris gave a soft rumble. *Yes, I know what you seek, and it is my duty to answer. However, it is not so simple as you may believe.*

The princess lifted her chin. "How so?"

I may be Magister, but my power requires a conduit. This is the human your kind will recognize as Magister in my stead. It will take time to transfer such strength and teach my new conduit to bear it.

"If you need a new leader for your city, Elsanna would be an excellent choice," Zaide said.

The dragon turned one golden eye his way. *She is a noble fighter and has filled her role well, but I have chosen another.*

Elsanna and Lark both gasped as he lowered his head to catch Tula's gaze.

The librarian looked left and right before she grasped the weight of his intention. "Wait. Wait, no! I don't want this!"

I understand, the Magister said, his powerful voice the most gentle it had ever been. *But my decision is already made.*

CHAPTER TWENTY-NINE

"THEY'VE BEEN in there a long time." Zaide tried not to pace, but he couldn't keep his feet still. He shifted in place and lifted one foot at a time to press the curled and pointed toes of his boots against the floor.

Lark studied the door to the Magister's quarters with a pensive wrinkle in her forehead, but otherwise, she struck him as unbothered. "I expect there is a great deal they'll need to work out before they're ready to speak to the rest of us. There are plenty of things to keep us busy in the meantime."

Except they waited on those things, too. Elsanna flitted between rooms of the palace, gathering reports from the guardswomen who came and went with news. Zaide paused to watch as the woman slid through the parlor again, a stack of papers in her hands. "Do you think the dragon made the right decision?"

"I don't believe that's for us to say." Lark propped her elbow on the arm of her chair and leaned against it. "I agree that Elsanna would have made an excellent leader, though. She has experience, and a strong reputation among the city's people."

"Her name is enough to scare people."

The princess offered a wry smile. "After seeing her fight, I understand why. They managed to injure her when she was in chains, but after she was healed with a drop from the spring, no one touched her in battle again."

Zaide gave his head a slow shake of disbelief. He'd seen it himself, but he couldn't grasp it. "I wish we could stay longer. I could have her help me, make me a better fighter."

She sobered. "Depending on how long it takes Tula and Magister Vorkaris to settle their differences, you may get your chance."

The door at the far end of the parlor opened a crack. Zaide expected another guardswoman, or maybe part of the palace serving staff, but Moros poked in his head, instead.

"Your Highness," the warden began, an unusual touch of hesitance in his voice, "I require your presence."

"My presence?" Lark touched her chest. "Not Elsanna?"

"Elsanna's presence would also be appreciated."

Zaide almost bounded into motion. "I'll get her." She'd just slipped into the next room over. The office was a mess, but the guardswoman had people working to right things.

He peeked through the door, afraid he might interrupt something, but the room was quiet, with only a handful of people present. The guardswoman stood behind a wide desk of carved wood, drumming her fingertips on its surface as she skimmed the paper in her hand.

He opened the door a little wider. "Elsanna, Moros needs you."

"Hm? Oh." She lowered the paper and rubbed her eyes. Unlike the rest of them, Elsanna had yet to rest. "Of course. Is this about the gathering of the Mage-Guard?"

"I don't know." Zaide held the door so she might pass, then trailed along beside her. Lark and the warden stood ready to go.

"My apologies for interrupting your work." Moros didn't look apologetic, but he rarely looked anything.

Elsanna waved for them to move. "What's going on?"

The scarred man led the way. "All members of the Mage-

Guard have been found and arrested. They are not agreeable. I would imprison them all, but they are numerous, and Jadora's prison is not equipped to hold so many."

"Are you sure?" Zaide asked. "The prison is huge."

"Its size may be impressive, but it is not well maintained, nor do we have a staff capable of preparing and monitoring that many cells at this time." Moros took them out the front of the palace and toward the side where the prison was hidden.

Lark wrinkled her nose as they passed through the yard where city guards piled the bodies of goborrins and laid their fallen comrades in long rows to be covered by sheets, but she said nothing.

Stoic, Zaide thought. For as delicate as she looked, she was stoic. A great deal of her demeanor had come across as standoffish and arrogant, but the longer he looked, the more he grew convinced that impression stemmed from strengths, not faults.

They rounded the corner and a long row of men in chains came into view. It stretched far beyond the entrance to the prison, and dozens of guards stood with them, making the space claustrophobic.

"It would seem our false Magister recruited far more people for his Mage-Guard than we realized," Elsanna murmured.

Zaide scanned the line. "They're all men."

She snorted. "Of course they are. Women who want to learn to fight join the guardswomen."

"I thought all the guardswomen were related?" he asked.

Elsanna shrugged. "They are. But after this many generations, most of the city can trace their lineage back to the Magister's first guardswoman. That's sort of how lineage works."

"Convenient," Lark said.

Moros pointed to the first mage-guard in line. "We will begin here and work our way down. It is not possible for all of these men to be guilty of sedition against Jadora."

The princess nodded. "A number of them merely accepted a job, not knowing what it may entail."

"So we need a list of questions to use to ferret out those who cannot be trusted to go free," the warden concluded.

Zaide gave the men a second glance. Some wore bitter scowls or cautiously stony expressions, but most were scared, worried, or exhausted. Somehow, he didn't think the screening would take long.

A steady stream of guards in plain armor came and went from the prison with supplies, but a small cluster of guards emerged together and headed straight for their group. When one of the guards moved to the front, it was clear they brought bad news.

"Warden," the man said. "We have a situation."

Moros turned. "Show me."

The rest of the group of guards remained behind while the one who had spoken guided them into the prison.

They passed the empty cell where Zaide had been kept, the corridor now brightly lit and filled with men at work. They stopped outside the confinement cells with their heavy iron doors. The man gestured toward one of them.

Moros touched a tiny, round disk of metal that looked like a rivet and pushed it to the side. It swung open to reveal a hole with a glass lens set inside, and he pressed his face close.

"What is it?" Elsanna asked.

He unsheathed his sword. "Move back."

The group scuttled backwards. Lark pressed close to Zaide's side, not for lack of space, and he brushed his fingers against her arm to offer reassurance.

The warden opened the door and slipped inside. Elsanna followed without permission, and the guard who had brought them put his head down.

A moment later, Moros emerged. "The Magister is dead."

"What?" Lark shoved forward and flung the door wide. Inside the cell, the man who had called himself Magister lay sprawled on the stone floor with his long black hair strewn about him.

Elsanna smoothed a hand over the dead man's robes, putting them back in order after her search. "No marks."

"He had nothing but his clothing when we left him here." Moros cast Zaide a sidewise glance. "Not even shoes."

And that punishment had been short-lived. Zaide slid into the narrow cell to move past Elsanna and search the walls with both hands. "How did this happen, then?"

Lark knelt beside his body and exhaled hard. "He could have been poisoned. He would have been given water by now, correct?"

"An angry guard who decided to take matters into his own hands?" Elsanna suggested.

Zaide found nothing, no secret switches or brushes of air that might indicate a hidden path an assassin could take. He lowered his hands and curled them to fists. "Or someone on the enemy side, making sure we don't get a chance to ask questions."

"And Jinohe is dead by my blade." Elsanna scoffed low in her throat.

"The two people who could have given us answers," Lark said.

Zaide had plenty to ask. How had the false Magister known about the dagger and the dragon, when even the librarians didn't? How had that knowledge slipped free of what the librarians knew to begin with? Dozens more passed through his thoughts, but in the end, he only let one free. "So how do we find out who he was?"

The princess pushed herself up. "It doesn't matter. His movement is over and he won't trouble us again."

"So we give up? Just like that?" The impulse to touch the Spectrum Blade and see if it agreed with his indignation was strong, and he didn't like it. He clenched his fists tighter.

Elsanna stood, too. "There's nothing else we can do. Come.

The tunnel in the cell across the way is being sealed, and we'll be in the way of the workers if we stay here."

"I'll write a list of questions to ask the mage-guards who have been arrested," Lark said as she slipped into the prison's main walkway and made for the front room. "Elsanna, I'll need your assistance to ensure they're attuned to the state of things in Jadora."

Zaide didn't know if he should follow, but Moros lingered in the front of the cell, blocking the way.

"What do you wish me to do with the body?" the scarred man asked.

Lark and Elsanna both paused to consider.

"We don't know who he is, where he's from, or what his customs may be," the princess murmured.

The guardswoman's lip curled. "I don't care. He dishonored himself and brought our city irreparable harm. Feed him to the pigs."

The memory of the previous Magister's bones in the grip of the chained goborrins made Zaide shudder. "Is that our official method of Magister disposal now?"

Elsanna answered with a mirthless smile. "Don't tell Tula."

He fought back another shudder and rejoined them in the hall.

As afternoon crawled near, people began to filter back in from the desert. Weary, disheartened faces filled the streets. The smoke was gone, but the scent remained, as did the ash and soot. Zaide paused his work now and then to watch people go by.

Guards and guardswomen wheeled carts past at regular intervals, their beds piled high with dead goborrins. Carrion birds filled the sky, their wings more ominous than smoke had ever been. The monsters were given a resting place in the desert, nothing more than a pit in the sand. Elsanna said it was better than they deserved. Zaide was inclined to agree. He watched another cart go by, then returned his attention to his work.

"There you are." Lark's silhouette blocked the sunlight, forcing him to pause.

Zaide sat on the ground, safely out of the way in the guardswomen's armory. A tangle of leather straps sat in his lap. "Elsanna told me I should stay out of the way. Tula?"

"Still with the dragon." She crept forward and eased herself to the floor beside him. "What's that?"

His nerves fluttered and he offered an uneasy grin. "For the Hymnflute. Or, it will be. The first one didn't work out so well, but I think I've got it now." He untwisted the straps but held tight to his needle and thread.

Lark cocked her head to the side, unable to make sense of it. "Uh-huh."

"It's a little clumsy, but it should be all right. Can I see it? I'll show you." He held out his hand. Even with as familiar as they'd become, he wasn't bold enough to snatch things out of the princess's bag while she wore it.

She folded back the bag's flap and removed the Hymnflute. Its little wooden flowers clinked pleasantly against its pipes as she passed it to him.

Zaide straightened out the straps and slid the artifact between them. It fit in the unfinished sling securely, though there was not yet a catch for the top strap. "This will fasten here." He tapped the front of the sling. "So it can't slide out if it gets turned upside down, but you'll be able to unhook it with a thumb and get the flute out fast."

Her eyes brightened. "I see."

"This will be the shoulder strap. The Hymnflute's not very heavy, but the leather's kind of hard, since I'm using scraps and didn't get a lot of options. I'm going to add some padding so it won't chafe." He slid the strap on overhead to demonstrate how it would hang at his hip. "Hmm."

"What's wrong?"

"I think I need to add a buckle or something. I made it my size. Not sure it'll fit on you, it might be too long. I wasn't thinking, I guess." He fingered the strap for a moment. There hadn't been any buckles in the box of scraps the blacksmith had offered when Elsanna gave permission for him to make something, so long as it kept him out of the way. There were a few pieces of leather cording, though. Maybe something with adjustable laces would work.

Lark offered a slight smile. "I'm sure you'll figure something out." She accepted the Hymnflute when he gave it back, then leaned forward to run her fingers across the uneven stitches. "I didn't know you could do this."

He settled back to work, finishing the joining point of two straps with his needle and thread. "It's generous of you to think I can. It's new. I'm not really good at it."

"You don't have to be, as long as you enjoy it and your work is serviceable."

"Well, it might be that." Zaide checked the length of the strap again, then dug through the box of scraps to find that cording. "At least for something this simple, it doesn't need to be pretty. Or complicated."

"Hm," was all Lark said.

She watched him work for a while, her knees drawn up and her arms folded atop them. Eventually, the city took her attention.

Zaide paused long enough to study her face. "You look sad."

"It's hard not to be. I feel like this was our fault." Her shoulders tightened and she tucked her chin, though her rich blue eyes remained focused on the scene beyond his borrowed workshop.

"It kind of was." Trying to undo a stitch so he could incorporate the cording let the needle prick his finger, and he paused to suck on his fingertip. He didn't need to elaborate. They'd both heard the dragon.

Lark snorted. "You seem very calm about that."

"I can't really stop to be upset about it right now. We've got to get the sword's blessing here, then head to Desheni for the last one, and then we're throwing ourselves back into the middle of the war. If I stop and think about everything that's gone wrong so far, I won't be able to keep going." The strap came loose when he tugged on it. He made himself focus on that now, as the burdens of all they'd been through bubbled back to the surface of his thoughts.

"What do you do, then? You can't just bottle it up and not deal with it."

Zaide gave a guilty shrug. "Ehh..."

"Zaide, that's not good for you." She shifted to sit on her heels, a stern frown plastered on her face. "You need time to sit and work through bad experiences. Talk to people, let them know what you're feeling."

"What, like you?" He grinned to soften the words. "You're shut up tighter than a river clam."

"That's different," she said. "I have to be."

"Says who?"

Her determined expression faltered.

"Yeah, exactly." He'd had a hole punch. Where did that go? He leaned back and felt around on the ground as he searched for it. "I know, though. It's one of those instances where you want me to do as you say, not as you do. I'm starting to figure you out."

She turned away. "You don't know anything about me."

"I know you don't want me to." Zaide shrugged.

The redness in her cheeks could have been frustration or embarrassment.

His hand bumped something. The hole punch. He straightened out the strap across the block of wood he'd found to hammer against, then pressed the punch to the leather. "I know being around you is like being around two different people, sometimes. Because you're Lark, and you're Dasienna. One of you is serious all the time. Duty-driven and determined to prove you can help save Amroch." He punched several holes and brushed the little circles of loose leather out of the way. "The other one smiles sometimes."

Lark snorted.

"Yeah, like that." He pointed the end of the punch at her nose.

"I didn't smile."

"Yes you did. You get a little smirk when you think something's funny, you just don't know you do it. Or that you have a sense of humor, apparently. Can you hand me that?" Zaide nodded toward a pair of shears.

"Those." She scooted them closer.

"And now you're Dasienna again, because you're being pedantic." He threaded the cord through the new holes and snipped off the excess.

The princess grew quiet, so he focused on figuring out a lacing pattern that would be strong enough to hold, but simple enough that changing the length of the strap wouldn't be frustrating. He settled on a simple criss-crossing order, then dug in the box. There had been a wooden toggle at the bottom. If he found it, that would do for the closure at the front.

It rolled away twice before he caught it. Once he had it in hand, he held out the holster. "Here, try this on. See if you like how it fits, or if I need to add a few more holes to the strap before I sew this thing where it goes."

Lark stood and slid the strap over her head. "This should do."

Zaide extended his hand again, and she shed the holster and gave it back. "I'll get this finished and bring it back for the Hymnflute after I clean up in here. It should be handy, having it right at your side instead of stuck in a bag all the time." He twisted the thick straps between his fingers for a moment, then stifled a sigh. "You should probably go check on Tula."

"You're probably right." She adjusted her bag and turned to go.

He threaded the thick needle. "Hey."

The princess paused.

"Lark's the one who's happy sometimes. Just for the record, I like her better."

She snorted and spun to leave, but not before he caught the faintest hint of a smile.

THERE IS MORE, *but together, those are the core duties of the Magister.* The dragon's voice left her head, leaving her mind to her own thoughts for the first time in what felt like ages.

"But I can't be the Magister," Tula insisted. "I'm—I'm not even a full-fledged librarian yet. I'm still an apprentice! There have to be a hundred people in the city better suited to it than me."

She hadn't stopped pacing since the dragon's announcement. It would have been a shock even without spectators, but the moment everyone's eyes had turned her way, she'd thought she might faint on the spot.

Vorkaris had not moved. He still lounged with his tail tip curling and uncurling like a cat's. *I understand, but that changes little.* He remained patient; she wasn't sure how. She had to have repeated herself a hundred times by now. She'd lost count of how many times she'd interrupted his explanation of her new duties.

The reasons behind her objection seemed good enough to her, but he still insisted she would be his conduit. Her, barely eighteen years old, Magister of Jadora. Revered leader of the Watcher, the powerful and impregnable city in the desert.

Or, *previously impregnable,* she thought with a grimace.

She paused her pacing long enough to spin and face the dragon. "But why can't you pick Elsanna? You keep saying no, but you haven't told me why! Why can't she do it? The city loves her, she's a good leader, she—"

She was not the one who unsealed the door. Your role in this was decided the moment you sought the dagger.

Tula froze. "What?"

It was sealed to protect it. Your studies told you this much. He lowered his head until his gaze was level with hers. *To lock its power away until need drove someone worthy of its might to break the seal and retrieve it. Someone worthy of* my *might.*

"But I didn't break the seal," she protested weakly. "Zaide did."

But you were the first of Jadoran blood to reach its chamber. You aided in its recovery.

She wrung her hands. "It has to be someone Jadoran?"

Not only Jadoran, but someone of the first Magister's bloodline. He blinked slowly, his golden eyes fixated on her face.

"The first Magister." Wringing her hands wasn't enough. She caught the edge of her robe in both hands and worried that, instead. "And the first guardswoman. All the guardswomen..."

Carry the first Magister's blood. Yes. His head tilted to one side. His expression never changed—she didn't think it could—but the angle from which he looked at her now struck her as sympathetic. *Had your little library's records not been tampered with, you would have known this. Unraveling the mystery of who has hidden knowledge from your people must be one of the first tasks we address, once your conversion to conduit is complete.*

"I'm not ready." Tula's voice cracked.

And if you wait until you feel you are, Jadora may never have a proper Magister again. His tail curled and swished in a steady rhythm. *Your friends wait for you, you know.*

She straightened and looked behind her. The room was

empty, the others having left some time ago to allow the two of them to talk. "But what if they're not?"

Vorkaris tilted his head the other direction. *Waiting?*

"Friends."

The rumble of his draconic laugh was hearty enough to shake the floor. *I can hear them. They are in the next room, worrying about you.*

Tula stared at the doors. She heard nothing, but surely the dragon's senses were better than hers. "Me?"

Your Bladebearer is concerned I may be treating you unkindly.

"His name is Zaide. I don't think we're friends, though." They'd interacted so little after their frustrating expedition to recover the Molten Dagger. Their time on the ship would have been the best time for her to make sure everything was smooth between them, but she'd devoted herself to the study of the artifact, instead. At the time, it had seemed most important. Now, all that research and effort seemed to be in vain.

I know who he is. And I know he is making the princess nervous, because he keeps trying to open the door. Watch. Vorkaris rose and padded toward the door, his movement startlingly stealthy, given his size. He lowered his head and crouched like a cat waiting beside a mouse's hole.

The door opened and Zaide shouted in alarm when it put him face-to-face with the dragon. The mental cackle that brushed Tula's mind almost drowned out the sound of the door slamming shut again.

She couldn't help a laugh of her own.

When the moment of mirth subsided, she wiped her eyes. The moisture was not all from laughter. "They're waiting for me, aren't they?"

They need you.

"They need the Magister."

The Magister is you.

Tears brimmed against her eyelashes. "I'm not ready."

You never will be. But... He tipped his horned head toward the door. *You won't be alone.*

Tula swallowed hard and made herself nod.

Good. Vorkaris turned and slid back to settle before her. His tail curled close around his haunches as he sank to his elbows—did dragons have elbows? She wasn't sure of the anatomy—and opened his large clawed forefeet before her. *Now, come. Let's awaken that nascent power within you.*

"Will it hurt?" She inched closer, until he could curl his claws to create a cage above her head. Warmth radiated from his scales and she shut her eyes.

I don't believe anyone has ever asked that before.

Her nose crinkled and she screwed her eyelids tighter shut. "That's not a very reassuring answer." Actually, it wasn't an answer at all.

Instead of giving her a proper answer, the dragon chuckled. *Relax.*

Tula couldn't relax, so she braced herself, instead.

Vorkaris spread his jaws, the rasp of his teeth separating warning her of what might come. But when he breathed over her, it wasn't angry fire or gloomy ash that poured over her, but a gentle roll of warmth and light. She cracked an eye open and was greeted by swirls of orange light that twisted around her body and sank through her clothing. The magic tingled as it sank into her flesh, and as it did, she grew aware of a strange new sensation.

Warmth.

Breath.

A pulse that wasn't her own.

She gasped and drew up her sleeve. Beneath the fabric, a glowing outline of a dragon etched itself into her skin.

The mark of your new power, the dragon said with a smug note of pride.

Tula whipped up her other sleeve. A dragon coiled there, too, wrapped around her forearm with its head nestled at her wrist.

"How far up does this go?" She pushed her sleeve higher and higher, tracing the contour of the glowing lines with her fingertips.

All the way. Their tails will be entwined on your back. Do you like them?

"I don't know," she replied honestly. She let her sleeves down.

He didn't seem offended. *Perhaps you will grow used to them, then. They will not always be visible. Only when your new power is needed.*

"And... how do I use that power?"

He snorted softly, and instead of smoke, plumes of steam spouted from his nose. *All in time, my little Magister. Right now, we have work to do. Shall we call your friends?*

Tula held the cuffs of her sleeves. "Okay."

The dragon extended his foreleg until he could catch the door's handle with one massive claw. He unlatched it and pulled while he turned Tula around with his other paw and nudged her forward with his nose against her back.

She stumbled along to the doorway, where she froze and held her sleeves tighter.

Zaide was closest by. He had one hand on his sword and a face full of worry when he made his way toward her.

"I'm fine," she lied. "I think we're done."

"Are you certain?" Dasienna asked as she approached.

"He's been talking about responsibilities and inter-city treaties and tax collection for hours," Tula said. "I don't know what else could be left."

The princess frowned. "I meant you." She touched Tula's arm, her hand gentle and supportive, an understanding light in her eyes. Of course Dasienna understood; she was the only one present who had lived through anything similar. Politics and responsibilities foisted upon her by blood had shaped the princess's life. Now it seemed they would shape Tula's, too.

Tula did her best to smile. "I'm all right." She wasn't sure of it, but maybe she'd have a chance to talk to Dasienna in private before they departed for Desheni. The thought of the expedition put a lump in her throat, so she swallowed hard and tried to clear it.

"Elsanna just left to get some food. She'll bring water and tea along with it, so you can have a drink," Zaide said, misinterpreting what made it hard for her to speak.

"Thank you." Tula wasn't sure it was polite to correct him.

Behind her, Vorkaris loomed, great and glowing and fierce. His presence was intimidating enough that Zaide took a step backwards, though Dasienna met the dragon's stare with a level gaze.

There is more for me to instruct her on before the day is out, but we cannot waste too many hours, the dragon said. When he wasn't angry, his mental voice was a perfectly reasonable volume. Tula dared say it was pleasant to listen to, and it left a warm sensation in her head after he spoke. Warm like his scales, like a cup of hot tea.

Come to think of it, hot tea didn't sound bad at all.

"The guardswomen have assembled in the palace yard. Elsanna has been itching to give them orders, but she hasn't known what to ask of them, beyond cleaning up the bodies of the dead." Dasienna's brow furrowed as she spoke. "I did not wish to overstep any bounds by making suggestions."

The dragon rumbled and pulled the second door open. That was one part of the palace that would have to be remodeled. At some point through the years, the dragon-sized doors to the Magister's quarters had been replaced with something more modest. Still larger than anything a man might ever need, but even with the opening being ten feet high and eight feet wide, it proved difficult for Vorkaris to wriggle himself in and out of the space. Instead of trying to depart now, he slid forward until his shoulders brushed the door frame and let his head and neck snake out alone.

I was the one who encouraged Jadora to kneel and be swallowed by the Allied Kingdoms of Amroch. I would not be offended by the heir's recommendations. The dragon's jaws split in a way that would have been frightening, had Tula not already learned it was his equivalent of a grin. *In fact, I would appreciate the chance to hear your thoughts. I would take comfort in knowing whether our future ruler bears sense befitting such a title.*

Tula winced. "That's rude."

I am a dragon. We are not known for our manners.

"Despite that, you appear to have no difficulty in wielding a silver tongue when it behooves you." Dasienna smirked.

Vorkaris rumbled his agreement with a mellow mental laugh.

Tula found herself leaning against the dragon's neck, her fingers tracing the outline of each large scale. "I have some suggestions, too, if I'd be allowed to make them."

Zaide made a face. "Aren't you supposed to be leading this place? You're the one who's going to be giving the orders, why wouldn't they want to hear your suggestions?"

Though she knew he meant it to reassure her, Tula found his words unsettling, and her heart raced. "Well, I... I don't know..."

"I'll start, then." Dasienna planted her hands on her hips and stood with her shoulders squared. "The south gate is, as of right now, our lowest priority. The people of Jadora are on their way back into the city, along with the merchants who have been waiting to gain access. The gate guards have tripled their numbers while they wait for further instruction, and they're doing an efficient job of screening re-entry and new visitors."

The south gate can wait, Vorkaris agreed.

The princess nodded as if she'd expected that answer. "Our main priority right now needs to be sealing off all other alternative entrances into the city. There are a large number of tunnels beneath the palace now, which intersect with the natural caverns. These need to be sealed. All of them."

That, the dragon took less well. A tingle brushed Tula's arms, where the magic dragon-marks were branded, and she stroked his neck with a soothing hand. "We need to leave one entrance.

A ledge in the crater is where Vorkaris sleeps. I don't think he'd appreciate having his volcano blocked off entirely."

Vorkaris appeared to be placated by her statement, for his voice was calm when he spoke into their minds again. *I fully intend to return to my rest when Jadora's affairs are settled. Political issues tire me. A path to my volcano will remain.*

"We can keep it connected to the palace," Tula suggested. "The rest of the tunnels should be collapsed."

"Can we do that without causing structural damage to the city?" Zaide asked.

Dasienna tapped a finger against her chin. "Maybe not collapsed, then. Magister Vorkaris, would it be possible to channel magma into the tunnels to seal them with rock, instead?"

Hmm, he rumbled. *It might be a good training session for my new protege.*

Tula gulped. "Can I... really do that?"

Perhaps. Perhaps not yet. It will take time for your new powers to mature.

"There's something else we need to address, too. Something else we need to know you're capable of." Zaide unsheathed the Spectrum Blade by an inch, then returned it to the scabbard.

The dragon huffed and lifted his head until he could glower downward. *You are an impatient brat.*

Zaide blinked up at him as if he didn't know what to say.

Tula patted the dragon's neck until he lowered his head. "I will bless the sword," she said.

Even Vorkaris looked at her in surprise, and warmth blossomed in her cheeks.

"I don't know how, yet," she added in a hurry, "but if I'm the conduit and the human Magister, it means I can."

"Can we pursue this now?" Dasienna asked. She turned to Tula with the question first, but then twisted toward the dragon. "I wouldn't dare claim it the most important task on the new Magister's plate, but when compared to the task of flooding hundreds of tunnels with magma, it seems restoring power to the blade is less likely to exhaust her."

"The tunnels can be sealed any time," Zaide added.

Yes, Vorkaris agreed, though with a certain amount of dubiety.

Tula's fingers twitched with a desire to wring the edges of her robe some more, but she kept them flat against the dragon's neck. "What do I have to do?"

"Resia had us take the sword to the spring beneath the forest's temple. She put it in the water and said something to cue the blessing." Zaide drew the shimmering blade from its leather sheath, the motion almost soundless.

"The words were recorded in my journal," Dasienna added. "I believe you studied them while we were on the ship."

Tula recalled them, simple and effective. "Am I supposed to do something like that? But I don't have a spring. My source of power is Vorkaris."

Zaide scratched the back of his neck. "There has to be some way." He tilted the blade so it looked as if the flowing iridescence coursed toward the floor. It was so like ripples of water, Tula almost expected it to drip from the end.

"Should he..." Tula removed her hand from the dragon at last. She wound the edge of her robe between her fingers and held it fast. "Should he lick it?"

The dragon was not amused.

Dasienna tapped her chin some more. "You're the mortal conduit for the Magister's power. Can you think of something that might reflect that?"

"He's done this before, hasn't he? Shouldn't he know?" Zaide asked.

Do not overwhelm the child with questions, Vorkaris growled.

Tula didn't know if she should thank him for the concern or be irritated that he felt she needed it. "That's a good question, though. You do know how to do it, don't you?"

The dragon swung his head back and forth in a slow

negative. *The blade was first forged in my flame, but like all dragons, my strength has grown. I fear an attempt to repeat the process would result in damage. I have seen no other blessings.*

"None?" The princess's brows drew together, a deep knot of confusion between them. "Does the process not require your power?"

Under typical circumstances, my human conduits should be able to pass their power from one human Magister to the next, allowing me to sleep for many generations. When I chose to hide the dagger, the blade was strong. I have never seen the process, and the conduits who knew it are now long dead.

Tula gave the edge of her robe a tug, then crept back to the door. "I have an idea. Let me through, please?"

The dragon blinked at her, but drew back enough that she could squeeze through the doorway.

"Come with me," she called.

The others had no choice but to tail her into the Magister's quarters.

At the far end of the room, a tall fireplace with a hearth as wide as the dragon's shoulders waited against the wall. Now that she got a better look at it, she realized it was a later addition to the palace. It made sense; dragons with glowing scales that emitted heat of their own had little use for fireplaces. It was well-stocked, though, and she pointed to the ashes as she knelt beside the tinderbox. "Put the sword in there."

Zaide gripped the hilt a little tighter. "I thought fire would damage it?"

"Just do as she says," Dasienna murmured. They exchanged looks, the way their eyes locked betraying the silent battle of wills, but after a time, Zaide acquiesced. He knelt to lay the Spectrum Blade in the ashes left from the night before, and Tula saw the hesitance in how his fingers trailed across the hilt before he moved back.

"Don't worry." She didn't know how reassured he would be when she wasn't sure of what she was doing, but she did her best to smile and put on an air of confidence. Doing what she had in mind bore little chance of harming the artifact.

With the sword in place, she drew a twig from the tinder and turned to the dragon. "Vorkaris, would you?"

He rumbled and gave a sigh. *Hold it overhead.*

She raised the twig.

Far overhead.

Tula extended her arm until she could reach no farther.

The dragon angled his chin upward and gave the tiniest puff. A controlled flame spouted across the twig and ignited the end, but the heat was intense enough to make her gasp.

Better your hand than your hair, he said with enough chagrin that she suspected there was a story to be told.

"Thank you." She cupped the flame with her other hand to shelter it as she brought the flame down and knelt at the edge of the hearth. Nearby, Dasienna had her notebook ready. Always a scholar. A kindred spirit, and one Tula would miss.

Zaide remained still but tense, his fingers flexing at his sides as if he itched to rescue the sword. After everything she'd seen, she wondered what his bond with the blade was like, but there would be no chance to study that now. A pang of sorrow hit Tula's chest and she gulped hard to keep it at bay.

"Okay, here goes." She made herself focus on the tiny flame, on the heat that graced her fingers.

It struck her as fragile; odd, considering its destructive force and what it had done to the city. She bit her lower lip and knelt at the edge of the hearth.

The flame was small, but it could grow. "Like you," she murmured as she touched the burning twig to the blade. "Like your power."

She'd never worked magic before. All Jadorans had it; it let them bear the desert heat and tolerate the fumes from the volcano that made visitors ill. But touching it consciously was different, and she wasn't like the men in the ranks of the arrested Mage-Guard or the librarians who wore the carved crest that marked them as competent in the power.

No, but you are the Magister, Vorkaris rumbled in her thoughts, and somehow she knew the words were for her alone.

She squinted and thought back at him. *You can read my mind?*

We are connected in more ways than one. With time, you will be able to read mine, too. Even when I sleep.

Tula didn't know if that would be a blessing or a curse. *I could use some mind-reading now. What am I supposed to do next?*

Whatever you've decided is best.

She stared at the tiny flame. A small power. Fragile, but ready to grow, to spread, to become something more. Slowly, she reached toward it with her other hand.

The others remained silent as she touched a fingertip to the flame. Its color morphed, a cool blue instead of bright orange, and when she drew her finger down the sword's central ridge, the flame followed.

Good, Vorkaris said with a small purr.

The flame spread outward to envelop the width of the blade, and as it faded, a soft white glow was left behind.

"Dragon fire's not meant for destruction," she murmured as she guided the flame to the tip of the sword. "Is it? It's powerful, but it's here to defend."

"As is the sword," Dasienna said.

The blue fire washed across the rest of the steel and faded, leaving the whole sword white. Tula nodded. "As is the sword, which is why we give the flame back." She pressed her palm flat against the blade's surface and willed that thought to enter it.

Warmth blossomed beneath her hand and a flash ignited to race outward, tip to pommel, glittering and fading at the edges of the blade.

Its color returned, warm reds shifting across its surface like they shifted in the veins of the Molten Dagger.

Zaide grunted softly and touched a hand to his forehead.

The princess lowered her pencil. "Are you all right?"

He feels it, Vorkaris said. *Don't you, boy?*

"I'm not even touching it." Zaide shook his head as if to shed whatever sensation coursed through him.

The dragon chuckled. *Soon, it won't matter. The blade has chosen you, and it is your eternal burden to bear.*

Something he hadn't asked for or claimed, something to carry without cease. Like her, with the mantle of Magister. Tula tried to smile as she inched back from the hearth so he could retrieve the blade, but the expression wouldn't come.

Her first act as Magister was done, and there was no going back.

CHAPTER THIRTY-ONE

THE SWORD FELT no different when Zaide pulled it from the ashes, no matter what had buzzed inside his head the moment Tula touched it with her blessing. He hardly knew what to think of that, nor had he made sense of what that sensation had been, but the sword had been silent since then. He touched it now and then, trailed his fingers over the pommel and cross guard, but nothing had graced his fingers.

The dragon's words had left their own burden on him. Soon, it wouldn't matter if he touched it? Zaide could only assume Vorkaris meant something would happen when the blade's power was fully awakened. Would it cross into a sense of awareness beyond the strange buzzing sensations he got now and then? Or did the Magister merely mean that connection would intensify? Considering the way the sword had shrieked into his mind when he'd struck down those guards, he wasn't sure he liked that notion at all.

"Are you all right?" Tula walked beside him, though she clung to the ends of her sleeves in a way he hadn't seen her do before.

Zaide made himself let go of the sword's grip and smoothed a hand through his hair. "Yeah, fine. Just tired, though those hot springs helped." They'd been a welcome surprise, too, but a benefit that made sense when he considered the sleepy volcano beneath the city. They had all taken time to wash and rest in the Magister's private springs, and removing the ash from his hair and skin had been a luxury all on its own.

"Don't miss them too much. There won't be time for any of that after we set out." Lark didn't sound tired in the least, though Zaide wasn't sure she'd napped like the rest of them. When he'd awoken and finally dragged himself from bed, she'd been at a table with a stack of books two feet high.

Studying seemed second nature to her, and seeing her tidy notes gave him an odd sense of shame. He'd never liked being the Elder's apprentice and didn't regret having escaped the role, but some part of him still wondered if he could have done a better job of meeting expectations. And wondered if Kolmar might not have suffered the same fiery fate, had he been better educated on what to expect.

Logically, both questions were absurd, and both could be answered the same way. He'd done his best. There was only so much he could do without the magic his peers bore, and now he knew the Elder had hidden a great deal of information from him, for reasons he couldn't begin to fathom. Had he any clue what sort of information that might have been, he might have been able to inquire on the subject at the Great Library. As it was, he knew only what hid within the pages of the few books they'd liberated from the cellar and taken to Amrochan, and those were almost solely about the artifacts they carried.

"Here we are," Tula sighed as they stopped at the foot of the library's stairs. Given all that had happened after their arrival, the library didn't look bad, but librarians in pale robes filtered in and out of the building with boxes and buckets of water, and every single one of them paused to give their trio a dirty look.

"I think we're unpopular," Zaide said.

Lark snorted. "Well, set a city's greatest treasure on fire, and you're bound to step on a few toes. Shall we?" She started up the stairs without waiting for a response.

All things considered, Zaide was surprised they were allowed in. The princess went first and Zaide second. Tula followed close behind him, though she kept her chin down and refrained from looking around.

For all that Vorkaris had awakened there, the damage wasn't bad. Most of the ash and soot shed by his wings had been cleaned up, and planks of wood covered the gaping hole in the floor where he had clawed his way through. Zaide hadn't yet puzzled out the logistics of that, and he frowned as he worked it over now. "How come the dragon was sleeping directly underneath the library?"

"So he would be easy to locate, I presume," Arkosh answered from nearby. The old man adjusted his spectacles and gave Zaide such a deep frown, he suspected the librarian disliked him even more than the dragon did.

"Have you found more information on the dragon's history as Magister of Jadora?" Lark asked as she joined the old man. Zaide hadn't known anyone was looking for it, but he couldn't claim surprise. The princess had probably set half the city to special tasks in the few hours of peace they'd known.

Arkosh shrugged. "Little. We found several mentions of the human Magister as conduit, but without the additional context, there's no way to know the source of power is the draconic Magister. But on that note, has he, ah..." He raised both brows, as if that was enough to finish the question. When everyone stared at him, he cleared his throat and went on. "Has the dragon announced the new Magister's presence yet?"

Tula stiffened. "I am sure the Magister will be revealed when the time is correct."

Zaide didn't dare question, so he could only frown. Why keep it a secret? Surely the librarians would be thrilled to have one of their own lead the city.

The old librarian deflated a bit, but nodded his

understanding. "Of course, of course. It would be foolish to rush, I know. I simply hope a leader chosen by the dragon itself proves better than the last few we've had."

"That's asking very little, Master Librarian Arkosh," Lark said. "Perhaps you ought to aim a little higher."

"Indeed," the old man sighed. "But that's neither here nor there, and it's not why you're here, besides. I have pulled all relevant information about the Desheni Shaman from our archives and have it set aside for you."

The barest hint of a smile graced Lark's lips. "Thank you. I knew you would deliver."

"I would not be worthy of my title as master librarian if I didn't." Arkosh led them to a table covered with books and notes.

The same table, Zaide noted with a smirk, that Tula had first used to help them locate information about the artifacts on their first visit. She made the connection, too, because she smiled to herself as she brushed her fingers against the table's edge. A moment later, her face fell.

Concerning, but he would have to ask later.

Arkosh gathered a stack of papers from between the books and presented them to the princess with both hands. "I've already taken notes on everything I feel you might need to know. The Shaman's identity is no mystery. Athradan is a reclusive leader, though, and you may have difficulty reaching him."

Lark skimmed the notes as she accepted them. "Reclusive or not, the Shaman must answer to my father. With luck, he'll be more receptive than our mystery Magister was, here."

"Yes, that's an interesting subject, as well. I've begun a report on that man and have made some headway, but I expect it will take more research to gather information." From the way the librarian's eyes brightened, that wasn't a bad thing. "We've uncovered two things, at least."

Zaide picked up a loose paper from the table. Unlike everything else he'd seen in the desert city, it was written in a language he understood. Something done for Lark's benefit, perhaps. "I'm surprised you were able to find anything on such short notice."

"Yes, well, palace staff do talk. Given the last few days, they've been more than happy to spill what they know. We are aware of his magic, at least, and know now that he used it to gain entry to the city." Arkosh sniffed and provided yet another paper. "There are few people gifted with the power of charm, but that means we'll be able to trace him. There will be a name in the gate logs, just the same as anyone else, and even a false name will give us a direction we may look."

Tula snapped her fingers. "I knew there was something off about him."

"He was too charismatic," Lark agreed. "I have some training for how to resist such magic. A necessary skill in a royal court, unfortunately."

"He seemed normal to me," Zaide said.

Arkosh gave a snort. "Of course he would. You're a young man, and less likely to be interested in his wiles."

"Oh." Zaide scrunched his nose, and Lark gave his arm a reassuring pat.

"Zaide's a sheltered boy, he doesn't think of such things. Thank you for this diligence, Arkosh. Please continue to research this individual, and forward any information you uncover to Amrochan. We plan to return to the capital after our visit to the Shaman, and I will study all future findings there." The princess tucked her collection of papers into her bag.

"Of course, Your Highness. It is an honor to research on your behalf." The old man touched a hand over his heart and offered a bow. "But, ah, if I may ask..."

Tula winced even before the librarian set his eyes on her.

Lark raised a brow. "Surely you don't mean to reclaim my librarian now?"

"Her duties have been neglected long enough. She must return to her post at the library."

Zaide planted a hand on her shoulder. "Actually, the Dragonster... uh, the Magister has already asked that Tula assist him for the time being. He's been asleep a long time, and he needs to catch up on Jadoran politics."

The old man gaped. "Tula? But her scores in history were atrocious!"

"She's a really good storyteller, though. She gets really animated, and I think Vorkaris likes that." Zaide flashed her a grin. To his surprise, Tula flushed and mouthed a silent thank-you.

Lark crossed her arms. "Did you really just call him the Dragonster?"

"Dragon Magister. It just mashed together in my head." He gave a vague motion to indicate the mental melding of the two words. "And my mouth, I guess."

The flat stare Arkosh delivered indicated he found it less amusing. "Thank the Maker you're leaving. Your tongue would get us all in trouble with that dragon."

"I don't think he likes me," Zaide said.

"He's not alone."

"Noted."

"I'll report back when I can, Master Arkosh," Tula put in before any further words could be exchanged.

The old man harrumphed. "See that you do. You've been off gallivanting for long enough."

"And her assistance is greatly appreciated," Lark said. "I will discuss the matter with Magister Vorkaris and ensure that she's returned safely to your care as soon as that's possible. For now, we must depart. I look forward to your future reports."

"You honor me, Your Highness. Safe travels." He touched his heart again, then turned to tidy up.

Tula spun on her heel and trotted to the door as fast as she could, and Zaide jogged to keep up.

"Why didn't you tell him?" he asked in a whisper.

Her golden cheeks turned rosy and she ducked her head.

A moment later, Lark caught up. "In that much of a hurry to reach Desheni, are you?"

"I think we've caused enough unrest in Jadora for now. It's time for us to move on." Zaide kept his tone light and teasing, but he cast Tula a worried glance. She'd been excited for every other adventure. Why wasn't she now?

"Good thing we're going straight out of the city, then," Lark said. "I asked that supplies be gathered for us and delivered to the south gate. I was told one of the guardswomen would meet us there."

Zaide stepped ahead and turned around to walk backwards. "Wait, just like that? No saying goodbye to anyone, or to the Magister, or—"

Tula cleared her throat and pointed.

The moment they were on the main street to the south gate, the dragon's form was visible, glowing a radiant golden-orange in the sun.

Zaide gaped. "The Dragonster is seeing us off?"

"I swear, Zaide, if you call him that one more time—" Lark cut herself off with an exasperated sigh.

They worked their way down toward the south gate, once an intimidating sight, now little more than a ruin. People ferried carts of rubble from the wall to the massive hole still in the ground, from where the goborrin armies had emerged and the bomb had almost been lost.

An endless stream of people flowed in from the desert, but they parted around Vorkaris and the small handful of figures who waited at the dragon's feet.

"Elsanna's there, too," Tula remarked as they grew near.

Vorkaris spotted them, and Zaide felt his hand twitch for the hilt of his sword as the dragon's eyes fell on him. There was still a hint of animosity there, and when they reached the group, he spoke before anyone in the greeting party could. "I'm sorry."

Elsanna blinked, as did Valla, but behind them, Moros remained as unperturbed as stone.

You've been a pest and I am happy to see you go, Vorkaris replied, *but I will accept the apology.*

"Do I want to know what prompted that?" Valla asked.

Zaide wasn't the only one who shook his head.

The guardswoman shrugged and deposited a pair of bags into his arms. "Elsanna provided the shopping list, but I added a few treats for the road. What we could recover of your belongings taken in the prison are there, too."

"There's no cold weather gear to be had in Jadora, but Magister Vorkaris allowed for the spending of Magisterial funds on such supplies, so you'll find enough money in this to get you properly outfitted." Elsanna produced a fat velvet purse from the ornate robe that covered her armor. More sensical armor, Zaide noted, and his attention didn't go unnoticed.

"The guardswomen will be wearing standard issue armor for a while," she explained. "Not just for protection until we're certain no one has smuggled any projectiles into the city, but because Vorkaris believes it would be best for all of Jadora's guard forces to display a unified front for a while."

The guards and guardswomen serve the city best when they are not separated. With time, the elite will be allowed to separate themselves into their own ranks once more. Right now, infighting between the ranks cannot be tolerated. Vorkaris blinked sleepily in the sunlight.

"Tired, Magister Vorkaris?" Lark asked as she accepted her bags from Valla.

Things are not normally so eventful immediately after my awakening. I did not anticipate it, but I expect I will be awake for some time.

"Sorry," Tula almost squeaked.

The dragon rumbled and touched the top of her head with a single clawed digit, like a person might pet a sparrow with a fingertip.

Moros stepped toward Zaide with a wrapped object in his hands. "We have brought you a parting gift."

"Me?" Zaide took it, the soft clink of metal against metal

confirming his suspicions, based on the shape. He folded back the cloth to reveal a long knife in a gilded sheath.

"There will be times ahead where actions must be taken, and the Spectrum Blade may not agree," the scarred man said. "Elsanna and I agreed it was best you be prepared."

The blade was slightly curved and tapered to a fine point, and Zaide brushed a thumb over its razor-sharp edge before he returned it to its sheath. "Thank you. I appreciate having it, but I wish I didn't need it."

"All of us wish it unnecessary," Elsanna said, "but we understand the ways of war. Promise you will keep the princess safe."

"On my life," Zaide said.

"Let's hope it doesn't come to that. Thank you for your assistance, Valla. Elsanna. And you as well, Moros." Lark smiled at each of them in turn. "With fortune, I fear you won't see the two of us again."

It would not be a tragedy, Vorkaris said dryly.

"We already know how you feel," Zaide muttered. "Tula, where are your things?"

The librarian stepped back with her hands clasped before her chest.

He froze in the middle of untwisting the strap of one bag. "What?"

"I'm... I'm not going," she said.

Zaide almost dropped his bag. "What? But the artifacts, your research—"

"I can't. I have to... Jadora needs me, and I'm tied here. I'm stuck." Tears brimmed on her eyelashes and she bit her lower lip as if that would keep them from spilling over.

His heart sank. "Tula..."

Her duties as Jadora's new Magister are great, Vorkaris said, his voice an ominous rasp across the top of Zaide's mind.

She nodded and clutched the front edge of her robe. "I can't research anymore. My people need a Magister."

The dragon rumbled. *It's fortunate they have one.*

"And a clever one, at that." Elsanna clasped Tula's shoulders and smiled. "Wouldn't you agree?"

Tula's face twisted with doubt.

The guardswoman laughed. "I'll do you a favor and not take that as an insult. We wouldn't want anyone to think you were leaving with the two of us on poor terms."

"What?" Tula shrank back a step.

Zaide caught her arm before she could go farther, though he felt a measure of incertitude, himself.

A ghost of a smile graced Lark's features. "You know, nothing has been announced yet. Not even to the librarians."

Vorkaris sat a little straighter, his tail curled around his haunches. *Upon further reflection and an opportunity to discuss the matter, I see the restructuring of Jadora requires a firm hand and an experienced leader. A time for magic and knowledge may come later. No one need know but us.* He winked one great golden eye and lifted his other forepaw to reveal a pair of bags.

Tula gasped.

"It may be in name only, but... for now, Vorkaris has bestowed me the title of Magister," Elsanna said. "I will oversee the rebuilding of the city and reestablishment of the city's government with new officials."

Zaide stepped back and fastened the sheath of his new knife to his left hip, opposite the Spectrum Blade. "Guess that means you'll be out of a job, huh, Moros?"

"I am likely to remain in position beneath Elsanna," the warden said.

Tula clapped a hand over her mouth to stifle an unladylike snort. Lark gave her a disapproving frown, but Zaide snickered, too. "No, he thinks that's hilarious. Trust me."

The scarred man's expression did not change, but the tiniest twinkle touched his eyes.

Mortals never mature, Vorkaris sighed as he pushed Tula's

bags forward. Instead of picking them up, she wrapped her arms around his foreleg in a hug.

"Thank you," she whispered.

The dragon wriggled his limb free. *I wish I could say the choice was purely altruistic, but there are many reasons for you to go on this journey. I don't believe Jadora is prepared for such a young Magister, but for you to appear before the Desheni may make their Shaman more agreeable to our cause.*

"I'll do my best." She scooped her bags from the ground and mounted them on her shoulders with a grin.

"And I'll keep her safe," Zaide said, though he regretted the words the moment they left his mouth. The dragon bared his teeth and leveled his horn-crowned head with Zaide's.

Should you fail to do so, you will wish you never woke after being dragged from my volcano's crater.

Zaide swallowed and nodded, unsure what else to do.

"We thank you for your aid, Magister Vorkaris." Lark stepped between them to take control of the situation, as diplomatic and perfectly timed as ever. "Both in allowing Tula to accompany us, preparation of supplies, and in the blessing of the blade. Should Jadora find need, know you may always call on my father, or on me."

I call on your aid right now, and request you remove your Bladebearer from my city before I force you to seek a new wielder for that sword, the dragon said.

"Then that is what I shall do." Lark turned Zaide around and planted both hands on his back to steer him around the dragon and toward the hole that was once a gate. Beyond, the desert glistened in the morning sun.

Wisely, Zaide kept his mouth shut until they were beyond the broken wall.

Tula pranced past them with a spring in her step. "Can you believe it? We're going north!" She twirled and laughed as they worked their way down the slope to the heated sands below, excited for the journey, though much of the beginning would be spent in the shade of the plateau.

The princess giggled softly. "Her enthusiasm is appreciated."

"Her presence is, too." He scrubbed a hand through his hair and offered a nervous half-smile. "They really had me going for a minute, there."

"I'm glad the two of you get along. It'll make the trip much more pleasant." Lark drew something from one of her bags as they walked and settled it over her shoulder. The harness he'd made for the Hymnflute. It rested comfortably at her hip, and she draped a hand across the artifact. "You lied to me, you know."

Zaide lowered his hand. "What do you mean?"

"You said all your hair was white. But your eyelashes are dark."

He blinked several times, suddenly more aware of his eyelashes than he supposed any man ought to be. No matter how he fluttered his eyelids, he couldn't see them. "Huh. Well, that was a lie by omission, I guess, because I don't think I've ever noticed."

Lark flashed him a coy smile, and he dared not think what that was supposed to mean.

Carrion birds still circled the city and crowded the sky, but beyond the desert's edge, the blue expanse was clear.

A cool breeze touched the air, and Zaide breathed deep.

They turned to the north as they reached the base of the city's plateau, leaving the shadow of wings and the weight of death behind.

GLOSSARY

Addare – (uh-dare) – An oasis city on the western coast of Amroch.

Amroch – (AM-roke) – The Allied Kingdoms ruled by King Sendassian. Originally a number of smaller kingdoms, unified as an empire for defense purposes.

Amrochan – (am-ROW-kan) – The capital city of Amroch.

Andriun – (AN-dree-un) – The Desheni Shaman's son.

Aren – A soldier stationed at the garrison outside Kolmar. Friend of Zaide and Resia.

Arkosh – A well-respected Master Librarian and one of Tula's mentors.

Beshnai – (besh-NIGH) – An isolated city on the northern coast of Amroch.

Broken-born – People born in the western kingdoms destroyed by Gadranus. Many seek refuge in Amroch, but face difficulty integrating due to their history in the war.

Bugrak – (BUG-rack) – Small, flat-faced and ugly gray creatures. Hunt in packs and use primitive weapons.

Captured Spring – One of the three artifacts. A vial that contains a self-replenishing healing tonic.

Chithal – (chee-thal) – A large port city and trade hub

Dasienna – (das-EE-en-uh) – The princess. King Sendassian's daughter.

Desheni – (duh-SHEN-nee) – A settlement named after the race of aquatic people who live there. The Desheni people bear blue-tinged skin, fin-like ears, webbed fingers, and gills on their necks.

Elder – Kolmar's chief overseer and most skilled mage. Zaide and Resia's mentor. Also known as the Paragon of Forest.

Elsanna – (el-san-nuh) – Chief of the Magister's guardswomen.

Estkel – (est-KELL) – A marshy city at the edge of the Ellean Sea.

Gadranus – (guh-DRA-nuss) – Breaker of the Shattered Lands, leader of the army that threatens to destroy Amroch. According to legend, he has been cursed to be reborn a thousand times as a punishment for his misdeeds.

Ganede – (gan-NEED) – Jadora's sister city. A port of trade on one of the peninsulas that frame the Ellean Sea.

Goborrin – (guh-BOR-rin) – Bipedal man-like monsters with pig-like faces and tusks. The smallest of the goborrins are the size of an adult man.

Jadora – (jah-DOR-ah) – Ganede's sister city. Referred to as The Watcher. A fortress atop a desert plateau.

Kolmar – (coal-mar) – A small forest village in the southwestern region of Amroch.

Lark – The name Dasienna uses while traveling to protect her identity.

Magister – The leader of the fortress city of Jadora. Also known as the Paragon of Fire.

Molten Dagger – One of the three artifacts. An obsidian dagger that appears to have veins of magma trapped within it. Contains fire magic.

Moros – The warden of Jadora's prison and Elsanna's sweetheart.

Murk – A soldier from the garrison outside Kolmar.

Paragons – Leaders entrusted with the protection of the three magic artifacts.

Parral – (puh-rawl) – A port city at the southernmost tip of Amroch.

Plain – A soldier from the garrison outside Kolmar.

Raddan – A lieutenant and medic in Amroch's army. Stationed at the garrison outside Kolmar.

Resia – (ree-see-uh) – Zaide's foster sister and the new Elder. Bears a strong magical bond with the forest and wields earth magic.

Salamander – Bipedal lizard-like creatures found in Jadora's caverns. They attack anyone they deem an intruder.

Sarma – Resia's mother and Zaide's foster mother.

Sast – A fortress outpost on an island in the Ellean sea. Unfriendly to visitors. Little is known about the city.

Sendassian – (sin-das-see-an) – King of Amroch.

Shaman – The leader of the Desheni. Entrusted with the protection of the Captured Spring.

Shattered Lands – The western kingdoms destroyed by Gadranus.

Spectrum Blade – The fourth artifact. A legendary weapon said to be the only thing that can strike down the cursed knight Gadranus.

Tinith – (ten-nith) – A marketplace large enough to be its own city.

Tula – (too-lah) – An apprentice librarian at the Great Library in Jadora. Fancies herself an archaeologist and adventurer.

Vale Hymnflute – One of the three artifacts. A set of wooden pan pipes that serves as anchor for Kolmar's Vale magic. It bears power over earth and wind.

Vale magic – A spiritual shield that lays over Kolmar's valley and protects the forest from evil.

Valla – (vah-lah) – A high-ranking Jadoran guardswoman. One of Elsanna's most trusted soldiers.

Verlin – Resia's father and Zaide's foster father.

Vorkaris – The Magister who sealed away the Molten Dagger. Also known as the Dragonster, according to Zaide.

Yithel – (yee-THEL) – A trade city along the river north of Amrochan.

Zaide – (zayd) – A broken-born refugee fostered in Kolmar after his mother's death. Accidentally involved in helping the princess recover the artifacts and saving Amroch.

9 781952 145193